# THE
# FALLING

# BOOKS BY ANNA TODD

After

After We Collided

After We Fell

After Ever Happy

Imagines

Before

Nothing More

Nothing Less

The Spring Girls

After: The Graphic Novel (Volume 1)

# THE FALLING

## A BRIGHTEST STARS NOVEL

# ANNA TODD

wattpad books · FRAYED PAGES

Published in Canada by Wattpad WEBTOON Book Group,
a division of Wattpad WEBTOON Studios, Inc.
36 Wellington Street E., Toronto, ON M5E 1C7
*www.wattpad.com*

First Frayed Pages x Wattpad Books edition: July 2022

ISBN 978-1-99025-980-7 (Hardcover)
ISBN 978-1-99077-857-5 (Trade Paperback)
ISBN 978-1-99025-998-2 (Trade Paperback - Canada Edition)
ISBN 978-1-99025-981-4 (eBook)

Library and Archives Canada Cataloguing in Publication and U.S. Library of
Congress Cataloging in Publication information is available upon request.

Printed and bound in Canada
1 3 5 7 9 10 8 6 4 2

Author Photo © Anna Todd
Cover design by Lesley Worrell
Cover image © XYZ images via Shutterstock
Typesetting by Neil Erickson

To you, the reader holding this book:

I hope you find comfort, solace, or distraction from any pain or loneliness you may be carrying—and at a minimum, I hope your heart feels a little lighter as you read these words.

You're never alone. <3

# THE
# FALLING

# PLAYLIST

**WITHOUT YOU**
The Kid LAROI

**YOU BROKE ME FIRST**
Conor Maynard (cover)

**ONE LAST TIME**
Ariana Grande

**PSYCHO**
Post Malone (feat. Ty Dolla $ign)

**I MISS YOU, I'M SORRY**
Gracie Abrams

**SHE**
Jake Scott

**WAVES**
Mr. Probz

**FAKE LOVE**
BTS

**EUPHORIA**
BTS

**TO BUILD A HOME**
The Cinematic Orchestra

**MONSTER (ENGLISH EDITION)**
Henry

**YOU OUGHTA KNOW**
Alanis Morissette

**IRONIC**
Alanis Morissette

**BITTER SWEET SYMPHONY**
The Verve

**3AM**
Matchbox Twenty

**CALL OUT MY NAME**
The Weeknd

**TRY ME**
The Weeknd

**SAFE INSIDE**
James Arthur

**1 STEP FORWARD, 3 STEPS BACK**
Olivia Rodrigo

**IN THE DARK**
Camila Cabello

**NIGHTS**
Frank Ocean

**BLINK TWICE**
Joy Oladokun

**SEATTLE**
Sam Kim

"Maybe I made a mistake yesterday,

but yesterday's me is still me.

I am who I am today, with all my faults.

Tomorrow I might be a tiny bit wiser, and that's me, too.

These faults and mistakes are what I am,

making up the brightest stars in the constellation of my life.

I have come to love myself for who I was, who I am,

and who I hope to become."

-Kim Namjoon

# PROLOGUE

The wind whips around the coffee shop each time the old wooden door creaks open. It's unusually cold for September and I'm pretty sure it's some kind of punishment from the universe for agreeing to meet up with him, today of all days. What was I thinking?

I barely had time to put makeup on the swollen pockets under my eyes. I held two freezing ice cubes to my face and moved around my kitchen while they dripped down my cheeks, melting quickly. It was humid in my house and the smell of cool Georgia rain filled the whole place, not that it took much. And this outfit I'm wearing? A simple fall ensemble that took me an hour of digging around my drawers and my closet—with a mini fashion show in front of my bedroom mirror—to decide on the same thing I usually wore to anything formal: an all-black outfit, pants with a crease that looked very grown-up and like I tried, even though I felt like wearing sweatpants. To go with them, I put on a thick black turtleneck and only discovered an annoying drop of toothpaste on it as I turned the speck into a big spot, rubbing it with water and a paper towel while driving. After so much effort, I look like shit. Complete shit.

Sitting here, my head aches but I'm not sure I have any ibuprofen in my purse. I'm thinking that it was smart of me to choose the table closest to the door of the coffee shop, in case I need to get away quickly. Or if he needs to. This little place in the middle of Edgewood? Another good choice—it's neutral and not the least bit intimate. I've been here only a few times, but it's my favorite coffeehouse in Atlanta. The seating is pretty limited—just about ten tables—so I guess they want to encourage a quick turnaround. There are a couple of Instagram-worthy features, like the succulent wall and the clean black-and-white tile behind the baristas, but overall, it's quite austere. Harsh gray and concrete everywhere. The whistle of an espresso machine. Loud blenders mixing kale and whatever fruit is trendy.

There is a single door: one way in, one way out. I look down at my phone and wipe my palms on my black pants. Another stain. I need to get my shit together.

Will he hug me? Shake my hand? Is he preparing for our reunion obsessively, the way that I am? Did he toss and turn like I did, thinking about what to say and how to present himself? The new awkward. Mature and like I've gotten my shit together, that's who I want him to think I am. A better version of the girl he knew so well.

I can't imagine him shaking my hand and using such a formal gesture. Not with me. But maybe he's just as anxious as I am, maybe his head is spinning with memories and regrets like mine? He isn't even here yet and my heart is pounding in my chest. For about the fourth time today, I can feel the panic bubbling just below my rib cage, and it pisses me off that I can't control the physical effect he has on me. It pisses me off even more that he will probably walk in completely calm and steady, his own version of masking. I have no idea which mood of his I'll get today, controlled or turbulent? Will he bring up the one thing I don't want him to? I haven't seen him since last winter and I don't even know who he is now. And really, did I ever?

There were little things I should have let go of, but there was one big thing that I still can't accept. Even now the thought twists my insides and makes me want to change my mind about this whole Atlanta ordeal. I could go check out of my hotel, pack up my carry-on suitcase, and drive two hours back to my house, a place now off-limits to him. Did he remember that? I'll be able to tell if he often thinks of me by the way he looks at me. He isn't a mystery anymore, he is now a memory. Maybe I only ever knew a version of him—a bright and hollow form of the man I'm waiting on now. I have to keep reminding myself that this trip isn't about him, it's bigger than him, bigger than both of us. Kael would be hurting. He would hide it like a professional soldier, but I knew he would be hurting. I didn't know how much contact he'd had with our friend over the last year, but I knew Kael couldn't afford to lose anyone else around him.

I suppose I could have avoided him for the rest of my life, but the thought of never seeing Kael again seemed impossible and worse than sitting here now, driving myself insane with anxiety. At least I can admit that. Here I am warming my hands on a coffee cup, waiting for him to come through that raspy door after swearing to him, to myself, to anyone who would listen for the last few months, that I would never . . .

He's not due for another five minutes. It feels like the longest five minutes of my existence, but if he's anything like the man I knew, he'll strut in exactly on time with a straight face, not showing one hint of emotion.

When the door tears open, it's a woman who walks in. Her blond hair is a nest stuck to the top of her tiny head and she's holding a cell phone against her red cheek.

"I don't give a shit, Howie. Get it done," she snaps, pulling the phone away with a string of curse words.

God, I hate this about Atlanta. Too many people here are like her, tetchy and forever in a hurry. Zero patience and not seeming to care that other people have shit to do, too. The city wasn't always like this. Well, maybe it was? I wasn't always like this, though. Or maybe I was? But things and people change. I have. He probably has. I look around the shop again and watch the door for a few seconds. If he doesn't arrive soon, I'm going to end up talking myself out of this whole meetup. I used to love this city, especially downtown. The dining scene is full of small, privately owned restaurants, not just chains, with actual chefs who create dishes that I've never even heard of but love. There's always something to do in Atlanta and everything is open later than it is around Fort Benning. The exception, of course, being the strip club—there's always at least one outside every military base. But the biggest draw to Atlanta for me back then was that I wasn't constantly reminded of military life. No camo everywhere you look. No ACUs on the men and women waiting in line for the movies, at the gas station, at Dunkin' Donuts. People speak real words, not just acronyms. And there are plenty of non-military haircuts to admire.

I loved Atlanta, but he ruined that.

We ruined that.

*We.*

That was the closest I'd get to admitting any fault in what went down.

"What are you staring at?"

Just a few words, but they pour into and over me, shocking every one of my senses and all of my sense. And yet, there's that calm, too, that seems to be hardwired into me whenever he's around. I look up to make sure it's him, though I know it is. Sure enough, he's standing over me with his hickory eyes on my face, searching . . .

reminiscing? I wish he wouldn't look at me like that. The small café is actually pretty packed, but I hardly notice. I'd had this meeting all scripted, and now, with five words, he's disrupted everything and I'm unnerved.

"How do you do that?" I ask him. "I didn't see you come in."

I worry that my voice sounds like I'm accusing him of something or that I'm nervous, and that's the last thing I want. I need to be cool and make it clear that he doesn't have the power to get to me, not anymore. But still, I wonder—how does he do that, really? He was always so good at silence, at moving around undetected. Another skill honed in the Army, I guess.

I gesture for him to sit down. He slides into the chair, and that's when I realize he has a full beard. Sharp, precise lines graze his cheekbones, and his jawline is covered in dark hair. This is new. Of course it is: he always had to keep up with Army regulations. Hair must be short and well groomed. Moustaches are allowed, but only if they're neatly trimmed and don't grow over the upper lip. He told me once that he was thinking of growing a moustache, but I talked him out of it.

He grabs the coffee menu from the table. Cappuccino. Macchiato. Latte. Flat white. Long black. When did everything get so complicated?

"You like coffee now?" I don't try to hide my surprise.

He shakes his head. "No. You like hot coffee now?" he questions.

I look down at the mug between my hands and shake my head. "No."

I hate that he remembers small things about me. I wish I could erase them all from his memory. And from mine.

A half-smile crosses his stoic face, reminding me of one of the million reasons I fell in love with him. A moment ago, it was easy to look away. Now it's impossible.

"Not coffee," he assures me. "Tea."

He isn't wearing a jacket, of course, and the sleeves of his denim shirt are rolled up above his elbows. The tattoo on his forearm is fully visible and I know if I touch his skin right now, it will be burning up. I'm sure as hell not going to do that, so I look up and over his shoulder. Away from the tattoo. Away from the thought. It's safer that way. For both of us. I try to focus on the noises in the coffee shop so I can settle into his silence. I forgot how unnerving his presence can be.

That's a lie. I didn't forget. I wanted to but couldn't. Just like sometimes I wanted to forgive him, but I never could.

I can hear the server approaching, her sneakers squeaking on the concrete floor. She has a mousy little voice and when she tells him that he should "so totally" try the new peppermint mocha, I laugh to myself, knowing that he hates all minty things, even toothpaste. I think about the way he'd leave those red globs of cinnamon gunk in the sink at my house and how many times we bickered over it. If only I had ignored those petty grievances. If only I had paid more attention to what was really happening, everything might have been different.

Maybe. Maybe not.

I don't want to know.

Another lie.

Kael tells the girl he would like a plain black tea, and this time I try not to laugh. He's so predictable.

"What's so funny?" he asks when the waitress leaves.

"Nothing." I change the subject. "So, how are you?"

"Don't do that. Don't act like we're strangers."

I tuck my lips together and look away before I reply. "Aren't we, though?"

He sighs and his eyes roam around the room before they land back on me. "Should I go?" he asks directly.

"I don't know, should you?"

He moves his chair out slightly and I reconsider. I don't really want him to go, but there are so many reasons to be mad at him and I'm afraid that being around him will soften me. I can't have that happen.

"Okay. Okay. Just sit. I'll be nice," I promise him, with a small smile that's about as convincing as my attitude.

I don't know what bullshit we're going to fill this coffee date with, but since we're going to see each other tomorrow, it seemed like a good idea to get the first awkward encounter out of the way without an audience. A funeral is no place for that. And I had to be in the city today anyway.

"So, Kael, how are you?" I retry this whole being-nice thing.

"Good. Given the circumstances." He clears his throat.

"Yeah." I sigh, trying not to think too much about tomorrow. I've always been good at pretending the world isn't burning around me. Okay, I've been slipping these past few months, but for years denial was second nature, a permanent habit I mastered between my parents' divorce and my high school graduation. Sometimes it feels like my family is disappearing. We keep getting smaller and smaller. Sometimes I feel like I'm disappearing, too.

"Are you all right?" he asks, his voice even lower than it was before.

It sounded the same as it did those damp nights when we fell asleep with the windows open—the whole room would be dewy the next morning, our bodies wet and sticky. I used to love the way his hot skin felt when my fingertips danced across the smooth contours of his jaw. Even his lips were warm, feverish at times. The southern Georgia air was so thick you could taste it, and Kael's temperature always ran so hot. Another thing I pretended to forget.

He clears his throat and asks again if I'm okay. I snap out of it.

I know what he's thinking. He can tell that I've left earth with my thoughts and he's trying to bring me back. I can read his face as clearly as the neon *But First, Coffee* sign hanging on the wall behind him. I hate that those memories are the ones my brain associates with him. It doesn't make this any easier.

"Kare." His voice is soft as he reaches across the table to touch my hand. I jerk it away so fast you'd think it was on fire. It's strange to remember the way we were, the way I never knew where he ended and I began. We were so in tune . . . so different than the way things are now. There was a time when he'd say my name, and just like that, I'd give him anything he wanted. I consider this for a moment. How I'd give that man anything he wanted.

I thought I was further along in my recovery from us, that whole *getting over him* thing. At least far enough along that I wouldn't be thinking about the way his voice sounded when I had to wake him up early for physical training, or the way he used to scream in the night. My head is starting to spin and if I don't shut my mind off now, the memories will split me apart, on this chair, in this little coffee shop, right in front of him.

I force myself to nod and pick up my latte to buy some time, just a moment so I can find my voice. "Yeah. I'm all right. I mean, funerals are kind of my thing."

"Tell me about it."

I don't dare look at his face. I don't want to see his grief or share my own, so I try to diffuse the intensity of what we're both feeling with some dark humor.

"We're running out of fingers to count the funerals we've been to in the last two years alone and—"

"There's nothing you could have done, regardless. Don't tell me you're thinking you could've—" He pauses and I stare harder at the small chip in my mug. I run my finger over the cracked ceramic.

"Karina. Look at me."

I shake my head, not even close to jumping down this rabbit hole with him. I don't have it in me. "I'm fine. Seriously." I pause and take in the expression on his face. "Don't look at me like that. I'm okay."

"You're always fine." He runs his hand over the hair on his face and sighs, his shoulders leaning onto the back of the plastic chair.

He's not buying it. He can feel my anxiety.

He's right. That whole fake-it-till-you-make-it thing? I own it.

What other choice do I have?

"How long are you in town?" he asks, scooting his chair a little bit closer.

Should I lie to him? Why don't I want to?

"For two days. Maybe less. I booked a room at the W."

"Oh, fancy." He smiles.

"It's so loud . . ."

He nods and thanks the server as she sets his tea in front of him. Her eyes take him in and she tucks her hair behind her ear with a big, beautiful smile that makes my stomach burn. I want to disappear.

He doesn't look away from my eyes.

"And so unlike you," he says.

"Huh?" I've already forgotten what we were even talking about.

"The hotel." He takes a drink of his tea and I try to catch my breath.

Being around him is still so dangerous for me. Sometimes warning signs and butterflies are one and the same.

# CHAPTER ONE

**Two years earlier**

I had hit the job jackpot. Not financially, but in all the ways that mattered. I didn't have to open the massage studio until ten, so most mornings I could sleep in. And being able to walk there from my house—bonus! I loved this street: the mattress shop, the ice-cream place, the nail salon, and the old-fashioned candy store. I'd saved up my money and there I was, twenty years old, on that street, living in a tiny house that I'd bought. My own house. Not my dad's. Mine.

The walk to work was brief—only five minutes and not quite long enough to be interesting. Walking along the alley behind the shops, I mostly tried to stay out of the way of the cars. The alley was wide enough for one pedestrian and one car at a time. Well, a Prius or some kind of small car would be an easy fit; unfortunately, people around here usually went for big trucks, so most of the time I pinned myself up against the bushes lining the alleyway until they passed.

Sometimes I'd create stories in my head about people in the world around me, a little bit of excitement before my shift started. Today's story featured Bradley, the bearded man who owned the mattress store on the corner. Bradley was a nice guy, and he wore what I came to think of as his nice-guy uniform: a plaid shirt and khakis. He drove a white Ford something or other, and he worked even more than I did. I passed him every morning, already at his shop before I started at ten. Even when I worked a double or a night shift, I'd see that white truck parked in the back of the alley.

Bradley had to be single. If he had a wife or children, surely I'd have seen them at least once in the year since I'd moved to this side of town. But no, it didn't matter if it was during the day, at night, or on the weekends—Bradley was always alone. He lived in the house next door to mine and he never seemed to have any company. All of his lights were usually off except one lamp in the living room.

The sun was shining, but not a single bird was chirping. No garbage truck was grumbling. Not one person was starting their car. It was eerily silent. Maybe that's why Bradley's presence seemed a little more sinister that morning. I looked at him anew and wondered why he combed his white-blond hair down the middle, why he thought it was a good idea to expose such a harsh line of scalp. Really, what I wanted to know was where he was going with that rolled-up rug in the back of his truck. Maybe I'd seen one too many episodes of *Criminal Minds*, but doesn't everyone know that's how you dispose of a body—roll it up in some old carpet and dump it on the edge of town? As my imagination was turning Bradley into a serial killer, he gave me the friendliest wave and a smile, a real one. Or maybe he was just that good at being charming and was actually going to—

I nearly pissed myself when he called out to me.

"Hey, Karina! Water's out in the whole strip!"

His thin lips turned into a heavy frown as he waved his arms around to show how upset he was. I stopped walking and lifted my hand to cover my eyes from the sun. It was harsh, shining its brightest, even though the air had a little bite to it. Georgia was so damn hot. I thought I'd be used to it after three years, but nope. I longed for the chill of those Texas nights. "I've been tryin' to get the water company out here, but no luck so far." He shrugged and held up his cell phone as proof.

"Oh, no." I tried to mimic his tone of frustration over the water, but honestly, I kind of hoped Mali would let us shut down for the day. I had barely slept last night, so I could have used another hour, or twenty, of sleep.

"I'll keep tryin' to call them," he offered.

His fingers reached down and touched his longhorn belt buckle. He looked like he was already sweating, and when he grabbed the massive rug from the bed of his truck, I almost wanted to help him. Almost.

"Thanks," I said. "I'll let Mali know when she gets in."

# CHAPTER TWO

The door was locked, the lights were off—even the hallway light that we usually kept on—and it was hot as hell inside. I cranked the a/c, turned on the oil warmers, and lit the candles in the lobby and in Elodie's workroom and mine.

My first client wasn't until ten thirty. Elodie's wasn't scheduled until eleven thirty. She was still snoring on the couch when I left the house, which meant she'd rush through the door at forty past eleven and give her client a sweet smile and a quick apology in that cute little French accent of hers and all would be fine.

Elodie was one of the few people in the world I'd do most anything for. That was especially true now that she was pregnant. She'd found out about the baby just two days after her husband's boots hit the dirt in Afghanistan. That kind of stuff was the norm around here. I saw it with my parents, with Elodie . . . and countless other women I met throughout my life who raised their kids mostly alone. Military wives are a rare breed of women. As much as I had endless respect for them, I never wanted to be one. My version of loneliness seemed easier than waiting for your love to come home—or, worse, not come home at all.

As soon as I started thinking about all the women and men who had lost their spouses, my heart sank and I could feel the cloud coming over my mind. I tried to distract myself but couldn't help the overwhelming sadness. I needed some music in here. I hated silence. I wasn't one to linger in silence; my mind wouldn't allow it. Recently, I convinced Mali to let me play more relevant music over the speakers while we worked. I couldn't handle another shift of relaxing spa tunes on repeat for hours. The sleepy sounds of waterfalls and waves got on my nerves and made me drowsy, too. I turned on the iPad and within seconds Banks was washing away the memory of all that soft, dreamy babble. I walked to the front desk to switch the computer on. Not two minutes later, Mali came in with a couple of big tote bags hanging from her thin arms.

"What's wrong?" she asked, as I took the bags from her.

"Um, nothing?" No *Hi?* No *How's it going, Karina?* I laughed and made my way to the back room.

The food in those bags smelled so good. Mali made the best homemade Thai dishes I'd ever tasted, and she always made extra for Elodie and me. She graced us with it at least five days a week. The little avocado—that's what Elodie called her baby bump— wanted only spicy drunken noodles. It was the basil leaves. She had become obsessed with them since getting pregnant, to the point where she'd pick them out of her noodles and chew on them. Babies made you do the strangest things.

"Karina," Mali said, smiling. "Answer me. How are you? You look sad."

That was Mali for you. *What's wrong? You look sad.* If it was on her mind, it came out of her mouth.

"Hey—I'm fine," I said. "Not wearing any makeup." I rolled my eyes.

"That's not it. You never wear makeup," she said, poking my cheek.

No, that wasn't it. But I wasn't just sad. And I didn't like that my mask had slipped enough for Mali to notice. I didn't like it one bit.

# CHAPTER **THREE**

Ten thirty came and my client was right on time. I was used to his punctuality, not to mention his soft skin. I could tell he used oil after his showers, and that made my job easier, massaging already pliant skin. His muscles were always so tight, especially around his shoulders, so I assumed he sat behind a desk all day. He wasn't military. I gathered that by his longer hair, curling at the tips.

Today he was so tense that my fingers hurt a little when they rubbed the patch of tissue at the top of his shoulders. He was a groaner—a lot of clients were—and he made these deep, throaty sounds when I loosened the knots he held in his body. The hour went fast. I had to tap his shoulder to wake him when it was over.

My ten-thirty client—his name was Toby, but I liked to call him Ten-thirty—was a good tipper and kept things simple. Never talked, except for that time he asked me out. Elodie freaked when I told her. She wanted me to tell Mali, but I didn't want it to become a thing when it didn't need to be. He was fine with my rejection—not the usual male reaction, I know. He hadn't even hinted at any attraction toward me since, so I figured things were okay between us. What's more, he hadn't asked me out while I was treating him. I had run into him while I was walking out of the nail salon next door on a day off.

Forty-five minutes past eleven and there was still no Elodie. Usually she'd text if she was going to be more than fifteen minutes late. The man in the waiting area must have been new, because I didn't recognize him and I never forgot a face. He seemed patient enough. But not Mali; she was about to call Elodie.

"I can take him if she's not here in five minutes," I suggested. "My next appointment can be moved an hour later, it's Tina." Mali knew most of our clients who came in and out of her spa; she remembered names like I did faces.

"Fine, fine. But your friend is always late," she scolded. Mali was the nicest woman but was made of pure fire.

"She's pregnant," I said, defending my friend.

Mali rolled her eyes. "I was pregnant five times and I worked just fine."

"Touché."

I kept my laughter quiet and texted Tina to see if she could come in at one fifteen. She immediately responded with a *yes*, like I knew she would.

"Um, sir," I called to the man in the waiting room. "Your therapist is actually running late. I can start you now if you'd like. Or you could wait for Elodie." I didn't know if he was partial to her for some reason, or if he simply wanted a massage. Now that we were on Yelp and booking online appointments, I never knew which clients wanted a specific therapist and which didn't care.

He stood up and walked to the desk without saying a word.

"Is that okay?" I asked.

He hesitated for a second before he nodded. Okay . . .

"All right—" I looked at the schedule. *Kael*. What a strange name. "Follow me, please."

We didn't have assigned rooms—not technically—but I had fixed up the second room on the left to almost perfectly fit my taste, so that was the one I used the most. No one else took it unless they had to.

I had brought in my own cabinet and decorations that included lots of fake plants and was in the process of convincing Mali to let me paint the walls. Anything would be better than this dark purple color. It wasn't exactly relaxing, plus it was dull, with chipped corners and edges that dated the room by about twenty years.

"You can leave your clothes on the hanger or the chair," I told him. "Go ahead and strip down to however you're comfortable. Lie facedown on the table, and I'll be back in a couple of minutes to see if you're ready."

The client didn't say a word; he stood next to the chair and lifted his gray T-shirt over his head. He was definitely military. Between his solid build and his nearly shaved head, he *screamed* soldier. I grew up inside and outside of Army posts my entire life, so I knew a soldier from a mile away. He folded his shirt and set it down on the chair. When his fingers tugged at his athletic pants, I left him alone to undress.

# CHAPTER **FOUR**

I pulled my phone out of my scrub pocket and read the first line of a text from my dad:

**See you tonight? Estelle is cooking and wants you to come.**

I could name at least a thousand things I'd rather do, but this is what the three of us—sometimes four—did every single Tuesday. I'd missed only one family dinner since moving out a year ago, and that was when my dad drove Estelle in our family RV to the boot camp graduation of some distant relative, so technically I guess I wasn't the one who missed it. They still had Tuesday dinner, on their family vacay, while back home Elodie and I shoved our faces with Domino's pizza straight out of the box.

I didn't respond to my dad because he knew I'd be there at seven. My "new" mom would be in the bathroom curling her hair while dinner kept warm in the oven. I'd be there on time, like I always was.

It had been at least three minutes since I got lost in my own world, and Elodie's client was waiting. I sent her a quick text to say **he better tip** with a smiley-face emoji so she would know I was teasing. I quietly announced myself, pulled back the curtain, and walked into the room. The lights were dimmed but still reflected the hideous shade of purple from the walls; it had always been my least favorite color. The candles had been burning long enough for the air to take on the clean smell of almond. Even after my restless night, the scent had the power to calm me.

He was on the table in the center of the room with the white blanket pulled up to his waist. I rubbed my hands together. My fingertips were too cold to touch someone's skin, so I walked over to the sink to warm them. I turned on the faucet. Nothing. I had already forgotten Bradley's warning, and for the last hour, I'd managed without water.

I wrapped my hands around the oil warmer on the edge of the sink. The burner was a little too hot, but it did the trick. The oil would be warm on his skin, and he probably wouldn't notice that the water wasn't working. It wasn't convenient, but it was manageable. I hoped that whoever worked last night's closing shift had put clean towels in the warmer before they left; I always made sure to do that.

"Any specific areas of concern or tension that you'd like me to focus on?" I asked.

No answer. Had he already fallen asleep?

I waited a few beats before I asked again.

He shook his shaved head in the face cradle and said, "Don't touch my right leg. Please," adding the flat "please" as an afterthought.

I had requests from people all the time not to touch certain parts of their bodies. They had their reasons, from medical conditions to insecurities. It wasn't my business to ask. My business was to make the client feel better and to provide a healing experience. I hadn't looked at his treatment form—actually, I don't even think I'd asked him to fill one out. Mali was the one who'd checked him in, so maybe she did?

"Will do. Would you like light, medium, or deep pressure?" I asked, grabbing the little bottle of oil off the cabinet shelf. The outside of the bottle was still really hot, but I knew it would be the perfect temperature when it hit his skin.

Again, no answer. Maybe he was hard of hearing. I was used to this, as well, working outside a military installation; all forms of difficulties and disabilities from war were familiar and welcome here.

"Kael?" I said his name, though I didn't know why.

His head popped up so quickly, I thought I'd frightened him. I jumped a little myself.

"Sorry, I just wanted to know what level of pressure you wanted."

"Any." He didn't sound like he knew what he wanted. Probably a first-timer. He put his head back into the cradle.

"Okay. Tell me if the pressure is too light or too firm and I'll adjust my touch," I told him.

I could be a little heavy-handed and most of my clients liked that, but I'd never worked on this guy before, and everyone was different.

Who knew if he'd ever come back? I'd say only four out of ten first-timers actually returned and only one or two would become regulars. We weren't a big salon, but we had a steady clientele.

"This is peppermint oil." I dotted the little bottle against my forefinger. "I'm going to rub some into your temples. It helps with—"

He lifted his head up, lightly shaking it. "No," he said. His voice wasn't harsh, but it let me know he absolutely did not want me to use peppermint oil. Okay . . .

"Okay." I screwed the lid back on the bottle and turned the faucet. *Damn it.* The water. I knelt down and opened the towel warmer. Empty. Of course it was.

"Um, just a second," I told him. He laid his head back into the cradle and I shut the warmer door a little too hard. I hoped he didn't hear it over the music. This day was turning to shit and I was only on my second client . . .

# CHAPTER FIVE

Mali was in the hallway when I pushed through the thin curtain to search for towels. "I need water. Or warm towels."

She put her fingers to her lips to tell me to hush. "There's no water. I have towels. Who didn't stock?"

I shrugged. I didn't know and didn't really care, but I needed a towel quickly. "He's been in my room for five minutes and I haven't started yet."

At that she moved faster, disappearing into the room across the hall and popping back up with a few hot towels. I grabbed them from her, shifting the steaming bundles from palm to palm to cool them off.

When I got back into the room, I waved the towel through the air one last time and rubbed it across the bottom of his bare feet. His skin was so hot to the touch that I pulled the towel away and touched the back of my hand to the top of his foot to make sure I felt correctly. *I hope he isn't sick?* I couldn't afford to get sick; that's the last thing my mortgage payment and electricity bill needed.

Literally. The days on my dad's Tricare were coming to an end and I couldn't afford health insurance on my own.

His skin felt so warm. I lifted the blanket a little and realized he was still wearing his pants. That was just . . . strange. I didn't know how I was going to rub his other leg, the one I was supposed to massage.

"Did you want me to avoid your legs altogether?" I quietly asked him.

He nodded in the cradle. I continued to run the warm towel across the bottoms of his feet, something I did to clean off any oil and dirt. The hygiene of clients varied. Some people came in wearing sandals after walking around all day. Not this guy, though. He must have showered before he came in. I appreciated that. These were the things you thought about as a massage therapist. I started on the balls of his feet, applying pressure there and moving to the arch of his left foot. There was a soft, bubbly line across the bottom of his left foot, but I couldn't see the scar in the dark. I slid my thumb slowly along the arch and he jerked a little. I was used to timing my hour sessions perfectly, about five minutes per leg, so I took the extra time to work on his shoulders. A lot of people carried tension in their shoulders, but this guy was off the charts—his were absolutely the tightest shoulders and back I had ever worked on. I had to stop myself from making up a story about his life and why he was so stressed.

To keep my imagination at bay, I thought about Elodie again: Was she awake yet? Does she know this client? I continued, keeping his legs covered by the blanket and working on his neck, his shoulders, his back. His muscles were defined, but not bulky or hard under my moving fingers. Being near the military my whole life has taught me that someone as young as this man could easily be carrying the weight of something for a long time, whether it was a rucksack or life itself. He didn't express enough of himself for me to make up the details the way I did with Bradley and most of the other strangers around me. There was something about this guy that kept my storytelling quiet.

His scalp was the last part I worked on. The soft pressure release usually made people moan or at least sigh, but nothing came from his lips. He didn't make a peep. I thought maybe he'd fallen asleep. That often happened and I loved when it did. It meant I'd done a good job. When the time was up, I felt like it had just started. I usually drifted in and out of thought during a treatment—my dad, my brother, my job, my house. But there was something about working on this guy. Did I know him? I remembered nearly every face I saw, and I definitely would have remembered his. So I came up with nothing.

"Thank you. Was everything okay?" Sometimes I asked, sometimes I didn't. This guy was so quiet that I wasn't sure if he'd enjoyed it or not.

He kept his face in the cradle so I barely heard him when he said, "Yeah."

Okay . . .

"Okay, well, I'm going to step out and let you get dressed. I'll see you in the lobby when you're finished. Take your time."

He nodded and I left the room, pretty sure I wouldn't be getting a tip.

# CHAPTER **SIX**

I heard Elodie in the lobby. She was talking to Mali, who was giving her a hard time for being late.

"I don't know if you saw my text, but I took your client—he's dressing now," I told my friend. It didn't hurt to let Mali know that everything was covered, no harm done. Elodie smiled at me and tilted her head to the side. She had this thing about her where she could get away with anything.

"I'm so sorry, Karina. Thank you." She kissed both of my cheeks. That was something I got used to the first week she moved in. I wasn't really fond of excess touching, but with her it was hard to recoil the way I normally would.

"I couldn't fall asleep last night. The avocado started kicking." Her smile grew wide, but I could tell by her eyes that she wasn't rested. I could relate. Not to the pregnancy, of course, but to the feeling of living in a constant state of tired.

Mali put her hand on Elodie's stomach and started talking to the baby. I half expected her to ask the bump, *What's wrong, why aren't you smiling?* but Mali was soft and kind around children, even the ones who hadn't been born yet. It made me a little uncomfortable, the way she was touching Elodie like that, but the idea of the baby kicking was exciting, so I smiled. I really was happy for my friend.

It worried me that she was here alone while her family and most of her friends were across the Atlantic Ocean. She was young. So young. I wondered if she'd had the chance to tell Phillip that she thought she felt the baby move yesterday, or if he would even get to check his email today. The time zones made it so hard for them to talk as often as Elodie or anyone with a soldier in their life would want, but she was handling it with grace, as she did everything. It scared the hell out of me, though—the fact that she was going to have a baby in a few months. Sometimes I treated her as if she was a child herself.

Elodie's eyes snapped to the curtain behind me, and she lit up like a Christmas tree, pushing past me to the client. She said a name that I couldn't hear completely, but it didn't sound anything like Kael. She wrapped her small body around him and hugged him so tight that even a soldier would wince.

"You're here! I can't believe you're here! How did you know where to find me?" She squealed and hugged him again. His expression remained blank even though she was clearly happy to see him. Something about his face bothered me to the core. Maybe it was the way it probably made his life easier to have a face that people couldn't look away from, that people would gawk at. It made me uneasy to see Elodie clinging to him. Nothing good can come from a man with a face like that.

Mali nodded to my next client, who was walking through the front door. "Back to work for you," she said, and I caught one more glimpse of Elodie's friend before Mali shushed me away.

# CHAPTER SEVEN

Tina was one of my favorite clients. She worked from home as a family therapist and, more often than not, let me use her massage session as *my* therapy. I wasn't open with too many people, but Tina had no one to tell my secrets to. It made me sad for her, though, thinking about how lonely she must be, eating dinner by herself in front of the TV most nights. Then again, aside from Elodie, that was pretty much my life, too. I guess I shouldn't feel too much pity. At least Tina had a big house.

Today's session with her felt like it was never going to end. I checked the clock again: ten minutes left.

"So, how are things with your brother?" she asked. I moved her hair to the side so I could focus on the tight muscles in her neck. Tina had recently cut her hair—"the Demi," she called it—but hated it and immediately started wearing hats to cover her dark strands. It still wasn't long enough to put into a ponytail. I thought she looked beautiful and wished my hair was as thick and soft as hers was.

I didn't really want to talk about my brother. Actually, I didn't want to feel the way I would feel if we talked about my brother. My day already sucked enough.

"The same. I've barely heard from him since he's been staying with my uncle. Who knows when he's coming back." I sighed, gliding my fingers down the lower part of Tina's neck.

"Is he in school there yet?" she asked.

"No. They keep saying they're going to sign him up but haven't." I tried not to think much about it, but my brain didn't work that way. Once I cracked the door open, the wood snapped off the hinges and everything rushed in.

"It sounds like they don't plan on it," Tina said.

"Yeah. I figured as much. He won't talk to me about it, and his scholarship to the community college expired last month."

Little pokes of stress rapped at my shoulders and down my spine. I understood that Austin couldn't bear to live with our dad any longer, but I was conflicted; he was my twin, twenty and headed nowhere but the clouds. He shouldn't be living in the next state over with our thirty-year-old uncle who smelled like Cheetos and watched online porn all day, but I also didn't want him to live in my house with me. I knew that wasn't a good idea, even if Elodie hadn't been sleeping on my couch. It was complicated. I still couldn't believe my dad had let him leave in the first place. But I really couldn't blame my brother. Again, complicated.

"Honestly, Karina, you can't take on full responsibility for this. It's not good for you, and at the end of the day, your brother is an adult . . . the same age as you. Or five minutes younger, if I remember?"

"Six." I smiled and moved my hands down to her shoulder blades.

I knew she was right. Austin wasn't my problem to solve, but that didn't make it any easier.

I moved my hands along her skin, using a compression stroke. "You have to decide what's best for you," she said. "You're starting a new chapter and you should have the most decluttered life possible."

Easier said than done.

"I'll ask my dad if he's heard anything from him and leave it at that." I hated asking my dad about my brother because, even if he was a mess right now, he was still his son, the golden child. I could never compete with Austin for Dad's affection, no matter how hard I may have tried.

Tina didn't say anything after that. She must have known that talking through the drama of "dinner with my family" would be too much for me this early in the day, so she enjoyed the rest of her treatment while my thoughts boiled inside my brain.

# CHAPTER EIGHT

I attended to three more clients after Tina, and each of them occupied my mind in different ways. Stewart—I called her by the last name stitched into her ACUs—was an Army medic who had the most beautiful eyes I had ever seen. She kept me busy talking about her next post, about how, with her job, she could be stationed almost anywhere in the world, so being posted to Hawaii was like hitting the jackpot. It was nice to see her so happy. Part of me wanted to hide in her suitcase and run off to Hawaii and start all over. Maybe my anxiety wouldn't follow me that far.

Some people loved to move around in the military, and Stewart was one of them. She was only a year older than me, but she'd already been deployed to Iraq—twice. And, man, did she have stories. At twenty-one, she'd had experiences most people couldn't even imagine. But when those experiences turned into memories . . . well, they started playing through her mind on a constant loop. Never waning, never quiet, those memories became background noise, tolerable, but always there. I knew all about it. My dad's brain was full of that clamor. With six tours between Iraq and Afghanistan, his background noise wasn't just a personal soundtrack, it blared throughout our house. His house.

I thought about all of this while Stewart lay on my table. I was glad she could open up to me, that she could unburden herself by talking and releasing a bit of her background noise. I knew better than most that it wasn't only the physical aspect of massage therapy that reduced stress, that helped a body come alive and quieted the mind.

It was almost poetry the way Stewart talked about her life. I felt every word when she spoke. She connected me to each experience, and when she told me about the things she had been through and what she had learned, she opened me up to a different perspective. She talked a lot about how, in the United States, fewer than 8 percent of Americans had ever served in the military. That included all the branches—every veteran who enlisted, even for one term. Out of more than three hundred twenty million people, fewer than 8 percent! It was hard for me to realize that fact, given the way I grew up, moving from post to post, trying to make new friends, trying to adapt to strangers every few years.

It seemed impossible to me, that small a number. From my great-grandfather to my dad, and my uncles and cousins who were scattered across the country (except that loser uncle my brother was living with), everyone around me wore a uniform or lived with someone who did. The world had never felt so big until Stewart and her statistics. I knew that, as of now, only 1 percent of Americans were actively in the military. I hoped I could someday live among the other 99 percent.

She talked a lot during our sessions, like Tina. But unlike Tina, Stewart didn't expect me to share. I could lose myself in her experiences, many of which forced me to bite back my tears. Maybe that's why her sessions went by fast.

# CHAPTER NINE

The water came back on right after Stewart left. I washed the sheets and towels in the few minutes I had between appointments.

Elodie managed to be busy with a client each time I finished with mine. I was dying to ask her how she knew that soldier with the strange name and quiet presence, but we kept missing each other. I usually stayed out of other people's drama—I had enough of my own—but Elodie hardly knew anyone here, and I was curious about this connection of hers. The only people she talked to were on Facebook.

My next client was a sleeper. He usually conked out within five minutes, which left me with the entire hour to think about my brother. Oh—and how much I was dreading tonight's dinner. I was slightly envious of Austin for being far away in North Carolina, sleeping past noon and working part time at Kmart.

I also thought about Elodie's friend, how he wore pants throughout his treatment and how the amount of tension he held in his body wasn't healthy for such a young guy. He couldn't have been older than twenty-two. If that. He had a baby face, smooth skin, and a sharp jaw.

My last client of the day was a walk-in who left me a big tip for a thirty-minute prenatal massage. Her belly was full and she seemed so tired. I almost asked her if she was okay, but I didn't want to be rude so I kept my mouth shut.

I walked by Elodie's room again. The door was closed, and for a second I even imagined that her soldier friend might be in the room with her. My imagination sure was out of control. Before the end of my shift, I helped Mali restock the back room and the towel warmers, and I folded the laundry. I wasn't in a rush to leave, especially on so-called family dinner night.

When I finally left for the day, I took Mali's delicious leftovers home with me. That whole thing about pregnant women eating for two might be an old wives' tale, but Elodie was walking proof of its truth. I carried the food in one hand and tried to call my brother with the other. Voicemail after two rings. Asshole.

"Hey, it's me. I'm calling to check on you. I haven't heard from you in a few days. Call me back. I'm going to Dad's for Tuesday dinner, as always. You suck for not being here, as always."

I hung up and put my phone in my front pocket. Around me, the sky looked like the sun couldn't decide to set or not, staying an orange color that made everything look a little nicer, a little softer. The parking spots in the alley were all taken. Bradley's white truck was there—parked sideways across two spots—and the truck bed was so full of mattresses it reminded me of that fairy tale about the princess and the pea. He walked out the back door and tossed a pillow into the pile.

"Water's back!" he shouted, waving his hand.

"Yeah . . ." I said, smiling. "Thanks for being on the water company!" I added.

Okay, that was awkward. I could feel it. Bradley didn't seem to notice or overthink my words the way I did—he simply told me to have a good night, locked the door to his shop, and climbed inside his truck. I knew I would mull over my awkwardness all through the evening. My brain usually worked that way.

Doors slammed, tires crunched over branches, and voices filled the rest of my short walk home. I thought about dinner at my dad's tonight and what forced conversation we would have during at least three courses. Half of it would be about my brother, of that I was sure.

I had to be at dinner by seven, which meant getting ready to leave my house by six forty. I needed to shower and put civilian clothes on, even if I was giving my appearance minimal effort. My dad had stopped commenting on my looks once I'd lost enough "extra pounds" to please him. Small mercies, I guess.

I really wanted to stay home and eat leftovers with Elodie. Sure, dinner once a week was better than living there—by far. But I hated the task of it. Every week since moving out I'd told myself the same thing: that I'd get used to the routine. I hated that my entire week revolved around Tuesday at seven. When I did my laundry, when I washed my hair, when I brushed my teeth, when I worked—it all had to fit around this dinner. I guess I wasn't as much of a grown-up as I thought.

# CHAPTER TEN

I was starting to hate Facebook. Every single time I opened the app, there was a newborn baby, a proposal, or a death. If it wasn't that, it was politics, with everyone shouting so loudly they couldn't hear what everyone else was saying. The whole thing was exhausting and I had barely posted in months. I never felt like I did anything important enough to share with people I hardly knew. And unlike Sarah Chessman, who had moved away my senior year at Spencer High, I didn't feel like every Crockpot meal or selfie was social-media-worthy.

But out of slightly bitchy curiosity, and a tiny bit of envy I'd never admit to, and because I had another few minutes to waste on my walk home, I went to Sarah Chessman's page to scroll through her boring life. Maybe it was the fact that I was walking home through the back alley and my feet hurt like hell, or that I'd be knocking on my dad's door in an hour, but Sarah's life actually looked legitimately eventful. She had a husband—a newly minted soldier stationed in Texas—and she was pregnant. I watched a ten-second video of her opening a box full of pink balloons, revealing the gender of her soon-to-arrive baby. Gender-reveal parties were starting to piss me off. What was the point? Why did people spend money on them? If I ever had one, who would even come?

I started to feel like a hypocrite for judging her, so I clicked back to my main feed. My dad had posted a picture of himself holding a fish in one hand and a beer in the other. He wore a smile that I had never seen in person. He always loved to hunt and fish; my brother and I couldn't stomach it. Austin could handle the gore a bit more than I could; he would go on hunting trips with Dad until we got to high school and girls became his favorite pastime. My brother, whom I had talked to nearly every day up until a few months ago but now could barely get on the phone, had already liked my dad's post. So did someone with a golden retriever as their profile picture. The golden-retriever friend had commented that my dad was "looking happier than ever."

It stung. It really stung. Probably because it was true. I had been hearing that phrase since he got remarried two years ago after a whirlwind romance of less than a year. We had barely unpacked our boxes from our move to Fort Benning when my dad met Estelle on Facebook, of all places. He commented on a mutual friend's picture and their romance took off from there. From the neighbors to the cashiers at the PX, everyone thought it was okay to congratulate my dad on how happy he was. No one thought about me . . . that I was in earshot, that telling him how happy he seemed *now* implied that he had been really unhappy before. No one considered my feelings. Not him, not Estelle, not the strangers. That's when I started clinging to people—boys, mostly. Some at my high school, some older. I was searching for something I wasn't getting at home, but I couldn't tell you what it was because I still haven't found it.

Most of all, I clung to Austin. Maybe it was the twin thing, or maybe it was the fact that our parents were never around when we needed them, when their guidance would have mattered. Staying close to my six-minutes-younger brother seemed to help for a while, but once we were out of high school, I started to consider that maybe Austin wasn't the person I had built him up to be. One of the weirdest parts of growing up was the way memories changed once the veil of naïve innocence disappeared.

Austin had once taken me to that party in Chesapeake Manor, where all the officers' kids were partying. He told me that everyone our age was drinking, that I should just relax. Then he passed out in one of the bedrooms with some girl from a high school across town and I was forced to sleep there, surrounded by loud, rowdy, belligerent boys. That's when one of them, the one who called me "Austin's sister" and had too deep a voice for a high school kid, swore I had a crush on him and shoved his tongue down my throat—repeatedly. Until I started crying and he got "weirded out."

Funny how my telling him to stop, my constant "No, no, no, please no!" didn't do it. Nope, it was the salty, hot tears streaming down my face that finally got him to go away. I guess he didn't like the way they tasted. Eventually I fell asleep on a couch listening to some war video game being played in the other room. Austin never apologized the next morning. He never asked how I had slept or where. He just kissed that random girl on the cheek and made a joke that she and I both laughed at, and then we Ubered home like nothing ever happened. Our dad yelled at me, not at him, and we both got grounded for a week, but three days in, Austin got to hang out with his friends, and since I didn't have any, I was stuck there.

I clicked on Austin's profile and thought about calling him again, but then Elodie opened the front door and surprised me. I hadn't even realized I was on my front porch.

# CHAPTER **ELEVEN**

My house is small: when you go through the front door, you're already in the living room. That's one of the things I like about it, the way it's all cozy and warm, everything there waiting for me. No surprises, except the faulty electrical work that I still haven't been able to fix correctly. The lights and TV were on when I got home that night, the room filled with the voice of Olivia Pope. And there was Elodie, standing at the door, greeting me with a nervous smile. Something was up.

I hadn't known Elodie that long, but I felt I knew her better than I knew the father who I'd lived with for a lifetime. We met at work on her first day hired. I found her in the cleaning supplies closet, crying because a client had yelled at her when the massage oil she used was too hot. We didn't have much in common, other than being the same age. And even that, well, I felt older some-how. I looked older, too. Elodie had this youthful air around her, a forever teenager, especially when she smiled. And when she was nervous or sad, she looked about sixteen. Maybe younger? That brought out the protector in me. I didn't have a choice but to grow up fast. Even at twenty, I barely remember a time when I was free of adult thoughts and worries.

Elodie tried her best to be the perfect young Army wife, but she was already at the center of so many petty rumors. The wives in Phillip's platoon made little jokes about her accent and called her a "mail-order bride," despite the reality that tons of soldiers met their wives online. I'm sure my client Stewart had some stats on that, too—about how many members of the military met their spouses on social media.

That didn't seem to matter to these women who entertained themselves by belittling Elodie. That's how a lot of military installations were—everyone bickering and jostling for position. Elodie's neighbors were snarky assholes who spent their days selling pyramid schemes on Facebook and bullying her over her grass being an inch too long. That's not an exaggeration. I was with her once when the "mayor" of her housing department pulled up, tires screeching, and scolded Elodie for letting her grass grow half an inch too long.

Yes, the "mayor" measured.

No, she didn't have anything better to do.

That's why Elodie preferred to spend her nights on my couch, or next to me in my bed, depending on where she fell asleep. I got the feeling she liked the couch the most. She didn't wake up asking for her mom or Phillip when she was on the couch.

I planned on asking Elodie about the guy, Kael, I had met earlier. Obviously, she knew him—but how? She didn't have many friends, as far as I was aware, and she didn't spend much time socializing.

While I was looking at my phone for a text from my brother, hoping for one—not surprisingly, there was nothing from him— Elodie walked to the couch, sat down, and tucked her feet under her. Her petite body was changing, her belly starting to swell. I wondered where the baby would sleep in my little house. The thought made me equal parts excited and terrified.

Elodie's favorite American show at the moment was *Scandal*.

She was binge-watching it for the first time, and while it was on, she was completely checked out. I wished I could find something that I loved as much, to distract my mind from its constant flow of thought.

"What season are you on now?" I asked, watching her spring up again.

"Two," she said softly, as she moved toward the kitchen.

She was being so quiet. I pulled my shoes off, and it wasn't until I dropped one on the floor and something moved in my peripheral vision that I realized another person was in my house.

A noise, a little like a shriek, flew from my mouth when I saw him. He was staring at me, the one-syllable client. He was sitting in my chair—the dark pink, used-to-be-red one that my nana gave my mom before I was born. I always loved it, and because it had sat in my dad's storage unit after my mom left, I decided it was mine to take. She left it, and us, and the chair was a tiny victory for me.

"Um, hey?" I said when my heart stopped doing little flips from the aftershock of surprise. How did I not see a whole human in my living room?

"How was work?" Elodie asked, looking at the TV while her fingers picked at the fabric on her frayed shorts, and then back at me.

"Good . . ."

I stared at this Kael guy and he stared back at me. When I would recall this later, the first time he was inside my house, the memory would linger in my thoughts, changing from a burning pain to pure bliss and back—again and again and again. But when it happened in real life, it happened fast. Before he was anything to me—before he was everything—he was just a quiet stranger with a blank face and distant eyes. There was something inscrutable about him, something so closed that I couldn't even begin to read him. He hated peppermint oil and hadn't wanted me to touch his legs during his treatment—those were the only clues I had about who he was. He stared at me for a few seconds, then looked away and stared at the wall for so long that I almost wanted to count the seconds until he blinked.

I smelled the popcorn right before the popping sound started. "I'm making popcorn," Elodie announced. She was nervous. What was going on here? Were they having a movie night? Netflix and chill? The whole situation was weird. He was fucking weird.

"Okay . . ." I excused myself. "I'm going to take a shower. Have to be at my dad's at seven."

I walked down the hallway. Elodie followed, chewing on her bottom lip.

"Well?" I asked.

"He arrived home last night. He was with my Phillip." Her voice was low, and I could tell she was gearing herself up to ask me something. My mom was like this, too, when she wanted something.

"Can he stay here for a day until he can get a hold of his . . ." She trailed off, stopping for a second. "Until he can get into his place. Sorry to ask like this, I—"

I held up my hand. "How do you know this guy?"

"Oh—I met him right before they left. He's a good guy, Karina. Honest. He's Phillip's closest friend over there."

"What's he doing back?" I asked her.

She shook her head. "I didn't ask. Should I ask?" She peered into the living room.

"I wouldn't now," I told her. "He can stay here, but if he ends up being a problem, he's out. So are you," I teased her.

She smiled at that and touched my arm. She was always so affectionate. Me, not so much.

"Thank you. You're the—"

"I know, I know. I'm the best. Now I have to shower so I'm not late to my dad's."

She rolled her eyes. "Yeah, you should thank me."

We both laughed and I shut the bathroom door in her face and sank against the wall. I'm not the kind of person to let a stranger, especially a man, stay in my house, but there I was, muddying my judgment for the first of many times when it came to Kael.

# CHAPTER **TWELVE**

My house was in dire need of a few-ish repairs. It'd been that way since I'd moved in nearly a year ago. Every day it was the same dance, bouncing from foot to foot, completely naked, waiting for the water to heat up. That wasn't even the worst of it. Once the water got hot, it didn't stay that way—not for long, anyway.

The water went from hot, to cold, to hot again. I could barely stand it. I loved my slightly shabby house, but there were a lot of things that needed fixing and it was going to take a while to get through them all. I tried to do some of the smaller renovations myself. Like the shower tiles I bought during an overly adventurous Saturday afternoon at the hardware store. I bought cans of paint, little tubes of white gunk to patch the holes in the hallway walls, some knobs to replace the ones on the kitchen cabinets, and some tiles for the bathroom. The knobs found their way onto the cabinets. I had to admit they really did update the cabinetry like HGTV told me they would. I wasn't necessarily good at home demo, but I really loved doing it with the little bit of money I had.

I painted the kitchen walls. Then I started the bathroom shower tiles. As in, I removed about half of them and replaced maybe . . . six.

I counted them.

Okay, so eight.

As convenient as it was to use the constant "remodel" as a way to discourage guests, most notably my dad, I really wished I had the money and skill to do everything I wanted to do to the house. One day I would. This house was my way to prove that I could take care of myself. I didn't know who I was trying harder to convince, myself or my dad. And did it really matter?

The water was finally warm enough to wash my hair. It shorted out on me only a couple of times. When I turned it off, the shower still dripped behind me as I rough-dried my hair. I thought again of Elodie's friend, the stranger in my house. He seemed nice enough, but too quiet. Was he rude or just shy? His demeanor didn't come off as shy at all. As I wrapped a hand towel around the leaking bath faucet and plugged in my hair dryer, I wondered if Phillip was the kind of guy who would mind his friend staying with his pregnant wife. I started to feel uneasy as I blow-dried the tips of my hair. It was impossible to blow-dry in less than thirty minutes and I had only about ten before I had to leave. That would have to do.

I had to do laundry—and soon. I didn't need to be super-dressed-up for my dad and his wife, but I knew my outfit—and Estelle's—would be topics of conversation at the dinner table. Outside of our apparel and the typical "Have you seen any good movies lately?" question, my stepmom had nothing to talk to me about. To be fair, I had even less to say to her. My dad's insult framed as a question, about my career, always came up toward the end of dinner. As predictable as the tide, he made me feel lousy about my job, no matter how much I loved it. It didn't matter. It wasn't enough. It would never be. He made me feel like shit.

I could hear Elodie's voice as I got dressed. It sounded like she was trying to explain *Scandal* to her soldier friend. She was the absolute worst at explaining movies or shows to anyone. She always got character names confused and would spoil the ending without even meaning to. As someone who hated spoilers, I now knew better than to ask her about anything she had already seen.

I barely had any clothes left in my dresser, so I shoved my hand in the Forever 21 bag next to my nightstand. There wasn't much of use in the bag: a pair of jeans one size too big and a brown button-up shirt that fit me everywhere but the chest. I stretched my arms out to see how much of an opening there was between the buttons. Ugh, too much. The last thing I needed was for my dad to comment on my clothes being too small. I ended up throwing on a black T-shirt with a little pocket on it and my go-to black jeans with a hole at each knee. I knew my dad would comment on them, but he always made the same jokes. "You have a hole in your pants." Or "I hope you didn't pay full price for destroyed jeans."

I finally made it out to the living room with about five minutes to spare before I had to leave. Kael was sitting in the same spot, his eyes looking like they were going to close at any minute, his T-shirt clinging to his broad shoulders. The chair looked so small when he was in it. He had to be at least six inches taller than me and at least ten taller than Elodie. The longer I looked at him, the bigger he seemed to grow.

Elodie darted out of the kitchen with a big bowl of popcorn. "Leaving?" she asked.

I nodded, digging my hand into the bowl. I was starving. I couldn't even remember if I'd had anything to eat today. I knew Mali's food was in our fridge and I would eat it as a late-night snack after barely touching whatever Estelle would be serving.

"I'm going to be late," I said, groaning.

"What would happen if you didn't go?"

Elodie and I often joked about my Tuesday date. We did that every single Tuesday, to be exact.

"They would disown me." I looked at Kael. He wasn't looking our way, but somehow, I knew he was listening. He was a soldier, after all.

"So, wouldn't be so bad, yeah?" She licked her buttery fingers and then wiped them across her shorts.

"Not bad at all, actually." I grabbed my water jug from the table by the couch. Elodie went a little far with the salt on the popcorn. "Do you want me to bring you home dessert?"

She nodded, smiling with a mouthful of kernels.

"I'll be back around nine thirty. Maybe later, but hopefully not," I told both of my houseguests. I found myself wondering what they would be doing after I left. The images in my head bothered me a little, not only because Elodie was married, but because this guy seemed off. Before I could even contemplate that, his voice surprised me as I reached the door.

"Can I use your shower?" His voice was soft as rain, and he looked at me patiently, a look I would come to know well.

Kael was familiar in the way that only a stranger could be. I hadn't seen him before today, but already I had memorized his face. The thick draw of his brow, the little scar above his eye. It was like I had come across him somewhere, or sometime, before. Maybe I had seen him in passing, at a store or on the street, in line for a coffee or to pay for gas. Or maybe he had one of those faces that felt familiar. There were people like that.

"Can I?" he asked again.

I fumbled a little. "Um, yeah. Of course. Of course, you can shower."

"Thanks," Kael muttered and stood up, heading toward the bathroom.

He looked so big next to my little leather couch. Actually, he looked so big next to everything in my house, even the china cabinet I bought off Craigslist, before I realized how dangerous it was to meet strangers in the back of the Walmart parking lot. I had a lot of stuff in my house, most of it old and previously owned. Until now, I'd never thought about how my home may have looked to others, but suddenly I felt insecure that he might be judging me. Did he notice the pile of dirty clothes desperately waiting to be washed, the stack of dirty dishes in the sink?

And why did I care?

"If there's that one pie . . ." Elodie struggled for the English word. "The one with the little cer—" She held up her fingers and I finished her thought for her.

"Cherries?" I had retained zero of what I learned from high school French class. Elodie nodded, but she didn't have to. I knew she could eat an entire cherry pie in one sitting—I'd seen her do it. And who could blame her? My dad's wife, Estelle, was a decent cook. If I liked her more, I would admit that she was a great cook. But I didn't, so I wouldn't.

I assured Elodie if there was cherry pie on offer it would be hers.

"Is he always this quiet?" I asked her. Then I shouted, "Towels are in the closet behind the bathroom door!" loud enough that he would hear me. Of course, he didn't respond, but I heard the cabinet creak, so I knew he'd heard me.

She shrugged and winced a little. "I don't know . . ."

"Yeah, don't remind me." I sighed, wondering again what I had agreed to.

She chewed on her lip the way she always did, and I gave her a somewhat reassuring smile. I left before another minute could pass.

# CHAPTER **THIRTEEN**

I was late. Not a five-minute, "Oh, there was traffic" late. This was big late, the kind of late that would end with my dad's dramatic sighs and a lecture about how Estelle had to keep the oven on to warm the food, but now the chicken was all dried up, and did I ever think of anyone but myself? I was already supposed to be at my dad's house and I was still sitting in my driveway. As I said, *late*.

I wasn't sure why I was prolonging my lateness by sitting in my car and staring out the windshield in silence. Sometimes I wished my car wouldn't start, so I wouldn't have to go, though my dad would complain even more and come pick me up. I hated any and all obligations that I had no control over. I didn't like to be told what to do and where to be, and yet I let my dad put that burden on me. He'd applied that kind of pressure my whole life— and I did nothing to stop it.

I checked my phone again: a missed call from a random number. When I called back, an automated robot voice said it was a collect call for my mother. I bet the bill collector would have more success finding her than I would. My mom was the last person I needed to think about right now, and I started to feel that sinking pit in my stomach that I didn't have the energy for tonight.

I went on Instagram out of habit and scrolled through pictures of girls I had known in high school who were now starting their adult lives or in the military themselves. Not a ton of people I went to high school with ended up going to college. For money or whatever reason, it just wasn't the norm like it was in movies. I stopped scrolling when I saw a picture of a coast, bright blue water, and white sands. This was the backdrop to a couple of lounge chairs shaded by beach umbrellas, and in the corner of the photo, two hands clinking glasses of what I guessed were piña coladas. The caption read "OMG if you think this view is nice, wait till we post pics tonight!!! The sky here is sooooo beautiful!" with a bunch of heart-eye emojis. The account belonged to Josie Spooner, a one-time friend and a complete social narcissist who posted every time she left the house. Her daily coffee cup with a quote about how she's "ready to kick Monday's ass!" or "Ugh, people suck. So bad. Don't feel like talking about it!" filled my feed often. What was the purpose of telling the world that she didn't want to talk about it—why post it? I didn't know why I didn't just delete her, or my whole account. I hadn't spoken to her since we moved from Texas. Then again, if I deleted everyone who annoyed me on social media, I would have zero friends.

I was mid–eye roll when I caught something out of the corner of my peripheral vision. It was Kael, dressed in his tan camouflage ACUs, striding down the grass and onto the sidewalk.

I rolled my window down and called to him. "Hey!"

He walked toward my car and leaned into the open passenger-side window. He had to duck down a little so he could see me. His eyes were bright in the setting sun. They were more than bright, they were striking. They were distracting; the unnerving cocktail of vulnerability and certainty in them seemed to sway me, to make me want to be kind to him.

"Where are you going? Was something wrong with the shower?

I know it can be a pain in the ass. The water goes from boiling to freezing in like one second and—"

"Shower was fine." He had one of his hands hidden in the pocket of his uniform pants and the other was resting on the window lining. The black ink tattoo on his forearm was in full view. I couldn't tell what it was without staring, and he was way too close to not notice.

"Are you going somewhere?"

"To my company," he answered softly.

"Right now?" I looked at the street to see who was there to pick him up, but there were no cars. "You're walking?" I asked, again engaging in way too much conversation with him. Every few seconds I forgot I was already late to dinner.

He shrugged. "Yeah. My truck's there." He looked down at his uniform. "And all of my clothes."

"But it's so far from here to walk. Why don't you call an Uber?"

He shrugged again.

Was he really going to walk three miles?

I looked at the digital clock on my dash: 7:06. I should be knocking on my dad's door right now, but here I was, sitting in my driveway, debating with myself whether or not to offer him a ride to his company. We were both going to the same place, after all . . . well, depending where his company was—Fort Benning wasn't as big as, say, Fort Hood, but it was spread out and took a while to get from one side to the other.

Without saying a word, Kael stood up straight, his upper body disappearing from view as he walked away. I called out for him again and leaned toward the passenger side, almost by instinct.

"Do you want a ride? I'm going through the West Gate—where's your company?"

He leaned down again. "It's near Patton, same gate, but I'm good. Thank you, though."

I was a bit annoyed and surprised by his blunt response, so it took me a second to say anything.

"I'll literally pass it on my way. I'm already late anyway, it won't kill me to be a tiny bit later." I said that, but I knew every second would count with my dad.

I could only see Kael's hands, because they were no longer in his pockets. He was fiddling with his fingers, picking at the skin around his fingernails. An anxious tick? I could have watched him stand there for an hour, taking in the tiny bits of character he was giving me. My mouth was physically dry, desperately drinking in the smallest details, the freckle on the tip of his thumb.

The way he dug at his skin reminded me of my brother. He had skin peeling around every visible finger. Austin used to get so antsy during car rides, especially those to visit our mom in her apartment right after she'd moved out. She bounced from place to place and my brother's hands bore the evidence of his pain and her instability. The first place on Clear Creek Road was right outside of Fort Hood . . . we ate frozen pizza off paper plates while my dad stood over us. The second one, only a block away from the first, was a little smaller and a little messier, and she said she lived alone but the soldier's boots by the door said otherwise. By the time she was in the third and final apartment, with a handful of roommates she didn't even try to hide, Austin had such thick scabs around every finger. One of Mom's roommates walked in smoking a cigarette and offered it to my brother, who was sixteen at the time. Our mom and dad screamed at each other for so long that night that I fell asleep on Austin's shoulder, and I woke up to my dad yanking open the car door and shouting that we were never, under any circumstance, to be around her without his supervision.

As I sat in the driveway, I shook my head, trying to jumble up the memories enough to lose them and stay present in this moment with Kael.

"Do you want a ride or not? I really have to get going," I repeated my offer, annoyed at myself for persisting.

"Aren't you already late? Elodie seemed pretty worried about you being late." He leaned down to look at me and I noticed his eyes on my cell phone screen. "More worried than you, at least."

I smiled sarcastically and plugged my phone into the cord connected to my car. "Are you going to get in or not? Last chance."

He made eye contact with me and held it just a second too long. I looked at myself in the rearview mirror while I thought of something witty yet sarcastic that I might say as I drove off, leaving him in the driveway.

He changed my plan by trying to open the passenger door behind me. I pressed the lock button to prove a point.

"This isn't an Uber," I told him, only half joking, and unlocked the doors.

He walked around the car, opened the passenger door, and sat down next to me. This was different. Usually my only passenger was pint-sized Elodie, but here was this big guy sitting next to me with his knees touching the dashboard, smelling like my coconut body wash.

"You can adjust the seat," I told him.

I put the car in reverse and my gear shift stuck for a second. It had been doing that lately. My reliable Lumina had been on this earth for more years than I had and was one of the few constants in life since I bought it for five hundred dollars on my eighteenth birthday. It was the first thing that was solely mine, and I didn't ask for a penny from my dad.

I was the only one of my friends to have a job in high school, working part time and weekends as a server at a local pizza place. My small group of friends would complain, trying to pull me away from work to go to parties, to the lake, to smoke weed in the parking lot of the elementary school where we hung out. Yes, elementary school. We were mildly delinquent, but at least I could pay for my own delinquency. All of them relied on their parents for allowance, and all three of them had since moved away. One went to Kentucky for college, one to Colorado for a change of scenery and a more exciting life, and one to Kansas for a soldier who promised to love her forever.

"Ugh," I groaned, and jiggled the gear, frustrated at my car and the lie of forever. No one could ever love someone forever. After all these years growing up, love itself was the biggest lie I'd been told throughout my life.

"Yeah, my car and my house are falling apart. I know," I said, before Kael could.

He looked over at me, confusion clear on his face.

"Didn't say anything." He shrugged and looked out the window.

I jiggled the gear one more time and it finally moved. I looked at him again and I swear there was a tiny bit of a smile on his face. It was hard to look away from. He annoyed the shit out of me and I hated that his first impression of me outside of the spa had been a big, bright banner of my failing life. My tires crunched down the gravel driveway and we were on our way.

I picked up my phone and saw my dad's name across the top. I didn't need to read the text to know he was asking me where I was. I also didn't need to respond, because why would I? I knew he'd lecture me anyway, and I'd rather keep it to one instead of two.

Yay for Tuesdays.

# CHAPTER **FOURTEEN**

The alley across the way looked deserted as we pulled onto the street. It was after work, with the shops now closed. Everyone had cleared out in the last hour, but Bradley's truck was still outside his mattress shop. Sometimes I would watch him drive from his shop to his house directly across the street with a truck bed full of mattresses, which always left me wondering what he was really transporting. Kael buckled his seatbelt across his chest and I ignored the annoying ding my car gave, the one that reminded me to put my seatbelt on. Luckily it was an old car so it would ding only once, sometimes twice. I always waited to put my seatbelt on later, a few streets away. I'm not sure why—a little bit of living recklessly, I guess.

As I got closer to my dad's house on post, the familiar creep of dread was washing over me. I thought about trying to start a conversation with Kael, but from what little I knew about this guy, talking wasn't really his thing. I glanced over at him and quickly turned on the radio. I had never been around anyone who made me feel this prickly awkwardness before. I couldn't explain what this felt like—couldn't even be sure that I disliked it—but I just had this weird desire to talk to him. What was that? The urge to pierce the air, the need to fill the space with words? Maybe Kael had it right by choosing his words sparingly, and the rest of us had it wrong.

My Spotify was playing a song I hadn't heard before, but I recognized Shawn Mendes's voice immediately. I turned the volume up a little, trying to contain my inner fangirl on hearing a new song from him for the first time. Kael didn't react at all to the music, even when I turned it louder and played the song twice in a row. He sat there, like a statue, in my car as I drove closer and closer to the impending doom of the dinner table.

My gas indicator light came on, a bright reminder of my disorganization and irresponsibility. When the Shawn Mendes song finished, it was time for an ad break: a testimonial for a weight-loss clinic, great for my psyche, and an offer for low-interest car loans. "Huge military discounts!" the voice promised, with a borderline drill-sergeant shout. Someday I would be grown-up enough to pay for ad-free listening, but that day wasn't here yet.

"I can play something else if you want," I told him, ever the cordial host. "What kind of music do you like?"

"This is fine."

"Okay." I replayed the new Shawn song a third time.

I exited the highway and was glad to see there wasn't a line to enter the base. I loved living on my side of town, close enough to the post, but far enough from my dad that I could breathe.

"Here we are," I said, as if he couldn't see the bright lights ahead of us.

He shifted his hips and pulled out a dog-eared wallet from the pocket of his ACU pants. He dropped his military ID into my open hand. The tips of his warm fingers grazed my skin and I jerked my hand away. His ID fell between the seats.

"Damn it. Sorry." I shoved my fingers into the slim slot and managed to grab the card just as it was my turn to approach the guards.

"Welcome to the Great Place," the soldier working the gate said.

"Really?" I couldn't help but tease him.

Ever since the soldiers were required to recite that ridiculous motto, I gave them shit about it. I couldn't help it. I did it in Texas and carried it on to Georgia.

"Yes, really," he said, his tone neutral. He inspected our ID cards and the standard decal stuck to my windshield.

"Have a good night," the soldier told us, though I knew he didn't care about our night.

He probably thought we were together, that I was some barracks whore driving us to this guy's small room, where we'd have sex while his roommate slept in the other bed. Who even came up with the term *barracks whore*? And why did I think it so freely, without considering that the soldiers were also sleeping with random strangers? I felt like shit knowing how easily the word *whore* slipped into my head. I made a mental note to get better at the way I think about other women.

"Uh—I don't know where I'm going," I reminded Kael.

"It's a right up here," he mumbled, as I was passing a street on the right.

"Right *now*?" I jerked the wheel to make the turn in time.

He nodded.

"Next light. Turn left there. There!"

"Dude." I rolled my eyes, stopping my car for a second.

"What?" The way he asked seemed like he'd forced himself to respond. I felt like he wanted to get out of my car as soon as possible and the thought sort of pissed me off. I didn't necessarily want to be playing taxi for a stranger who was allegedly Elodie's husband's bestie. I barely knew Phillip as it was, and his friend acting this way didn't exactly improve my opinion of Elodie's man.

"Sorry. Just go up a little further. It's there on the right. The brown building." He gestured in the general direction.

The buildings were nearly identical. The only things differentiating one from the other were the numbers painted on the sides. The one we were passing was either 33 or 88; the black paint was faded so I couldn't tell.

"Yeah, they're all the same big brown buildings here at the Great Place."

I swear I heard the tiniest hint of a laugh, just a small puff of smoke, enough to show that he was at least mildly amused by my comment. Sure enough, when I looked over, there it was—a sliver of a smile spread across his lips.

"It's here." He pointed to a massive parking lot. Kael kept his finger pointed at a navy-blue truck parked in the back of the mostly empty lot. I pulled up next to it, about a car's length away.

"Thanks . . ." He looked at me like he was searching for something.

"Karina," I told him, and he nodded.

"Thanks, *Karina*."

I tried to calm the swarm of bees in my stomach as he climbed out of my car without another word.

# CHAPTER FIFTEEN

I don't know what I expected Kael to drive, but this beast of a truck wasn't it. When I sized him up—literally and figuratively—I came to the conclusion that he'd drive something practical, like a black sedan or a medium-sized white pickup truck. But it wasn't this massive dilapidated blue thing with rust circling the wheel well and covering most of the passenger side. The truck-jeep-car thing said BRONCO in bold letters and had two big circle headlights. The tires were so oversized that the truck somehow made Kael look small. His truck-jeep thing was actually really cool, but it needed some work. The more I noticed about the car, the more I realized it suited him perfectly. Like the saying that dogs and owners start to look alike after a while. Or is it husbands and wives? Either way, his truck simply fit him. He had the standard Georgia plates, peaches with the corny slogan, and *Clayton County* printed across the bottom. I had no idea where that was.

I wondered if he actually was from Georgia or if he bought the car here. You never knew with soldiers. Cars seemed to drop from the sky above. If his hometown was really in Georgia, I wondered how he felt being here with home not far away. Or did it feel far away? The perspective depends on your situation. I would feel distant even if I was in the same county as my dad and his wife, but maybe Kael had a good relationship with his family and felt close and content and okay with that. I didn't know this about him, but now I wanted to find out.

I kept watching Kael; I don't think I'd ever seen someone like him. He wasn't doing anything spectacular like men in the novels I'd read and films I'd seen, but there was something inside of him that made him sort of glow compared to other people. He was charming, too, but in an unassuming way. He knew who he was, and he gave me this almost competitive feeling, this little burn in my stomach to try to be on his level. He was Elodie's friend—and he was going to be sleeping in my house! Was it going to be weird? It was absolutely going to be weird. I yanked my visor mirror down and checked my appearance. The light surrounding the mirror came on, but Kael didn't notice. He was calling someone and standing at least ten feet away from where I was in my car.

Yikes.

I swiped under my eyes. The mascara on my lower lashes had left little flakes of black across the top of my cheekbone. I was pale. Abnormally so. I slapped and pinched my cheeks a little and sucked in my lips and counted to ten. It was what the girls my age were doing on Instagram and getting thousands of views doing so. It worked, but I looked way too frazzled for this evening. I should have finished styling my hair. I turned to scan my backseat, hoping to find one of my gigantic cloth scrunchies. I had at least two in my car at all times. Minimal time spent, with the illusion of effort. I watched as Kael stuck his hand under the metal sheet above his front tire and felt along the surface. He tried to call someone else and I finally found a white hair tie and pulled half of my hair up. A lot of loose pieces of my wavy hair came down. I messed with them a little, and then put gloss on my lips. I glanced at my reflection one last time, and when Kael hung up the phone, I closed the mirror.

The more I watched him, standing there in the dark, pacing around with his iPhone going back and forth from his pocket to his cheek, the more I felt uneasy about this whole situation. I thought Elodie's excitement over his arrival might be her loneliness getting the better of her—someone familiar taking the place of the husband she missed so much. She was so lonely lately that some days she cried all night. This Kael guy was the closest person to her husband, and I was the closest friend she had, so I needed to be on guard with him, making sure he was not just spying on his buddy's pregnant wife. Soldiers did that more often than you'd think.

I was about to Google Clayton County and his license plate number when he opened my car door and leaned down, totally dominating the space, or lack of, between us. I leaned away from him; it almost felt like I *had* to.

"You can go," he told me.

I didn't know him well enough to decipher what he was really thinking. It almost felt rude. I wanted to challenge him, to taunt him for being locked out of his car, but I was about to piss myself; I was already late and had no room to be snarky. But I was curious about this soldier.

I looked at his truck and back to him. "Can you not get in?"

He sighed heavily and shook his head. I could see the frustration emanating from his body. He seemed like someone on the brink of losing a very carefully crafted control. So different from the man standing in my hallway minutes ago and sitting calmly in my car on the drive over. His breathing was dancing the line of composure and chaos. In my twenty years on this earth, I'd come across many a frustrated man. Why did this one spark my curiosity so uniquely?

"My keys are supposed to be here on my tire. But I'll find my way back, it's cool."

"I'm so late to this thing I have to do, but honestly—"

"The dinner? I don't think you should be any later than you already are," he cautioned.

So he was paying attention.

"Yeah, the dinner. I can't take you back before . . . but maybe I can call my dad and cancel. It's not like—"

Kael interrupted me. "It's cool, for real."

I couldn't just leave him here. There were barely any cars parked in the lot, and I couldn't see other soldiers walking or standing guard anywhere. I really didn't want to leave him stranded.

"Why haven't you left yet?"

I opened my door and got out of the car. "I don't know. I feel bad," I replied. "It's a long walk back. Do you have another set of keys somewhere? Or a friend who can come help you?"

"All my friends are in Afghanistan," he said.

My chest burned.

"Sorry," I said, leaning my back against my car.

"For what?"

We kept eye contact until he blinked. I quickly looked away.

"I don't know. The war?" It sounded so stupid coming from my mouth. An Army brat apologizing to a soldier for a war that had started when they were in kindergarten. "Most people wouldn't have asked me, 'For what?'"

Kael's tongue grazed his bottom lip; he tucked it between his teeth. The parking lot lights above us clacked on, buzzing, breaking our silence.

"I'm not most people."

"I can tell."

The lights shone through the windows of the barracks across the street, but it didn't seem like he lived there. That meant he was either married or higher-ranking than his age would suggest. Soldiers below a certain rank could live off-post only if they were married, but I couldn't imagine that a married man would be sleeping on my chair right after a deployment. Besides, he wasn't wearing a ring.

I was checking out his ACU jacket for his rank patch when I saw his eyes on me.

"Are you coming with me, Sergeant, or are you going to make me stand in this parking lot until you call a locksmith for your car?" I looked at the patch on his chest, his last name stitched in capital letters: *Martin.* He was so young to be a sergeant.

"Come on." I put my hands up, begging. "You don't know me, but this is what will happen if I leave you here. About five seconds after I drive away, I'll feel guilty, and I'll obsess over it the entire way to my dad's. I'll imagine you getting hit by a car or passing out or something. Some awful death scenario, and then by the time the dinner is over it'll be worse. Way worse." I rolled my wrist in a circle and looked him right in the eyes.

My mouth was dry. I was talking a lot, and not slowly. It didn't seem to annoy him and I wasn't even getting that little bubble of fear of rejection from basic contact with other humans like I usually did. I continued, more animated.

"I'm talking apology texts to Elodie, who'll be stressed because she worries about everyone, and then we're talking the guilt level of stressing out a pregnant woman, and good Lord, who knows what will happen to the baby?"

"The Lord," he said randomly. I studied the scar in his eyebrow as he spoke. It was small but somehow made his look more interesting.

"What?"

"You said, 'Who knows what will happen.' So, I answered you." He didn't smile, even when I nearly cackled. I covered my mouth with my hands to keep my laughter in.

This guy was the kind of funny everyone wanted to be. The kind who could just say random stuff like "the Lord" and it was effortlessly funny. He was probably never awkward, and he seemed like he knew he was good at humor. He didn't physically show it, but I could hear it.

"Are you always funny?" I asked him.

He shook his head, looking away from me. I stared at him, but he didn't let up or look at me.

"Anyway, I'll have to drive around trying to find you if you haven't made it back yet. It's messy, Kael, and probably easier if you just get in. I'm sure my dad's called me at least five—"

"Okay, okay." He held up his hands in mock defeat. I nodded, smiling in my victory, and you know what? He almost smiled back.

# CHAPTER **SIXTEEN**

No matter where we were stationed, my dad always chose to live within the gates of the post, in the housing that was offered. From both of the Carolinas, down to Georgia, to Texas. I didn't mind it so much when I was young, because the small handful of friends I had lived very close by, but as we moved, then moved again, and again, it got old fast. I started to hate the groomed cul-de-sacs, all the American flags and impeccable yards, and the lines of cars at each gate every single time we left the post. The older Austin and I got, the more we hated it. But our dad loved his Army life: the commissary and the PX convenience store, both tax-free, and the company where he worked every day just down the street. He felt empowered in this domain, but as Austin and I grew up, we started to feel trapped.

Austin and my caged feeling was nothing compared to our mother's. When we were younger, she was alive and bright with the excitement of a new place, a new environment every time we moved. But as the weeks went by she would begin to pace around the new house, picking at little things, rearranging the dolls in her open glass cabinet, to introduce her own bit of chaos to the pristine quarters my dad expected her to maintain. She was always up, up, up or down, down, down. There was never an in-between.

There were these hours of madness that seamlessly morphed into days of lunacy. They began in small stretches of mornings when the curtains were never opened, lunches weren't packed, and my dad yelled about the empty coffeepot or the laundry left in the dryer for days. My mom would start to smoke again on the porch, staring at the replicated identical houses on the street. When it got really bad the couch turned into her bed and Austin and I knew better than to comment on our parents' sleeping in separate parts of the house. We also sort of enjoyed the peace that came with their distance.

As I stared at the road in front of me, Kael's quietness allowed me to continue thinking about the slow unraveling of Mrs. Fischer the First. Her decline was subtle, with each episode lasting only a few days and mostly peaking when my dad was at work. She had two personas for most of our life, and we watched her switch gears in an instant from military wife to a woman falling apart: the paranoia, the anxiety, the messiness of her ashtrays on the porch, and the stains on her clothes. By the summer after eighth grade, her mania had completely taken over. She woke up later and later, took fewer showers, stopped dancing, and even stopped pacing. She would stare at the wall in silence for hours, and even her fairy tales turned sinister and eventually burned out.

"You think I'm funny?" Kael's voice drew me out of my memories of my mom just as a knot in my chest was beginning to move up toward my throat.

He was eyeing the green light above us. I pressed the gas.

"What?" I faltered, clearing my throat. I was reliving my childhood while he was still on a question I had asked him. My chest was aching, and focusing on his cool voice and his steady eyes helped fade the image of my mom.

He turned his body toward me. I kept my attention on the road. We drove past a Subway and it reminded me of my brother always craving their cookies when he was stoned.

"People don't usually ask other people if they're funny. It kind of ruins the joke," he said, and stared out the window.

I gave him an annoyed look. "Do you want me to apologize for asking you about your humor? Is this a thing?" I turned onto the main road and tried to figure out where I was.

"No. Not a thing."

"Okay, so we're going to my dad's house and not only am I late, which he hates, he's kind of . . ." I exhaled, trying to pinpoint such a complicated man with one word. "He's sort of—"

"Racist?" Kael asked.

"What? No!" I felt a little defensive over his question, until I turned toward him and saw the look on his face. It said that he figured that was what I was going to say and that I couldn't find a tactful way to say it.

I didn't know what to think about that.

"He's not racist," I told Kael as we drove. I couldn't think of anything my dad had ever said or done to make me believe he was. "He's just kind of an asshole."

Kael nodded and leaned back in his seat.

"This dinner will drag on longer than it should. Too much food for three people. Too much matching cutlery, too much everything."

Kael nodded again. Ugh, his silence here wasn't helpful. He wasn't prepared for my father.

I made sure to stay on the main road, really the only route I could navigate without getting lost in the sprawl of Fort Benning. We were less than five minutes from my dad's house. But I was more than half an hour late. It would be fine. I was an adult, and something came up. They would get over it. I repeated that to myself and began to concoct an excuse that didn't necessarily involve a stranger staying at my house.

My phone vibrated in the cupholder between us, and I reached for it the moment I saw that it was Austin calling. I couldn't remember the last time he'd returned one of my calls.

"I'm going to get this, it's—" I didn't finish explaining to Kael.

"Hello?" I spoke into the phone but got only silence.

I lifted it from my cheek. "Damn it." I'd missed the call. I tried to call him back, but he didn't pick up. I hated feeling like I let him down by missing a call or not being there for him, even though he had no problem ignoring my calls and casually treating me like an inconvenience.

"If you see the screen light up, tell me. The sound doesn't always work." I looked down at my phone and Kael agreed with a nod.

"Another broken thing," I swear I heard him say. But when I asked him what he'd mumbled, he shrugged.

I turned onto my dad's street and tried to spend the last two minutes of the drive conjuring up an achievement, or something I could stretch to sound like one. I would need something to talk about after the scolding for my extreme tardiness. My dad always asked his darling wife and me the same questions. The difference was, it only took her planting a flower bed or going to someone else's kid's birthday party to get praise, when I could save a small village and he would be like, *That's great, Kare, but it was a* small *village. Austin once saved a slightly larger village and Estelle created two villages.*

It wasn't healthy to compare myself to his new wife or to my brother—I was self-aware enough to know that. But the way he cosseted her still bugged the hell out of me. And then there was the fact that Austin was my dad's doppelgänger, and I was my mom's. We were twins, but he looked like him and I looked like her. This worked out better for my brother than it did for me; to my dad, I was a copy, and a constant reminder of my mother.

"We're almost there. My dad's been in the Army a long time."

Kael was a soldier; he wouldn't need more of an explanation. He nodded beside me and looked out the passenger window.

"How long have you been in?" I asked.

I heard him swallow before he spoke. "Little over three years."

"And you've already deployed?"

He nodded. "Twice."

I was curious to know more, to ask him if he liked being in the Army, but we were pulling up in front of my dad's house.

"We're here," I warned him. "It's like a whole fiasco. Three courses. Lots of small talk and coffee after. Two hours, minimum."

"Two hours?" He blinked.

"I know. I know. You can take my car if you want to skip it, as long as you pick me up later."

"No, dinner's cool. Anything else I should know?"

"My dad doesn't do strangers. We could lie and say you're my brother's—Austin's—friend? He's my twin."

"Austin. Got it." Kael opened the passenger door and leaned down to talk to me while I was still in my seat.

I checked my hair in the mirror. It was almost dry. The air was thick with humidity and it showed. I wiped away the little black specks of mascara under my eyes.

I grabbed my phone. Austin hadn't called back. The pounding guilt was there again for not answering the call. It was only one call, I reminded myself.

"I'll tell you, however awful you think it's going to be, it's gonna be worse than that." The more I thought about it, he probably should have stayed in the car. I didn't even know him and he wasn't exactly friendly—but neither was my dad.

"Mhm," I thought I heard him say. I looked up as the passenger door shut. The reality of just how bad an idea it was to bring a stranger to Tuesday dinner was sinking in.

# CHAPTER SEVENTEEN

I was fidgety, wiping my hands on my legs. I always did that when I was nervous. We walked up the sidewalk as the little solar light trail was turning on with the sun going down. The house was brick, recently power-washed, and clean as always

"I'll do the talking," I said to Kael, as we approached the door. "Let me explain why we're late. Why *I'm* late." Then it dawned on me who I was talking to. A soldier wouldn't have a problem being quiet, especially not this one.

I really could have used a shot of tequila, or some magic pill to get rid of the race of thoughts tearing at my mind. Distracted by my anxiety, I started to knock on the white wooden door, then realized what I was doing, opened it, and took my shoes off, suddenly mortified that Kael could see I didn't have matching socks on. He politely took his boots off, setting them next to my little sneakers.

"One of the many rules in this house," I whispered to him, and he nodded, looking me in the eyes instead of around the room.

He followed me into the kitchen, which was filled with the aroma of honey and cinnamon, and what might have been ham. It smelled like a holiday.

"Hey! You made it. I was getting a little worried . . ." Estelle greeted me like she usually did. Fake. Whether it was excitement or worry, it was all fake.

"Sorry I'm late," I said. "I had to stay behind a little at work, um . . . and then I was helping Elodie's friend. I mean, Austin's friend. Well, he's sort of everyone's friend." I turned to introduce Kael. I was clearly freaking the hell out and we had been in the kitchen for maybe thirty seconds, max.

Estelle wasn't doing the best job, either, at hiding her surprise over the extra body in the room. "Oh, well . . . hey. Hi! I'm Estelle." Her big earrings shook with her head, and I found myself sort of using Kael's body as a shield from her.

My dad was seated at the head of the table when Kael and I entered the dining room. He might have been reading the *Army Times* or listening to the radio, but no, he was sitting in his king chair in silence. Just waiting. His confused look turned to stone as he stared at us in the entryway. I took him in, sitting there with his craggy face and sparse white hair. It was really thinning now. So was his papery skin. Everyone on my dad's side of the family turned to snow early. It looked beautiful on the women—at least it did in photographs—but I secretly hoped I would take after my mom, as I always had. She was eternal summer.

My dad moved his eyes off me without any expression on his face and looked at Kael, who took a step back. Instinct or nervousness—who knew? My dad was only a few inches over five feet tall and he was intimidating, even sitting down. He could be soft at times. And when he didn't want to, he could cut like a knife.

I was waiting for the fallout for being late when my dad finally stood up to shake Kael's hand, his eyes moving to the name on his chest.

"Martin, nice to—"

Estelle interrupted the conversation as she entered the dining room carrying a bowl with a big wooden spoon sticking out of it. She always wore slightly different versions of the same outfit: jeans with a little flare at the bottom and a button-down shirt with a pattern. With the exception of the fitted dresses she showed off in pictures on her Facebook, she always dressed the same way. I had never really seen Estelle less than put together, even during that first year of their marriage when we all lived under the same roof. My brother and I would come downstairs before school and she would offer us eggs or toast and have fresh coffee left over from my dad, who left early each day for physical training. Her perfect outfits were a kind of uniform.

Today's top was striped blue and red. She told me once, while staring at both of our bodies in the mirror in the hallway, that she liked to buy these fitted shirts because of the way they flattered her shape. She twisted her torso like a model when she said it, as if she was having fun bonding with her new husband's daughter. It had been excruciating and made me feel like complete shit about the way I looked. I already had a complicated relationship with my body, and the last thing I needed was my new size-two stepmother telling me how to dress. Bonding for her was triggering for me and I don't know that I'll ever have the courage to tell her that.

"So, um, Kael is Elodie's husband's friend," I said, avoiding eye contact with my dad. "And he knows Austin. He's going to eat with us, okay? He's locked out of his car." I didn't want to go through all the details, so I hoped my fragmented word vomit made enough sense to avoid further questioning.

Estelle motioned for Kael to sit next to my dad. Kael glanced at me, then toward my dad. They shared a look I couldn't recognize, and as Kael went to sit down, I held my arm out, motioning for him to sit on the other side of me, as I took the chair next to my father. No need for Kael to occupy the hot seat.

"I'm assuming you've heard from your brother?" my dad inquired, skipping the niceties and small talk.

I pulled out my phone. "I missed a call from him."

"He's on his way."

"He's on his way where?" I asked.

"He's coming here, Karina." My dad took a long, slow drink of water as I wondered why the hell Austin would turn up at our dad's house. "He was arrested last night. Neither of you knew about it?" My dad's eyes were a carbon copy of my brother's. Bright blue ice.

I half stood up from my chair. "What? For what?"

"I don't know, exactly. The precinct won't tell me since he's over eighteen. If it had been on government property I could easily have found out," he said and huffed. My dad wasn't used to not getting what he wanted. I could see the faint twitch of his eye masking the disappointment and shame he was going to pour all over my brother once he arrived.

"And how is he getting here?" I asked. Whatever this incident was that got him arrested, it must have been the reason he'd been calling me on my drive over. And I missed the call. Guilt bit me a little harder.

"Driving." My dad shrugged.

Estelle sighed, still fussing over her presentation on the table. Moving effortlessly with stealth, she leaned over me to adjust the bread basket and reposition a napkin holder on the other side of the floral centerpiece.

"He's driving himself?" I immediately had a bad feeling about this.

Dad nodded. "He should be here in a couple hours."

Kael sat there with an almost diplomatic look on his face. His eyes were tracking whoever was speaking; he didn't look panicked or stressed or the least bit bothered. Something felt cold and political about his presence.

"Where is he going to stay?" I asked. "Will he have to go back to North Carolina to deal with the arrest?" I hoped it was only a minor infraction, something like public intoxication, which he'd dealt with before, not like the aggravated assault that got pinned to him that summer when Dad saved his ass because it happened on post; my dad's power was used as currency.

"He's staying here. And we don't need to talk about this anymore right now. Not in front of your . . ." He looked at Kael, but Kael's eyes were on me. "Friend," he pronounced.

Kael was still looking at me. I felt a bit dizzy from the intensity of his attention. Like the effect of a massage. I slowly started to feel my tensions releasing, enjoying the way my body was responding. Imagining that I could read his mind and he was saying something to calm me, I started to feel less dazed and confused. Maybe things would be okay?

"If you don't have anything useful to say about your brother, let's talk about something else," my dad said, moving the conversation off the subject of Austin's arrest. "Lighten up the mood."

"Okay," I said, wondering what was coming next.

"Okay?" he echoed.

My dad's stone face fell for the smallest of seconds. He was playing his usual mental chess game with me. The difference was that I, for whatever reason, suddenly felt like it was stupid, a waste of time to play a passive-aggressive game with him.

Kael was watching me, and stealing a quick glance at him felt like the courageous hit of a cigarette.

"Yeah. Whatever you want to talk about, Dad." I nodded, looking up at Estelle, my father, then back to Kael.

Kael gave me a little smile followed by a nod. I shrugged. Barely a connection, but his tiny bit of approval felt so reassuring to me. This time with him was feeding the starvation of my loneliness.

Estelle clucked around my dad as he tapped his thick fingers against the table, ready to keep up the sparring match with me. She did this during every single meal. No matter what was happening around her. Even if we were going at it, or he was scolding my brother for getting pulled over for the fifth time. And even now, with a stranger watching, she was making my dad's plate as he critiqued his only son's failing in life. When he and I would raise our voices, she would just keep moving and serving the table. Kael accepted mashed potatoes from her, and I watched him as she scooted carrots onto his plate.

"Would you like some ham? Or are you a vegetarian, vegan? Everyone is something these days." Estelle winked at Kael.

She was laughing at her own lame joke, and he sort of smiled at her to be polite. There was no way he actually found her charming.

Not that she wasn't charming. She was, very. She was exactly what my dad required in a wife. Someone who could ignore everything except his needs. Someone who never broke her role, someone the exact opposite of my mom. My mom was a hurricane and Estelle wasn't even a drizzle. Actually, Estelle might be the umbrella in this scenario.

"The glaze is a family recipe. Here, take some of this." She held up a gravy boat full of dark, syrupy liquid. When she bought the thing off eBay, she told me it was "from a real plantation," like that wasn't a gross thing to say, let alone buy. I was thankful she didn't repeat that story with Kael sitting here. And a family recipe? Come to think about it, I didn't know a thing about her family.

"Karina's always boycotting something. Whatever documentary on Netflix she watches, she'll buy right into what they're selling." My dad was clearly doubling down. "She goes vegan for a month, then changes her mind again with the next one. Wants to save the whales. Hasn't let me plan our annual SeaWorld trip in years."

"Wow. How awful of me to care about the world."

"I care about the world," my dad said. "But I show it in a get-it-done productive way."

I really didn't want to get into a global-scale argument with my dad in front of Kael, or Estelle, or under any circumstances, really.

"Are you eating meat right now?" Estelle whispered to me, but everyone could hear her. Her voice was soft, with a condescending drip.

I nodded. My face was on fire with embarrassment. Why do they both do this? Being here always made me feel like everything about me was inherently wrong, like I was endlessly failing.

Was it them or was it me?

That was the question I was constantly trying to answer. The post-parents'-divorce therapy question: Was my dad doing something damaging to me, or was this my own reaction to the way I felt about him?

My dad chomped on his food loudly. Opened another beer. Nope, it was definitely him, not me. Right now, at least. I didn't even like when he drank. He was always on my mom's case about drinking, and the moment she moved out, he started having beer with dinner. Every evening.

Kael quietly thanked Estelle for helping him make his plate. I was starting to think he was enjoying himself. Either that or his manners were impeccable. I wasn't sure which was worse.

"I'm not that hungry," I told Estelle when she passed me the gravy boat. My stomach gurgled, proving me a liar.

"Don't be a child," my dad chided, then smiled at me, in a sorry attempt to soften his words. "I'm sure it's cold by now, but you should still eat."

And there it was. I was surprised he hadn't mentioned my late arrival ten times already.

"I'm not being a child. I'm just not that hungry. I had a long day. Part of the reason I was late." I hated bickering like this, but my father brought out the worst in me. Especially when the subject was my brother, and now that there was an audience, I felt even more pressure.

"You have some growing up to do, clearly," he said, with a sip of beer in his mouth. God, he pissed me the hell off.

I wanted to tell my dad off, to count on my fingers and toes all the ways he was wrong—that he was a horrible father and example—but nothing came out. I just sat there feeling shame. I couldn't even get excited over my brother's arrival because my dad was obviously going to make it a point to knock me down every time I tried to get up.

"Both of my kids need to grow up." My dad looked at Kael, but Kael either didn't notice or didn't care, because his eyes were on me.

"I wonder where we get it from," I snapped, under my breath.

"Where are you working now?" my dad asked me.

"Same place as last Tuesday," I said, wishing I hadn't driven so I could have another glass of wine.

Kael didn't say anything, but the very, very tiny lift of his top lip told me he liked my response to my dad.

Something about Kael being there made me want to . . . show off? I didn't want to come off as a brat or emotionally unstable, but I wanted it to be clear that I could hold my own with this decorated-by-the-Army man, who happened to be my dad. I wanted Kael to think I was cool, but not trying to be cool.

"Martin? Or Kael? What should we call you?" Estelle, the stage director, asked.

77

"Either is fine." He was sitting up straight with his back aligned perfectly with the chair. I sat up, correcting my horrible posture.

"You're in the same company!" Estelle read the patches on Kael's uniform. "Honey, look. He's in your company."

My focus darted to my dad. He was thinking about it, his eyes sort of rolling as he thought through the roster of nameless, faceless soldiers he oversees from his throne.

"There are about two hundred people in the company." My dad had the nicest voice when he was talking to Estelle. He was borderline a totally different person. But small hints of annoyance were there behind the smile despite the soft push of his voice. He was still being condescending to his beloved new wife, just in a nicer way than he would if he were talking to me. Or my mother, for that matter.

"Oh, of course. Aren't most of your guys deployed right now?" Estelle turned her attention back to Kael. She hadn't touched her food since sitting down after serving everyone.

He nodded.

"How did you—"

"Let's eat," my dad interrupted. I was glad he stopped her; she was moving beyond polite to nosy at this point.

"I'm sure the last thing he wants to talk about is deployment," my dad said. He scraped his knife against his plate, cutting an already diced carrot. He always did that and no one ever said anything, even though the noise was ungodly annoying. I could see leftover scratches on my plate, in between the ham and the pile of carrots.

All of us, even Estelle, began to eat our dinner in silence. My thoughts went to my brother, hoping he was close by now, and hoping even more that this latest incident would be the one that finally made him grow up. I had a feeling it wouldn't be, though.

# CHAPTER EIGHTEEN

"Well, that was nice. I'm so glad you came," Estelle said. "Hope you had enough to eat . . ." She seemed to be fishing for a compliment as she looked at Kael, who nodded politely. She turned and handed me a Tupperware with pie inside for Elodie.

"I know it's not cherry, but I think she will still like it." She stood near the front door, awkwardly waiting for me to hug her. Sometimes I did. Sometimes I didn't. It depended on my mood. It was more of a half-hug night.

"Let me know when Austin gets here. I'd stay and wait, but I have work in the morning, and Kael needs to get home."

My dad waved from his chair in the living room, not caring enough to say a proper goodbye.

Kael stood in the doorway, half in, half out.

"Do you have plans this weekend? We're driving up to Atlanta on Saturday for a few days, if you want to—" Estelle offered. My dad looked at her pointedly. Kael looked down at his boots.

"I'll be working." I loved Atlanta, but no way was I going with them. And wouldn't their plans be changing with Austin coming to town?

"That's too bad." She tucked her dark hair behind her ear. She had shiny, wide earrings on. "Maybe next time."

"Maybe," I said, descending the porch steps.

My dad and Kael were both dead silent.

"It was so nice to meet you, Martin. Drive safe." Estelle smiled as I motioned for him to get off the porch. I wanted to leave, and fast. Once he caught up to me, I practically ran down the driveway and yanked my car door open.

"I told you those dinners are the worst."

Even after suffering through it, Kael didn't have a word to say.

"Do you have a family?" I assumed he wouldn't answer, but anything was better than silence as we drove away, and I began to think about my brother and the trouble he continued to cause. I needed a distraction.

"Do I have a family?" he repeated, the words bouncing around in the small space of the car.

Muttering, I tried to correct myself. I was starting to feel nervous again. "I mean, obviously you have a family, otherwise you wouldn't exist. But are they like that? Three courses, matching plates, all the beer, all that shit."

"No," he said, staring out the windshield of my car. "I don't think many families are like that."

"In a good way or a bad way?"

"Both." He shrugged, buckling his seatbelt. "It depends if you're looking at the intent, or the impact that intention has on other people."

I slowed down to stop at the stop sign. I looked at him when the car was fully halted. "Huh?"

He turned, fixing his eyes on me. "Her intention is to impress you. To please you and your dad. The decorations, the folded napkins, the elaborate meal. She obviously cares not only what your dad thinks, but what you think." He used his index finger to point at me.

"Continue," I said, beginning to drive again. I was concentrating on our conversation and slowed down to below the speed limit.

"She wants to impress you, to make you see the effort she's putting in." He took a breath. "To you it's all performative, and the impact it has on you is, well, it's hell to even be there. So what I'm saying is that intention and impact aren't connecting in the right way. But each of you *thinks* what you are doing and feeling is right."

"Did you read that in a self-help book?" I scoffed at how wise he sounded, how maturely he was dissecting my family when I wanted to be a brat and complain about how awful my evil stepmother and father were.

"I think I did, actually. But I came up with my own interpretation after almost dying a few times," he said, and I nearly choked on my breath.

"Sorry, I—" I began.

He held up his hand. "Sorry for what? Why is it your first instinct to say 'sorry'? Did you send me to war? Did you hold my hand while I enlisted? Do you profit millions from sending me off?"

I was sort of stunned at the way he was speaking to me. It was like something inside of him had woken up and crawled out to play. There was a harshness laced with truth there, and honestly, I had never really thought about how a soldier felt after coming back from war. Especially a young one. I villainized my father for missing half of my life and I made sure to stay away from other soldiers, for the most part. Until now.

"Well, did you?" he repeated.

I shook my head. "I almost apologized again."

"I know." Kael turned his body so he was leaning toward the window, his face out of my eyesight while I drove.

As I skipped ahead in my playlist and Shawn Mendes started again, he reached to take his phone out of his pocket.

He didn't do what most people our age did and mindlessly scroll, he checked the screen and put it in the cupholder. He didn't seem bothered the least bit about the uncomfortable silence between us. His disaffection, mixed with the relief that dinner was over, allowed me to start to relax.

A few minutes went by and I found myself softly singing along to the music. I wasn't great at singing and wasn't trying to be. The song ended and I looked over at Kael, surprised to see that he was already looking at me. I didn't feel the embarrassment that I was expecting. I smiled at him and kept on driving. An old Mariah Carey song that reminded me of my mom trying to hit the high notes came on and I swiped up on my phone and closed Spotify altogether.

We were on the highway now, only about five minutes away from my place. I didn't want to ask him if he had anywhere else to go; it felt rude.

"You seemed to like my stepmom," I half asked, half told him.

"How?"

I thought on it for a second. "I guess just that you were nice? I'm an asshole. I want you to dislike her or at least call her out for being snobby or obnoxiously fake. I think it bothers me that she's the opposite of my mom. She's not fun. My mom was really fun when I was younger. She was spontaneous and would never have made such a fuss around a dinner. And absolutely not on a weekly basis. Every fucking Tuesday? Like, who does that?"

Kael's expression didn't give me anything in return, but I still felt the urge to keep going.

"My mom used to listen to music every time she was in the living room or kitchen, and not on a fancy speaker that plays throughout the house." I looked at him to make sure he was at least paying attention if he wasn't going to speak. He was. I could feel it in the way he was watching me.

"She basically had a soundtrack to every moment of her life and would dance around the living room listening to Van Morrison, waving her arms around like a bird or a butterfly. She wore sparkly clothes and shoes, and colorful feathers, beads, and sometimes even sticks in her hair. She had soft eyes."

"Is she alive?" Kael asked. I was so thankful not to be on the highway anymore. The town's quiet streets were a much better place to handle such a blunt question about my mom.

"Yeah. I mean, technically."

He raised both his brows. "Technically?"

I nodded, pulling to a stop at the red light. "She isn't around, but she's not dead. Not today." I thought about it. "Not that I know of, at least."

There it was. My oversharing, which made most people uneasy. I continued to do it even though a really shitty boyfriend I had in high school told me to stop telling people "uncomfortable" things about myself. He said it was weird, so did my brother, and a few therapists I managed to scare away. But it didn't stop me. I drank in Kael's face as he smiled a little, and I silently rejoiced that finally someone got my dark humor and didn't get uncomfortable. Kael found me funny, I could tell. Maybe he was the only person in the world who didn't think I was weird?

"My point is that my mom was cool. Effortlessly. She was confident. And so likable. Everyone who met her loved her. She was moldable. Sometimes vibrant, sometimes bland. Sometimes appearing as a brilliant piece of art and sometimes just a blob sitting on a sculptor's table, waiting to be morphed into the next version of herself. She wasn't like Estelle. She didn't have to wear jewelry and heavy makeup and heels around the house. Estelle is like glass, once she shatters there won't be anyone there to put her back together, but my mom . . . she was like clay."

Until now, I had never thought or spoken about my mom in this way. I usually condemned her for leaving me and didn't really take the time to appreciate who she was—or might still be.

I closed my eyes and leaned my head against the headrest of the car. I couldn't think of a single time that I sat in my car without music playing, just talking to another person. The thrum of my engine cutting through the thick Georgia air was all I could hear. That, and the whisper of my mom's laughter as she shook her hair. Her hair always tickled my face, and the two of us would laugh until our stomachs hurt.

"She would stand over me and shake her hair, like a wild woman. I loved it. I can't imagine Estelle doing that. Or laughing in general."

Not a peep came from Kael; he didn't even move. If I hadn't witnessed him blinking, I'd have wondered if he was okay. He had this "thing" about him, and I didn't understand it. I kept trying to make him fit into a box—was he charming, warm, friendly, genuine? He didn't quite fit anywhere exactly, but he somehow put me at ease. It wasn't a familiar feeling. It was sort of scary how fast I could see myself getting used to this. This must be why people want boyfriends? To have a comfortable, settled feeling all the time.

Boyfriends? Friends? What in the world is wrong with me? I kept the conversation focused on my mom. It felt nice to be able to talk about her, and who knew when I would next have this chance?

"Anyway, my mom, she wasn't materialistic. She didn't care about overpriced purses or flashy earrings. She shopped at thrift stores and made her own jewelry half the time. The fanciest we ever got was for our birthdays. She was obsessed with birthdays, even more than Christmas-level obsessed. She used to go all out for them. It was this huge thing, more like a birthday week. We didn't have a ton of gifts or anything, but she was creative and thoughtful. She would make us pancakes and cut them into the shape of our age. She did it every single year until I was seventeen."

I paused.

"If you want me to shut up, I will." I laughed nervously, realizing that this guy hadn't given me anything and I was telling him stuff I had never told anyone. Half of me saw the red flags, and the other half ignored them because it just felt good to be around him. It crossed my mind that I could make up anything I wanted about my mom if I felt like it. I didn't have to tell him the truth about her. I could make her out to be the villain who abandoned her kids, or a sympathetic free spirit who escaped the ties of a life she was forced to live but never wanted.

He shifted in his seat and cleared his throat. I stopped talking.

"Go on."

There was something too casually cool about him. He was close to the line of arrogant and I could feel how sure of himself he was. I envied it. The way he knew exactly who he was and didn't have to say it or show it off. His attentive listening made it clear he wasn't a narcissist. I've met enough of them to know.

"One year she really went to town. The year before . . ." I paused. I wasn't ready to decide which version of my mother I would put in the story I was telling Kael. "She decorated the whole house in those lights from Spencer's, even a freaking disco ball. Do you remember that store? They had the most absurd T-shirts and penis-shaped everything."

He nodded.

"They had these disco lights and my mom put them around our living room and kitchen. All of our friends came over. I mean, I only had like three friends, most of the kids came for Austin. We always had a packed house. I had this boyfriend, Josh, and he brought me cornbread. That was my birthday gift."

I didn't know why I was going into such detail, but I was so lost in my own memories that I just kept going.

"I never figured out why he brought me cornbread. Maybe his mom had it lying around? Or was it a snarky joke about my weight that I didn't get at the time? . . . I don't know. But I remember getting this karaoke machine and thinking it was the coolest present ever, and my mom went into her room and locked the door during the party so we could feel older than we were and not be chaperoned the entire time. Of course, we ended up playing one of those stupid party games and I had to kiss a boy named Joseph, who actually overdosed on heroin a few months ago . . ."

I could feel Kael looking at me, but it was the weirdest thing—I couldn't stop myself from talking. We were at another red light. The sky was pitch-black and the red lights were reflecting off his dark skin.

"Wow, I'm talking a lot." I clammed up, embarrassed. I couldn't believe I had spiraled into conversation about the drug epidemic and everything. My cheeks flushed.

He looked over at me.

"It's cool. I like hearing your take on the world." His voice was so soft.

*Who was this guy?* So patient, so reserved, yet so in touch with the moment. I tried to imagine his friends, the lucky people who actually got to know him. Like Phillip, Elodie's husband. Phillip was buoyant and friendly, and Kael . . . well, I didn't know what the hell to think of him.

My brother was the only person I'd had to share reminiscences of my parents with. He had an aversion to reliving our childhood, and he no longer wanted to dwell on that part of our lives, but not me—well, I lived in the past most of the time. Even so, I'd never had this type of conversation with anyone other than Austin.

"My take on life?" I repeated. "You've heard enough about that. What's your life like?" The light turned green. I wished it would have stayed red for another minute, another hour, maybe even an entire day.

He looked a little perplexed.

"There isn't much to say. My life is that of a soldier. I live alone. Sleep and wake up alone. Go to war with my guys and hope to come back alive."

Now I was the one who was speechless.

"So you don't have a girlfriend or anything?"

"No way." He immediately shook his head.

"A boyfriend?" I just had to ask. I took him in, his uniform, his young face, his voice that spoke as if he were a generation older than he looked.

He shook his head. "Neither. There's no point in dating. I'm a soldier. Why make anyone else suffer while waiting for me to die?"

His loaded response kept us both quiet as we turned onto my street.

I parked my car in the driveway. The wind whipped around us as I pulled the keys from the ignition. Dirt covered my windshield with each sweep of air. Paving my driveway was rapidly moving up on my to-do list.

As we climbed out of my car, his voice surprised me. "Do you date soldiers?"

I laughed, grabbing my purse from the back floorboard, and the wind helped me slam the car door.

"No way. I don't date much . . . I mean, I could if I wanted to. I just don't have the time. Or the energy. But no, I don't date soldiers, ever. Like you said, what's the point if they're always gone and can die at any moment?"

Kael stared at me, our eyes touching in some odd sort of

agreement. He was a soldier who didn't allow intimacy into his life, and I was a messy twenty-year-old who hardly knew what intimacy meant, with a promise to never date a soldier. Problem solved. Not that there was a problem to begin with, but now I knew that I could truly tell this stranger anything, since he would always be that: a stranger.

# CHAPTER NINETEEN

Elodie was asleep on the couch, her small body sprawled out at awkward angles. I sat my purse down on the floor, kicked my shoes off, and covered her with her favorite blanket. Her grandmother had made it for her when she was a kid. The stitching was really worn now, almost threadbare, but she slept with it every day. Her grandma had passed a few years back; Elodie cried every time she talked about her.

I wondered if she missed her family. She was literally on the other side of the globe from them and pregnant, with a husband away at war. She didn't talk much about missing the life she had before becoming an Army wife. She didn't mention her parents much, but I got the impression they weren't keen on her running away to the U.S. with a young soldier she'd met on the internet.

I couldn't say I blamed them. Elodie moved a little when I turned off the TV.

"Did you want to watch that?" I asked Kael. He was so quiet I forgot he was even here. I also forgot that he would be sleeping over at my house. He was holding the pie I'd brought back for Elodie that I had neglected to bring in from the car.

"No, it's cool. Where should I put this?" he asked, looking down at his full hands.

Oh, this man of many words.

I continued, "Um, the fridge is fine."

He walked through my house, boots off but full uniform still on.

"Do you need clothes to sleep in?" I asked. We were both in the kitchen now.

"I'll get the rest of my stuff tomorrow."

"I have some of my brother's clothes here if you need something—"

"I'm fine. I've slept in this many times." He pulled at the tan camouflage jacket.

Kael and I were only feet apart. His dark eyes were focused on me. I waited, thinking he had something to say, but no words came. Just those eyes reading my face. I was so tired that I barely had the strength to hide it. I felt like crying as he stared at me, though I had no idea why. The kitchen felt so small and I felt so weak; the pressure of being around my dad and Estelle for hours after a long day at work had worn me out.

"You okay?" Kael's voice was soft, just enough to keep me standing upright.

I nodded and my eyes filled with tears. *Why? What the hell is wrong with me?* The more I tried to stop the tears, the more my eyes filled. I was beyond tired. Tired from working, from the stress of my bills piling up, from everything. I had forgotten that my brother was on his way and he still hadn't called me.

"Sorry, I don't know what's wrong with me." I blinked up at the dim ceiling lights. One was out. Of course it was.

"What did I tell you about 'sorry'?" He half smiled and lifted his hand into the air between us, hesitantly petting my head.

The tears poured over at his gentle affection. He somehow knew that I needed someone to be there, to tell me things would be fine.

"Wow. I'm sor—" I stopped myself from apologizing again. He's right, I do that a lot. Most of the women I know do.

"Almost did it again." I smiled, pulling myself through my random meltdown in the center of the kitchen. It was a real smile. I was confused and frustrated and tired, but I wasn't embarrassed. The thought that maybe I should be crossed my mind for only a brief moment. Embarrassment is one of the worst emotions people are forced to feel. I've spent my life trying to avoid it.

Abandoning his typical emotionally unavailable look, Kael offered a smile that was bigger than mine, still a tiny bit awkward but he held his composure. He had a few different levels of smiles. This one was probably a six, if I had to guess. I wondered if I would ever get to see his totally unabashed level-ten smile. Would I ever see this man full of happiness, with weightless shoulders? I shook my head at myself, forcing the thoughts into quietness.

"I'm going to go to bed. I had a really long day and I'm so tired that I'm all over the place." I waved my hands between us, shifting the weight of my body to my left, and moved past him.

I purposely avoided eye contact and forced my gaze to follow the straight line ahead of me to my living room. I desperately hoped Elodie wasn't awake and listening to us. She wasn't really the sneaky type, though. She usually led with her opinions and voice. I admired it. Envied it, even.

The night sky washed over my living room, where Elodie slept. Her elbow was still bent oddly over her head and her legs were dangling off the cushion.

"Should I wake her? So you don't have to sleep in the chair?" I turned to Kael as he stepped behind me to lock my front door. The dead bolt, too.

"I'm fine with the chair."

He was standing close to Elodie now, staring at her face, her belly, and her face again. Her perfect porcelain skin, even with a small breakout on her forehead, looked incredibly appealing and charming. She was stunning from every angle. I hated that having Kael around made me compare myself to my best friend and feel unusually insecure. I'm not like her, but I don't mind the way I look most days. I think I'm pretty. Mostly.

This is what boys did to us. Logically, I knew it was a me thing, not her, but it still felt like shit. Which in turn made me feel guilty for thinking anything but loving things about her. Ugh, my head spun around and around.

Kael looked at me again, trying to read my face. I always loved meeting people who read and considered others' emotions. I've met only a handful of empathetic people in my entire life and definitely wasn't expecting that characteristic from a random soldier who's currently couch-surfing at my place.

"If you're okay, I'm going to bed," I reassured the both of us.

He nodded and sat down in the chair. That was his way of backing off, I could feel it.

"Do you need a blanket?" I asked from the entrance to the hallway.

"If you have one," he said, almost under his breath.

I grabbed an old comforter from the closet and quietly brought it to him. He thanked me, and I nodded. I still felt overwhelmed, but Kael's silent watchfulness and the quiet familiarity of my home made it easier to breathe. I crept down the hallway again and stopped at the bathroom to pee and brush my teeth. My routine made me feel like I was accomplishing something. Red flag. I was seeking approval, and according to my last therapist, that was a habit formed from my childhood. This learned behavior then turned up in my relationships, like with my ex-boyfriend Brien, and has now manifested into mostly keeping myself out of them. I washed my hands and rubbed them with lotion, then spit out my mouthwash. I'd brought a T-shirt and shorts into the bathroom, so I slipped them on and turned the light off.

The floor creaked as I walked out. I tried not to look at Kael from the hallway, but I couldn't stop myself. He was awake, his eyes wide when they touched mine. He looked away and closed his eyes as I went into my room, feeling relief as soon as the door shut.

I lay in bed and listened to the soundtrack of my house. The fridge kicking on and off loudly, the dull drone of the a/c. I listened particularly for Kael to make the smallest of sounds. It occurred to me that I wasn't worried, even for a second, to leave Elodie alone with him in the living room. *Trust?* An unfamiliar feeling, but a nice one. I tried and tried to quiet my mind as my body began to fall asleep.

I felt so restless. I turned over, grabbed a pillow, and put it between my legs, hugging it close. I thought about how it would be really nice to have someone next to me in bed. I like living alone, but there were times like tonight when I couldn't sleep and just wished I had someone to bare my soul to as the dawn came and quieted us both.

Outside of my family and Elodie, it had been almost a year since I'd had human contact that wasn't work-related. I had never really had that in large or consecutive doses, but Kael was making me feel a bit like I had a crush on him. That little patter of your chest when they look at you, the uncontrollable spells of word vomit. I didn't know Kael well enough to actually have a crush, and I hadn't been around men for so long that I'd forgotten what cute ones can do to our brains. I guess that doesn't really apply to Brien; he was attractive, but it was his charm and the spreadsheets inside his mind that drew me to him. He gave me attention, told me I was hot and smart and should leave this Army town and move with him closer to Atlanta. His job as a government contractor was ending soon, and he wanted to be closer to his parents. As if they weren't close enough. His mom knew every time we fought. His dad gave me a worried fake smile every time I talked about my job. He was my longest relationship, and, God, did he make me never want to have another one. He liked other girls way, way too much, and that's what ended us, all three times. I went back twice out of loneliness, or was it self-pity? I didn't know, but this was the longest I'd gone without going back to him.

He was the only boy I'd dated since I moved here, since high school, when I barely dated at all. Making out with senior boys who didn't know my name apart from "Austin's sister" wasn't exactly dating. Brien's manipulative charm was addictive, and I had hoped that one day he would actually understand me and find me good enough for him and his parents, although that day never came. But now, after these few months, the spell had finally worn off and he barely crossed my mind anymore.

I rolled onto my back, sprawling my legs and arms out. I moved my arms up and down like I was making an angel in the snow. I should be grateful I get to have the whole bed to myself and I should stop thinking about men, in general. Not Kael, not Brien, not my dipshit brother, and especially not my dad.

# CHAPTER **TWENTY**

I woke up with my cell phone on my chest. It felt like the heat was on. I checked the time: almost four in the morning. I had to be up at eight so I could run to the grocery store, get gas, and be ready for work by ten. Thinking of my to-do list was stressing me out in the middle of the night, making my brain too awake to go right back to sleep. I rolled my T-shirt up, turned my fan on high, and lay back down, letting the cool air fill the room and brush across my skin.

Opening Facebook on my phone, I went to Elodie's friends list and typed in Kael's name. Nothing came up, so I searched for him again. I changed my search to "Mikael Martin" and found a profile with fewer than one hundred friends, which seemed odd to me, but made sense for what I knew of him so far. I didn't talk to 99 percent of the people I was "friends" with, but I still had almost a thousand. That seemed excessive, having a thousand people I never spoke to have access to me.

His profile picture was a group shot of Kael with three other soldiers. They were all dressed in ACUs and standing next to a big tank. Kael was grinning in the picture, maybe even laughing—that's how bright his smile was. It was weird to see him like that, his arm around one of the guys. Maybe this was his level-ten smile that I had been wondering about? I zoomed in on it. My stomach tingled. I went back to his profile, but apart from his profile picture and Fort Benning, Georgia, I couldn't get any information from his page at all. Everything was private. I almost asked to be his friend, but it felt stalkerish to send him a Facebook request while he was sleeping on a chair in my living room.

I clicked out of his profile and went onto Instagram to see if he had one, though somehow I knew he didn't. I typed his name in and searched, but nothing came up. I went to Elodie's page like I had on Facebook, and still nothing. So he wasn't an Instagram kind of guy; I liked that. I closed the app and threw my phone to the empty side of the bed and sat up. It was so hot in my room that I was starting to think Elodie might have accidently turned on the heat instead of the air again. My throat was dry. I could feel sweat on the back of my neck when I tied up my thick, curly hair.

Kael and Elodie would both be sleeping in the living room, so I made sure I was quiet when I walked down the hallway and into the kitchen. I knew the floor plan of my house so well I could easily navigate every inch in the darkness with only a little guidance from the night-light plugged into the kitchen outlet.

I grabbed the jug of water out of the fridge and chugged it until I couldn't anymore and my throat burned from the cold. Every night when I was a kid, my mom had brought me a cup of ice water to help me sleep. I stopped craving it a few months ago but still kept a jug in the fridge, just in case the need for that comfort returned. I closed the fridge and almost screamed when I saw Kael sitting at the kitchen table.

"Shit, you scared me." I wiped my wet lips with the back of my hand. "Sorry if I woke you up. It's so hot in here."

"I was up."

I took a step closer to him and it took his eyes raking down my body, down my rolled T-shirt to my stomach and my exposed thighs, to realize I was barely dressed. It was dark in the room, but he could definitely see at least the outline of my body. I pulled my shirt down, attempting to undo the knot I had tied at the hem.

"Why are you up? Were you just sitting here in the dark?"

Kael's head tilted just a bit, like he was confused by what I was saying, and he looked down at my legs. I immediately felt a wave of insecurity, thinking about the dips of cellulite peppered across my thighs. He looked back up at my face.

"Can I have some of that water?" he asked.

I flushed, wondering how the hell I hadn't noticed him sitting there as I made my way to my fridge and chugged water out of a plastic gallon jug.

I nodded and opened the refrigerator door. "It's just tap water. I buy one of these"—I held up the jug labeled *Spring Water*—"every once in a while, and just refill it with tap water. So it's not actually spring water."

"I can handle tap water."

His sarcasm surprised me. I smiled at him and he smiled back—also a surprise. He took the container from my hand and lifted it to his mouth without touching his lips. I hadn't been able to see what he was wearing, or not wearing, in this case. He had taken his uniform jacket and tan T-shirt off, and camo pants hung so low on his waist that they revealed briefs I could almost read the label of but knew I shouldn't try to. I looked back at his face as he took another drink.

"So why are you up? Getting used to the time difference?" I asked.

He handed back the jug and I took another swig. I was still hot, but the kitchen was much cooler than my bedroom. The cold tile felt good under my feet. I checked the thermostat just inside the living room, near the hallway. It was set to seventy, and it felt like seventy in here, just not in my room. Was I getting sick? I couldn't afford to—literally.

"I don't sleep much," Kael finally answered.

"Ever?"

"Never."

I sat across from him at the dark wood kitchen table.

"Because of where you just were?"

"Not your father's house," he said with a hint of irony, but with no trace of humor in his face. Not in the strong, straightforward set of his jaw. Not in his cloudy eyes that were bloodshot from not sleeping.

"Ha, ha." I rolled my eyes, trying to stop my brain from imagining him in Afghanistan.

"War, of course." His eyes were on his hands now, not my face. He licked his lips, allowing a small laugh to escape. "I wonder if I'll just be saying that my whole life, you know, like the Vietnam vets I meet at the VA hospital. Still telling stories from fifty years ago."

My stomach started to ache thinking about this quiet young man in a war zone, being woken up by shells or rockets or whatever terror he went through, while I complained and whined to myself over unimportant things and the little miseries of my life. Perspective was a bracing slap across the face.

"I guess it's weird being back here." He sighed. "Like I'm not sure what to do with myself."

Between his honesty and the vulnerability cast across his face, I thought I might be having this conversation in a dream. It was like I could read his mind and feel his pain, even though he was doing a good job trying to conceal it. I was an expert in avoidance and knew emotional masking when I saw it.

"Do you have to go back?" I asked, hoping he would say no.

In my mind, an alarm was blaring, screeching to warn me, or maybe Kael, of how I was starting to feel about him. I had known him for less than forty-eight hours, yet I wanted to protect him, to keep him from going back there. To just make sure he didn't get lost . . . in any of the ways one could. A list ran through my head as we stared at each other for minutes that felt like an hour. Why did I even care? I took his face in, wanting to keep a copy of the way his eyes were steady, not darting all over, his lips were half open, words hesitating to escape. His focus went to the wall behind me. I felt like he was reading my mind, detecting sympathy that might be easily construed as pity. I didn't pity him. I just felt . . . I couldn't make sense of what exactly I was feeling. When it came to Kael and the Army, it was none of my business. He knew what he had signed up for. But that was the logical side of my brain; I knew I felt otherwise. I was lying to myself about the *consequence* of serving, like signing up made it okay, and that emotion turned my stomach.

"I don't know yet," he responded, and we both fell silent.

"I hope you don't." The words were out before I could care how they sounded.

I hated the idea of Kael at war, so far from here. Hiding in the darkness of sandpits, building makeshift posts only to have them destroyed by rockets in the middle of the night. My entire body got angry when I thought about his life there, so many people's lives lived and lost there. Part of me felt like I was betraying my childhood, my family lineage of soldiers and airmen, but I guess I wasn't as patriotic as I was expected to be. Not if this is what it meant. I had never been, and neither had my mother. You couldn't convince either of us that violence would ever be the solution to anything, no matter what the issue was.

Kael's head rested on his bent hand. His eyes were fluttering closed.

"I want . . . to stay here," he whispered, barely coherent.

My whole body heaved. This military life was so unfair sometimes. I wanted to ask Kael if he felt like this was his purpose in life, or what made him join the Army. Everyone had their reasons, but what were his? Was he like most of the young soldiers I knew? Had he been persuaded to join by the poverty around him and the promise of a steady paycheck and health insurance?

"I really—" I started to say, but his eyes were fully closed. I stared at him in the dark and watched his face relax, feature by feature. His eyes stopped swirling behind his eyelids, and I felt myself drawn to sleep as I watched him unwind before my eyes. I drifted off, not caring that I was away from my bed.

# CHAPTER **TWENTY-ONE**

The morning came fast. I had dreamed about my brother, his face bloodied in an alleyway. Our dad calmly talking to a deputy of some sort, myself crying, and Kael was there. We were in another place, a foreign one that I knew I have never seen. It was weird and obviously not realistic, but it stuck in my head as I got ready to leave for the grocery store. Kael was nowhere in sight when I woke up at the table, the sun filling the room. Elodie was still asleep on the couch, lying on her side now and looking much more comfortable than she had before. I skipped showering because I just couldn't deal with the water going in and out today; it was already going to be busy enough. I did my hygiene regimen, including the skin care I'm trying to get a handle on. That's part of growing up, isn't it?

I threw on a navy-blue dress that Elodie bought me when she went to Atlanta with her group of Army wife friends. It was short, but not too short, and had five little fake pearl buttons going down the center of my bust. They were fake buttons and the dress had pockets. Peak Karina happiness when it comes to fashion in one dress. I'd worn it only once, when I tried it on, and now that I was wearing it in my room, my waves took wonderfully to the dry shampoo and were less frizzy than they normally are, and my skin wasn't peeling from overexfoliating. I looked . . . cute. Pretty, even. Pretty cute?

The dress was a little tight around my hips but not too bad. The skirt was the ideal length. It had thin straps that tied on my shoulders, making it perfectly adjustable. I covered as much of my cleavage as I could, but I also sort of liked the way the top of the dress was shaped, like half an oval, dipping down into the roundness of my chest. The thin cotton was so soft and fell against my hips and flared out at my thighs in little creases, like a cheerleading skirt, but more stylish. I smiled at my reflection and I wished I could bottle this little moment of love for my body and save it for the next time that I really, really needed it—like when I order an outfit online or, even worse, try on clothes for an hour at the mall and leave with nothing but resentment for my body and myself.

Not today. I didn't feel any resentment as I twirled and pinched my cheeks to see if that viral video actually works. The color doesn't last more than thirty seconds, so I swooshed on a little bit of the blush that Elodie gave me. I hadn't bought my own makeup for months. I had priorities, and makeup couldn't be one of them right now so I lived through Elodie's hand-me-down, nearly finished makeup. No complaints—she always has great brands. I look at my face one more time, adding a quick layer of mascara and a lip stain. I look pretty rested for a girl who'd slept at the kitchen table half the night. I usually don't have mornings like this, where I become best friends with my reflection. I should get better at that . . . at least I'm trying.

When I walked out of my bedroom, I was fastening my sandals around my ankles. The heaviness of the platform made it harder to put on while moving down the hallway, but I managed by leaning against the wall. Kael was in the kitchen, sitting at the table, on his phone. He was dressed in his uniform again. Not shirtless, not jacketless, as he was last night, in the dark moonlit room with lavish purple shadows bouncing from his chest, his cheeks . . . the way his face changed as he fell asleep in this little kitchen, and I stared at him until I finally fell asleep there too. I peered into the living room to see that Elodie was still sleeping. I really didn't understand how she slept through everything. That must be so nice. I wish my brain would allow me the liberty of napping, sleeping in, or even just the minimum of sleeping an entire night without waking up more than twice.

Kael still hadn't looked up from his phone, and I felt my roaring confidence plummet the more he scrolled. He hadn't yet seen me put an effort into my appearance, and for some reason, I wanted him to notice. I cleared my throat, lightly stomping my heavy sandals against the hard kitchen floor. His eyes darted up, looking at my face first, then my neck, particularly the little beaded necklace there. He looked at it intensely enough to see the *K* charm dangling from it.

It felt as if his eyes were studying each single bead, then he moved to the straps on my shoulders. My hand moved up to twirl the beads around, letting myself enjoy this moment. My body slowly filled with confidence again as he quickly moved his eyes to my thighs and back to my eyeline. If I was imagining all this, why did his breathing change? It felt primal, like there was a little hint of something he couldn't control . . . . It made me feel high.

I wondered who would speak first, or if we would just stare at each other until something broke the tension. Unless I was misreading the moment. I could be inventing this: a flicker of hunger mixed with a look that bordered on desire as he homed in on my face. My lips. He licked his again. My lungs became wild, filled with hornets. My mouth was dry.

Kael stood up and I took a step away from him. I felt the need to protect myself from him, from myself. Not in a dangerous way, just in a this-won't-end-well way. He stared at the space I put between us like it offended him. I took another step back. My hormones were out of control; this is lust. I hadn't felt lust in my twenty years on earth. I couldn't decide if I love or hate the feeling, but it's definitely lust. Not a stupid crush, no false expectations of love and forever, just a physical attraction to a man. That's it. Lust.

He finally spoke, pulling me out of the mental rabbit hole I was floating down.

"Are you going to the store now?" He didn't look me in the eyes. I felt like he was purposely avoiding eye contact. It pissed me off. But it excited me. Lust, lust, lust. Now I see why it's one of the seven deadly sins. It's so distracting. And random.

I nodded while walking past him to open the fridge and drink some water before I went out in the heat. He watched me move around the room and I chugged straight from my water jug again. What was the point of acting sophisticated in front of him anyway?

"Is it cool if I come to the store with you? I don't need much."

Was he inviting himself to hang out with me? Why couldn't I help but smile? I covered my mouth and cursed my dream, the one that played a big part in the way I was feeling around him this morning. Damn my vivid imagination.

I nodded again. I couldn't say much to him, and I knew he never really had much to say to me, so we agreed to a quick shopping trip, back by nine thirty, so I could change, brush my teeth again, walk to work, and not be late.

I was searching quietly for my keys. I thought I'd put them where I always did, on the table by the couch.

"I can't find my keys." I rubbed my forehead. I tried my hardest not to get stressed. The more time I spent looking for the damn keys, the less shopping time I would have.

"Oh, shit. Sorry, I have them." Kael pulled them out of his pocket and dangled them in front of his chest.

Before I could ask why on earth he had them, he started explaining. "I filled your tank up. And may have driven it to the hardware store down the street, since your porch light doesn't work."

I didn't even know what to say. We made our way to the car and, sure enough, as I powered up, my gas meter went straight to the *F*.

"Thanks." I struggled to look at him. "You didn't have to do that, and I was going to replace my light."

"You said you had to work and I was up early, so I just did it. Not a big deal." He shrugged.

I didn't know if it bothered me. I felt like it should bother me because I didn't even know him, and I definitely didn't need him to pay for my gas or change out the lightbulb on my porch. I remembered the way he seemed to be surveilling my yard as we approached the porch last night, him even grabbing the Tupperware full of dessert that I'd forgotten about. He was a soldier, after all, and they just can't help but assess their surroundings at all times. But also, maybe, just maybe, he was a person who does kind things for other people? I hadn't ever met someone like that, but maybe that's what all this was and I was way overthinking it, allowing my imagination to get the best of me.

"Um, okay . . . do you have Venmo? For the gas?"

He laughed sarcastically as I continued our drive to the store. "You aren't paying me back for a tank of gas. You were late to your dinner because of me. I won't take the money, so there's no point in arguing with me." His tone wasn't combative, it was just certain. Certain enough that I didn't argue it.

We continued our drive, through the main gate and to the commissary; the tension from last night was gone. I sighed in relief. I was definitely just tired and borderline losing it. Today was a new day, a new Kael, and a new me. I parked and he led the way to the entry door. The sun was so bright, I had to cover my eyes.

"When will you get your clothes back?" I asked him, as we entered the crowded store.

"Not sure. I can't get a hold of anyone."

I wondered what that meant. Who couldn't he get a hold of? And why were they keeping his stuff from him? A scorned ex, maybe? The thought irritated me.

The cart we had chosen had a creaky wheel that got stuck on every turn. I'd handed Kael my grocery list in the parking lot, assigning him to hold on to it.

I looked at him, pressing him to say more. "Should we go back there again? To find your keys? Maybe they're in the parking lot. It was dark."

"*We* don't need to go back there. I'll figure it out."

*Shit.* "Okay. Don't you need a ride to get them?"

"No. I don't."

I felt like we were suddenly in an argument in the cereal aisle but I'd missed what we were fighting over. He grabbed a box of Cinnamon Toast Crunch and placed it in the cart. At least he had good taste in cereal. He was keeping his groceries in the seat at the front of the cart where kids usually sat while parents tried to keep them entertained and cooperative.

I ignored his rejection and kept shopping. We needed only a few things, and I was ready for our little trip to finish, since he was clearly in a bad mood. I really didn't react well to people shutting down; it's made me paranoid since I was young, made my mind spiral. I knew I needed to say something before my mind fully went there. I stopped walking for a second, and he halted, too.

He looked confused now. But I was getting better at reading

him. Granted, it had been only two days, but still. I was cracking him open, slowly but surely.

"If I said something that bothered you, or did something . . ."

"Huh?" He cocked his head to the side and studied my face, the cart, our surroundings. "What makes you say that?"

There were people walking by, looking at us as we stood right in the center of the aisle.

An older white man passed us, keeping his eyes on Kael and me just a beat too long. I noticed his lingering stare, shifting back and forth between us, and the hairs on my neck prickled. The man disappeared around the corner. I almost mentioned it to Kael, but I started wondering if I was just paranoid, and decided not to give the rude man any more attention than I already had.

"I don't know. I just feel like you're . . ." I tried to explain myself. I hated that I was so easily at a loss for words sometimes.

He wrapped his hands around the handle on the cart and took over pushing it.

"If something was wrong, I'd say it. I'm just in my own head." His tone wasn't condescending or wrapped in a lie.

I appreciated the honesty. It made me feel like I understood what he was doing instead of making it all about myself. And maybe, unlike with my family, the silence didn't need to be filled while grocery shopping. Kael looked at the list again and pulled the pen out of the sewn-in holder on his ACU jacket. He marked off three items, using a dash next to each one instead of striking them out, the way I always did. I found the tiniest things about him fascinating, and my thoughts began to form themselves into a little cloud that turned into a daydream. I used the silence between us as we browsed the aisles to think about how different we were, why my brother hadn't called me, and what I needed to do before I could leave for work.

The commissary was crowded as always, but I felt less stressed over the crowd and more at ease than I had been since we'd left the house. Kael still hadn't spoken as he put three boxes of granola bars into his part of the cart.

"I have some—"

"Not anymore." He rubbed the back of his neck with his hand.

"You ate my granola bars?"

He laughed. If I hadn't turned around, I would have missed it. "Mostly," he replied, smiling a little.

Kael stayed 'in his own head' for the rest of the grocery shopping, and he found everything on my list before we got in line behind three extra-stuffed carts. The low prices on groceries with zero tax were worth braving the crowd.

"So many people," I said to him as we waited.

Kael nodded, looking over at me. His elbows were leaning on the cart. "So many people giving their money right back to the government," he said, nodding at all the people in uniforms and their spouses.

"You're always complaining." I heard the voice before I saw her approach. It was a soft, feminine voice to match an equally beautiful face. "Martin, never thought I'd see you at the commissary. What the hell are you doing here?" She laughed, knocking his arm gently.

She was wearing ACUs that matched his. *Turner* was written on her name patch. She was below him in rank; I could tell by the difference in the patches on their chests.

"Just getting some actual food," he responded to her.

She smiled at him in a way that made me feel like I was intruding on them. Her teeth were so straight, I could tell she'd had braces in her past, and her dark brown eyes had thick, maybe fake, eyelashes sprouting out of them. They were so pretty and delicately placed that it didn't matter if they were real or not. The color of her hair matched them perfectly. Her boots were scotch clean, and she wasn't wearing a bit of makeup. I wished I didn't feel so instantly threatened by the presence of another woman. I was feeling a little more sure of myself this morning, but I was sort of distracted by her beauty as they briefly caught up.

I was hardly on her level, or Kael's, and I knew they were probably aware of that. They were sure of themselves, enlisted into an organized, structured career, and both immediately charming. I felt awkward and embarrassed by my thoughts.

"When did you get here? I heard you were sent back but didn't know it already happened. Where are you staying?"

He sighed. "With a friend."

The girl looked at me, smiling still.

"Turner. And you're?" she asked me, reaching out her hand. It felt so formal to handshake in the line at the grocery store, but there I was. Unsure what to do with my body and my mouth.

"This is Karina. She's Phillip's wife's friend," Kael answered for me, gently pressing her hand down between us so I didn't have to shake it.

Her chin pointed up. "Oh, the French girl?"

I couldn't read her. I couldn't tell if she was being judgmental of my friend or if she was merely stating a fact. She was a blank sheet of paper that I couldn't read a word from.

"Yeah," he spoke for me again.

I felt like hiding behind him. I wasn't usually so easily intimidated, and I tried to reclaim how I felt when I looked in the mirror this morning. That confidence had evaporated and I was collapsing in on myself as the noise around us continued to escalate.

Turner stood there for a few seconds, waiting for one of us to talk. I knew she couldn't care less if I spoke, she wanted to talk to Kael.

ANNA TODD

"Well, see you? I'll call you later. Does everyone else know you're back?" she asked, leaning toward him. He moved a sly step away from her. At least it wasn't only me who he kept at a distance.

"No. Don't tell them," he said to her.

"I'll try to keep my mouth shut." She laughed to herself, flirting with him. If I could see that, he definitely could. And in front of me? How did she know I wasn't his girlfriend? I guess she must know him well enough to not assume that. The thought rubbed at me, making my lungs burn. I would do anything to be back in the quiet comfort of home.

Neither of them said bye, but she walked away after what felt like an hour.

"Do you know her?" Kael asked me. I blinked out of my unnecessary jealousy and shook my head.

"I don't think so."

"Hmm," he said under his breath.

"You do, though," I reminded him. If he could ask me if I did, why couldn't I do the same?

Of course, when I did, he gave me a simple "I do."

It was finally our turn to load the groceries. He stopped me from lifting the gallon of milk.

"I can lift milk." I rolled my eyes.

He looked down at my wrists. "You need those hands for work. More than I need mine. I know you're capable, I'm trying to be a nice guy."

I glared at him. "I was trying to be nice, too."

"I know. I'm just fucking with you. Let me put the milk up there." His voice was lighter than it was a moment ago, a different tone than I had ever heard come from his lips. It made my skin tingle. I looked away.

"Fine," I teased back.

My throat was aching.

Kael managed to move around me in the small space as I went to the cashier. He knew exactly how to toe that fine line between being open and closed. The music overhead was louder; it had to be. A song from my childhood, one that my mom used to scream out the window as we drove from garage sale to garage sale on the weekends, played through the loudspeakers. With each of these memories, I began to feel more and more unsettled. Why were all my thoughts of her so fond lately? I still should be too pissed to care that she's gone. When would my mother stop haunting me?

Kael and I didn't talk again as we checked out separately. We both had to show our ID cards, his active duty and mine a dependent ID. He was a gentleman and helped me load my car and carry the bags into my house, and he even asked if he could help unpack them. I hated that my brain was trying to figure out why he was so nice to me. I mean, he was also sort of rude, but he did thoughtful things. I wish I had a friend to confide in, to talk about this feeling that was distracting me. My mother always warned me that love was the most dangerous thing humans could feel, aside from greed, which would be the cause of the end of the world, but that was another issue for a different day. It wasn't that I was emotionally unstable, I could say I was attracted to this stranger who I've only known for two days, but I was a logical person. It was more the feeling of owing him something for his kindness. I couldn't accept kind gestures or compliments from people if I didn't feel worthy of them.

But as much as he made me feel flustered and a little bit paranoid, I was starting to kind of like the way I felt around him. We weren't doing anything wrong. Nothing. We were grocery shopping, sharing a living space, and talking about nearly every thought I had.

"Everything okay?" he asked, after all the groceries were put away. It took half the time with him helping and I didn't have to tell him to recycle the paper and plastics. You'd be surprised how many people I knew who didn't recycle.

"Yeah. I'm fine. Just in my own head." I summoned his words and used them to avoid answering his question. He let out a breath and didn't look directly at me. My eyes followed his movement from the fridge, to the cabinet to grab a glass, and back to the fridge. He poured himself some water, splashing a little onto the floor. I liked the way he silently used my kitchen as his own. He had become familiar with my little house in such a short time.

"So we'll be gone until like five, but we always have our phones on at work. If my brother comes by, let him in? And try not to let him leave."

Kael nodded. I watched as he cleaned up the splashed water that I'd assumed would dry on the floor with the rest of the random spillage that had accumulated since I'd mopped two weeks ago.

Elodie came walking down the hallway with her short hair soaked, staining the shoulders of her gray T-shirt. She was wearing her black scrubs that had an elastic waist, her favorite.

"You look so pretty, wow. Doesn't she, Martin?" Elodie enthused, looking straight at Kael. He looked at me, then at her, and nodded.

"She does."

Without giving me time to process Kael's compliment, Elodie circled around me with approval, touching the soft curls in my hair.

"I mean it. So beautiful." She squeezed my body and tapped her index finger against my necklace.

"So cute," she exclaimed. Her blue eyes lit up. "Oh! And the shower is finally fixed! It was so nice to have such hot water!"

"What do you mean?" I made my way down the hallway toward the bathroom.

"The temperature! You had it fixed, right?" she asked. I passed her, shaking my head. Sure enough, when I went into the bathroom and turned the shower on, it was immediately warm. I turned it to cold. Immediately cold. The pressure was even stronger, like a normal shower. Such luxury. I hoped it wasn't temporary. I was instantly looking forward to taking a long, hot shower when I got home from work tonight.

"I'm glad it is, but have no idea how . . ." I started to say. My eyes landed on Kael's and he licked his lips, turning his cheek slightly away from me.

"You!" It dawned on me. "Did you fix it?" Somehow, I knew he did, even though I couldn't imagine why he would bother.

Kael nodded sheepishly. "It wasn't a big thing. It was just a loose pipe, a broken bolt. It took less than five minutes."

Elodie walked toward him, her hair dripping as she moved. "You are so nice. Oh, thank you, thank you," she told him, hugging one of his arms. He looked down at her dangling on his arm like she was an alien. He didn't nudge her off, but he definitely didn't seem to welcome her overtly physical affection. Yet another piece of evidence to add to my list of all the ways he's emotionally unavailable. I found myself wondering what it would be like to receive affection from him and what it would take for him to welcome it from me. He was so confusing to me. So polite, yet so cold. So easy to talk to, yet so quiet himself.

First the full tank of gas, now fixing my shower. Of course, it was nice of him, but it also made me feel helpless. I hated owing people anything.

I couldn't bring myself to thank him in front of Elodie. I knew that seemed rude, but I would clear it up with him later, when we were alone.

*If* we were alone—my brain edited the thought as it surfaced.

"Okay." I chewed on the inside of my cheek. I didn't know what else to say, so I ended up awkwardly stepping away from the two of them, using my very real reason to leave, work.

"I really gotta go, I can't be late. See you at eleven. Please, for my sake, don't be late!"

"I won't! I promise!" Elodie shouted, as I approached the front door. I slid my work shoes on and didn't look back at Kael as I walked out. He did something nice for me. More than one thing. The gestures weren't only thoughtful, but practical. I appreciated it, I did, but I also didn't want him to make a habit of doing things like that, of fixing my things.

# CHAPTER TWENTY-TWO

My morning at work was the same as always: two elderly retirees and one married soldier who came in at the same time almost every week. He never made an appointment, but I always kept the spot open for him. He was nice and easy, tipped well, and didn't groan and moan while I did my job.

I now had "free time" to help clean up around the spa and avoid walk-ins—as much as they could be avoided. I didn't like the uncertainty. It was always uncomfortable, and those clients hardly ever came back. It didn't matter what their body looked like; all types of bodies came through those doors. I found it refreshing and hopeful on those rare occasions when women didn't put themselves down during a treatment. I wanted them all to let their insecurities go while in my room. It was both comforting and disheartening to know that other women thought of their bodies in the same harmful way that I did. We always suspect that others are thinking or talking about us, when most of the time everyone's too worried about themselves to focus on anyone or anything else.

I was pulling out my second round of towels from the dryer when I thought of how uninteresting a part of my job this was— "side work" is what we called it when I was waiting tables. I'm constantly running out of towels, filling the fridges, loading the washer. I spend probably as much time on freaking towels as I do actually treating people.

Mali popped her head into the break room.

"That guy came here for you," she told me while we folded towels.

"What guy?" I immediately thought of Kael.

"The one you used to like," she said. The way she wrapped *like* around her tongue made me feel like a child.

*Oh. Brien. Great.*

"When?" I asked.

"About ten minutes before you got here."

I dropped a towel onto the pile before I folded it. "What? Why didn't you tell me?"

She snickered. "Because I can't have you getting back together with him. He's bad news."

She shrugged. I gaped at her, grabbed the towel, and threw it at her.

"I'm not going to call him, by the way." I may have been a little defensive. But, I didn't think I would, even if I was curious. We had literally nothing else to talk about.

Okay, so maybe Mali was right.

"Mhmm." She nodded yes with her lips jutted out sarcastically. The deep wrinkles on her bronzed skin made her look extra-serious. I knew she was mostly teasing and she was also right about him. She'd never liked Brien, and even cut off the electricity in the lobby when he came to see me the first time after our breakup. In her defense, I was crying, and he was accusing me of something that I couldn't even remember anymore. That must've meant I was innocent, right?

Truth was, I wasn't as sad as everyone thought I should be after we broke up. And another truth was, I'd used him to fill something missing inside of me. That's what most relationships actually boiled down to.

Mali interrupted my sour memories of Brien. "We have a walk-in," she said.

Her back was hunched so she could see the little security television screen. I couldn't make out whether it was a man or a woman, but I knew Elodie had just started on her two-thirty appointment, and we were the only two working until four. Two more therapists, Kandace and Joanie, would be working the evening shift, which meant I wouldn't have fresh towels in the morning, because the two of them did the bare minimum when it came to closing. Again, the damn towels.

"I'll take the walk-in." I jumped up. "I don't have any more appointments today and I really don't want to fold any more towels."

I pushed through the curtain in the lobby to find Kael walking around the small space, almost pacing. There were only a few chairs, and along with the front desk, furniture dominated the entire lobby space. I watched him walk back and forth before I moved past the curtain. He was wearing gray sweats and a gray T-shirt. Seeing him in normal clothes meant that he'd gotten his stuff from whoever had the key to his truck.

"Hey," I greeted Kael. The Thai food Mali brought us for lunch was now jumbled with nerves in my belly.

"Hi."

We stood there, enveloped by the thick smell of incense and the dim lights of the lobby. The old PC tower on the floor hummed between us.

"Is everything okay?" As I asked, it dawned on me that he might be there for a reason.

"Yeah, yeah. I came to get a massage, actually. I didn't know if you had time or not." He held up his hands.

"Really?"

"Yeah. Do you have time?" His voice was soft, an unsure question.

I nodded and brought my hand up to my mouth. I didn't know why I was smiling, but I was, and I couldn't stop.

# CHAPTER **TWENTY-THREE**

I pulled back the curtain to my room and he entered first. He smelled like soap, and he looked so much younger without his uniform. I still couldn't guess his age.

"I take it you got your stuff?" I pointed nervously to his outfit. He nodded.

I clicked my tongue, not sure if he wanted me to press more, and since I was at work, the lines were slightly blurred. He was my client here, not my friend. Even at home, he's not exactly my friend, either. This whole thing was so confusing.

"Well, I'll give you two minutes or so to undress and I'll be back," I told him.

Kael stood by the table with his arms crossed. His sweats hung on his hips and his skin glowed in the candlelight. I couldn't remember the last time I liked looking at someone as much as I did Kael. It fascinated me. He fascinated me. I didn't know what it was about him, but he got more attractive every time I looked at him.

I moved out into the dimly lit hallway and took a deep breath. I told myself that it wouldn't be weird. I did this all day, every day. He was just a regular client—a stranger, really. I barely knew him, and on top of that, I had already given him a massage. I pulled my phone from my pocket to see if Austin had called me back yet. Nothing.

I couldn't believe how much of a shithead my brother was being. I knew he was here and capable of texting me back. I texted my dad. Anything to distract myself.

I could hear Mali talking to her husband down the hall. Something about extending a hot-stone promotion we had going this month. She was always trying to come up with new promotions and semi-free marketing for their small business. It was impressive to watch her keep this place full of a steady clientele, even though there was a lot of local competition, with massage spas outside of each gate. Most massages were about forty bucks, some more, some less. Some sort of shady, some not. I tried my damnedest to bring her into modern times, but she still fought me along the way. I opened my phone again to check for a text from my brother. I couldn't wait to cuss his ass out for not replying to me.

A text from my dad popped up on my screen.

**Austin is okay. He's asleep right now.**

Not only is my brother ghosting me, my dad is the one to tell me that he's fine. *Fuck both of them.* I shoved my phone into the pocket of my uniform. It had already been a few minutes.

"Can I come in?" I touched the heavy curtain.

"Yeah."

He was facedown on the massage table, his head in the cradle, the white sheet resting right at his waistline. He was shirtless. Of course he was, he was here for a treatment.

"Do you remember what you liked and didn't like last time?" I asked, out of habit, the way I started every appointment.

"Everything was fine."

I ran my hand down his bare back. Rising goose bumps appeared in the wake of my fingertips. I shivered. I needed to turn the music up and forget that the client on the table was Kael, or I wouldn't make it through the hour.

"Okay . . . so I'll apply the same pressure and see where we go from there?"

He nodded.

I ran my fingertips up his back again, just like I did with every other client. My fingers were shaking, and I was almost afraid to touch him because it didn't feel right to *want* to touch a client. Maybe this was a mistake. Should I see if Elodie would switch with me? I knew that realistically that wouldn't work, and I also sort of hated the idea of her touching him. What the hell was going on with me? I was fine before he came here. We'd spent the whole morning together and I was totally fine.

I grabbed a towel and tried my best to go through the motions. The warm towel glided easily across the bottoms of his feet. He was wearing his sweats on the table again, the gray fabric peeking out of the bottom of the white sheet. I almost pushed them up a little so I could rub his ankles more thoroughly, but something told me not to. He was wearing the pants for a reason, and though I could admit to myself that I really wanted to know what that reason was, I knew that he would tell me if he wanted me to know.

I pressed my thumb into the pad of flesh right under the line of his toes and he groaned. I eased up and his tense body relaxed again. He rolled his ankle to get rid of the feeling. It was a sore spot for a lot of people.

"Sorry. It usually releases tension. It's a pressure point."

I walked back around to the top of the table where his head was and reached for my oils.

"No peppermint, right?" I asked him.

"No, thanks. I hate the smell."

*Okay, then.*

"I can use one without a scent. Will that work?"

His head nodded in the cradle.

I rubbed the warm oil between my hands and started at the base of his neck. The cords of his muscles were thick around his neckline and down his shoulders. In a way, he looked like someone built to fight, to protect, but sometimes he seemed so boyish, silly, even, someone who should be kept out of harm's way.

A giggle broke out in the hallway, and I heard Mali shushing the laugh over my music.

"Elodie," I told him. He stayed quiet as I moved my hands across his soft skin. His shoulders held a little less tension than they had yesterday. Holy shit, it had been only a day since he came in for Elodie! One day. One night at my dad's house, one middle-of-the-night talk, one grocery-shopping trip, and suddenly I'm acting like I have some sort of crush on him.

I continued to talk to Kael about Elodie, reminding myself of our tiny little connection that all stemmed from bad timing and a petite French woman.

"I met her in training for my therapist's license. She had just gotten here from France after researching programs for military spouses." I remember how thick her beautiful accent used to sound to me. "She was very determined and taking the first day of work so seriously. I was drawn to her almost immediately. She's smart and charming. I couldn't believe she married a soldier," I explained.

His shoulders danced with slight amusement.

"No offense." I paused, relieved that he found it funny. "Phillip's as nice as I think he is, yeah?" I asked Kael, while we were on the subject. He stayed quiet for a few seconds.

"He's a good guy."

"Promise? Because he brought her here from another country with no family and no friends here. I worry about her."

"He's a good guy," he said again.

I needed to stop grilling him and just do my job. He didn't come here to talk to me. He came here to get a treatment for his aching body.

I moved down his back and up his arms, settling into my normal groove. I did the same thing in most treatments, medium pressure, using a little more oil than most other therapists did. The song playing was an older Beyoncé song that I loved as a teen, and I let the music fill the quiet air until about twenty minutes later, when I asked him to roll onto his back.

He closed his eyes when he turned over and I took the liberty of studying his face as I placed a warm towel over his eyes. His sharp jawline, the light stubble under his chin. He took a deep breath when I tucked my hands under his back and raked them up his skin, pressing and stretching the muscles in his back.

The moment I moved away from his shoulders, his hand reached up and yanked the towel off.

"I can't have that on my eyes," he said, his voice cracking.

I grabbed the towel from the floor and he sat up.

"Sorry—" he began.

I shook my head, lifting my hands up. "It's okay. I should have asked . . ."

He was recently back from a deployment, and I wondered if his reaction was related to that, or if he simply didn't like his eyes being covered. Maybe the towel was too hot? The list of things Kael didn't like was building. The smell of peppermint, his lower body being massaged, towels covering his eyes . . .

His eyes were wide, his hands were gripping the sides of the table. "If you want to stop, it's okay. I'm really sorry that—"

He shook his head and unwrapped his fingers, one by one, from the table's edge. He let out a breath and closed his eyes.

Seconds later, I almost asked him what sounded good for dinner. I thought about telling him how I convinced Mali to let me choose my own music for the treatment room—and how much I loved the Beyoncé song that was playing. Should I ask him if he liked the smell of the caramel cake candle that filled the room? Something about him made me want to speak. All the time. I wasn't sure what to make of it.

Only two minutes had gone by since I'd had him roll over. Fuck my life, time was going so slowly. It was unprofessional to talk a client's ear off without them talking first. I repeated that to myself a few times.

"Everything good?" I asked finally. The words were practically bursting out of my mouth.

He nodded. "How's your brother?" His question surprised me.

"I don't know. I thought he'd come to my house as soon as he arrived to Benning, but I guess not," I said. "He's asleep at my dad's now. My dad's the one who told me that. I still haven't gotten to talk to Austin alone. It's so frustrating. He must have really fucked up. Otherwise, he would have called me by now. I can't even believe he's staying with our dad. Like what the hell?"

Kael kept his eyes closed. I was kneading my fists down his shoulders and arms. His eyes clenched shut.

"Sorry, that's a longer answer than you probably wanted. I seem to do that a lot." I laughed, but it sounded so fake. Probably because it was. I realized I had said too much, and really should be protecting my brother from a stranger's judgment.

Kael's eyes opened for a second and he leaned his head up, forcing eye contact. "It's fine. I don't mind it."

I looked away and he laid his head back down. "Thanks, I think," I teased, and my stomach flipped when his face broke into the biggest smile I had seen on him yet.

# CHAPTER **TWENTY-FOUR**

I walked into the lobby and only Mali was there. She wasn't paying any attention to my arrival and was busy cleaning. I was waiting for Kael when I got Elodie's text with the *BuzzFeed* link. She was the queen of "Is It Your Fault You're Single?" quizzes, and "Are Women Taking Over the Self-Employment Industry?" articles. This one was "25 Things You Need to Know About *Twilight*." Trust me, I already knew every detail of those books and films and enjoyed crushing all the "hardest" quizzes. Elodie didn't share my love for vampires falling in love with humans, so she mostly took the "What Kind of Toast Are You?" or "Choose a Day of Meals and We'll Tell You Where to Travel" ones.

I started scrolling through the list and wasn't surprised by how basic these "facts" were. It was public knowledge that *New Moon* was Robert Pattinson's favorite book in the series. I kept reading, smiling at the pictures. *Twilight* was my comfort series and had been since I was a teenager. I had all the merchandise and my mom let me see each of the movies at midnight the night they released. I cried in my room when Kristen and Rob broke up. As I zoomed in on a picture of them in the quiz, I caught something moving from the corner of my eye. My phone fell out of my hands and Kael reached for it. He looked at the screen and then at me. I was mortified. Kristen's stunning face stared up at me, even more zoomed-in than it was when I'd dropped it.

"Sorry, I—" I started to say.

"Do you apologize every time you speak?" he interrupted me. My cheeks burned.

"Um, no. I just . . ." I paused. He was right. *Sorry* was probably the most overused word in my vocabulary.

"What are you apologizing for? Being a *Twilight* fan?" he was laughing at me, biting his lower lip as it curled.

I joined him, smiling even though I was still slightly embarrassed.

"My sister started reading the books last summer and read them all in one week."

A sister! My brain created a spreadsheet of questions to ask him.

"How old is she?" I started with one question instead of twenty.

"Fifteen."

I wondered what she was like. If he was a sweet, protective older brother, and if she was as beautiful as he was.

"Aw. Does she live close?"

He shook his head. "Yes and no. Closer than most soldiers are to their families. But her and my ma are in Riverdale. Here in Georgia."

"Ah, like the show?"

He nodded, smiling a little. I really, really wanted to see him smile like he did on my table a few minutes ago. That big smile made me crave another.

A phone started to ring, and I pulled mine back out of my pocket. It wasn't mine. Kael swiped his finger across his phone and put it back in his pocket.

"Well, I hope everything was okay with your treatment today."

"Thanks," he said, but didn't answer my question.

I rang him up and handed over the credit card slip to sign. I'd never felt anxious seeing a client scribble his name across that little black line before, so this was new. And, of course, Kael wasn't giving anything up, which left room for me to fill in the blanks. First, I wondered if he'd come back for another massage. Then it was *What's going to happen after he stops crashing on my couch?*

He left me a twenty-dollar tip on a forty-five-dollar massage. It was more than generous. Certainly more than I usually got. I felt a little weird about it, like he was giving me charity or something. Or paying for my time, which I guess he was. But I did need the money, so I took it with a smile. Okay, the smile was mostly forced, but he couldn't tell. At least, I didn't think he could.

I thought about how I had talked through half of his massage. It probably didn't make for the most relaxing experience.

"Sorry I talked so—"

Kael cut me off before I could finish. "No," he said, and offered me a friendly shrug. "No more sorrys. It's cool."

Moving on to something else, I pointed to the dark green walls. "I want to change the color."

He studied them and asked, "Well, what color do you want to paint them?"

"Something more neutral and modern. Do you think it's overly decorated in here?" I asked.

He looked perplexed.

"Do you feel like you're in an expensive spa in a big city, instead of here, in this strip mall?"

"I guess." He shrugged. Kael answered with a word or two now and then, but mostly it was my voice that filled the lobby. We were in a public area—not exactly a private therapy room—but he was still playing the strong, silent type.

"Do you want a receipt?" I read the prompt from the credit card machine.

"Of course." He held out his hand.

"*Of course*? Such certainty over a credit card receipt?" I teased him. I was beginning to love doing that. He reacted differently nearly every time. It was fascinating.

"Responsible," he said. He almost smiled as he tucked the receipt into his wallet. It was leather, light brown, and obviously well used.

"Sure," I said, and snorted. "Whatever you say."

"Better hope you don't get audited." No smile this time, but he did give me a raised eyebrow.

Mali was watching everything closely now. When Kael came out into the lobby after his session, she had been busy nearby, humming to herself while wiping the fingerprints from the glass door. Now she'd given up even the pretense of cleaning. I had forgotten she was even here, honestly.

"See you tonight?" I asked, as he approached the door.

"Yeah. For sure."

He waved to me and said a polite goodbye to Mali, calling her ma'am and all. The door closed and she turned her attention to me.

"Mhm?"

"*Mhm* what?" I closed the cash register and stuck the tip in my pocket.

Her eyes fell on the door again and a Cheshire-cat grin spread across her face. "Oh, nothing."

"Stop gossiping," I told her, as I disappeared down the hallway.

Her voice followed me. "You're not painting my walls!"

I rolled my eyes and went back into my room.

# CHAPTER **TWENTY-FIVE**

I was keen to go home while the sun was shining—for once. That's why I didn't stay to clean as thoroughly as I usually did. I still put a load of towels into the dryer and opened a couple of boxes of products and put everything away, wishing my coworkers would do a little more to pick up the slack around here.

The alley was busy when I left. Bradley was helping a customer load a king-size mattress into the back of a truck when he waved to me, friendly as ever.

I pulled out my phone to open Instagram when my brother's name popped up on the screen.

"Austin, what the hell is going on? Are you okay?" I didn't bother with *hello*. I had no time for formalities.

"I'm fine. It's fine. Really, Kare, it's not that big of a deal. It was just a fight."

"A fight? With who?"

He sighed for a second. "Some guy. I don't know. I was out somewhere and this guy was giving a girl at the bar shit."

I rolled my eyes and pressed my body against the bushes lining the alleyway so a church van full of kids could pass.

"So you're telling me that this whole thing stemmed from your chivalry?"

Austin was good at spinning things. He would make a wonderful publicist for a messy celebrity—or a horrible husband.

"Yes. That's exactly what I'm saying," he said, laughing.

His voice was calming—it was like hearing an old song you had forgotten you loved. I'd really missed him.

"Right. So how much trouble are you in?"

"I don't know." He paused.

I thought I heard the flick of a lighter. "Dad bailed me out . . . which sucks, because now I'm going to owe him money."

Unbelievable. I wish I had his ability to look the other way and not worry about things. He knew he would figure it out—or someone would figure it out for him—before it got too serious.

"Yeah, because owing Dad money is your biggest problem."

"I didn't kill anyone, okay? It was your standard bar fight."

I laughed. I could *feel* his magic working. I was starting to feel almost okay about his arrest, and the ink on his paperwork wasn't even dry yet.

"How did you manage to get into a bar? We're not twenty-one for another month."

This time, it was his turn to be amused. "You're not serious."

"Yes, I am!" But I was joking, sort of.

There was this thin line between me worrying about my brother and just wanting to have fun with him. I was by no means a stickler, or super-responsible, but I was light-years ahead of my twin. The difference was incredibly noticeable. I was the worrier and he was the free spirit. Only in this case was I like our dad.

I knew my loser uncle was taking Austin to bars with his gross older friends, probably introducing him to women who downed too much alcohol, wore too much makeup, had too much experience . . . too much everything.

"You're a worrier. You and Dad."

I groaned. I didn't want to worry. I didn't want to be the nag-ging older-by-six-minutes sister. And I certainly didn't want to be anything like my dad.

"Don't lump me in with Dad. Come on. I don't want you to be in trouble. That's all."

I was almost home.

"Yeah, wouldn't want to mess up this bright future of mine." It was meant to be funny, but a hint of sadness filtered through.

"Do you want to come over tonight? I miss you."

"I can't tonight. I'm meeting up with someone. But tomorrow? And Dad and Estelle are going to Atlanta for a few days, leaving on Saturday, so I'll have the house to myself."

"House party!" I laughed at the memory of Austin's streak of failed house parties throughout high school. Most of the kids our age had been too afraid of the Military Police to go to a party on post, but fewer people actually made the parties more fun.

"Totally."

"And I was totally joking. You're not going to have a party at Dad's house."

"Uh, yeah. I am."

He could not be serious. Our dad would lose his mind if Austin had a party at his house. I couldn't bear to think of the consequences.

"You are not. I mean, throwing a party a few days after you get arrested? What is wrong with you? We aren't in high school anymore!"

It was stuff like this that made me return to my family theory, which was that Austin had inherited my mother's ability to live without consequence and charm her way through tricky circum-stances. My little brother was always so good with people. He could be thrust into any situation and people would flock to him. What's that saying, *like bees to honey*? He had all the honey. Me—I was the opposite. I fluttered around people like Austin, easily charmed, like my father.

"Speak for yourself."

"How do you even know enough people here to have a party? I mean—"

"Look, I gotta go. See you sometime tomorrow. Stop worrying. You should come over. Love you."

He hung up before I could get in another word.

*Oh, Austin. I love you, but sometimes you make some really shitty life choices.*

# CHAPTER **TWENTY-SIX**

I was surprised to find my front door locked. I dug for my key and let myself in, grabbing my mail from the box on the way. My little mailbox was falling off my house. Another thing to fix. As I flipped through envelopes, a realtor's brochure of fancy, expensive houses in Atlanta was on top. I searched for the smiley realtor—Sandra Deen, was her name. The price for a house in Buckhead, with a sparkling swimming pool, was three million dollars. Yeah, I freaking wish, Sandra.

Until I hit the lottery or my random idea of opening up a chain of high-end spas takes off, it's the little white house with the dangling red mailbox for me. When I got inside, the house was heavy with silence. I went through the rest of my mail—nothing interesting, mainly bills and flyers—and because the entire house smelled of Elodie's popcorn and it made my stomach growl, I grabbed some pretzels from the pantry.

My house felt different with no sound. It felt strange not hearing the name Olivia Pope every few minutes. I was completely alone. No Elodie. No Kael. We didn't agree on a time or anything, but I guess I'd assumed that he would be at my house when I got off work.

Where else would he go?

I microwaved the last of the leftovers from Mali. I washed a load of dishes. Sat at my kitchen table. Grabbed the paperback I was reading to pick up where I had left off. I tried to focus on the story, but I kept thinking about Kael, wondering how he would be when he got here. If he was still coming. Would he be more talkative than before?

I loved to torture myself with second thoughts, so now I wondered if I had misconstrued the whole situation. Did Kael want to come over? Was he under the impression that I wanted him to come over? I started to convince myself that he might be thinking I was weird or pushy. Or both.

Ten minutes later, I was back to reality. No way would Kael be sitting around overthinking our conversation—wherever he was. I was totally overreacting.

Overthinking. Overreacting. Not exactly skills I could put on my résumé. I put the book down without having read a word, then picked up my phone and went through Facebook, typing *Kael Martin* in the search box. No change in his profile. And I still couldn't bring myself to send him a friend request.

I clicked out of his page and went to my inbox, as if I was expecting an important email or something. I was pacing around my room before I knew it, going in circles, getting myself worked up. I stopped dead in my tracks when I caught a glimpse of myself in the mirror. With my dark hair pulled back, my eyes wild, I looked like my mother. Frighteningly like my mother.

I lay on my bed and grabbed my book again, but soon felt like I needed a change of scenery, so I went to the living room and flopped on the couch. I checked the time on my phone. Almost seven. I picked up where I'd left off on my last dog-eared page—I had never been a bookmark kind of girl—and let Hemingway's brutal tale take me to the First World War. It wasn't the distraction

I had hoped for, though. The closer I got to sleep, the more Kael's face appeared on multiple characters. He was a drill sergeant. A wounded soldier. An ambulance driver. And he looked at me like he recognized my eyes.

I woke up on the couch, the sun bright on my face. I looked around the living room, gathering my thoughts. Elodie was in the shower; I could hear the water running.

And Kael hadn't come back.

# CHAPTER **TWENTY-SEVEN**

It would be four days before I saw him again. When we finally crossed paths, I was sitting on my front porch, trying to get my feet into a new pair of shoes I had seen on Instagram. I knew that the IG model I followed had most likely been paid to wear them, but I still had to have them. Per the caption, they were "The Best!" and "SOO comfy!!! [heart-eye emoji]." Maybe for her. I could barely get the first one on. I mean, the damn thing wouldn't go over my heel. I was tugging on the shoe, leaning back on the porch like some kind of idiot, when Kael pulled up in his gigantic jeep-truck thing. Nice timing.

He must have gone shopping, since he was head-to-toe in civilian clothes. Black jeans, a rip on one knee, and a white cotton shirt with gray sleeves that looked almost identical to one that I had. The only difference was that mine said *Tomahawks* on it and had a picture of an actual tomahawk.

A friend from Texas had given it to me; well, she left it at my house before she moved. It was from her old high school in Indiana somewhere. I wondered if her midwestern home had been like the place where my mom grew up, a little town that was hit hard by the advances of technology, causing factory after factory to close down completely. I also knew horror stories from the place, like when the hyper schoolchildren had gone on field trips to sacred Native American burial grounds—what they called "Indian Mounds"—and stomped all over them while being taught a false history of dangerous savages. No mention that these people were victims of genocide or that we had taken their land and forced them into poverty today.

Come to think of it, I didn't really want to wear that shirt anymore.

Kael stopped short of my porch.

"Hey, stranger," I said to him.

He tucked his lips in and shook his head, then nodded. I guess that was his way of saying hello.

"Looking for Elodie?"

Little Mama was spending her evening at the monthly family readiness group meeting for Phillip's brigade. She was determined to make the other wives like her before the baby came. I didn't blame her. She needed all the support she could get.

"I'll tell her you stopped by."

"No, actually. I just—" Kael paused. "I went to get a massage, but you weren't working." He looked in the direction of the alleyway toward the shop.

"Oh." Now, that was a surprise.

I scooted over on the porch and made room next to me. Sort of. I had been blowing the seeds off dandelions in between my slightly manic thoughts, so Kael had to move a pile of bald weeds before he could sit down. He dropped them softly into the palm of my hand.

"I could use some wishes for sure," he said.

"There's more if you want." I pointed to my weed garden. I hadn't meant to harbor all those dandelions, wild daisies, and creeping something-or-other, but there they were by the corners of my concrete porch. Surrounded.

"I'm good," he told me.

He looked so different in regular clothes.

"I see you went shopping?" He was obviously okay sitting in silence, but I wanted some conversation. Plus, I wanted to know where he'd disappeared to.

Kael pulled at his T-shirt. "Yeah, sorry about that. It's been kind of a crazy few days."

I had to ask. "Crazy? How?"

He sighed, picking up a dandelion stem from the steps. "Long story."

I leaned back on my palms. "Yeah."

"When do you work again?" he asked, a moment later.

A plane flew overhead right as I started to answer. "Tomorrow. I'm filling in for someone."

"Do you have any openings?"

He was looking at me, his dark eyes hooded by his long lashes. "Maybe."

"Maybe?" He raised his brows and I laughed. He was soft today. I liked this relaxed version of him. Kael the civilian.

"I'm going to a party tonight," I told him. "It's at my dad's house."

He made a face.

"Yes. Exactly. Only worse, because my brother is being an idiot and throwing it while Dad and Estelle are off in Atlanta at the Marriott, eating lobster tails and boozing with expensive wine." I rolled my eyes.

My dad never took my mom anywhere like that. They never had adult time without my brother and me. One of the many reasons their marriage didn't work out. That and the fact that they were the two least compatible people on earth.

"Your dad doesn't seem like the kind of guy who wants a party thrown at his house," Kael observed. "Especially when he's not there."

If only he knew. "Oh, he's not. That's why I'm going to chaperone."

He made a noise—something between a grunt and a laugh. He was actually amused. I was really liking this, the way I was starting to read his face and guess what he was thinking.

"Aren't you a little young to be chaperoning?"

"Ha, ha." I stuck my tongue out at him . . . then snapped my mouth shut as soon as I realized what I'd done. I was flirting with him! I didn't know how to stop. Who was this person, sticking her tongue out at a boy?

"How old are you, Mr. Expert-on-Ageism?"

"That's not what *ageism* means." He corrected me with a smile.

I scoffed. I was equal parts charmed and surprised.

"Okay, Mr. Know-It-All, how old are you?"

He smiled again.

So soft.

"I'm twenty."

I shot up. "Really? I could be older than you?"

"How old are you?" he asked.

"Twenty-one next month."

He licked his pink lips and bit on the bottom one. It was a habit of his, I'd noticed.

"I turn twenty-one tomorrow. I win," he said with a smile.

I opened my mouth in an O. "No way. Show me your ID."

"Really?" he questioned.

"Yes, really. Prove it." And then, because I couldn't help myself, I added, "I want receipts."

He pulled his wallet out from the back pocket of his jeans and handed it to me. The first thing I saw was a picture of two women. One was older than the other by a couple of decades or so, but the resemblance was there.

I looked up at him, apologizing for the lack of privacy. The picture was obviously old and important, otherwise it wouldn't be in his wallet. Across from the picture of the women was his military ID card. I read his birthday. Sure as sin, his birthday was tomorrow.

"So, you're older than me by like a month." I gave in.

"I told you."

"Don't brag."

I leaned in to Kael with a playful shoulder bump. He didn't move away from me. And I froze with hopeful anticipation. On my sunny porch, in ripped jeans and with soft eyes, he paused for a moment and pressed his shoulder back into mine.

# CHAPTER **TWENTY-EIGHT**

"I haven't sat on my porch in so long. This is nice."

It was just me and Kael, with the occasional passing car for company.

"I'd sit out here almost every day when I first moved in. I couldn't believe it. My porch. My place." I stopped and smiled. "It feels good, you know? The street in front of you, the house behind you."

Talking to Kael was like writing in a diary, sort of.

"I've always loved sitting out front. Wherever I've lived. Did you notice that swing on my dad's porch? We moved that swing with us when we were growing up. It came from base to base, from house to house—kind of like my dad's recliner."

I could feel Kael listening, encouraging me to go on.

"When we first moved to Texas, we didn't have a big enough porch, so we kept it in the shed. It's heavy wood . . . you can see where it's splintered in a few places and where it's worn down on the arms a little. It's not like that plastic outdoor furniture you get now. What's it called—rosin?"

"Resin," he said, helping me out.

"That's it—resin." I was thinking about my mom now, how she would sit out front on the porch steps in the dark and stare up at the sky. "When we were in Texas my mom practically lived on our porch, all year round. I always wondered what she was looking at. What she was thinking about when she stared at the dark sky for hours."

I thought about the nights when she didn't have the swing and how she would just sit there, a little lost, but still focused on the sky.

"She always made up stories about the sky. The sun, the moon, the stars. She really lived in her own head, a lot like me, I guess." I paused. "She was quite dramatic. She told me once that she believed God was made up of all the stars and that when one burned out, a little bit of the good in the world died with it."

Kael's eyes were on me, and I was aware of how the heat was spreading on my cheeks. The way I was talking . . . well, it was like I was thinking out loud. I barely realized it. I knew that it sounded cheesy. I'd read things like that in books sometimes or had seen it in movies, but it hardly seemed possible, in real life, to instantly connect and feel so comfortable with a stranger. What a cliché. Yet there I was, being opened by someone I hadn't even known for a week.

"I mean, it was way more complicated than that, obviously. That was the quick version. There were civilizations whose entire religions were based on the galaxy of planets and stars. My mom used to tell me all about them. I mean, it makes sense, doesn't it? They were here first."

Kael spoke up. "Were they?"

His words seemed important, there were so few of them. I guess that's why when he asked me questions, I wanted to really think about my answers.

"I'm not entirely sure," I finally said. "What do you believe in?"

He shook his head. "I'm still figuring that out."

"I think that's okay," I told him. "There are so many different religions . . . too hard to get people to agree on one thing. I think it's okay to take a little time, learn a little more. Don't you?" Such a heavy question, and wrapped in the most casual bow.

He sighed, blowing out a puff of air. I could hear the whisper of his words coming together but couldn't quite make them out. The longer he sat on his opinion, licking slowly at his lips, chewing on his cheek, the more I anticipated his answer. Time melted as I waited.

"Thinking for yourself is better than being blindly led," he said at long last. "I just want to be a good person. I know a lot of people inside and outside the church who are both bad and good. There's so much out there that's bigger than us . . . I'd rather focus on how to make things better than wonder how we got here in the first place. For now, at least."

He sounded so sure. These were the deepest thoughts he had shared since we met.

A car door slammed, and my phone buzzed with a text from Elodie. She was going to someone's house—someone named Julie—where all the wives, except her, would start their evening with a few drinks and catty conversation. I dimmed my screen and put my phone facedown on the concrete porch.

"I have a lot of shit to make up for before my life is over." Kael's confession startled me. His voice slipped a little at the end and the gravity of what he was saying ate at me. My throat burned and I swallowed, trying to dilute it, but it didn't work. It was physically painful to think about the kinds of things Kael had seen at his age—at *our* age.

I wished I was someone who wasn't so affected by the emotions around me. It would have been easier not to take on other people's troubles, not to make them my own, but I'd always felt so much, ever since I was a child. I was always either burning or floating, moving from one extreme to another. "Karina feels things deeply," my mother said of me. "She takes things to heart."

Kael cleared his throat. I wanted so badly to ask him what he had to make up for, but I wanted him to tell me at his own pace, not because I asked. I could feel him next to me, brewing, but I kept my eyes on the sky, blinking and watching as blue swirled into orange. I pictured him with a gun strapped to his chest, a boyish smile. I didn't know what he'd experienced over there, but that blank stare on his face . . . I had to say something.

"I don't think it works like that. Your life isn't a debt for someone else's sins. You're a good person, you deserve to be safe."

My words fell short of all that I wanted to say, but I wanted him to feel everything I felt for him in that moment.

"Safe?" he asked, as the clouds drifted over us. "From who?"

# CHAPTER **TWENTY-NINE**

Somehow between our talks of gods and war, Kael accepted my invite to the party tonight. I was a little nervous for him and Austin to meet. My brother liked everyone, but I really wanted Kael to like him, and this house party probably wasn't the best way to make that a reality. I drove there, and when we arrived I didn't hear loud music or see bright lights as we pulled up. And nobody had spilled onto the lawn. That had to be a good sign.

"Doesn't seem too bad," I said.

The stately brick house was in the far corner of a quiet cul-de-sac, with a field at the back and other houses all around. I had to park on the street because three cars were already in the driveway—two of which I didn't recognize. Plus, there was my dad's van, an ugly white thing that he hadn't touched in at least a year. I'd come to hate that van after ugly arguments and resentments that spilled over from the front seat displaced the happy memories of our one Disney road trip long ago.

My parents didn't have typical husband-and-wife shouting matches. Even as a child I remember wishing for some of the honest anger I had heard in other families. Theirs was worse. My mom would use a cold, flat voice to deliver her punches. She hit hard, and she knew instinctively where to strike, how to make it hurt the most. I was a needy girl and wanted her anger and passion to reassure me that she cared. I think my dad wanted that, too, but she either couldn't or wouldn't give it. My dad and I both navigated her cold indifference the best we could.

Kael's phone lit up in his hand. He glanced down and put it into his pocket. I felt important. Prideful as it was, I still felt it.

We were walking up the grass when someone I didn't recognize came out of the house and walked toward the street. I saw Kael watch him until we were safely inside. It wasn't anything obvious, a slight tilt of the head, an almost imperceptible scan of where this other guy was and what he was doing. It made me wonder what Kael had experienced, and what he might fear. I tried not to let it affect my mood, thinking about what he had seen in Afghanistan. I was sure that was the last thing he wanted to talk about at a party, the night before his birthday.

I led Kael into my dad's house for the second time in a week. Brien had been there only a total of maybe three times during our entire four months of dating. He liked my dad . . . well, he liked trying to impress him while staring at Estelle's boobs. She was new back then, her boobs, too.

*Ugh* Brien was the last person I should be thinking of. I looked at Kael to edge him back into my mind, but also to make sure he was still following me up the steps.

Someone's music was playing on the TV screen when we went inside. It was a Halsey song, so I knew I'd like at least one of these random people. I was relaxing a little now, since the party wasn't out of hand. Austin had been right about the party—so far, anyway. Everything was more low-key since it was a Sunday night. There were only about ten people there, and everyone seemed to be older than high school, thank God. And there was no sign of Sarina or any of her other friends, and as far as I knew, she was Austin's only recent high school hookup. He said she lied about her age. I didn't know if that was true or not. No sign of Austin, which meant he was either outside smoking or in some room with a girl. As long as it wasn't my old room and the girl was of age, I didn't care.

Five or six people were dotted around the living room. The rest were in the kitchen, crowding the booze counter. There wasn't much to speak of: a bottle of vodka, a much bigger bottle of whiskey, and tons of beer. We stayed in the kitchen, moving around a guy and a girl who seemed to be mid-argument, and passing a man wearing a gray beanie. I couldn't see his hair, but I suspected he was a soldier, based on his build. My brother always seemed to gravitate toward people in service, even when we were in high school.

Austin and I made a pact from a young age that neither of us would ever even consider enlisting, but he still had a natural draw to Army life. Whether it was out of habit or comfort—the pull of the familiar and all that—I didn't know. His curiosity scared me sometimes.

Kael stood near me by the kitchen sink, not touching or speaking, but close enough that I could smell the cologne on his shirt. The smell was sweet, and it made me wonder if he had other plans tonight. I grabbed a plastic cup from the stack and poured in a little bit of vodka and a lot of cranberry juice.

"Want one?" I asked Kael.

He shook his head no. He seemed tense. Whether he was more tense than usual, I couldn't say. He looked at me as if he wanted to say something but couldn't. His eyes leveled on the cup in my hand.

"I'm only having one since I'm driving," I explained, slightly defensive. Guilt didn't really feel appropriate, since I could crash upstairs in my old bed if I needed to. I still hadn't seen my brother, and we had been there for at least twenty minutes.

"I don't drink much." I didn't need to explain myself further, but did anyway.

Kael's attention was all over the kitchen. His eyes were a bit robotic, scanning every detail of the room. It was like he wanted to be present, but his mind was wandering back and forth between here and somewhere else. I tried to guess where, and even considered straight-up asking him, but the idea made my heart pound.

"I'll take a beer," Kael said, after I downed half my drink.

I handed him a can from the bin in front of me, next to the partition between the living room and kitchen. Shelves full of eight-by-tens of my dad and Estelle, and me and Austin when we were young, stared back at us. My mom had long since been erased from the record.

Kael studied the beer for a moment, rolling it in his hand before popping open the tab.

"Natural Light, huh?" He raised his brows. They were so thick they shaded his deep-set eyes and helped hide him from the world. Like he needed help with that.

"Yep. The best of the best." I took a gulp of my vodka mixture. I felt it fast, my cheeks and tummy warming up.

Kael took a drink of the watery beer. I lifted my cup to touch his can. "Happy birthday! You'll be drinking legally in about three hours," I joked.

"And you in a month," he said, taking a swig of the beer and making a face. I didn't blame him. I much preferred vodka over heavy bubbles of beer. It was my go-to when I drank. Drink less, feel more.

Another plus with vodka: I knew exactly how much to drink before I would get too drunk. I'd pretty much mastered vodka. I'd been drinking it since Austin and I had gone to that seniors-only party back in Texas.

Austin and I were probably the only freshmen there. We scanned the place when we arrived, but it didn't take long until Casey, a preppy seventeen-year-old, made a beeline for Austin. She was one of the popular seniors. *Popular.* I hated that word. Austin didn't, though. He knew it was his way in. The moment he complimented Casey's eyelashes—it was something lame, like, "You have the longest eyelashes"—well, that was it. Five minutes later, they were tongue to tongue, and I was left to wander the party by myself.

The only person who talked to me was a boy who had a mustard stain on his shirt. He had sharp canines, like a wolf, and he smelled like orange Lysol. I left him in the hallway by the bathroom and found the vodka bottle in the freezer. It was cool going down. That's probably why I drank so much so fast. Too much. Too fast. I ran to the bathroom with my hand covering my mouth, holding in the vomit. Unfortunately, I ran into Lysol guy again, and he looked at me like I was the pathetic one. Maybe I was? I mean, I *was* the one pushing people out of the way to get to the toilet.

But that was then and this was now. This party was different. I was different. I had learned to hold my liquor. And I was no longer the girl who couldn't walk away from a creepy guy without second-guessing herself. I felt safe with Kael. Interested and interesting. Like I was the senior at this party.

# CHAPTER **THIRTY**

Kael was taking everything in. He wasn't obvious about it, but he was watching. Analyzing. Paying attention.

We made eye contact and he surprised me by being the one to break the silence between us.

"Exactly how I thought I would spend my twenty-first birthday," he said, taking another gulp of beer. And another.

Someone turned on an old Usher song and I smiled into my cup. People were definitely trying to set the mood if they were playing old-school Usher. I was liking this group, even though I tried not to. I was a sucker for nostalgia.

"Wow. Usher. Well, take all the sarcasm out of what I just said." Kael smiled.

I hadn't known this guy long, but, wow, I loved it when he was this way. Unguarded and funny. I laughed at him and he took me in—my mouth, my eyes, my mouth again. He wasn't subtle about it.

Was he aware of the way he was looking at me?

He had to be.

My head felt fuzzy, and it had nothing to do with the vodka.

"Kare!" Austin's voice boomed over everyone and everything,

including the blender being used to make some sort of neon mixed drink that I hoped wouldn't be splattered all over my dad's bathroom floor later.

"There you are!" He wrapped both arms around me. He smelled like beer himself.

He hugged me tight and kissed my hair.

"Look at you," he said, holding his plastic cup in the air. I knew he was drunk. He wasn't wild. He wasn't belligerent. But buzzed for sure.

"Did you get a drink?" Austin's ice-blue eyes were bloodshot. I reminded myself that he had just gotten out of jail, that he probably needed the drink.

The fact that jail was a part of my vocabulary was something in itself, but I refused to be anything but chill the entire night. I was there to chaperone, and now that Kael was there, I wanted Austin to have fun.

"Yes." I held up my cup and Austin nodded as if to say "Good."

"Did you meet everyone?" His words were slightly slurred. His hair was messy, tousled, hitting the middle of his forehead.

"Not yet. I just got here."

"You look happy. Are you happy?" my twin asked me.

His cheeks were flushed. I put both of my hands on his shoulders.

"You look drunk. Are you drunk?" I taunted him. In a loving way, of course. He was drunk. I was happy. But I wasn't going to talk about that or the circumstances of his recent arrest in front of an arguing couple and Kael.

"I am. As you should be," Austin told me with conviction. "It's so good to be back." He raised his hands in the air. His happiness was contagious, giving me a burst of energy I hadn't felt in a while.

Austin raised his cup to mine and then moved to Kael's. It

took a second for him to register that Kael wasn't someone he had invited.

"Hi." Austin extended his hand to Kael. I cringed, wishing I had poured double the vodka into my drink.

"Hey, I'm Martin. Nice to meet you." The two guys shook hands like they were making a billion-dollar deal.

"Martin." Austin let that one sit for a second. He looked at me, silently asking me who the hell this guy was, and I widened my eyes, telling him to behave. He smiled.

"Nice to meet you, man. We have drinks in here, pizza on the way. She knows where everything is," he said, pointing at me with his cup. "You guys should come out to the living room with me."

Kael looked at me and I shrugged. I knew it was either the best or the worst idea to follow Austin back to the living room.

"Here, refill your drinks and come with me."

I tried to make eye contact with Kael, but he was looking at Austin, who was asking how long he had been in the Army. Austin could tell that Kael was a soldier. Even without being told, he could tell.

I knew that Austin wouldn't embarrass me by asking too many questions in front of Kael, but I also knew by the way he was looking at me that he was going to ask a hell of a lot of questions later. The arguing couple disappeared down the hallway, probably to have make-up sex in the downstairs bathroom.

"I'm glad you came," Austin said to me, leading us into the living room.

He looked at Kael again and I rolled my eyes. Austin and I mostly stayed out of each other's dating lives. Not that there was much on my end to be nosy about. I had had only one serious boyfriend, and the more time that passed, I came to realize we weren't as serious as I thought. I had been told *I love you* only by someone who didn't mean it. Austin was different, falling in love every week. He somehow managed to stay honest about it, channeling his need and loneliness into physical contact. If it was the thing that made his life a little better, who was I to judge? I had that same itch, just no one to scratch it.

# CHAPTER **THIRTY-ONE**

Kael and I were smushed together on one end of the couch. Not squished. Not smashed. *Smushed.* Austin and a guy who had introduced himself as Lawson were on one cushion; Kael and I were on the other.

"You look so familiar," Lawson said to Kael after a few minutes.

Kael reeled off a few things that sounded like Army lingo and Lawson shook his head. "No, that's not it."

"You say that to everyone," Austin said. Then he grabbed a video game controller from a basket under the entertainment center. "Who's ready to play?"

"Not me," Lawson said. "Time to go. I have to be up at five for duty." He and Austin stood up and did that handshake thing guys do where they slap their palms together and make a fist.

Once there was more room, I moved over a little on the couch. We weren't smushed anymore, but my thigh was still touching Kael's.

"Do you want to play?" Austin lifted a controller to Kael, who shook his head.

"No, I don't really play."

*Oh, thank God.*

"Who wants to play?" Austin asked again, holding up a controller to see if he had any takers.

The front door opened and a familiar face walked in. I couldn't remember his name off the top of my head, but I knew he and Austin used to hang out before he went to our uncle's house to *keep out of trouble*. Yeah, because that had worked out so well.

"Mendoza!" Austin rushed to the door to greet the guy in the Raiders shirt. Austin always collected people around him. He was good at it.

The guy, presumably Mendoza, hugged Austin. His eyes landed on me as I stared him down. My cheeks flushed. He looked next to me, to Kael.

"Martin! What the fuck are you doing here!" he said, pulling away from my brother. He walked over to the couch and Kael stuck his hand out between us. It took me longer than it should've to realize that they knew each other very well.

"Thought you were staying in tonight." Mendoza's honey-colored eyes were on me.

"I was going to," Kael said.

Mendoza looked at me again, then back at Kael. "Right," he said, smiling.

"You two know each other?" Austin pointed between them. I sat there, observing. Confused. Austin was as surprised as I was.

"Yeah, man. He's my fucking brother." Mendoza's voice was loud and happy. If it were a color, it would be yellow. Where Kael's was more of a dark navy blue.

Wait, were they actually brothers? They were different races, but that didn't mean anything, really. Or was this soldier talk, always calling one another family?

"We were in basic together. And we deployed—"

"Mendoza, this is Karina," Kael interrupted, looking at me.

"My sister," Austin said to both guys.

"We met before. I don't know if you remember," I said.

It shouldn't have rattled me that Kael and this guy knew each other, but it did. Military bases always seemed so small, but they were really their own cities with hundreds of thousands of people. When someone said, "Oh, your dad's in the Army. I bet he knows my cousin Jeff, he's in the Army too!"—it didn't really work that way. So, Mendoza knowing Kael *and* Austin, and sort of knowing me, was a coincidence, to say the least.

"I do. We met a couple times." Mendoza cocked his head to the side. "Didn't we go to the castle one night? What was that, like last summer?" I thought back to the end of summer, riding in my dad's van, which had been too full of Austin's friends. Definitely squished.

"We did," I told him. "I forgot all about that." Brien was there, too. We had just met, in fact. I didn't mention that.

"Your brother and that damn castle." He laughed, and Austin flipped him off.

Kael was looking at us both like we were crazy.

"Have you heard about it? Dracula's castle?" I asked. It sounded ridiculous out loud.

He shook his head and I continued to explain. "It's not really a castle, but it's this big stone tower that everyone says was haunted."

"IS haunted!" Austin argued.

"*Is* haunted," I said, rolling my eyes. I had gone to Dracula's castle at least five times with Austin since we'd moved here. I didn't know if the story about the kid getting electrocuted at the top was really true, but the old tower had earned a reputation for being haunted by ghosts. "Actual ghosts!" is what everyone said. There were all kinds of stories.

"Anyway, so it's a tower and people drive up there at night to drink and try not to get caught," I explained to Kael.

"She's acting like she's cool now, but she's always the first one to run back to the car." Austin held up his drink to Kael and Mendoza, laughing.

"Oh, fuck off." I shot him a look—more laughter followed.

Mendoza started to taunt Austin. "Oooh, looks like sis has grown up since I saw her last," he said, picking up a bottle of dark liquor from the table.

"Shots, anyone?" he asked the room.

Everyone took a shot of warm liquor. Everyone except Kael, that was. There were shouts of "To Austin!" and "Welcome back, bro!" Austin gave a mock bow to acknowledge his friends as they celebrated his return. I wasn't sure if any of them knew that he had been arrested. Looking around at these guys . . . well, I wasn't sure if any of them would even concern themselves with something as trivial as a night in jail. But maybe I was being hard on them.

We all migrated back to the kitchen to cheer Austin's return to Fort Benning. I put my shot glass in the sink and gathered up a few more. A guy in a bright blue T-shirt that said *Bottoms Up!* grabbed his glass back from me and went for a refill. Definitely a soldier. He was with a younger-looking guy wearing a brown band tee. Also a soldier. I kept forgetting how removed I had become from life on post. Sure, I still saw soldiers at work and at the grocery store. I still smiled at them while going through the gate to the Great Place, but I didn't have any friends who were soldiers. Not one.

Not unless you counted my client, Stewart. She was the closest thing I had to an Army friend. But even though I liked and respected her, even though I felt close to her, I couldn't really claim her as a friend. As Mali liked to remind us, clients were not our friends.

I turned on the hot water and rinsed out a few shot glasses just for something to do. I was glad Austin didn't see me. He would have made some crack about my being *responsible*. It wouldn't have been a compliment. God, it was so weird having him back, being at my dad's, being surrounded by all these people. No doubt about it: this was Austin's world, and I was only visiting.

I wasn't the same person as I was before he left, though. It felt good to remind myself of that. And Austin, as much as he gathered people around him, he latched onto them, too. Which was risky in his case, because he was often the one to run, like our mother. And he often left broken hearts behind, also like her.

I walked over to Kael, Austin, and Mendoza.

"Another?" Mendoza asked.

"No way." I shook my head and held up my hand, the universal symbol for *no, thanks*.

My stomach still burned as the tequila settled inside me. Mixing vodka and tequila was definitely going to have me suffering tomorrow. The flavor was strong—pretty good, but so strong compared to the cheap vodka diluted with sweet cranberry juice that I usually drank.

"Come on. Anyone?"

Austin's eyes were on Kael, who was also saying no. He didn't need to put his hand up or shake his head. Apparently, "no" is all the answer you need when it comes from a guy.

Austin turned to Mendoza and refilled his glass. "He's trying to get as many shots in as possible before his wife calls for bedtime." Austin heckled him.

By the way Mendoza smiled when my brother teased him, I could see their bond. He was a nice guy, this Mendoza. I could feel it. It was never easy to predict the people I would meet through my twin, because he never had a type. Soldiers were usually involved, but that could be more of a geographical thing. Mostly strays. Mostly friendly. But every pack had a few wild cards.

"Well, she did let him come out this week," another male voice taunted. I turned around to see the guy in the *Bottoms Up!* T-shirt holding his shot glass in a way that was slightly menacing. He had a square face, tiny lips, and a bad crew cut.

Mendoza laughed still, but it didn't reach his eyes. Not like it did when he had joked with Austin. The guy in the T-shirt snickered, pointing a Bud Light bottle at Mendoza. "How many kids you got now, anyway?" This question was delivered with a straight face.

"Three," Mendoza replied, humorless now. Something shifted in the room. I could feel it. Kael stiffened next to me. Austin inched closer to the two jerks.

"Three? That's it? I thought I saw you driving out of the commissary with like ten—"

"You're not funny, Jones. Neither are you, Dubrowski. Comedy's not your thing. Now move along or get out," Austin snapped, pointing his chin toward the door. His eyes may have been glassy, but he was fully present. He wasn't having any of their shit.

The room was silent, except for the obnoxious intro music to the video game that was playing on a loop in the background.

"Chill, we're leaving anyway," *Bottoms Up!* said.

No one made a sound as Jones and Dubrowski set their beers on the counter, opened the back door, and left. Mendoza and Austin stared at each other for a second. I tried not to look, but I caught a glimpse of it.

"Who were those guys?" I asked Austin when the door shut.

"They're in my new company," Mendoza answered. "I thought they were cool and felt bad because they're so young and just got home and don't have any family here, you know?"

"Quit being so fucking nice!" Austin slapped Mendoza on the back and we all laughed. "See where it gets you? Now let's have a drink and not waste any more time or tequila on those pricks."

"This isn't any old tequila, my friends." Mendoza held up the bottle. "It's an Añejo, aged to perfection. Smooth as butter." He showed me the label and I nodded, reading what I could as he watched me, before moving it to Kael.

Añejo or not, I knew I shouldn't drink much more. Even with my mother's tolerance for all vices, I could tell the alcohol was settling into my bloodstream. My cheeks were red—I could feel them.

But Kael was less blurry somehow.

You know those moments when someone suddenly looks different to you? Like you swipe and a filter covers the picture? Everything about them becomes a little deeper in color, a little more vibrant?

Kael was leaning against the counter in my dad's kitchen of all places, answering trivial questions from my brother, when it all started to change. There was something about watching him there with Austin, the way he was standing with his back straight, his eyes a little more wild than usual. He was still the definition of composure, but there was something emanating from him in that moment.

Something strong and dark. I had to see more.

# CHAPTER **THIRTY-TWO**

"Martin, where you from?"

"Atlanta area. You?" Kael took a drink of his beer. And then another. I remembered that he said he was from Riverdale. Easier to say Atlanta, I supposed. I liked being in on one of his secrets.

Austin crossed his arms. "All over. Fort Bragg, Texas, and a couple others. You know, Army brat."

Kael nodded. "Yeah. I can't imagine, man."

The doorbell rang. "Pizza? I hope so. I haven't eaten all day," Austin said, disappearing from the kitchen.

"Are you hungry?" I asked Kael.

"Kind of. You?"

I nodded.

"Shall we?" I gestured toward the living room.

He nodded, smiled at me, and tossed his beer into the trash.

"Do you want another one?" I asked, looking into my almost empty cup and debating a refill.

"I'm good. One of us has to drive," he said.

"Ah," I said, biting my lower lip. Kael's shoulder brushed against mine. He was standing so close to me. "I can stay here."

His eyes widened a little.

"You can, too. There's plenty of room."

We had stopped walking, but I couldn't remember when. He was looking down at me and I was looking up at him. The curve of his lashes shaded his brown eyes. The way he smelled like cinnamon. For the first time, the scent didn't remind me of anything except him. My brain was short-circuiting, not connecting thought with my tongue.

"I mean, you don't have to stay here. You can use my car, or an Uber. Whatever. I was just suggesting because I'm obviously not driving, and your car—" Kael leaned toward me. I had to work hard to catch my breath.

"I'll get another beer," he told me in a whisper. He paused there, so close to my mouth, that the bottom of my stomach ached.

He moved away, casually, and grabbed for another beer. I swallowed, blinking.

Did I think he was going to kiss me?

I *so* did.

That had to be why I was breathing like I had run up a flight of stairs.

I gathered myself as quickly as I could.

"Uh, yeah. Me too," I said, voice hoarse and audibly awkward. I pulled open the freezer door to grab some ice. The cold air felt so good against my hot face. I let it roll over me for a few seconds before I filled up my cup.

Kael was waiting for me by the wall, sipping his new beer. My insides wouldn't settle. Gah, he made me feel on edge one second, yet so calm the next.

We were both quiet as we walked into the living room. There seemed to be the same number of people in the house—minus the two assholes—but the crowd felt dense now that everyone was crammed into the living room. It didn't help that my heart was pounding in its cage, no matter how hard I tried to calm myself.

Austin was talking to the pizza delivery man. I watched as he handed over some cash, shoving a wad back into his pocket. As far as I knew, Austin had been working only a few hours a week at Kmart, which he supplemented by asking my dad for money here and there. My brother was never good with money. Even when he worked summer jobs, he'd spend his check the day he got it. I wasn't much better, so I wasn't judging, but where did that cash come from? It didn't make sense.

"Kare! Grab some plates?" Austin yelled to me, passing out pizza boxes to the group.

I didn't know what was going on, but my brain couldn't handle any more tonight. I wanted to have fun, to not worry about things that I couldn't control. I had been trying that for years—maybe tonight would be the night that I actually followed through with it?

Black jeans were a girl's best friend. They stood out from the usual indigo. They made your legs look longer. And that dark wash was great when you were out on a date and needed to do something about greasy pizza fingers. Not that I was on a date. Was I on a date?

There was just this way that Kael was looking at me that made me wonder. The fact that he'd agreed to come to the party at all made me wonder. But as with everything with this man, I couldn't be sure.

We were still sitting next to each other on the couch. Kael's empty plate rested on a napkin on his lap. The plate was clean and the napkin was spotless. My plate had a splinter of hard crust on it and a bit of stray pepperoni. My white paper napkin was splotched with pizza sauce. My black jeans didn't show my greasy handprints, though. Small mercies. I wasn't neat and tidy. Not like Kael. And certainly not like Estelle, the perfect housewife, whose picture was hanging in a thick black frame above us. A black cloud was more like it. I couldn't see her face, but I could feel her bearing down on me. I knew that picture well—it had been taken on one of their many vacations. My dad was next to her, wearing a big smile and a Florida tan. A beachfront *American Gothic*.

Kael leaned up to grab a pizza box. "Can you hand me a napkin?" I asked.

Another guy might have made a crack about the red sauce massacre I had going on, but he didn't say anything, just grabbed some pizza and napkins, then leaned back into the couch cushion. I could feel the heat rising off him. My imagination was playing with that. My body, too.

"Want some?" he asked. He offered his plate, which had two thick slices, glistening with cheese.

I shook my head, thanking him.

"I see you have a new twin." Austin pointed to Kael and mostly everyone looked at him, then me. His shirt and jeans were practically identical to mine, only my shirt was plain gray. I thought back to the photograph of my dad and Estelle, standing side by side in their matching Hawaiian shirts from Old Navy, and burned with embarrassment. Kael cracked a smile. A very small smile, but it was there, all right.

"Ha, ha," I said, rolling my eyes. "You were gone awhile, sooo—"

Laughter bounced around the room.

"Fair enough." Austin took a bite of pepperoni pizza.

Cheese slid down the slice and he caught it with his tongue. He was so much like a younger teenage boy sometimes, as if he had stopped maturing after tenth grade. It was part of his draw, I guess—the innocence of him. He really did have a good soul, and it was easy to see. He was the kind of boy who would start a fire and then save you from it.

I wondered if this new girl understood what she was in for, if she knew she was playing in the brush on a hot day. A pretty brunette with a smattering of freckles across her cheeks, she had deep blue—almost navy—eyes. Her shirt set off her coloring, and the style of her loose peasant top resembled her hair—ruffled sleeves falling in waves down her arms, mimicking the curls in her long tresses. She was sitting on the floor by Austin's feet, looking up, a flower tilted to the sun. The attraction she had to him was clear as day. The way she almost willed him to turn his face to hers, to say something, anything, to her. The way her shoulders were angled toward him, pulled back to expose her long, graceful neck. She wasn't sitting cross-legged like the others on the floor. The awkward child's pose was not for her. She had folded one leg on top of the other, ankle to knee, and she was tilted sideways so that her legs formed an arrow pointing toward my brother. This girl was vulnerable and open. Calculating, too.

Body language could be so obvious.

Did Austin know that she was planning their first kiss, their first date?

The paper plate in his hand slipped a little and she lifted the corner for him. He looked at her, smiling, thanking her, and then she did this pouty thing with her lips, and a flippy thing with her hair. It was impressive as hell, even to me, and I wasn't the intended target. I looked away from my brother and the girl. I'd seen this movie before.

"Mendoza seems great," I said to Kael.

"Yeah. He is." Kael looked at his friend, who was offering his special tequila to someone who had just come in. I thought I had seen the guy before. In the kitchen, maybe. I remembered his black-and-white checked T-shirt. From the way he reeked of cigarette smoke, it was clear that he had been outside for a smoke break. At least this group of friends was respectful enough not to smoke inside the house, unlike some Austin had had in the past.

"He's married?" I asked.

Kael's forehead scrunched up a little and he nodded.

"Cool." I was about out of small talk. I could have talked about the weather or the alcohol, but that would have seemed desperate. I was buzzed from the drinks and getting paranoid about Kael's silence, and while I may have been anxious, I wasn't desperate. I wasn't going to be the needy girl at a party. A party at my dad's house, of all places.

Kael nodded again and then . . . nothing. I should have been used to the barriers he put up, the distance between us, but he had let down his guard since coming to the party, so much so that I was beginning to forget it had even existed. But there it was, brewing next to me.

And that was why I didn't like dating. Or whatever this was.

I knew I was being ridiculous. I mean, it had been only about twenty minutes since I'd decided to admit to myself that I was more than just attracted to him. I was completely fascinated. Enamored. We had been standing side by side in the kitchen and I could feel that heat of his. It didn't matter that we weren't touching. I could feel myself being drawn toward him. It was strong, this pull. Almost animal in its intensity. I lost myself in the physical for a moment, and then my brain took over and started to dissect the reasons he wouldn't like me, or why this couldn't—wouldn't—work. I was such a romantic.

I looked around the room, to friendly Mendoza pouring Austin and the ruffly brunette a shot. To the three guys sitting on the floor, and the voices coming from the kitchen. Everyone was alive in their own way, talking, listening, drinking, laughing, playing with their phones. Everyone except the one person I really wanted to connect with.

My frustration grew and grew inside my head, and by the time Austin and the girl were making out (which took less than five more minutes) I couldn't sit there anymore. I needed some air.

I got up from the couch, and if Kael noticed, he didn't care to show it.

# CHAPTER **THIRTY-THREE**

I sat down on my mom's swing, feeling the heaviness of the situation with Kael. Not for the first time, I thought of it as a mood swing. My own little joke. Only it wasn't funny.

I'd lost track of the number of times I'd made my way out to the porch at this house. If I was feeling anxious and alone, if I wanted to think something through or just daydream, I'd head to the swing. I was out there a lot after my mom left; sometimes I thought maybe she would be sitting there. And when Dad was talking about shipping Austin off to live with our porn-king uncle, you'd find me on the swing. There was something soothing about the gentle back and forth as the seat pushed into its arc and then returned. I could be close to full-on panic, but after a few minutes on the swing, my breathing would slow, and I'd feel myself calm down. Most of the time, anyway.

When Brien and I were on the rocks, I'd planted myself out here, trying to get some perspective. But more than once, Estelle had followed me out to see how she could help. She'd give me this look that I could tell she thought was sympathetic. To me it just seemed obnoxious, like she was trying to sell me something. A used car, maybe. A used stepmother was more like it.

She'd say things like "I was young once, too, you know." That was my cue to say, "Oh, but you're still young," and, "You're so pretty." But I wasn't going there. I wouldn't have given her what she wanted even if it had been true. Then she'd tell me that everything was going to be okay, that what I was going through was tough, but she understood how I was feeling. That bothered me the most. How could she possibly understand what I was feeling when she didn't know me, and I didn't know myself?

And there I was again, sitting on my dad's porch, not really knowing what I was feeling. I wanted to get closer to Kael, but I felt stung by his silence. I wanted to ask him to join me on the swing, but I felt too timid. I wanted . . . whatever it was I wanted, I wasn't getting it, so I had sulked off like a little kid.

I was kicking my feet a bit and starting to move the swing when the front door creaked open and Kael stepped out onto the porch. He leaned against the railing, watching me with glassy eyes. He looked older, somehow. I wasn't sure if I liked it.

The streetlight hummed as it cast a dim glow over my dad's yard. I could make out cars, trees, houses—but only the outlines. I wasn't sure if this was because it was getting dark or because I was pretty buzzed. I didn't particularly care. It had been a while since I had had anything to drink other than a little wine and I felt this hazy glow. Actually, I felt pretty damn good.

Rocking gently back and forth, I was aware that my breathing was syncing to the rhythm of the swing, and that made it easier to pretend that I hadn't noticed Kael. No way was I going to be the first one to say something. I kept my mouth shut and my thoughts to myself. God, this guy was tough to figure out.

Maybe it was the way he was with me—observing, nonjudgmental. That was rare. So often you could feel people sizing you up, trying to figure you out. *Who are you and what do you have that I want?* Not Kael. He just noticed. I liked that. But it didn't seem fair, somehow. He knew a lot about me, and I hardly knew anything about him. The things I did know I could count on one hand. Almost reflexively, that's what I did.

One: he was charming in that strong, silent way.

Two: he had this almost magnetic draw that attracted people to him.

Three: he made you want to know what he thought of you. (Or was that just me?)

Four: he was insanely attractive.

Five: his family lived in Riverdale, and he knew what *Twilight* was.

Maybe I could get to ten, but I liked the drama of one hand.

Everything about Kael seemed so complex, yet uncomplicated at the same time. He hadn't said much to me while we were inside, other than to ask if I wanted a slice of pizza, but he had clearly followed me out. So why was he standing there with that force field around him, shifting his weight from one foot to the other and looking at me as if words were a burden too heavy to carry? I started to say something to break the tension, but stopped myself just in time. No way was I going to make this easy on him. I'd give him a taste of his own medicine and see how he liked it.

The sky was darkening now, filling with the most gorgeous stars. I knew everyone thought they were magical, diamonds hung aloft in the sky and all that, but even though I found them beautiful, I mostly found them sad. Stars seemed so fierce and bright, but by the time they got to us, they were dying, almost gone. And the biggest stars? They burned the fastest, as if their intense radiance was too much for them to hold on to. Damn. There I was getting sappy. I always thought of how fragile things were when I drank. I could move from beauty to despair in the blink of an eye. Or the twinkle of a star. As I said, *damn*.

"Can I sit with you?" Kael finally asked. Had he seen the shadow cross my face?

I nodded yes and moved over to make some room.

"This is *the* swing?" he asked.

I nodded again. I still had a dose or two of his own medicine to give him. Not really. I was just trying to stay cool. If I was going to second-guess myself, I might as well be cool about it.

"She didn't take it with her?" he asked into the night air.

I jerked my head, looking at his face. "What?"

"When she . . ." He could see that he had struck a nerve, but he couldn't exactly backtrack.

I blinked. He was referring to my mom, of course. Despite his reserved nature, he sure liked to ask questions that packed a punch.

"Left?" I finished for him. "No, she didn't take anything."

*Not even us.*

*Not even* me.

I didn't really feel like talking about my mom, but I was happy he asked—happy that he had remembered the swing. He was a good listener; I'd give him that. We sat with nothing but the stars between us for a while, which was fine by me. All I wanted was to sit next to Kael, to know he was there. In that moment, it was enough.

The peace didn't last long, though.

"Oh, man, you wiped out!"

"No, hey, Austin—watch!"

"Dude! You are crazy. I mean, what the fuck!"

It was just a lame video game, but it had put Kael on high alert. It was hard not to notice how hyperaware he was of his surroundings. I couldn't imagine how tough that must be, to never be able to relax. It must be exhausting. He turned to say something but was interrupted by wild shouts from inside the house.

"You got him, man. Killed him with one shot!"

"Fuck yeah! Dead as a fucking doornail, man!"

I shook my head. Kael clenched his jaw.

At least we agreed on something.

"Am I making you uncomfortable?" Kael asked, picking at his fingers.

How the heck was I supposed to respond to that?

"Do *you* think you're making me uncomfortable?" The best way to avoid answering a question was to repeat it. I had learned that from my dad.

He let out a breath. "That's not an answer. But yeah, probably?" he said, cracking a smile. I loved the way his whole face changed when he smiled.

I couldn't help but laugh. "Well, my answer is no. But one minute you're ignoring me and the—"

"Ignoring you?" he asked, startled.

"Yeah," I explained. "You were kind of blowing me off."

He seemed genuinely surprised. Almost hurt. "I wasn't trying to." He hesitated. "It's kind of hard to adjust to being back here. It's only been a week and it's so . . . different? It's hard to explain. I don't remember it feeling this weird last time I came back."

"I can't even imagine," I told him. Because I couldn't.

"It's the small things. Like using those coffeemakers that brew individual cups or being able to shower every day and wash my clothes in an actual machine."

"I'm guessing there aren't any Tide Pods in the Army," I said. My dad always hated them—even when he returned and could use them, he refused. He liked old-school powder and it grossed me out.

"Sometimes. Wives would send packages to their husbands and we would all get the hookup," he said.

I wondered if anyone sent him packages, but I didn't ask. It was my turn to laugh now, but I didn't. If I wanted to connect with this guy, to find out who he was, I needed to take the first step. Stop deflecting. Build a bridge. Find some common ground and all that.

"You know," I started, "my dad always came back acting like he just got home from *Survivor*. It was kind of a joke in our house. Not that it was funny." I was so bad at this. I was overthinking every single word that came out of my mouth.

"It's fine." He smiled, obviously amused by my ramblings, and looked me straight in the eye. "Honestly, Karina. It's fine. You're fine."

I kept going, more relaxed now—more reassured. "He would crave the weirdest things and eat Taco Bell for a week straight after coming home."

Kael nodded slowly, sucking on his lips. "How many times has he gone?"

"Four."

"Wow." Kael blew out a breath. "I'm over here complaining about two," he said, laughing weakly.

"That's a lot, though. And you're my age. I'm over here complaining about zero."

"Did you ever think about joining?"

I shook my head so quickly.

"The Army? Nope. No way. Austin and I always said we wouldn't."

I sounded like one of those twins you read about in sappy books where they make lifelong promises to each other. One lives in the shadows and the other has to live out their twin's legacy. I didn't want to think about which role I played in that saga.

"Why not? Just not your thing?" Kael asked.

"I don't know," I started. *Careful, Karina,* I warned myself. I didn't want to offend him, but my mouth was known for spitting out words without my brain's approval. "We agreed on it one day. I don't remember what even triggered it. My dad was deep into his third deployment and . . ."

I could picture the smoke as it billowed through the hallways. I smelled the fire before I saw it.

"And my mom made . . . well, let's say she made a mess in the living room. A charred mess."

Kael looked at me, puzzled.

"She said it was from a glue gun, like for crafts? But it was a cigarette. She fell asleep on the couch with a lit cigarette in her hand and had barely woken up when I came rushing down the stairs to find the room filled with smoke. It was crazy."

As I was telling Kael this, a few people came out of the house, a few people went in. Party traffic. The last guy to come out was wearing a plain white T-shirt with a red stain on the chest. I stopped talking when I saw him and kept my imagination from turning a pizza-sauce stain into anything else. Kael kept his eyes on me the whole time. It was intense, the way he looked at me. The bottom of my tummy ached, and eventually I had to break eye contact with him. Pizza-stain guy walked down the steps and got into his car. I recognized him from the kitchen. He was one of Austin's quiet friends. The quiet guys always left first.

"And what did your mom do when you found her in the room full of smoke?" Kael encouraged.

"She was walking toward the door, straight ahead, like she was going out to buy milk or some orange juice. She didn't yell for us. She didn't look for us. No . . . nothing."

Kael cleared his throat. I gauged his expression to make sure he wasn't uncomfortable with the details.

"So . . . you know those quizzes where they ask you what you would save if your house was on fire?" I looked at him.

"Not really," he answered.

"I guess that's a Facebook thing. They ask what possessions you would save if your house was burning down and your response is supposed to reveal your personality. If you say you'd save your wedding album, that says one thing about you. But if your choice is to save your vinyl collection, that says something else."

Kael raised his eyebrows, as if he hadn't ever heard of anything so absurd.

"I know, right?" I continued with my story. "Anyway, it's so insane, but the smoke was growing and as I rushed up the stairs to get Austin, I remember thinking, *That quiz is the most ridiculous thing ever. Who would even think about possessions at a time like this?* But there I was, in the moment, thinking about that stupid quiz—so what does that say about me?"

"I think it says that your mind was keeping you from panicking. I think it says that you have good instincts."

I let that sink in for a moment before continuing. "When I got to Austin's room, I shook him awake. We ran downstairs together—he was leading now, squeezing my wrist so hard, and when we got outside to the lawn, our mother was standing there just watching the smoke. She hadn't tried to set the house on fire, nothing like that. But oddly, she wasn't alarmed. More like she didn't even realize what was going on."

"Karina . . ."

"It was like one of those old movies, you know, where the madwoman starts the fire and gets mesmerized by it, like she goes into a trance—" I laughed a little, not wanting to be awkward. "Sorry, all of my stories are over the top."

"Karina . . ." God, I loved the way he said my name.

"Oh, it's—" I was going to say, *It's okay.* That's what I always said when I told this story. Not that I told it often. But the thing was, sitting in the dark with Kael beside me, urging me on, listening, not judging . . . Well, I knew that it wasn't okay. It wasn't okay at all. I could have been killed. Austin could have been killed. It was so not okay. But what was not okay was usually my reality.

"You're a good storyteller."

That was a kind thing to say. Not, *God, your mom sounds like a wackjob.* I was a good storyteller. I liked the sound of that. I liked the certainty with which he said it.

"Yeah, well, I don't know what even got me started talking about this . . ." I did that a lot, told long tales with lots of side-tracking and other mini-stories in between.

"You not wanting to join the military," Kael reminded me.

"Right." I pulled myself together. "I mean, my dad was gone so much of the time and coming home from deployment but still being constantly absent while training. He was always so unhappy. My mom, too. The lifestyle basically broke her. You know . . ."

He nodded.

"So my brother and I promised after that fire that we wouldn't live our lives that way."

"Makes sense," Kael said, looking around the yard, then back to me. "Wanna hear my side?"

I shook my head, teasing. He smiled.

"I get that. For real, I do. But to me, a Black kid from Riverdale, joining the Army changed the trajectory of my life. It was the thing that changed my whole family. My great-grandpa's dad was a slave, my grandpa couldn't find a regular fair-paying job, and my mother struggled her whole life, always encouraging me to find a way to leave, and here I am, you know? Until now, the only job I'd ever had was bagging groceries at Kroger, and now I drive a decent car, can help my mom—" He stopped abruptly.

"Don't stop—" I urged him.

That earned me a small smile. "All the shit like that. It's hard, yeah. Really fucking hard sometimes, but the Army was the only way I was able to afford living on my own, getting a college education, having health insurance."

I sat, digesting. He had extremely valid points, given that his opinion of the Army was the opposite of mine.

"I get it," I told him.

"There are two sides to everything, you know?"

I nodded, whispering, "Yeah. Two sides at least." I tilted my head and asked, "Is your mom proud of you now?"

"Oh, of course. She tells everyone at church and anyone who'll listen that her son is a decorated soldier. From my town, it's kind of a big deal." It was beyond adorable to see him turn shy and even a little embarrassed.

"Local celebrity," I teased, leaning into his shoulder.

"Right," he said, smiling. "Not like Austin," he joked, as we heard my brother yelling again.

"What's your mom like? I bet she's—"

"We should probably go inside. You're the chaperone, and if it stays this loud, the MPs will definitely come."

I was well aware that he was avoiding my question, but I had already gotten more out of him than usual, so I decided not to be greedy. It was almost his birthday, after all.

# CHAPTER **THIRTY-FOUR**

The party had quieted down after a few warnings to my brother about the Military Police coming. The coffee table was littered with beer bottles and plastic cups; the game controller sat idle in front of the TV. Limp bodies covered the couch and a few people had made themselves comfortable on the floor. It was mostly guys (and mostly soldiers), except for the girl who earlier had been entwined with Austin. She was sitting alone on the floor now, moving slightly to the music, her shoulders doing this chill dance. Basically, she was doing that thing you do when you're all alone at a party and you want to say *It's fine, I'm fine, everything's fine.*

"Do you need another drink?" I asked Kael.

He held up his beer, shaking the empty bottle. "Yeah, please."

We made our way out of the living room, stepping carefully over denim-clad limbs. The kitchen was empty of people. Estelle's attempts at what she called French Country décor—a dish towel that said *Café*, a ceramic rooster, a little metal *Boulangerie* sign that Elodie says Estelle pronounces wrong—were visible among the litter of empty bottles and pizza boxes. Still, seeing Kael here against the backdrop of so many familiar things, feeling him next to me, watching me, in the small space of this kitchen, made me anxious . . . He seemed outsized now, larger than life, and when I scooted past him, I almost elbowed him in the rib cage. He inched farther away from me, toward the fridge. Of course, I needed to get ice from the tray in the freezer.

"Sorry," he said, nearly tripping over my feet to get out of my way.

"It's fine," I told him, my words blending together.

He made me feel . . . *nervous*. Maybe that wasn't the right word. I didn't feel tense or panicky, the things that usually come with nerves. He made me feel as if everything was so much closer to the surface, raw and more alive. When I was around him, my brain processed everything so fast, but everything felt still and calm in the cracks of him opening up to me. I felt bright and quick and stable and level all at once.

My heart raced when I glanced over and caught him looking back at me, his long fingers toying with the necklace around his neck. Maybe it was the effect of the vodka, but as I refilled my glass, I could feel Kael's eyes on me, as if he was taking me in, head to toe. He wasn't appraising me in that skeevy way some guys do when they are so obviously checking someone out. It wasn't like that at all. When Kael looked at me, it was as if he saw me, *the real me*—who I was, not who I was trying to be. He held my gaze for a moment, then lowered his eyes. My chest fluttered. Forget butter-flies—these were blackbirds. Big, glossy blackbirds flapping their wings, making my heart take flight. I took a deep breath to calm myself down. I felt him looking at me and tried to ignore the pang at the bottom of my stomach. I put the bottle back on the counter and mixed in apple juice. Someone had cleared out the cranberry.

"What's that going to taste like?" He was standing right behind me now. Whether he had moved or I had, I couldn't say. I saw his shadow in the metal sink and hoped like hell that he couldn't hear the wild beating in my chest.

I turned slowly to face him. He was so close.

"Either great or not." I shrugged.

He took a half-step back. My body didn't calm.

"And you're willing to take that risk?" he asked, smiling behind his drink. I wanted to tell him that he didn't need to hide it—his smile, that was. That I really liked it when he was funny when he teased me. But I needed a few more shots to be at that level of bold.

"Yeah. I guess so." I put my nose to the glass and took a sniff. It wasn't so bad. I took a sip. It wasn't horrible. But maybe I should microwave it to pretend it was a cider?

"Good?" he asked.

"Yeah," I said. I lifted the cup between us. "Wanna taste?"

"No, thanks." He shook his head, holding up his beer.

"Do you always drink beer?" I asked him.

"Yeah, mostly. Not in a while, though," he said, smiling but trying not to. "Because of being gone. Of being over there," he clarified.

"Ohhh, because you were gone. Right. Gone. Over there." I was an idiot, echoing everything he said. But it took me a second to catch on, regardless of how many times we had repeated the word *gone.*"Wow. Yeah, adjusting to being back must be so weird."

Every time he reminded me that his life was drastically different from mine, I felt shaken. I noticed his glassy eyes again . . . his beautiful brown eyes. Maybe he was as buzzed as I was. I leaned toward Kael to ask if he was drunk, to ask him if he was okay. That's when Austin barreled into the kitchen with Mendoza right behind him. Way to kill the moment.

"Hey, guys! It's awfully quiet in here," Austin howled, clapping his hands together as if he were trying to frighten a small animal.

Kael and I stepped back from each other, as if by instinct.

Mendoza rested an almost empty tequila bottle on the counter by the kitchen door.

"My man. You leaving?" Austin asked, as Mendoza nodded and clasped his shoulder. "Thanks for coming." Austin continued, "I know it's hard to get out."

"Yeah." Mendoza turned to Kael. I felt like something significant was going on in front of me, but I wasn't really able to decipher it.

"Next time bring Gloria," Austin said, reaching for the tequila bottle. "One more before you go?"

Mendoza looked at the thick, white watch strapped to his wrist and shook his head. "No way, man. I have to go home. Kids get to be a handful, and Gloria's tired. The baby is keeping her up all night."

"I didn't mean you." Austin touched Mendoza's car keys on his belt loop. "But for me?"

Mendoza took the bottle and emptied the remaining tequila into Austin's glass. It wasn't my responsibility to worry about my brother. This was his party and I was already over being the house mother. Not tonight.

"It was nice to meet you, again," I told Mendoza when he said bye to me.

"Take care of my boy," he whispered. Then he hugged Kael and went out the back door, leaving me to wonder what on earth he meant.

# CHAPTER THIRTY-FIVE

"Man, I love that guy. He's a Grade A fucking guy."

Austin was over-the-top cheerful, even for him. It made me a little afraid of what was coming next. It wasn't that I was worried about him getting into trouble. Not really. It was hard to see him standing there swaying like that.

"My sister! My beautiful sis." Austin wrapped his arm around me. His movements were fluid and his pale cheeks were red. He was clearly smashed.

"Isn't she beautiful?" he asked Kael. I froze. I hated when Austin talked about my looks.

Kael nodded yes, clearly uncomfortable.

"You've really grown up. Buying your own house and shit," he said, squeezing me. "I mean, there you are, holding down a steady job and shit. Paying bills—"

"And shit?" I finished for him.

"Essactly," he said.

Something on the bridge of his nose caught my eye. I moved toward him. "Did you actually break your nose?" I asked, lifting my hand to his face. He jerked away, laughing me off.

"It didn't break. It just, um . . . it moved over a little." Then he turned to Kael with a goofy smile plastered on his face. "Be careful with her, bro. I'm not going to be that guy who's like threatening dudes over his sister or anything like that. Nothing like that. I'm just saying, my sister, well . . . she flips on you and, man . . ." He used his fingers like a knife under his throat.

Kael cast his eyes downward, giving no indication of what he thought about what he'd just heard.

"I'm kidding. She's a peach." He hugged me again. "A real peachy peach of a sister. Aren't you?"

Oh, yeah, totally smashed.

The kitchen was getting busy now, with people coming in to refill their drinks, as if a shift change had been announced or something. It wasn't until Kael looked at me that I felt like a kid. I probably seemed so immature, borderline wrestling with my brother, who was completely out of it.

"Right. Thanks for the news bulletin," I said, maneuvering out of his arm. "Your new little friend is waiting for you. She looks lonely. I saw her a few minutes ago sitting by herself on the floor." I nodded toward the living room.

"Katie? She's cute, huh? She's going to school to be a nurse," he told us with pride.

Kael made a face like he was impressed, but I wasn't as drunk as Austin was, and I could tell that Kael was humoring him. He mostly hid his mouth behind the dark beer bottle.

"You mean the little girl wants to be a nurse when she gets to be all grown up? After she's out of high school and into the big world?" It was how I was with Austin—teasing him about stuff. It was part of our twin dynamic. We didn't have that mythical twin thing where we could read each other's minds or feel each other's pain. Nothing weird like that. Okay, I understood him on a level that I didn't feel with most people. And I felt a closeness to him that I couldn't explain. But a lot of siblings felt that, especially when they'd gone through their parents' divorce and all the mess that came with it.

So, really, my comment was not intentionally mean-spirited, it was just part of the teasing that went on with Austin and me. Only it sometimes caught other people in the middle of our fun . . . like the comment he made to Kael. (The comment that I swore to myself I wouldn't obsess over until later, when I was alone.)

"She's nineteen, okay? And she's going to actual *nursing school.*" Austin lifted his plastic cup to his mouth, pouring out the last drops of the Añejo he had been downing the whole night.

"I'm sure she is." I rolled my eyes at Austin. "And the next Barbie will be—"

It took me a moment to register that everyone was looking over my shoulder to something behind me. *MPs,* I thought for a split second. *Damn. We're busted.* I turned around to face the officers, to give them some sort of excuse or attempt some type of negotiation. Only when I turned around, I saw that it wasn't the MPs at all. It was the girl in the ruffly shirt, and she had heard every word I'd said.

*I was the one who was busted.*

The girl's face fell. My face fell. We stood there in silence. Caught. Two deer in the headlights.

I had insulted her, insinuating that not only was she in high school, but that tomorrow night, my brother would be making out with someone else. Which not only made my brother seem like a total douchebag, it was rude as all hell to her.

Her eyes welled up with tears.

"Sorry . . ." I said. "I'm so sorry. It wasn't anything against you, I just meant—" She looked so young when she pouted like that, her bottom lip quivering. *Damn.* I didn't want to give her a half-assed apology or make something up to make her feel better. But I couldn't tell her that she really *did* look like she was in high school and I sure as hell couldn't tell her that, in all likelihood, my brother *would* be making out with someone else—if not tomorrow, then the day after.

I stood in the doorway for a second, not facing the group, contemplating apologizing to her again—and thinking of how to smooth things over with Austin, too, even though he wasn't likely to be that annoyed with me. He knew my sense of humor better than anyone. And he gave as good as he got.

But Austin spoke first.

"Nice, Kare. Real nice." He moved toward the girl and put a comforting arm around her. "This here is my sister, Karina," he said, squeezing her shoulder. "Karina, this is—"

She cut him off. "You can call me Barbie," she said through her breaking voice.

The room erupted with laughter. Big, bold, sidesplitting laughter. Score one for Barbie. And who could blame her? Certainly not me. I let myself exhale.

Everything would have been okay if we'd stopped there. Awkward moment confronted and dealt with. Move on, folks, nothing to see here. Only Austin had to open his big mouth.

"Don't worry about her," he said, throwing his chin in my direction. "She's pissed. She's always pissed."

The word sounded slippery. Mean. I opened my mouth to say something, but apparently he wasn't finished yet.

"She likes to play the big sister. The only grown-up in the room. Just ignore her."

I felt slapped. Hard. I knew I had hurt the girl's feelings and I really did regret that. But I hadn't done it on purpose. He knew my sense of humor better than anyone, and he gave as good as he got. It was a lame joke between a brother and sister, and it was rotten luck and bad timing that it went awry. But what Austin said about me hurt. It really hurt.

I wanted to say something in my defense—anything—but I didn't want to make a scene. If I got upset in front of everyone, it would prove Austin's point and make everyone think I was crazy or that I was *always pissed*. I left the room with a growing ache in my chest. Now it was my turn to cry.

# CHAPTER **THIRTY-SIX**

*Shit, Austin. Since when did you think of me as always pissed? Worrying about you wasn't being pissed. Someone had to do it, and obviously you aren't too concerned with your future, since you just got sprung from jail and the first thing you did was throw a party with plenty of booze and underage drinkers. On post. At Dad's house.*

Those were the thoughts swirling around in my head as I walked up the stairs to my old room. The air inside the house was thick and getting thicker. I had to get away. I needed a break from Austin. From the vodka. From the party. I wasn't sure if I needed a break from Kael, and for a moment, I had almost forgotten he was even there.

*For a moment.*

*Almost.*

There was no way he'd missed the exchange. He probably thought I was being catty, that I was a bitch. It wasn't true. It really wasn't. I tried not to give other girls a hard time. We had it tough enough. Hormones. Periods. Underwire bras. Double standards. Douchey guys. We needed to stick together, not stick it to one another. I really believed that. But . . . there was always a *but*, wasn't there? I couldn't help my instinctual assessment of other women. Giving them the once-over, trying to determine who they were, with what kind of agenda, and where they ranked in our invisible hierarchy. It seemed so petty to put it like that, and it wasn't that I was comparing them to *me*—more like I was comparing myself to *them*.

Ruffly shirt girl was prettier than me. She had beautiful clear skin, slender hips, and long legs. Her hair was amazing. She dressed to flatter herself, to bring out her best features. I dressed in what was clean(ish) or what was on sale. I wasn't competing with Katie, Barbie, or whatever her name was. (Okay, that was bitchy.) I really wasn't. First of all, she was in a totally different league than I was, and second, her target was my brother. That was clear from the get-go. So this comparison thing, this competition . . . it wasn't about guys.

If it was, why would I compare myself to the girls on IG or on TV, like I did when Madelaine Petsch looked out at me from the screen? She was flawless. Even with my ultra-high-def TV, she had the smooth skin of a porcelain doll. Not a blemish, not a spot or bump. It almost made me want to go vegan, if that's what it did for you.

I thought about this sort of thing a lot. I tried to figure out where it came from. Where all my insecurities came from. I really didn't care that guys looked at other girls more than they looked at me. It was just that some girls made me feel *less than*. I couldn't explain it, not really, but it was hard to get out of my head. And the thing was, I knew it wasn't just me. I thought about Elodie, beautiful blond Parisian Elodie, with her pretty cheeks and doe eyes. She'd sit with a mirror in her lap, picking at her face, saying how horrible her skin was, that her eyes were uneven, and her nose was off-center. Did all women do that?

This was when I missed my mom the most. It would have been nice to be able to talk to her about this sort of thing, to have someone to confide in, to have her listen without judgment. *Has it always been like this?,* I'd ask her. And she'd tell me, *No, it was never this bad, social media and selfies and the Kardashians have made everything so much worse.* Or she'd say, *Yes, it really has always been like this. I used to compare myself to* Charlie's Angels *back in the day.* Then she'd get out her old photo album and we'd laugh at her eighties hair.

Who was I kidding? That would never have happened.

# CHAPTER **THIRTY-SEVEN**

My bedroom door was closed. Was someone inside? It wouldn't have been unheard of to find a soldier passed out on my bed, or a couple hooking up. Not Austin and Katie, though. They were still in the kitchen, probably talking about me. Katie would be over her hurt by now, and, smart girl that she was, she would have turned the situation around to her advantage, used it to get closer to my brother. United against a common enemy and all that. And Austin would have known that he was onto a sure thing, so he'd likely be going on about how annoying I was, how I'd always been so uncool. He had two sides to him, one that fiercely defended me, no matter what. And one that used me as a prop, a pedestal that elevated him to cool-guy status. I didn't need three guesses to know which one was down in the kitchen.

No matter how hard I tried, I couldn't rid myself of the habit of imagining what other people were thinking or saying about me. I did it all the time, even though I knew no good would come of it. It was like picking a cuticle, scratching and nipping at it until it started bleeding. I was doing that now, picturing everyone in the kitchen, wondering what they were saying or thinking. Even the ones who didn't know my name, they'd think of me as that prissy chick who badmouthed sweet Katie. Someone would ask who I was, and they'd say, *Oh, that's Austin's sister,* and then they'd remember me as the girl who went around picking up empty bottles and pizza boxes as if she was working the night shift at Fridays.

Ugh.

I hated the way my brain worked. I tried to tell myself that I didn't do anything too horrible, that people would understand I was mostly joking. I never would have talked like that had I known she was there, even if what I said was true.

I was grasping now.

Wasn't it funny how people always demanded the truth, yet mostly couldn't handle it when it came along? In all fairness, I was the same way. Demanding the truth, yet holding on to the lies. They came in handy when you wanted to guard yourself against the truth—lies, that is.

I paused in front of my room; I didn't really think anyone would be inside. This get-together was way calmer than most of the parties Austin had thrown in the past, before he went to stay with our uncle. And I had to admit that Austin seemed a little different now, more stable. Or maybe I wanted him to have calmed down; thinking this way protected me from seeing the truth.

I knocked, then waited before opening the door into what turned out to be an empty room. I stood for a moment before entering, taking everything in. Even the smell. God, the air intoxicated me with a feeling of nostalgia, like the scent of my former life. I had been trying so hard to start a new chapter, turn a new page . . . whatever it was people did when they tried to move on. I stood there looking at my old bedroom while thinking of my new bedroom. Such a stark difference.

This room was the same as it ever was. The same purple bedspread with little white flowers all over it. The same matching curtains with a burn mark on the corner from my one day as a smoker. I got grounded for that. My parents didn't notice the burnt curtain, lucky for me, but they had caught the cigarette smoke as it wafted down the hallway. After that I was forbidden to hang out with Neena Hobbs, the only girl in my grade who was allowed to shave her legs—and who had made me want to smoke like she did.

My dresser was cluttered with the usual teenage girl stuff. Old tubes of glittery lip gloss that had been expired for years. Bundles of headbands and hair elastics. Notes from my best friend, Sammy. Well, Sammy was my best friend until she married a soldier and getting a hold of her became impossible. Gel pens in every conceivable color. Everything had a memory attached. Some more than one. I couldn't bring myself to toss a thing. Not the hair accessories I had worn for years through multiple hair colors and multiple bad haircuts. Not even the sticky lip gloss that my mom snuck me when my dad said I couldn't wear makeup until high school. I picked them up now and rolled them around in my hand. They had names like Berry Beautiful, Pucker Pink, and Sweeter Than Sweet. Funny, though, once you got them on your lips, they all had pretty much the same rosy color, the same sugary and sticky shine that always caught in my hair.

I hadn't been in my new place that long, but this room already seemed like a time capsule. Come to think of it, this was the first time I'd stepped into the room since I'd moved out. I wiped my finger in the dust on my dresser. Estelle made sure every room in the house was clean, except this one. *What about Austin's room?*, I wondered. Did she do her Martha Stewart thing in there? Probably. She had different rules for the men in her life.

I realized that I hadn't changed any of the furniture since seventh grade or so. I remembered sitting in that purple beanbag chair when Josh, the cornbread-gifter and the first boy who kissed me with tongue, broke up with me. I was fool enough to believe him when he made the excuse that his mom had told him he needed to work on his grades, keep his head clear, and stay away from girls if he wanted to pursue his supposed football career. But he started dating one of the popular girls the very next day. Word around school was that he had dumped me for her. Seventh grade really did a great job of inflating my insecurities. And, spoiler alert: Josh was now in and out of jail, not on a football field.

That beanbag chair was the indoor equivalent of the porch swing, full of drama and dreamy memories. There were a lot of teenage tears in that fabric—no wonder I have a visceral reaction today to the color purple.

The nightstand was stacked high with my old books. My econ textbook from senior year peeked out beneath a hardcover copy of *You* by Caroline Kepnes that was collecting dust. I had bought a second copy of *You* when I realized I'd left the original at my dad's and didn't want to go back there to retrieve it. Dad and Estelle hadn't been married very long then, and I hated being around the newlyweds; I left every chance I got. That made two copies—three if you counted the audio. I bought that to hear the characters come to life in a voice other than my own. It was one of my favorite books and I was happy to keep a copy at both houses. It became one of the few stories that my dad and I both loved. I reached for it and cracked open the spine. I could use the distraction: *YOU walk into the bookstore and you keep your hand on the door to make sure it doesn't slam. You smile, embarrassed to be a nice girl...*

When I heard the knock on the door, I nearly jumped out of my skin.

"Shit!"

"Karina?"

"WHAT?!" I sounded angry, like you do when you're scared.

"Karina, are you okay?" It was Kael. "Can I come in?"

"Come in," I said, and nodded, though he likely couldn't see me through the crack in the door. He entered slowly and, once inside, gently closed the door. The little click sounded so loud. So definite.

"You okay?" he asked, as he walked toward me, stopping a few feet away from the bed.

I sighed. "Yeah," I said, shrugging, closing my book.

"So do you always read at parties?"

When he said that, it reminded me of a novel I was reading last year—an angsty good girl–bad boy trope. I had a love-hate relationship with those books, but was currently waiting for the next one in the series. So I was in love at the moment.

"I just . . . I don't know. I got overwhelmed? That girl"—I raised my hand in the air, holding the book—"she heard me say that stuff, and now Austin's being a dick and she probably feels like shit."

Kael nodded. "You didn't know she was going to walk up."

"Still."

"Try not to worry about it. I know you're going to beat yourself up over it, that's just who you are—"

"You know *what*?!"

Now he was the one who looked caught. It was clear that he hadn't meant to say what he had. Or maybe he'd meant to word it differently. His mouth hung open a little.

"What do you mean *that's just who I am*?" I accused. He'd better not have meant what I thought he did.

He took a breath. "I meant that I know you worry about a lot, and you put a lot of pressure on yourself. A lot of blame."

I wanted to stand up, to tell him to get the hell out of my room, but I sat there, holding tight to my book, keeping my legs crossed underneath me.

"And you know that how?" I asked, not really wanting to know what he was going to say. I had already become this girl to him, the one he needed to check in on, maybe take care of. I despised the idea of that.

No way was that going to be me.

No way was that me.

"Come on," he pressed me. He no longer looked unsure about what he had said or would say; he looked annoyed.

"You're acting like you know me. You've been around for, what—a week? And half of that time you were MIA."

"So you missed me when I didn't come back?" he asked.

Why was he talking so much all of a sudden? And how could I get him to stop?

"That doesn't matter. My point is that you don't know me, so don't say that I'm doing something or being a victim or whatever." My voice sounded screechy and dramatic.

"That's not what I'm doing." He sighed, rubbing his cheeks with both palms. "And I sure as hell didn't say anything about you being a victim."

"You said, 'You put a lot of pressure on yourself.'"

"Never mind," he said, defeated. "Forget I said anything."

I felt so angry, so embarrassed and upset. I didn't know I was directing all my feelings toward Kael. He came up to my room, I assumed, to check on me. That was a nice thing to do.

"I'm sorry," I said. "I'm frustrated and I'm taking it out on you. I guess this fits, since I'm"—I hooked my fingers into air quotes—"'always pissed.'"

"I don't think you should be too hard on yourself. People do shitty things. It's what we're made for," he told me.

He was trying to change the subject, and I was grateful because I felt like crap. Any sort of buzz that I was feeling was basically gone at that point, but Kael still looked different than he had before tonight, even without my vodka glasses.

"Humans are made to do shitty things? That's depressing," I told him. But I kind of liked the way it sounded, cynical as it was.

He sat down next to me on my bed and the metal frame creaked. He was too big for my bed. He looked like a grown man in a dollhouse. I felt like he was going to lecture me about something, maybe ask if I did my homework. His knowing eyes were focused on me, and in a rare occurrence, he didn't look away or stare at the floor.

"That's life," he said.

"Life is depressing?"

"Every life I've come across," he replied, his eyes still on me.

I couldn't disagree with him, though it made everything feel so heavy.

"Yeah. I guess you're right."

"You told me about the way you and your mom made sense of things, believing that when stars burn out, the good in the world dies along with them." He chuckled softly. "That's the most depressing thing I've heard, and I've seen and heard *a lot*." He drew out the end of the word.

I laughed at that and continued to look unabashedly into his eyes. He was a good head taller than me sitting down, and his black jeans and dark skin looked so nice against each other.

Kael's hands moved to his leg and my tummy flipped, thinking that they'd move to me next, that he was going to touch me. But instead, he rubbed at the top of his leg.

"What's wrong with your leg?" I asked him.

For all the voices downstairs, I couldn't hear anything except the slowing of Kael's breathing and the sound of the air conditioner vent blowing from the ceiling.

"It's . . ." he started to say. I watched the words hesitate on their way out. "It hurts sometimes. It's not a big deal."

"Can I ask what happened?"

He closed his eyes and didn't say anything as the seconds passed.

I remembered his first massage and how he kept his pants on the entire time, the way I thought I saw him limping, but couldn't be sure. "You don't have to tell me. I could . . . maybe . . . I could help, you know?" I offered.

I was sorry for asking in the first place, but he leaned down and grabbed the bottom of his jeans and started to roll up the fabric.

It was such an intense moment, the air so still between us.

And then the silence was broken by the ringing of a cell phone. Kael's cell phone. I jumped from the suddenness of it. Kael let go of his pants and stood up, pulling the phone from his pocket. His face changed as he stared at the screen and silenced the ringer. My heart was racing, beating inside of me.

"Everything okay?" I said.

His handsome face was distorted into a scowl as he looked at the number. He ignored the call. I thought a text popped up, but I couldn't be sure. "Yeah," he said.

I didn't believe him.

He shoved the phone into his pocket and looked at me. My eyes went immediately to his right leg and he stepped back. Then he scanned the room like he was looking for something he couldn't see.

"I . . . I, um. I have to go," he stammered.

He moved so quickly, like a soldier, and he opened my door before I could stop him. His name was stuck in my throat as he turned around to look at me, as if to say something. Our eyes locked for half a second before he seemed to change his mind and turned away from me. I didn't know what to think about what had just happened. We had been so close. I had opened up to him and he was opening up to me . . . and then he was gone.

I was so overwhelmed with everything that I didn't even understand why I burst into tears the moment he disappeared from view.

"Happy birthday," I managed to say, after he was long gone.

# CHAPTER **THIRTY-EIGHT**

I woke up with a headache like I'd never had before. My mouth was like the inside of a hamster's cage and my hands felt too big for my body. Even my hair hurt. I rolled over and buried my face in my pillow so that I wouldn't have to open my eyes. I rummaged through the bedding to find my phone and I felt the cool glass screen against my fingertips. When had I climbed into bed and under the familiar purple bedspread? Slowly, I turned over. Even more slowly, I opened my eyes.

Two missed calls and a **Where r u?** text from Austin. *Great.*

The person I was thinking of was Kael.

It was bad enough that he was the last person I thought of before I fell asleep. Did he have to be the first person I thought of when I woke up? I could picture him sitting there on the bed next to me. I could almost feel the impression his body made on this small bed. And I could see his face as he walked out the door, leaving me behind.

I had to do something about this situation.

I had to keep away from this guy.

Where did he get off thinking that I would be there for him whenever he felt like showing up? Who did he think he was with this on-again, off-again bullshit? This guy was playing me with his "So you missed me when I didn't come back?" attitude.

Last night he had opened up, let down his guard, and let me inside. He talked. He listened. He laughed. And the way he started to roll up his jeans . . . we were getting so close, and then he turned back into the stranger Elodie's husband happened to know.

I never wanted to see him again.

I needed to see him.

I didn't want to know where he went last night.

I needed to know.

I should never have let him stay over that night Elodie brought him home. I should never have brought him to my dad's for dinner. And I sure as hell should never have brought him to last night's party.

I didn't like my anger and regret. How dare he make me feel this way.

Lesson learned. *Remind yourself about that, Karina, as you go about your day.*

*Shit! My day!*

I had to work. I did a quick phone check for the time. It was eight thirty and I had to be at work at ten. It didn't matter that I felt like hell. No way could I get my shift covered on such short notice. Anyway, I needed the hours to pay that last cable bill, so I was going to have to suck it up. I was used to that. At least I didn't have anyone scheduled until after lunch. I'd be the one taking walk-ins. That wouldn't be so bad, though, because most clients didn't talk much at all during their first treatment. That was something, at least. I usually dreaded walk-ins, but today I preferred that to seeing anyone I knew.

Rolling out of bed was the hard part. The first hard part, that is—more belly flop than roll. I shimmied into my pants, then my T-shirt, and I pulled one of my vintage hair scrunchies off my dresser and stuck my hair in a ponytail, replaying the events of last night.

I didn't want to admit it, but I was starting to feel that addictive pull. Addicted. There was no other word for it. His beautiful face. His strong body. His confident voice. I loved the way he didn't bother with small talk, as if he knew instinctively what was important. I could tell that the other guys looked up to him. But what else was going on? What was it that made him shift from being another random guy at a party with a beer to a soldier, hypervigilant and on guard? What had Mendoza been trying to tell me about *his boy*?

Mendoza's voice in my head was drowned out by the sound of my brother's snores as I passed his room. I was glad he was asleep. I didn't want to talk to him. Or anyone else, for that matter. Just a quick pee and I'd—

"Oh, crap! Oh . . . I'm so sorry. I had no idea anyone was in here." I backed out into the hallway, trying to avert my eyes. Not knowing if I should leave or if I should wait until she came out, I was trying to figure out what the etiquette was in a situation like this.

The bathroom door opened and Katie appeared. "You sure know how to make an entrance, don't you?" She had a toothbrush in her hand and her hair was brushed neatly to rest just above her shoulders.

"Hey, um, hi." As if this wasn't awkward as hell. "Hey, I'm sorry."

"This is getting to be a habit with us. Me surprising you. You apologizing to me." She laughed.

I guess it was kind of funny.

"Look, it's okay," she said. "Really. No harm done. I was caught off guard last night. By what you said, I mean."

"Yeah, about that . . ."

"No, it's okay. Really. Well, the stuff about me still being in high school wasn't cool at all, but that other stuff, about your brother, you didn't tell me anything I didn't already know."

"Wait. You mean—"

"I'm not an idiot, Karina. I've heard a lot about your brother. But like you, I don't listen to everything I hear." The look on her face was a knowing one. Her blue eyes homed in on me. She certainly didn't seem like a high school girl now.

"And that means?" I was hazy from the hangover and the embarrassment of walking in on her like that, but what the fuck? Her candor shocked me. Had I underestimated her? "Are you referring to my brother, or Kael?"

"Maybe another time, okay? It was a late night." She paused to make an exaggerated stretch, causing the oversized T-shirt she was wearing to ride up high enough to show me that Nurse Katie was overdue for a bikini wax. "I'm tired and I really want to get back to bed. Besides," she added, "it's chilly in here."

And with that, she turned on her heels and went back to join my brother.

# CHAPTER **THIRTY-NINE**

Elodie wasn't there when I got home. I couldn't remember if she had to work or not—I barely remembered that *I* had to work—and I didn't pay attention to whether or not her car was in the driveway.

I took a quick shower, but I still felt like death when I got out. Brien used to keep a hangover kit in his apartment. Extra Strength Tylenol for a headache. Benadryl for puffiness. Pedialyte to replace essential minerals. And Alka-Seltzer to soothe the stomach. He was like a depraved Boy Scout, always prepared. What I wouldn't give for a couple of Tylenol now. Forget the ex-boyfriend, take the meds. That sounded like a good plan. I searched the entire house but came up empty-handed. I even fumbled through the drawer with the packets of soy sauce and chopsticks, just in case I'd find one of those little individual packets of Tylenol or Advil in there. I wouldn't even have cared if it was expired. Even though the drawer was full, there were no pills of any kind, but I did find an old fortune cookie, which I cracked open.

*You don't need strength to let go.*
*All you need is understanding.*

Actually, fortune cookie company, I really needed some aspirin.

I made a cup of coffee and sat at my kitchen table, staring into space. My mom, my dad, Austin, Kael—every stressor in my life seemed to be weighing on me, hard. Tapping me on the shoulder, pulling the muscles in my back. I wanted to bang my head against the wall, to cry or scream and shout, but I had to leave for work. As everyone kept reminding me, I was the responsible one. *Just do the next thing*, I told myself. *Put one foot in front of the other and do what needs doing. That's how you'll get through the day.*

With that little pep talk in mind, I made my way out of the house and through the alley to the salon. The doors were unlocked when I got there, the OPEN sign bright in the window. Mali was behind the desk, checking in a middle-aged man and woman for a couple's massage. I was glad I came in as they were being escorted to the room so that I didn't have to take them. The woman looked really excited about it. He looked annoyed, as if his wife had dragged him there to work on their relationship or something. You could always tell. That's why couple's massages were my least favorite thing. I'd rather rub a client's thick, callused heels, and I really hated doing that.

"Good morning, sweetie," Mali said when she returned. "Or maybe not?" she asked, her eyes searching my face. She could always see right through me.

"Hangover," I offered. I thought it was best to admit at least half of my problem.

She took in my wet hair, puffy face, and bleary eyes. "Hmm," was all she managed.

It would be a long day if Mali, of all people, started getting on my nerves.

"Is Elodie here?" I asked. I couldn't see the calendar from where we were standing.

"Yes, and on time," Mali told me, nodding in approval, and maybe making a little dig at me.

"Elodie's not late that often."

"Your client is here," Mali said abruptly, looking toward the door.

"I don't have any clients scheduled—"

"Not true," she said. "Here. Look at the schedule." She pointed to the name scribbled on the little blue line that said "10:00"

"Did someone move their appointment? I can't read this," I said to Mali.

The bell dinged behind me, and Mali turned to address the customer in her sweetest voice.

"Mikael? For an hour deep-tissue at ten? That you?"

I nearly choked on the air when I turned around and saw Kael.

Sure enough, there he was, wearing a gray T-shirt and joggers. They were black, tight on his legs, with a big Nike swoosh on the thigh. He looked exhausted, or hungover. Like I was.

"Kael," I said, as if I had to tell myself that he was actually standing there.

"Hey," he replied.

*Hey?*

Was he here to talk to me? Or to get a massage? Both?

It was all too much.

He waited patiently while I collected myself and checked his name off the schedule. I stared at Mali until she walked away reluctantly and with a smirk imprinted on her face. I looked at Kael and felt the tape of the last twenty-four hours unwind.

I didn't like him, I told myself. That addiction stuff was nonsense. It was just that it had been a while since I'd been in close contact with the male species, so of course he was getting inside my head. I was lonely, that was all. Everybody got lonely. It was only natural.

205

"Right this way." My voice was cool, professional. He wasn't the only one who could be aloof. I pulled the curtain back to enter my room, and as I did, Elodie popped up around the corner, a little French jack-in-the-box.

"Hello!" she said, her voice high and cheery. She scared the hell out of me, and I jumped away from Kael.

"I left before you woke up. I had—" She stopped talking when she saw who was with me.

"Kael? Hello!" She double-kissed his cheeks and I moved out of their way. In fact, I leaned my back against the wall. An appropriate metaphor, I thought.

"Elodie. Hi."

They talked for a moment, good-natured casual conversation. But when he put his hands on her elbows—a friendly and completely appropriate gesture—I felt a wave of anger swell. That's when I knew I had completely lost my mind.

"I'm really hungry all the time. I can't seem to gobble down enough food." She laughed as she said this. Kael gave her a faint smile, and I found myself secretly pleased that it wasn't the big smile he'd given me—the one I couldn't get out of my head. Yep. Mind was lost.

"Well, I'll see you around," Elodie said, and made her way back to Mali.

I walked into the room without even looking at Kael. I was usually more polite to clients; I would never turn my back on them. But I did now. Let him follow behind me. Let him feel what it's like to see someone's back disappear through a door.

# CHAPTER **FORTY**

The room was dark, so I lit a few candles. It was one of those small tasks that helped me ease into the day. Almost a ritual. Mali had a couple of those Bic automatic lighters in each room, but I preferred matches. I loved the scratch as you ran the match head over the striking surface, the tiny little explosion that brought the flame to life. So much better than the nervous *click, click, click* of those lighters.

I was aware of Kael, standing just inside the doorway. He might have been evaluating his escape route or maybe even considering a quick getaway. Who knew? I ignored him as I lit the candles. Almond, from Bath & Body Works. Yes, I knew the scent came from chemicals, but like most people, I couldn't splurge on the organic ones.

"I'll come back in a couple of minutes, give you some time to undress," I said, but he pulled his shirt off as I made to leave, so I didn't get a chance. I exhaled a small harrumph to express my displeasure, then turned around to face the wall. I could sense the tight movements of his shoulder muscles as he lifted his shirt over his head.

"I could have gone out."

"I only need to take my shoes and shirt off," he told me.

He was still a client, regardless of whatever this was.

I stared at my dark purple wall and tried to imagine it navy. I was still undecided on what color to paint it, but yesterday Mali had finally approved changing the wall color—for my room only—so that was a win for this crazy week. The clean, masculine aroma of the candle was working its way through the room, and I felt my breathing slow. I stared into the flame until I heard the table creak and the soft pull of the sheet. I counted to ten once he stopped moving.

"Same pressure as before?" I asked. He was lying there on the table faceup, his stomach exposed. The thin blanket and sheet were pulled up only to his hips.

He nodded. *Great. Back to this.* His eyes were open, following me around the room.

"Usually I start with the back, which means that the client lies on his stomach," I told him.

"The client," he said. "Right. That's me." Kael turned over and rested his head in the face cradle. I grabbed a hot towel from the warming cabinet and tried to think about him simply as my first appointment of the day—but who was I kidding, he was more than that. Was he playing some kind of game with me, being present one moment, gone the next? It sure felt like he was. Yet another reason I stay away from dating, and men in general. I couldn't keep up with the games, I wasn't good at them.

I placed a hot towel on his back. The moist heat would help relax his muscles and make the treatment more effective. I took another hot towel and wiped his arms and feet. In silence, I focused on his soft skin, taking in his scent: cedar and campfire, I think. And definitely bar soap. Kael was not the body-wash type.

I started to pump peppermint oil into my open palm but stopped when I remembered he had refused it in prior sessions—that curt *no* being one of the first of his monosyllables. I rubbed my hands together to warm them, although I would have loved to surprise him with icy fingers on his warm skin. A little bit of payback for the merry-go-round he had me on.

I was getting myself worked up again. In fact, I was about two minutes away from telling him to get off the table and get the hell out, or at least explain what his deal was. I was already regretting having opened up to him. All that stuff he knew about my mom, my dad . . . about me. I turned the music up on my phone. Banks. Let her tell Kael that I was tired of his waiting game. I made sure that the music was loud enough for him to hear the words, but not loud enough to disturb any other patrons. See—still professional.

Kael's black sweatpants weren't torn at the hem, or faded to purple like most of mine were. Black cotton can do that, turn the color of eggplant. And it always happened to my clothes after a few washes. Another problem I had with purple. And today, the purple glow of everything in the room was annoying me.

In that moment, I felt fortunate to have seven brains in my head, all thinking different things at the exact same time. Again, the flash of us alone together. Kael dropping his emotional armor. Leaving those invisible bodyguards outside. It was my own little streaming service, and thank goodness I could switch between channels so that the next fifty-five minutes wouldn't be awkward, for either of us.

Comedy? Drama? Home improvement?

*Take your pick, Karina.*

It was good for me to think about other things while I rubbed the balls of his feet, while I ran my palms up his left calf. Tylenol. I'd drop by the drugstore after work and pick some up. What else did I need—shampoo? I tried to push the leg of his pants up a little, but it was tight at the bottom. His phone started to ring in his pocket, but he didn't answer. I couldn't bring myself to be nosy enough to ask who it was. I've never seen anyone ignore so many phone calls.

I was about to tell him that most clients prefer to turn off their phones, that they find the interruptions jarring. But who was I kidding? Kael wasn't like most clients.

I moved up the back of his thigh, around his hips, gliding my hands along his bare back. I tried to think of what movie I'd watch when I flopped down on the couch after work, but it was hard to think of anything other than the muscles along his shoulders, so prominent under his soft, dark skin. Right under his shoulder blade, there was a spot so knotted that it had to be giving him some kind of pain whenever I pressed into it.

"Does this hurt?" I asked him.

"Yes," he replied.

"Like all the time or right now?"

"Aren't those the same thing?"

"No." I pushed the side of my thumbs into his muscle.

"Oh, yeah. That hurts all the time."

"You didn't say anything before." I hadn't remembered feeling it the last time he was here, and there was no way the muscle would pull that tight in a matter of days.

"Why would I?" he asked. I wished I could see his eyes as he spoke.

"Because it hurts?" I pressed harder than normal, and he groaned. The tissue separated under the pressure of my touch. "Because I asked you?"

"Everything hurts," he said. "My whole body. All the time. I'm used to it."

He was so casual when he spoke about what his body had been through. I was close to finding out more, but his phone ringing saved him from letting his guard down with me.

# CHAPTER **FORTY-ONE**

I loved my job. Healing people, offering them relief, both mental and physical, and being able to alleviate pain and soothe others using my hands. My career was my passion. But I didn't love the stereotypes. I had worked hard to become a massage therapist, taking classes in anatomy, bodywork, physiology, even psychology and ethical business methods. I had practiced countless hours, passed my massage and bodywork exam, got my license. All that and still I had to deal with those classless jokes about happy endings.

I remember the first time someone implied that I was a sex worker in scrubs. He got a gleam in his eye when I told him that I worked as a massage therapist. I had been sitting in a coffee shop, minding my own business, enjoying a latte and a book, when this older guy sat next to me and asked me what I was reading. We chatted for a bit—he seemed nice enough. That is, until the conversation came around to what each of us did for a living. He told me that he was a lawyer at this prestigious firm. I could tell that he was trying to impress me by name-dropping some big clients and talking about billable hours.

I told him that I was a newly licensed massage therapist and that I was really happy to be starting my career; I was going on about wellness and the whole mind-body connection and the undeniable growth of the self-care wellness industry, when he raised his eyebrows, leaned in close to me, and said, "Oh, you work at a massage parlor?"

I explained to him that calling it a *parlor* was offensive in today's world, and he let me know how tired he was of being called "offensive."

Most clients were respectful and seemed to understand that very few sex workers hid behind the professional label of massage therapist. I wasn't naïve and knew where the stereotype came from—that work was its own lane on another highway. I had nothing against women who decided for themselves to be sex workers and, out of respect for their choices, I hoped they could work safely, with self-determination. There had been a recent bust of a little massage place on the other side of town, and that shook me up a bit. I had applied for a job there before Mali hired me, and I got the creeps thinking about how close a call that might have been for me. It also made me appreciate my boss even more. The way she ran a tight ship, looking out for our best interests.

I prided myself on professional relationships with all my clients. Was I crossing the line with Kael? I tried hard to focus on the treatment I was providing, without so much as a gratuitous glance at his body, no matter how difficult that was. I had never thought about a client in this way before, and I wasn't going to start. Well, it had already started, but it wasn't going to continue. As he lay on his back with his eyes closed, I tried to distract myself with physiology, by naming all the chest muscles. *Pectoralis major. Pectoralis minor. Serratus anterior.* I remember learning in class that women are biologically wired to prefer men who have strong chests and shoulders, something about testosterone levels. So, really, I wasn't being inappropriate. It was biology.

Kael's voice cut through the dark, surprising me. "This is a great song."

I wanted to tell him that Kings of Leon was one of my favorite bands of all time and that their first album was the closest thing to a masterpiece my ears had ever heard. But after he left last night's conversation—again without an explanation—I was done opening up to him. And certainly not in this setting.

When I finished working on the top of his thigh over his pants, I moved up to the end of the table where his head rested. My fingertips trickled down his scalp, pressing firmly against the soft tissue of his neck. His eyes, which had been closed when I worked on his legs, opened slowly.

I fought my impulse to ask where he went last night or why he came here today. I decided to try to keep my tantrum to myself and not let it spill out.

I skated my fingers down his chest, circling around the span of him. The way his tight muscles felt breaking up under my fingertips, I could almost feel the tension releasing as I touched him. This was the best part of my job, seeing the relief of any type of pain. That's why I did this.

"You're quiet today," Kael said.

My hands stopped moving.

"You haven't said much," I countered.

"I just said I like the music."

I rolled my eyes, pursing my lips together. "Bravo for having good taste in music?"

"Wow. Attitude is strong today," he said in a playful tone.

"Sorry, I'm tired and hungover." I'd thought of the easiest excuse. "You saw how much I had."

He was quiet for a few beats of the song.

Kael's hand shot up from under the blanket, his fingers wrapping around my wrist. I definitely wasn't expecting him to touch me. It made me take a step away, but not so far that he had to let go. His fingers were as warm as a towel out of the heater, pressed against my pulse. I knew it was pounding under his fingerprints. My insecurities told me he was searching for a weak spot.

I had so many things to say. So many things to ask. But my thoughts were blocking my words. I didn't have a clue of what he had locked away in that head of his. I didn't know where to begin processing everything about him, especially what happened last night. I genuinely didn't know if I had created something in my head and was reading the entire situation wrong. The more I swiped through the memories of the night, the more blurry they became.

"Look." He sat up, still gently holding my wrist, his thumb brushing my palm. His touch made me dizzy, and I thought for a moment he might reassure me with some actual answers.

"I'm sorry that I left last night. Something came up and I had to go. I had to be there."

I freed my arm from his grip. "Something you can't talk about? Why can't you tell me what was going on?"

His brow raised. "I don't know. I didn't really think about it." He looked down at his hands. I wasn't sure if that made it worse or better that he didn't think about how that made me feel.

"I'm, um, not the best at this. I don't usually get into confrontation with my friends. And if I did, we would handle it the way soldiers do—physically, until someone apologizes."

"How mature." I rolled my eyes. Combat soldiers were forever mentally sixteen when it comes to fighting. I knew they were trained to be that way, but it didn't make it less obnoxious.

"I've talked to you more than ninety percent of the people I know," he said, leaning back on his elbows, putting more distance between us.

I started pacing around the small room. *Friends?* Even though I knew damn well we were just that, if that.

"I'm not asking you to be my boyfriend or tell me where you are at all times, I don't have the space for complication in my life right now," I rambled. "You come and you go, and I've had enough of that in my life. I know we just met, but—" I stopped myself from continuing. I didn't even know what I was going to say, and that scared me into silence.

When he realized I wasn't going to continue, he spoke.

"Got it. I'll communicate better next time and try not to add stress to your life. Don't worry, I'll only be here for a few more months . . . at most."

I processed his statement. It was a cup of cold water splashed against my face. In that moment, I was so glad he was looking toward the wall and not at me. It made it so much easier to answer him.

"Ah, yeah, only a few months."

I felt myself shrinking again, knowing that I made a big deal out of nothing. We are at most temporary friends. He's leaving and I have enough shit to sort out in my life without worrying about men in any capacity. Like, what the hell am I even doing with my life?

"Let's agree to enjoy each other's company until you leave," I suggested, as a kind of truce.

"A drama-free friendship until the baby is born?" he offered.

It took me a second to remember Elodie and her baby. So at least he would be around until the baby was born. That was good news.

For Elodie, I meant.

Kael sat upright and looked at me. "Or not?" He looked unsure.

I nodded, not knowing what else to say. My brain shut down and closed in on itself, and once again I was the silent one.

# CHAPTER **FORTY-TWO**

There are times when you don't need to say anything. Times when everything is easy and you can share a room or a moment without having to fill the space with words, when everything just falls into place.

Kael must have felt it, too, as he lay there on the table.

"I've been spending a lot of money on massages," Kael said, attempting small talk.

"Self-care," I said. "And I can tell that you really, really need them."

We both laughed then, and relief poured through me. The way his laughter mixed with mine sounded like soft music. It was one of those moments I wished I could bottle up and keep in a vial around my neck, the way Angelina Jolie had saved her lover's blood.

Okay, now, that was a weird thought. Why did my mind ricochet like that? I wished I could stay focused on one thought for longer than three seconds. His treatment was close to the end now. Only fifteen minutes left.

"Are you still mad at me?" Kael asked.

I shook my head and scrunched up my nose, making a disgusted face.

"What are we, twelve? I wasn't mad at you, I was annoyed because you gave me no clue what was going on, so I thought I did something . . . or pried about something you didn't want to talk about." My voice dropped off. I felt self-conscious for bringing up his injury, but that's where we had paused the conversation when he jumped up and left the house.

"Well, I'm sorry for that. I really didn't mean to make you upset or question yourself. You didn't do anything wrong." He looked up at me.

"Thanks. I think." Most people weren't as generous with apologies as he seemed to be. Either he actually meant it or he was a really good liar. I was really bad at accepting sorrys. I just wasn't used to them.

The massage had turned into a conversation, with no objection from the client. I turned the music down a notch. "The Hills" was taunting both of us. Raspy and suspenseful, the song fit perfectly between us, filling our occasional silence.

*I only love it when . . .*

"Last night was fun. I haven't been out since I got back, and it was great to see Mendoza relaxing and enjoying himself."

"If it wasn't because of me, why did you leave?" I finally asked.

"It was a friend thing—" Kael's expression changed.

"Friend?" I asked, and it clicked. "Oh, you have a—"

"Not that kind of friend," he said. He wanted to reassure me, and that was thrilling. A line of electricity charged through me.

"One of my guys is having a rough time right now. He's been really fucked, uh . . . . His wife called and I had to go over there." Kael's expression was stone.

I was confused. He was opening up, but I needed more. "So, again, if you were going to help a friend, why didn't you tell me? I would have understood if you told me—"

217

"I'm not in the business of telling people's business."

"Was it Mendoza?" I moved across the room, stopping directly in front of Kael.

He sighed. He bit down on his lip. "It's not my place, Karina. I'm not talking about what he's going through."

"Your silence serves you well when you want." I meant for my words to burn him, or at least make him sweat. I had a bad habit of this, saying things to people to get a reaction. But Kael didn't give me the reaction and he stayed quiet. I appreciated his loyalty to his friend, but I wished he felt like he could confide in me.

"We should finish your massage, and I should keep quiet. Unlike you, I can get fired."

"Deal."

I turned my attention back to my work. Lifting his arm and bending it gently at the elbow, I pulled softly, and as I did the thick muscles in his back shifted in response. I worked my way down his biceps. They weren't beefy in that artificial way, jacked up on supplements and daily visits to the gym. He was solid under my hands, and I knew it came from hard physical work. Army work.

I used my forearm to apply pressure to the knot under his biceps, where he had a scar that looked like an unfinished *M*. The pink-tinted skin was puffy and soft. It took everything in me not to run my finger over it again. I tried not to think about the pain he must have felt when it happened, whatever it was that had cut at his body.

The scar was deep, like from the lashing of a serrated knife. It made my heart ache for him. I slid my fingers down his forearm, the part of his body that was the deepest in pigment. He had a soldier's tan, which was like a farmer's tan, but worse, because they were in the desert getting baked by the sun. No rain, no fresh air to breathe in. Just smoke and IEDs. Body and mind damage.

I couldn't even imagine what he'd gone through . . . I lifted his hand into mine and pressed my thumb against the base of his palm and held it there. I felt his fingers go slack and moved the pressure along the center of his hand.

Was it only the night before that we sat together, side by side on my childhood bed, with alcohol washing over our thoughts and tongues? I started to think about Mendoza, wondering if he was okay. He hadn't been gone very long when Kael got the phone call.

"That feels so good," Kael said to me when I bent his wrists, pressing against the sides, slightly pulling at the same time.

"I just learned it," I told him.

"Really?"

"Yeah, I saw a YouTube video and tried it on myself first. It felt great. Especially for people who use their hands a lot."

"Wait, you learned it on YouTube?" he asked me, lifting his head a little. I gently pressed my palm against his forehead to lay him back down.

"Yes. It's helpful." I was proud of myself for mastering a new technique. The internet was usually a flaming dumpster of *you never know what you will get, but welcome to the party!*

"You're such a millennial."

"So are you." I positioned his arm back at his side and moved around the table to the other.

"Technically, I think we're Gen Z."

"Ew, no one actually says 'Gen Z' out loud." I rolled my eyes back.

"At least tell me you have an actual license and didn't learn everything on YouTube?"

"Of course I have a license. And you should let me finish my job, your time is almost up." I moved to the top of the table and applied gentle pressure to his closely shaved scalp. As I grasped his ears to release tension, his lips parted and he breathed deeply. I ended every treatment this way, and I was usually glad to be wrapping up. But now I wished for more time. With him. Just like last night . . .

"All done. Happy birthday, by the way."

"Thanks. It's just another day for me."

Kael swung his long, muscular legs off the side of the table. The stoic soldier had returned. He paid, tipped well, and left without another word.

# CHAPTER **FORTY-THREE**

I was never so relieved to be done with customers for the day. Mali had asked me to take a walk-in after that confusing session with Kael. I don't know if it was my general distraction or if it was the client, but nothing I did was good enough for her. The pressure was too light, then it was too heavy. The room was too cold. Could she have two blankets—but when they made her feet too hot, could I take one away? And could I please blow out the candle because the fragrance was giving her a headache?

And though the session felt like a test from the universe, she could do little to keep me from thinking about Kael. My mood had improved and my imagination started to invent a sympathetic story about this woman. I made every accommodation and even tried to rationalize her behavior: was she overworked or in a shitty marriage? Maybe this was the only time when she could let her anger out. Better me than her kids, or family, or even herself. I started feeling sorry for her; everyone has a bad day. Even when she said my nails needed to be clipped . . . but then she left without giving me a tip and I may have flipped her off as she walked out the door.

The new client Mali gave me for one o'clock was okay, thank goodness. The walk-in after that was fine, too—a pretty young woman from the yoga studio the next block over. Her skin was soft and she fell asleep almost as soon as she lay down, no tense muscles to work out.

I was happy to call it a day and to be heading home. *Thank God.* Mali had offered me some ibuprofen, and that helped turn down the volume in my throbbing head. But I still felt like complete crap. I was anxious and annoyed and nothing was helping. All I could think of was flopping down in bed with the blinds drawn and the covers over my head. After a full day of appointments and such an emotionally turbulent week, I craved darkness and quiet.

I walked along the alley and as I rounded the corner to my house, I saw him waiting for me on the porch. My biggest problem and biggest relief wrapped up and delivered directly to my front door.

Kael.

He seemed distracted by something, sitting there with AirPods in and a faraway look in his eyes. He was so in his own world, he almost didn't see me approach.

"Did you come for a refund?" I asked, trying to keep it light. I wasn't at all bothered that he was there. I wasn't nervous. No, I wasn't. Nope. Not at all. I was cool. I hadn't let him get to me, not the way he thought he did. Not me.

"No refund," he said, shaking his head. "I think we should finish our conversation."

"Oh? And which conversation is that?" I was playing it coy and he knew it. Cat and mouse.

"About last night." He waved a hand between us.

"We definitely finished that conversation. Drama-free friends, remember?"

"But did we finish it?" He paused, then said quietly, "It felt like you wanted something more."

"What?" I laughed at that. "We're not dating. We don't even

have each other's phone numbers," I said through a forced, fake laugh, reminding myself and him.

Kael pulled his phone out and mine started to vibrate in my pocket. The familiar 706 area code appeared with a number I didn't recognize.

"I got yours from your boss." He smiled. "I think she has a sweet spot for me."

I was shocked that Mali would do such a thing. "Mali doesn't have a sweet spot for anyone! And that's illegal."

"Technically, yes."

"Well, anyway, illegal or not, we're definitely not dating, that was my point." I backpedaled, sort of wishing I had let it go and moved on.

"Agreed. But what do people who are dating actually do? I mean, besides sex, obviously."

I shrugged. "They run errands together. They pick each other up from doctor's appointments and airports. They grocery-shop. And do things to make each other's lives easier," I explained, acknowledging to myself that we were already slipping into these domesticated routines.

Kael held an orange in his hand. It was a big orange, but small in his hand, with the little Sunkist sticker still on it. He was massaging it gently with his thumb, but hadn't broken into the peel yet.

"Have you never dated anyone?" I was curious.

"Yeah, I've dated. It was enough to last me a lifetime."

"Oh, that much?" I asked, trying not to sound as alarmed as that news made me feel.

He responded quickly. "The Army and dating don't go well together."

"So you're telling me you never considered getting married? Everyone else does it."

"That's hardly the reason to tie my life to someone else's. Getting married has to be about more than easy benefits and a better paycheck. It means something more to me."

"Good point." At least we were on the same page when it came to the casual marriages around us. "So did you stop dating when you enlisted?"

"No. I never truly started. I always knew I was going into the Army, so there wasn't a point. Why even consider it until I'm out? What about you? Why are you so against it?"

I picked at the weeds by my legs. The way he said *Why even consider it* pressed against my stomach. No matter how consuming my thoughts of Kael had become, it was obvious that he was temporary in my life: getting out of the Army, and probably leaving soon to go back to his hometown, no roots to keep him here. Everything I knew about him confirmed that I likely wouldn't see him again.

"It's not that I'm against dating. I just haven't met anyone whose company I like more than my own."

Kael smiled, his fingers toying with the sticker on the orange in his hands. I reached for a dandelion. I didn't want to blow it yet.

"I don't mean it in a narcissistic way, but in an I-don't-want-to-share-my-playlists-and-Netflix-account-with-just-anyone way."

"The ultimate commitment," he teased.

"It really is." I was laughing, but I meant what I said.

I didn't want to bend who I was, or what I listened to, or what I liked to watch, for someone else. It wasn't a fear of commitment, it was about compromising who I was and what I believed. I saw firsthand what making those compromises did to people and knew I would never, ever allow that to happen, no matter how I felt about the person. The most any ex had changed about me was Brien's encouraging me to read self-help books. Some made sense, and others were filled with toxic positivity that made me feel like shit about myself and where I was in life. I'm still on the fence about pop-psych, but I hope one day I might find the right book.

We both were quiet, roaming around the insides of our own heads. At the moment, mine looked like a vandalized art gallery, and I wondered what Kael was seeing in his.

"Is it the loss of control you're worried about?" Kael asked.

*Whoa.* Is he calling me out?

My reaction caused him to raise his hands in defense and continue in a lower voice. "I'm asking because if you found the right person, they wouldn't change you. They would have a part in making you into a better person, right? Isn't that what love is?"

I chewed his words for a minute before I responded. The dandelion danced as I started to spin it between my fingers.

I answered him honestly. There was no reason to lie or pretend I'm an expert on love and relationships. "I have no idea what love actually is."

The words hung as a placard on the concrete wall of my mental gallery. As I blew the flower to dust, I closed my eyes and pictured Kael and I in that gallery, standing in the corner, away from all the noise, taking in what the words meant. *What love actually is.*

Kael and I sat silently on the porch, and I can't explain how or why, but I knew he was in the same mental space as me, having the exact same thoughts as me. I didn't even have to open my eyes to know that his eyes weren't open anymore.

# CHAPTER FORTY-FOUR

I had forgotten to make Elodie a pitcher of sun tea, and I realized there was only an hour or so of daylight left. Jumping up, I told Kael I was heading inside to fix it, and he offered to help, even mentioning his mom's "special method" for making it. More domestic-couple behavior! Now that we were inside the kitchen, I started to feel a bit more rational. His idea of being drama-free friends made all the sense in the world. I couldn't keep thinking about it. There was no need to. It was like practice-dating in a way, and Lord knows I could use the practice. This way, my mind and heart wouldn't end up hurting—drama-free friends with an expiration date. Whatever I was walking into, I would be prepared.

"So, what's the first step in this friendship?" I asked him, as I began to fill up the jug of water in the sink.

"I think you may be too late to get this done today," he advised, pointing to the sun setting behind the trees out the window. I dumped the water as Kael pulled out a wooden chair at my kitchen table and sat down.

"Hmm, I think we're past step one. We've done the grocery-shopping bit."

I nodded, leaning back on my cute farmhouse sink. "And you've met my parents. Well, my dad and my brother."

"And a party. We've actually been through quite a bit. In a really short time."

"Yeah, we have." I looked away from his dark eyes on me. Turning around, I kept my back to him and busied myself with washing a few dishes. I really, really needed a dishwasher, but that was a luxury way down on the list. I had my eye on one, and considered getting a credit card, but the thought of owing money that I barely had made me more anxious than hand-washing my dishes.

"Let's do some basic get-to-know-each-other questions?" His tone was playful, far from the composed man I met a few days ago.

"Okay." I shot him a glance over my shoulder, but was skeptical. "Go ahead."

He gestured to the empty chair next to him.

I stepped to the table, sat down, and scooted my chair to put a few inches between us. If Elodie walked in and saw us here she would definitely have something to say about the two of us sitting so close, alone in the house.

"I'll ask you a question and you answer honestly and we go from there. Think of it as my birthday gift." He smiled at me. I wanted to kick him for being so adorable.

"This is what friends do. They get to know each other's hobbies and taste in music. Favorite foods, all that," he assured me.

He was so confident—in his words, his smile, even the way he leaned back on the chair with his arms crossed. I felt that familiar pull from the bottom of my tummy down toward my legs.

"Okay, okay. Enough small talk, ask something." I needed to be distracted from the way Kael's mouth made me ache as he licked his lips while peeling the skin off that freakin' orange.

"I only brought one, but we can share," he said. I loved this playful version of him.

"Some friend," I joked, and he shook his head.

"Hey, we're just starting out. I get to have a few hiccups."

"Touché." I paused, looking around the kitchen. "Anyway, you're the one who doesn't tell me anything about himself."

"You go first, then," he offered. I thought about what I wanted to know about him. There was just so much.

Music. That's what popped into my head first. I'd ask about music! "What's your favorite band that no one really knows?"

He turned to me, his eyes wide, happy.

"So many. I love unknown bands. It's most of what I listen to. I just open Spotify and type in my mood and they usually get it pretty spot-on." He opened the app and showed me his screen. "This morning I listened to a band called Muna. I found them recently. They're great."

"Muna isn't unknown. There's a rumor they are going to be opening for Harry Styles on his upcoming tour." I told him how I loved their music and how Elodie and I would try to get tickets to his concert as soon as they went on sale. I'd need to pick up a few more clients before I could afford resell tickets.

"Harry Styles, huh? If you could go to any concert, ever, who would it be?" he asked me.

I nodded a solid yes and thought about what concert I would choose if I could see anyone. Alanis Morissette had always been my go-to answer, but with Kael, I chose what I actually thought of first. It felt freeing, to be honest in this way. I liked how he brought me out of myself. I didn't give him the answer I thought he wanted. I gave him the truth.

"Shawn Mendes," I told him.

"Shawn Mendes? I never would have guessed." He smirked.

"And you?" I asked.

"Me, well, I would probably say either Amy Winehouse, before she . . ." He paused. It was lovely, a mark of respect somehow. I smiled, urging him to continue. "Or Kings of Leon on their first tour. Back when they were virtually unknown."

"I'm going to make a playlist of unknown bands before our next . . . hangout session, or whatever we're calling this," I said.

"Our next not-a-date," he said. I think we were both relieved to hear the word "next."

"Right," I said, feeling both relieved and excited.

"So," Kael said. "Here's another question for you. If you could describe your brother, Austin, in one word, what would it be?"

"Hmm." I tapped my nose, thinking of one word to describe my twin. "Well-intended?" I finally answered. But I was unsure. It wasn't the word I was going for. Not exactly.

"That's two words," he said.

"Actually, it's hyphenated, so that counts as one word." He liked that. I could tell. "He has good intentions," I continued. "He makes bad choices to go along with them."

"I get that," he said. And I really felt that he did.

"My turn," I said. "What about you? What about your little sister?" His expression hardened almost to say I had crossed a line. Then, just as quickly, it went back to normal. After a moment he answered me: "Powerhouse."

"Powerhouse?" I repeated. What a lovely way to be viewed by someone, especially by someone in your own family.

He nodded. "Yeah, she's brilliant. And doesn't let anything stop her. Her high school, it's one of those fancy private schools where they focus intensively on one subject. Science is her thing. She tested high enough to get into the school back when she was nine, but my mom can't drive and wouldn't let her ride the city bus alone until she turned fourteen. Now she takes the bus on her own, across town, every morning, and every afternoon."

"Wow" was all I could manage. Of course Kael's sister was

brilliant. It was impressive and ironic to compare this teenage prodigy riding a bus across town to get to her gifted school to my twenty-year-old dropout brother who managed to get himself in trouble even when he stayed home.

Kael turned the game back to me, and I continued with a basic question. "What do you like to do in your spare time?"

"Get massages"—he smiled at me—"and work on my place. I bought a duplex while I was deployed. Remember when you took me to the parking lot to get my keys? They were supposed to be left there, sitting on my tire, but they weren't. Turner, the soldier we saw at the commissary, tracked the keys down and brought them to me." He casually mentioned her like I hadn't visualized a thousand scenarios involving the two of them since I'd met her.

"Anyway, I bought this run-down duplex and I'm fixing up the empty side now, and slowly working on my side so I can rent it out and eventually move into another one and repeat the cycle. Maybe spread out toward Atlanta when I can. Real estate is one invest- ment that hardly ever decreases in value."

"I bought my house for the same reason," I told him. He broke a piece of orange off and popped it into his mouth. I could smell the sweetness from where I sat. My mouth watered.

"Well, the remodeling part. I don't think I'll ever own more than this." I waved around the kitchen. "But I'm totally fine grow- ing old and dying here because it's mine." I touched my chest. "I couldn't stand living with my dad and Estelle anymore, so I found this little house and I've been slowly, I mean, s-l-o-w-l-y, fixing it up." I dragged out the word for emphasis.

He laughed, inching closer to me. "I noticed."

"Don't you think I'm doing a good job?" I asked. "Didn't you see the shower tiles?" Kael was flipping houses—he was semiprofessional at this point—and I bet he cringed at the number of unfinished projects scattered around my house.

"Yes, you are. You're doing it on top of working and you live alone. Well, sort of alone."

"'Sort of' is right. I do as much as I can, when I can." I knew I procrastinated when it came to hard projects. I went through phases alternating between doing a ton and doing absolutely nothing for a few weeks at a time.

"What room do you feel the most at home in?" he asked, looking around the kitchen.

"Are we back to our game?"

He nodded.

I put some thought into my answer. "I'd have to say my room. I love my living room for hanging out with Elodie and sprawling across my couch on a weekend without having to wear a bra or socks." *What the hell, Karina!* I felt my cheeks turning red, but continued. "And I love my kitchen for being open and cute. It's easy to cook in, doesn't get too hot. My bathroom will hopefully be a favorite after I finish it. But for now, my bedroom, specifically my bed, is my spot. Me and my phone and I'm set."

He was close to me, so close that I could smell the fruit on his breath. I didn't know if it was me or if it was Kael, but one of us was inching closer to the other as we continued our little game. By the time Kael and I had asked each other random questions like how long we could hold our breath and what noise could he listen to all day, every day without being annoyed, we were inches away from each other, both leaning out of our seats.

It was a magnetic pull. An irresistible attraction. He was by far the smartest, most philosophical person I had ever met. He had the answer to everything; he knew exactly who he was. I really loved that, and his conversation drew me out. I told him how I first fell in love with figuring out life on my own. I told him how I would never change who I was for another person. I didn't exactly know who I would become, but I knew it would be on my terms.

"I could listen to you talk all day," he said, surprising me.

"No one has ever said that to me before."

"It's become one of my favorite things to do. I'm going to miss this when I leave."

His eyes were on my mouth.

My heart was beating out of my chest.

"I wish you weren't going," I confessed to him.

"One day you'll regret saying that." Kael's breath covered my cheeks.

His lips were so close to mine. Was he going to kiss me, here, now, out of the blue, with the dew of orange on his lips?

My mouth begged for his to inch closer, to touch mine. I had never wanted something more than I wanted him to kiss me, there in my kitchen.

Was he going to kiss me?

His lips soon answered my question. He leaned over and put his soft mouth on mine. Everything went quiet then. The traffic on the street outside. The faint sound of the TV. Even the noise in my head went quiet. I had no words. No thoughts. Just him.

He was timid at first, gentle . . . until I pushed my tongue between his lips and tasted him. His fingers cupped the sides of my jaw and down the skin of my neck. He pulled me closer and I sighed, feeling relief from a pain I didn't know I felt.

The flooding relief was immense but short-lived when Kael gently pulled away, kissing the corner of my mouth while whispering, "I'm so sorry."

The high I felt was ripped away, replaced with a different kind of pain taking stabs at me. The look on his face wasn't just surprise, but remorse.

"I'm sorry. I really don't know what I was thinking," he continued, wiping his mouth with his fingers. "I shouldn't have done that."

I nodded, almost agreeing in silence, but it felt like a rejection. "Yeah, you really shouldn't have." My words didn't match what I was really feeling, but I wasn't going to let him know that. I stood to leave the kitchen, wanting the safe haven of my room, wanting to curl up into a ball. That was it for me and oranges.

# CHAPTER **FORTY-FIVE**

I hadn't heard from Kael at all the next day, and by the time I got home from work I was so exhausted that I barely wanted to undress, let alone shower. Dad and Estelle were still in Atlanta, so thankfully, no Tuesday-night dinner. Elodie wasn't home, and she hadn't told me where she was going. The whole day at work I tried to avoid her, because I didn't want her to sense that something was off with me. I felt like she would know that Kael had kissed me when she looked at me. I didn't plan on telling her. It wasn't that I didn't trust her, I just didn't want anyone to know. I didn't know why, but I wanted to protect whatever this was with Kael from anyone's judgment or questions.

No matter how much I adored Elodie, managing her curiosity and keeping her entertained were more than I could handle today. I was emotionally drained and, after having two no-shows and a very high-strung walk-in who didn't tip, I really wanted the house to myself. I collapsed into the cushions of my couch and closed my eyes. I couldn't remember the last time I'd felt this way.

After a quiet nap, and realizing how badly I needed to relax, I decided on a pampering shower, using nearly every product in the bathroom. I shaved, twice, and even double-shampooed my hair, just to feel more lavish. After the long, hot shower, I combed out my hair, braided it the best I could, and put on the only matching pajama set I owned. They were soft, a silky rose fabric that clung to my body—a gift, of course, from Estelle. Hardly my comfort zone, but I had to admit they looked pretty flattering; if only I had someone to appreciate me wearing them.

My nails were up next. I was really leaning in to this self-care thing everyone kept talking about online. Tiny flakes of sky blue were left on my fingernails, and instead of picking at them like I always do, I grabbed the acetone and cotton balls and headed to my bedroom to get a bottle of white nail polish from the basket on my dresser, along with a candle that I had "borrowed" from my stash at work. On my way to the kitchen I collected a towel from the hall closet in anticipation of my mani-pedi. A cup of tea seemed the perfect accompaniment to my spa-at-home preparations . . . but Elodie and I had finished the supply of tea packets that we'd brought home from the salon. So a cup of microwaved water with a spoonful of honey in it would have to do. I carried the steaming liquid carefully to the living room, pausing to turn on my speaker and Bluetooth, as the honey dissolved into the clear water.

My wrists were a little sore from the no-tip client who was full of demands. He barked at me every time I spoke and didn't want to pay for a deep-tissue, even though he continuously asked me to use more and more pressure. The joints of my fingers had a dull ache, a manageable but not ignorable type of pain. I decided to paint my toenails first.

Actively not thinking about Kael caused me to think about him. It scared me how comfortable I had become with his proximity, his quiet and intense presence in my house. He had rapidly become a subtle, essential part of my life. But he was very, very clear from the start that we would never be a thing, and I went along with it, acting as if I was used to spending all my time with a guy and not calling him my boyfriend. But after last night, this turned into a more dangerous reality. I had to constantly remind myself not to read too much into that kiss. Even if it was the best kiss of my life . . . But I know exactly what happens when you expect something from people. It never ends well.

I felt the cold polish touch my skin and I jumped a little, dragging the white paint farther down my toe. Thinking too much about him distracted me from being able to paint my toenails properly. I really needed to get it together. I took a sip of the steamy sweet water in my mug and felt the wetness from the end of my braid moistening my back through my PJs, when a knock at the door made me jump. A visitor was the last thing I wanted right now, and I definitely wasn't expecting anyone, but there it was. I stood up and looked around for my phone so I could check to see if anyone had called. Austin? I couldn't find my phone, so I gave up and tiptoed to the door as the knocking came again. This time harder. Like the side of a fist pounding against my fragile screen door. I yanked it open to see Kael standing there; his hand was midair and he looked surprised to see me. It had started to rain again, and a mist floated around Kael, clinging to the cotton of his sweatshirt.

"Hey, sorry—is Elodie here?" he asked, trying to look past me.

He was wearing black pants and a gray sweatshirt that had big letters across the front and some sort of seal under them. I tried not to look for too long, but instinctively caught his eyes with mine. A car passed us with its brights on. I loved the way tires sounded on rain-slicked pavement. The street was busy with a continual shushing noise. Even the rain couldn't keep traffic away.

"Elodie's not. I'm here alone."

As I started trying to think of all the things I wanted to tell him about my shitty day at work, Kael smiled at me. It wasn't a big smile, but it was there, and the corners of his lips turned up, his eyes bright under my porch light.

"Wow. Home alone on family-dinner Tuesday? Who would have imagined?"

"Ha, funny guy is back? It's actually quite nice to have some quiet. I had the worst day today." I licked my lips and kept the bottom one between my teeth for a moment. I didn't even know where to begin.

He looked around, down at my pajamas. I followed his eyes with mine and became hyperaware of how thin the material was, how tight, and how braless I was. He was a friend, a gentleman, and he looked away from my body.

"Well, I'll go so you can enjoy your castle to yourself. If you see Elodie, can you tell her that Phillip's been trying to call for like an hour and he's getting worried. He has less than an hour of phone privilege before he leaves for his next mission, if she can talk." He effortlessly walked backward as he spoke, down the porch steps and into my grass. The blades shined under the streetlight, and the rain was picking up.

"If she comes home, I'll let her know," I called after him. I felt an unexplainable urge to stop him from leaving. My brain couldn't react as fast as he moved, and I stood alone on my porch, watching him get into his truck. As one of my hands waved to him, the other was at my chest, trying to hold my heart still. So he really wasn't going to mention the kiss? It's not that I wanted him to, but I did. I couldn't decide what the hell I wanted.

He drove away and I stood there, wishing Elodie was home and that I wasn't so awkward when he was around. I would have traded my alone time, even the long shower, for him to be sitting in my living room. I was surprised as the thought hit me, and even more surprised at how true it was. I really, really wanted him to come back. Maybe I could call Elodie and tell her to come home and keep me company until this pang of loneliness went away? Her husband was trying to get a hold of her, so it would be a win-win.

Deep down I knew that her company wouldn't fill the void. I tried to push aside thoughts of wanting to be alone with Kael. Feeling brave, I rushed around my house, looking for my phone. When I found it in my room, I clicked on his name and dialed before I could overthink it. My heart raced. This felt different. I felt high. Outside of my body and mind. *Why?* When he answered on the second ring, my voice spilled over onto the line.

"Karina?" He said my name so calmly, almost like he was suspecting I'd call.

"Um, yeah. Hi. Can you . . ." An excuse didn't come to me. "Do you want to come back?"

He instantly sounded alarmed. "Is something wrong? Did you get a hold of Elodie?"

*Elodie.* Our ever-present liaison was there, again. He wasn't asking about me, he was asking about her.

"No. Never mind. I . . ." The words felt like sand being poured down my throat. "Sorry for bothering you. I haven't heard from her. Yeah, so bye." I hung up and threw my phone back onto the bed. This time I wouldn't forget where I put it.

Now that Kael and I weren't hanging out, I got panicky about our situation. I felt the need to label it, to make it fit into this box that I had created in my mind of how we *should* be. We shouldn't have kissed, even though it was by far the best kiss I had ever had. Literally in my existence. But now we were both ignoring that it even happened, and I began to question everything again. A feeling of rejection bore a hole in my chest. I hated the idea of embarrassing myself in front of him, as I had just done.

I tried to distract myself with physical activity, splashing water on my face and walking back to the living room to finish my toes and start on my nails. I turned the music up louder and desperately tried to think about something else. If my life were more interesting, I would have plenty of things to obsess over. Thinking I heard a knock at the door, I paused the music, but found silence. The crickets chirping around the yard were the only distant sound. I started the song again, the chorus played, and I sang along with Halsey until I heard the banging again.

"Karina?"

I couldn't tell if I was imagining Kael shouting my name, but I made a promise to myself that if I was, I would eat a melatonin gummy, maybe two, and go to bed before my delusion got any worse. When I heard it again, I stood up, polish bottle in hand, and walked on my heels, trying not to mess up my toenails. He said my name again as I got closer to the door. When I opened it, he was holding his phone and it was ringing on speakerphone.

"The number you have reached—" The generic voicemail greeting began to recite a number. My number. I recognized it as it played between us. If I was a blabbering mess earlier, I couldn't even imagine how I would seem now.

"Hey," I said to him.

His eyes lit up again. "Hey?" He exhaled, and laughter followed.

I couldn't help but smile. Half of me hated that I was already feeling so giddy, but I was also relieved that he came back.

"You're here."

He nodded. "I'm here."

"Sorry for calling, I—"

"Nope. No sorrys." He walked past me, his cologne leaving a trail behind him as he took of his shoes at my front door. I followed him. The knot in my stomach was loosening instead of tightening, quite the opposite of what I expected. I shut the front door behind us.

"What's going on here? A party and I wasn't invited?" Kael kicked his foot out to touch my red speaker with his sock.

"Hardly." I waved my hand around, gesturing to the nail polish remover and my cup of hot water with honey. "I was enjoying having a night in. Pedicure, long shower. All that."

He sat down on my chair, where he usually did, and leaned forward, resting his elbows on the tops of his knees.

"That sounds nice. Very unlike you, but nice. Am I crashing?"

I shook my head and crossed my arms over my chest, remembering again how sheer the fabric was that I had on.

"Did you eat already?" he asked me.

I shook my head again, causing some of my hair to come loose. My hair was nearly dry, wavy from the braid, and definitely wild. I ran my hands over the strands. *Yep. Definitely frizzy.* I sat down on the floor and reached for a pillow from the couch to put on my lap. "I don't really have much in the fridge. Like borderline nothing. I need to go to the commissary again but I haven't had the time. I didn't get enough of the things I needed when we were there. I'm working on a grocery list for my next day off."

I was rambling again. My explanation was long, but as usual Kael didn't seem to mind.

"Are you hungry?" he asked me, clearly moving the conversation on.

I shrugged. I wasn't, really, until he asked, and it reminded me that the only thing I had eaten today was a piece of toast on my walk to work.

"I am," Kael added.

Was he offering to have dinner with me? I didn't want to chance totally misreading this whole thing. I didn't say anything and continued to let him lead. After about a minute, the silence between us settled. My gaze strayed toward the floor, staring at the spot where the carpet met the dark wood.

He spoke first. "We can order food. I'll open Postmates."

I somehow knew he wouldn't ask me why I called him back to my house. Drama-free. No more kissing. No more boundary-crossing. He will order us dinner and act like nothing happened. I studied him as he scrolled on his phone, dissecting him the way I did everyone. He was hard to break down; he was much, much harder to understand than most people. He wasn't simple, but he wasn't messy. He was calm in that way, where I was tripping over words and thoughts.

"Italian or Indian?" he asked.

"Is the Italian a chain restaurant or family-owned?" I wanted something that was made with love and thought. That was the kind of meal I needed now for comfort.

He smiled a little. "It's Olive Garden."

"Indian, please. I can add my order and Venmo you for it if that's cool?"

He shrugged and didn't look up from his screen. About two minutes later, he set the phone next to my ankle. Indian food reminded me of my ex and the one month we spent eating it every weekend. I always got the same thing with Brien, whatever he ordered for me. I clicked back onto the cart and opened Kael's order. His selections looked so good. Cauliflower and potatoes with a spiced sauce I hadn't heard of, but it sounded great. With Kael, even something as simple as a food order felt intimate, revealing. But I knew that was silly; it was only a meal, after all. I added another order of the same dish to the cart and handed his phone back to him. He didn't look at the phone longer than a second before he touched the screen and put it back into his pocket.

A few minutes later, Kael's calm had taken over the whole house and I had that familiar urge to start talking about the most random things. I rechecked my little setup and looked at Kael. He seemed content as I made eye contact with him. His face didn't change, he was staring at me, blank expression. No annoyance, no smile. Just content and still. I tried to let his ease wear off on me even more.

I opened the nail polish, wiggled the polish brush around the bottle, and started to finally paint my fingernails, swiping the brush over my thumb. Even though I took my time, half of the polish got on the skin around the nail. I sighed. I was so bad at this. One of the first things I would do when I made grown-up money would be to get regular manicures. It was a small luxury that I really enjoyed. *One day, Karina, one day.*

I grabbed the bottle of acetone and a half-used cotton ball to fix my mistake. I tried again, using my other hand this time. I could feel Kael still watching me, but I didn't feel pressured or rushed. I went even slower, but the strokes were uneven. My hands were shaking a little. I definitely needed food. I was so glad it was on the way.

"I'm just hungry, so my hands are acting funny. I'm always bad at painting nails, but usually a little better than this. Do you know how long until the food will be here?" I was rambling. "Not trying to rush you," I added, wishing I could clamp my mouth closed. But no matter the scenario, with him around, I couldn't seem to do that.

"The app said it would be an hour, but sometimes it comes sooner."

I reached for the cotton ball again, and Kael's hand wrapped around mine, stopping it in the air. His touch was so unexpected that I thought I had spilled something on him, or the top had come off the polish. I looked up to his face and drank in his eyes, how far the corners of his pink lips were turned up, how set his jaw was. My fascination with him was all in the details. Nothing seemed wrong. I was confused.

Kael reached for the polish bottle. It was Marshmallow, a creamy white color from Essie. Their signature square bottle looked doll-sized in Kael's free hand, the one he wasn't holding mine with.

"Do you want me to do it for you?" he offered, and I let out a breath.

Blinking, I searched for a sign that he was teasing me but found nothing. I slowly pulled my hand from his and put them both in my lap.

"What?" he calmly asked, dipping the brush back into the small bottle.

I didn't know what to say. It felt so binding, or like a big deal, but was it? Was the way my stomach danced because I couldn't imagine any of the men in my life offering something like that? Or was it because the men in my life weren't thoughtful and had firm ideas of gender roles? Kael lifted the brush, hurrying me along in my mental analysis.

"I have a steady hand. Technically trained, and you need to rest yours anyway. You use them for work every day and they've been bothering you."

"My hands are fine. Have I said that they weren't?" I wasn't sure, honestly.

"You rub them all the time." He nodded to my left hand that I just so happened to be slowly rotating in a small circle.

I froze and Kael smiled in a way that was both comforting and cocky. He was in a playful mood, it seemed. I wanted to savor his being here—the way he was making me feel—while I could; Phillip would come home, Elodie would have her baby, and Kael would be gone by this time next year. This companionship would not be mine for much longer.

My guard and boundaries tangoed with my rationality and reality as I looked at Kael. There they were again, those boundaries, after I was promising myself not to cross them less than ten minutes ago. I imagined them as big white doors inside my brain. I made sure to keep them away from my heart. We could choose Door A, where Kael paints my nails and I talk his ear off while we share dinner, or Door B, where I could keep my polish and my thoughts to myself and share a simple, friendly, drama-free meal.

"Just let me try it. If I suck as bad as you do, you can do it yourself."

He was so convincing and made his little act of service feel so casual. I couldn't come up with any logic that mattered more than how happy I felt in that moment.

"If you really don't want me to—" Kael began.

"No. Go ahead. I mean, yes. You can try," I blurted, wanting to say something before the offer was withdrawn.

He smiled at that. I couldn't see Door B anymore; any trace of a boundary was gone.

"It's not like I'm *that* bad," I teased.

He grabbed the towel I had brought out, unfolded it neatly, and placed it under my hands.

"Okay, so I'm not a professional. Just keep that in mind," he cautioned, focusing intently on my thumb, with one hand holding the polish.

"My ma sometimes . . ." He brushed the pad of his thumb across the top of my bare nail and a warmth ran through me. It was sweet and felt like melted honey. "Sometimes her hands would shake, so I often helped her as I got older."

I looked at Kael as he moved expertly from finger to finger. The image of him as a teenager, helping his mother paint her nails, made my heart want to explode. Of all the things Kael had told me about his family, I treasured this the most. He didn't say much as he worked, and I mellowed, trusting him completely without any further protest. I just watched him, my eyes opening and closing, as we listened to the rain pick up outside, pounding softly against my roof.

# CHAPTER **FORTY-SIX**

"I wonder if my nails are dry yet?" I moved my hand in front of my face, slowly studying my fresh nails. "I'll check—"

"You should wait!" he interrupted me.

I made the mistake of touching the paint too soon, and my fingerprint branded half of my thumbnail.

"Damn it. But still good as new." I continued to wave my hands in the air and blow on them every few seconds. I had been dozing and was relaxed and still sort of drowsy; I could have fallen asleep if I wasn't so hungry. The rain was steady and the heat had kicked on, blowing warm air out of the floor vents. I felt at ease.

"Remember how we were talking about *Twilight*?" I asked him, as my nails finished drying.

"What?" He laughed at that.

"I mean, not right now. Not even today, but you remember, we talked about it."

Kael nodded, though clearly confused. "Yeah?"

"Anyway, there's this character named Jasper who can control people's emotions—well, not only humans', vampires', too. That's his power. You know they all have powers, the Cullens, at least." I looked down at my new manicure, then up at him, smiling with delight. I felt so happy. It was weird.

"Right. Go on."

"Anyway, he does this thing where he can calm people, and I feel like you do that. Not in a vampire way. Obviously."

"Obviously."

I read the words on Kael's sweatshirt. It said Georgia Southern on top of a picture—was it a bird? I couldn't tell. The words and emblem were faded, the material of the lettering flaking off. It looked vintage, but not in a pretentious way.

"So, you're a huge *Twilight* fan, huh?" he asked, humor in his tone.

"Everyone is."

He licked his lips before he spoke. "I think that's a stretch."

"Is it?" I questioned with sarcasm.

We were flirting, I think? I wasn't very good at it, though he obviously was since I was grinning like an idiot and he had barely spoken.

"I mean, I wouldn't say *everyone* is a fan." He shrugged. "I can appreciate it for what it is."

I started to feel a little defensive. What did he mean by that? I couldn't stand the condescension.

"So you guys can watch a bunch of men chasing a ball, but romance fandom is dismissible?" I asked the question, thinking about how many times I'd wanted to speak my peace on this subject.

He raised his hands. "No, no, no. Not dismissing romance at all. I just like my vampires a little more murderous? I don't have anything against *Twilight*. Put your weapon down." He smirked. "My sister loves it."

"What's she like?" I was dying to know more about his family, about him.

He shifted his body closer to me as we sat together on the floor.

I could tell his eyes were reading mine to see if he could trust me. *Please trust me*, I wanted to beg him.

"She's . . . she's all the things I'm not."

I felt like he let me in, even if the door was barely cracked. I kept my focus on his face. In the tiny twitch in his jaw, I could sense his protectiveness of her, and in his eyes, the adoration for her. I was ashamed that it made me a little jealous. Not in a romantic way, not even close, but in a way that I really, really, really wished I had someone who loved me that much.

"When did you see her last?" I wanted to ask more before he closed the door on me.

"Before I deployed."

"Wow. It's been nearly a year?"

His face fell. When Kael's guard was down, he showed emotion so clearly.

"So, Jasper. That whole emotion-control thing," he said, setting a boundary. A firm one. He was changing the subject to keep me out of his personal business. My stomach twisted, but only I knew it. I was playing the part of a chill girl who you can hang out with . . . order takeout and talk about *Twilight*. Kael's line in the sand was drawn, so I followed him through my pretend Door B and moved the topic back to vampires.

"He was also a soldier," I added, trying not to show much emotion. I was happy that he let me in, even for the few seconds it lasted. I waved my nails in the air to try to make them dry faster.

Kael's hands touched the tiny stubble on his chin. I knew it would be gone soon, due to regulations and all.

"He was," he said and nodded. "Wait, wasn't he a Confederate soldier?"

My hand covered my mouth. "I've never thought about it like that," I admitted. *Yikes.*

Kael rubbed his hands together inches from my face.

"Well that changes things," I instantly decided.

"People can do things that you don't like, and you can still like them." He paused a for a moment. "Especially fictional characters. They're meant to make us question ourselves, aren't they? Sometimes the shittiest ones can teach us the most. That's the point, the balance between good and evil and all that."

"But a Confederate soldier is . . ."

"Bad. Pretty fucking bad," he affirmed. "But you didn't write the thing. And you don't like that part of the character. Just as I don't love that main guy, Derek, from *American History X*. He's an ex-Nazi and a total piece of shit, but it's one of my favorite films and he does the right thing in the end. Sometimes we find comfort in stories that aren't perfect. People are complicated, you know?"

"Everyone has a backstory," I said, my voice less confident than his, but he made me feel like he wanted to hear me. "When I was younger, I would always make excuses for everyone's behavior. My dad said it's the thing that made me weak."

Kael's voice was soft but quick to come. "You mean empathy?"

I looked away from his eyes and up at the ceiling.

"I guess so," I said, fragments of traumatic experiences flipping through my mind. Every time I gave someone a pass I was trying to do the right thing. But in the end my dad's harsh judgment became the only lens that mattered.

"Making excuses for someone's bad behavior isn't always the same thing as finding the reason why they are that way." Kael looked at me patiently.

I nodded. He was so intelligent when he spoke that he could take something like a vampire film and turn it into a meaningful discussion without sounding like a pretentious douche. Kael made my multitude of thoughts make sense in a way most guys his age never had.

"Yeah. I've found my peace with Jasper, flaws and all—and I guess I'm realizing that most of my comfort things are bad examples," I admitted, listing them off in my head. *Gossip Girl, The Vampire Diaries, One Tree Hill.*

He agreed. "Mine, too."

"Alice deserved better," I said, wondering where the line between writing and opinions lay.

"Yeah, she did."

"What else comforts you?" I dared to ask. I don't know what I was expecting as his response, but the question was out before I could process it.

I kept my focus on his face as he seemed to be thoroughly considering my ask, and was quiet for the longest ten seconds of my life. Kael looked straight ahead, staring at the brown tapestry hung on my wall. My mom got it from some flea market, I didn't remember in which state.

"Being around you."

The boldness of his confession sucked the air from my lungs.

His bright eyes turned to me. I was speechless and very caught off guard, to say the least.

"And you? What brings you comfort?" he asked.

I could feel my mind going into its own version of fight-or-flight and I was a little surprised by the way I felt. I was afraid to say that I loved being around him, too, that it brought me comfort to connect with him and that I was growing more and more attached each time I saw him. But what did this mean? He finds being around me comforting? I didn't know what to make of that.

"I . . . um." I hesitated, realizing that I had somehow moved closer to him.

Kael's finger was warm when it touched my lips. I both froze and caught on fire. I felt dizzy. He pressed the pad of his index finger into my wet lips and kept it there for no longer than a second. I could barely breathe and was trying with everything in me to remain calm and think before I reacted. For once.

Studying Kael's face, I sprinted through the possibilities of what this moment could turn into. I hated that the hourglass in my mind was moving faster, the sand pouring through the gap mercilessly reminding me of our limited time together. Our eye contact made me nervous; he was looking at me so intensely that my cheeks warmed. I wanted to tell him that I had never felt as much comfort from a person as I did from him, at least not in real life. I wanted to tell him that I would miss him terribly when he left. I wanted to admit that I liked him—more than just being grocery-shopping, stargazing buddies. I couldn't and wouldn't, but fuck, did I wish I could.

Kael's eyes were on my mouth. I was very aware that my chest was likely beet red, the revealing pajamas not doing me any favors. I closed my eyes, thinking maybe he would kiss me again, and if he didn't, I couldn't bear to look at him much longer. I felt so much and couldn't find a single word to say. When my lids shut, there was a sense of relief from his flame. My heart pounded.

His phone vibrated on the floor between us and I tried to read the name on the screen when my eyes snapped open. He scooped it up too quickly and I felt embarrassed that I was violating his privacy. He ignored the call, but his energy shifted instantly. I must have looked like such a freaking idiot with my eyes shut, like I was waiting for him to kiss me. Who said that's even what I wanted? *Not me.*

Suddenly, it was like our little bubble popped and reality

swallowed him up. His features felt harsh, his warm eyes became cold as they turned away from me and stared at the wall. I sank. I was pulled back into my thoughts on overdrive, wondering what I said or did wrong this time. Who kept calling him? Maybe he was secretly married? I couldn't think of another explanation for his odd behavior.

I thought about Brien and how often he would "shush" me. How many times he would gently tap my leg under the table if I was talking too much in front of his friends. If I was embarrassing him. Kael isn't like him, I reminded myself. He's just making sure neither of us cross a line that we can't reverse. I had a lapse of judgment. No big deal.

I paused, fidgeting and lightly pushing at my cuticles.

"Important call?" I asked him, hoping I didn't sound as immature as I felt.

He shook his head. "Obviously not, since I ignored it."

His tone wasn't rude, but his words had a bit of defensiveness that rubbed me the wrong way.

"Dinner will be here in five minutes, if you want to wash up," he mumbled.

"You don't have to talk to me like I'm twelve," I said and rolled my eyes. I wasn't completely sure why, but I felt slighted and moody.

"Madam, your dinner will be delivered in precisely three hundred seconds."

I cackled, a real laugh, suddenly back to being amused. This thing with him was exhausting but exhilarating.

He grabbed the pillow from my lap and I kicked my leg out at him. He suddenly tossed the pillow back at me and used his hand to push it down a little across my crotch area. *Oh my god!* His eyes were on mine and I squeezed the pillow, shoving it tightly between my legs, now remembering why I had it in the first place. Kael's cheeks were a bit more red than usual. Or was I imagining that his embarrassment matched my own?

Both of our backs were against the couch and we sat facing forward with our legs in front of us. Mine were crossed at the ankles and I still had the pillow on my lap. I couldn't catch up with my breath, even though we had barely moved. I turned my head. I just had to look at him, to try to make some sense of what we were doing.

His chest was rising and falling the way mine was. This wasn't exactly what friends did. We were crossing the line like we did last night when he kissed me. Why stop now?

"What?" I looked into his eyes, not sure what I was asking.

"What?" he repeated, shifting again, so his face was inches from mine.

Him kissing me or not was no longer the thing I feared, it was this different type of intimacy, this comfort. I tried to calm my heart and my head. No matter how good it felt to be with Kael—how much I wanted this right now—I knew it was never, ever going to work. He was leaving and I wasn't ready to date anyone, especially a long-distance soldier who I barely knew. We had an arrangement. An agreement.

"I . . ." We both spoke the same exact word at the same exact time.

Kael's expression looked like he was sizing me up, deciding what he was going to do based on what he thought I was going to do. All logic was gone as his tongue grazed over his bottom lip, making it shine under the light. I wanted to taste him again; it was all my mind was full of.

I tried to be logical even though it felt impossible.

"Do you think this is a good idea? What we're doing right now?" I could barely get the words out through my deep breaths.

"It feels like it is."

"But do you *think* it is? What will happen if we kiss again?"

"Karina." Kael turned his entire body toward me. "Please don't ask me questions that I can't answer. Not tonight. Please." His voice was a whisper as his hand cupped my ear.

All of my shame and embarrassment and second thoughts about feeding the hunger I had for him quickly melted out of my body and mind. I couldn't keep my eyes open when his thumb gently massaged the lobe of my ear. My neck instinctively rolled back and he lifted my head, firmly cradling my neck with his other fingers.

I let him take over. I didn't want to stop whatever questionable decision we were about to make. His lips were even warmer than his fingers as they brushed against mine. The tiniest of contact. It tickled in a daze-inducing way. He pushed against me, bringing his body to hover over mine. My back pressed against the edge of my couch as his mouth opened mine. A wave of relief, calmness, excitement, silence, screaming, rolled over me. I lifted my hands to his shoulders and guided his body to trade places as I climbed onto his lap, feeling his arousal against the thin silk of my shorts. I could feel the wetness in my panties as I kissed him again and again.

The door shook with a knock just as Kael's fingers dug into my hips, pressing me closer. I jumped off of him, my knee hitting my cup of tea and splashing it onto the floor.

"Elodie! Oh my god." I wiped at my mouth and tried to calm myself down. I was quickly coming out of the trance, realizing I would have to face Elodie if she caught us like this. Or my brother, which would be even worse . . .

"It's probably the food." Kael stood and went to open the front door. Of course it was the food. *Geez, Karina, paranoid much?*

Kael set the plastic bag between us without saying a word about the second kiss or what would have happened if the delivery man hadn't interrupted. He unpacked the bag and opened each container, describing the dish to me without teasing me for having copied his order. He handed me my food first and waited to see my reaction before taking a bite of his own.

"Incredible," I said with a mouth full of food.

His smile distracted me from wondering if we were going to pretend like it didn't happen, again. I didn't want to know the answer to that—not right now, at least. So there we sat, bonding over the foam boxes on our laps, browsing through Netflix, and joking and bickering like an old married couple. The boundaries had all slipped tonight. I hoped it wouldn't destroy me when I fell.

# CHAPTER **FORTY-SEVEN**

Kael was parked in the back of the spa when I got off work the next day, his huge Bronco dripping water from its massive body. He was wearing a long-sleeved shirt with his company's name printed on the front and blue jeans with frayed bottoms, as if he had worn them for years. I wanted to touch the soft, worn denim and feel the thread of the fabric against my fingertips.

"What are you doing here? How did you know when I would be off?" I was surprised to see him waiting with a freshly washed truck. Surprised, but thrilled.

"A little birdie told me," he said, pulling his sunglasses off his eyes and opening the passenger door for me.

"Does that little birdie happen to have an adorable French accent?" I asked.

He shrugged. "That's confidential," he said with a straight face. I could see a little gleam in his eye. How was it possible that I missed him so much when he had stayed at my house until almost midnight, leaving right before Elodie got home? I didn't know if I could hide Kael's visit from her if she so much as mentioned his name. Even if I told her the minimum, that he was at the house, she would want something, a little snippet of gossip, a morsel of a taste of my personal life, but unfortunately for her, I didn't kiss and tell. Oh, god, the kiss. It made my cheeks glow, my heart sink and float, sink and float.

"What are you doing here?" I asked Kael again. I was hesitant to climb into his truck, not knowing exactly where things stood with us.

"I came to hopefully get you to go on a date with me."

"A date? I thought we said we weren't going on dates, that we were just going to hang out until your discharge? We seem to keep doing the opposite of that."

He shoved his hands into his pockets and stood there, next to the open door.

"I disagree. We're technically hanging out." He shrugged. It was hard to argue with him when he looked this relaxed, this innocent and playful. I knew if I went with him, I'd have a great time.

"Semantics," I argued.

"Maybe, but would you like to hang out with me tonight, since you don't work until eleven tomorrow?"

I said yes without even pretending to have to think about it. There was no point. We both knew I would go anywhere he asked me to. He held me by my elbow as I climbed up into the seat, and he shut the door behind me. The fact that he opened doors for me was something I appreciated in a guy. The gesture wasn't lost on me—it was an old-fashioned and small thing, but I actually really liked the thought behind it and it made me feel safe. Kael was a gentleman without even trying. As he stood there, looking so confident in himself and in me, I knew this was all temporary and had my guard up not to get used to it. I hoped there would be men out there like him. If I could find someone who was half as smart and thoughtful and opinionated and socially and emotionally aware, I'd be lucky.

"I have something planned for you. Nothing too fancy, I put

together some music"—he paused, sheepishly—"and I want to take you to dinner at my favorite spot in town."

I was getting more excited by the minute.

"You made a playlist? How cliché, but also awesome." I couldn't wait to hear what Kael had assembled.

I was in fake-dating bliss.

"Wait, am I dressed okay? I'm still in my scrubs. I can change if you want to stop by my house."

Kael shook his head. "You look great. You don't need to change. Unless you really want to?"

I didn't really want to. Yes, I wanted to dress cute and look as pretty as I could to hang out with Kael, but at the same time I felt comfortable. Even with no makeup and wearing my favorite black scrubs, I did actually feel pretty.

"I can stay in this," I told him, settling it.

This is what life must be like every day for people who are in love. Not that I was in love, but this was companionship that's good for one's heart and self-esteem. Kael thinks I'm cool enough to hang out with, and though I tried not to value myself based on other people's opinions of me, his opinion mattered.

"I found like five bands I think you've never heard of. One is called Chevelle. I once knew this guy in basic training who would scream their lyrics over and over. They were from his hometown, and by the time we graduated, I knew almost all of their songs by heart. I don't know if you'll like them now, but if you had listened to them before you fell for Shawn Mendes, it might have been a different story."

"Leave Shawn out of this," I told him with a smile.

"I saw that poster in your room at your dad's."

Kael turned onto the highway as daylight was disappearing from the sky.

"He's the John Mayer of our generation," I argued.

Kael snorted. "John Mayer is the John Mayer of our generation."

A few minutes later, he was quiet, and I was happy as we listened to music and drove down a long, curvy road that I had never been on before. I would always remember the way the sun and moon danced in the sky that night and what a sense of calm his silence had started to bring over my body.

I listened to his voice when he asked me random questions that he had clearly put some thought into:

"How many siblings do you wish you had?"

"Which is your favorite character on *Friends*?"

"How many times have you watched *The Lion King*?"

"If you could have dinner with five people, dead or alive, who would they be and why?"

I was starting to get too comfortable with him, there in the front seat of his Bronco. And yet I could almost feel the chaos brewing somewhere nearby. Everything was going too well. I was totally lost in his world now, impressed and moved by every thought he had. I loved the way his tongue wrapped words up to sound pleasurable and profound. The depth of his thoughts and the way he spoke were incredibly attractive; his mind at work was so appealing to me. I thought I knew what connection was like, but watching it play out on a TV screen was nothing compared to real life. There's a joy here, a level of peace with Kael that I had not known in my twenty years on this earth. Being with Kael was like meditating; it was so good for my mind and my soul felt better when he was around. He was lighthearted and heavy, both at home and away. Biting whiskey and smooth wine. I loved the way he contradicted everything about himself—his purposeful silence, his wise youthfulness, his unexpected softness. He was a fascinating man, and I couldn't wait to learn more about him.

We made it through an entire playlist and began to make a second one together. I quietly sang along to a Halsey song. We got to the restaurant early and sat in the car, talking through the next few songs. The place was a cool little Chinese restaurant with nicely decorated patio seating, hanging lanterns, and lush green plants covering the space. We were only fifteen minutes from my house, but I had never noticed this place or the cute fragrance store next door.

"This street is so charming—" I saw my brother's name pop up on my screen. I thought about ignoring his call, but decided against it.

"It's Austin, sorry." I turned Kael's radio down and picked up the call. Music boomed through his side of the line and his slurred words were tumbling through, becoming inaudible.

"Kareeee, come get me. Please? Fuck Katie, Katie and her boyfriend that I didn't know she had. She said it was her ex-boyfriend, but they're trying to jump me . . ." Austin slurred his words. "Kare, please come get me."

I sat straight up in my seat. "What do you mean? Who's trying to jump you? Where are you?"

Chaos. No longer brewing. It was here.

# CHAPTER **FORTY-EIGHT**

I couldn't say no. Austin gave me the location and I asked Kael to drive me straight there. He put the address in his phone and pulled out of the parking lot, the restaurant lanterns fading in the background as we drove. Thanks to Kael's ability to drive in crisis mode, it took us only about eight minutes to get there. I called Austin once a minute until we arrived, but he didn't pick up. By the time we pulled up, two guys were rolling around in the middle of the street; a red T-shirt and a black T-shirt were all I could see. There was a crowd watching. Another guy pushed through and hit the guy in the black T-shirt in the ribs. I recognized it was Austin as he grunted on the ground. I pushed past Kael and he grabbed my arm.

"Stay here." He put his palms on my shoulders and moved me a few feet away before he disappeared into the crowd. There were three trucks parked in the cul-de-sac and about ten people huddled together, cheering and booing.

I tried to figure out where we were. The street was a row of similar houses, all quiet and with the porch lights on. There were a few people outside, yelling to stop the fighting and saying that they had called the Military Police. We weren't on post, but we were right outside the gate, so if the cops came it would be Military Police, not civilian. It was the last place my brother needed to be getting caught fighting.

I scanned my surroundings quickly, on my way to find Kael and Austin in the crowd. I shoved to the front of the adrenaline-fueled chaos trying to reach Kael in the middle of the brawl. He pushed one of the guys off Austin and Austin swung at him in the air.

"Stop it!" I recognized Katie's voice before I saw her. I beelined toward her.

"Come on, Nielson, let's get out of here!" someone said in the background. A couple more lines of toxic encouragement were thrown out before I saw Kael block my brother from getting hit in his ribs again. I screamed.

"Stop it!" Katie yelled again. I reached where she was standing, close to the fight, her face streaked with mascara tears.

"What happened?" I asked, grabbing her by the shoulders. Kael was yelling Austin's name, trying to break up the fight.

"My ex, and Austin—" She started crying hysterically. It was useless trying to talk to her and I kept moving through the crowd.

Sirens whirred through the air as Austin got his arms around one of their necks and brought them to the ground. Kael was shoving a guy with a bloody nose toward the crowd. They started to scatter, except Austin and the guy he was wrestling in the grass. One by one, the trucks pulled away, Katie with them. I locked eyes with her as she climbed inside the cab of one of the trucks. This had everything to do with her and there she went, driving away from the storm.

I yelled Austin's name as she passed. Begging him to stop, to get up and get in the fucking truck! Kael grabbed Austin by the waist and tossed him to the side. He propped himself up on his elbow, sitting up, ready to go back at it.

"Austin, STOP!" I screamed again, desperate to connect with him, to snap him out of this before it was too late. If he got arrested again, he would be fucked. The siren cut off and the voices got louder. There was a small group of onlookers left outside now, mostly neighbors yelling and arguing all at once; it was complete chaos.

Everything happened so fast.

The MPs rushed out of their cars, heading straight for us. I screamed as they got closer, and I realized they were going for Kael. I tried to run toward him as my brother was shoved to the ground. An elbow or fist was flying toward my face, so I lifted my hands up to block myself and heard Kael's voice booming.

"Not her!" His voice shook me.

When I couldn't see him anymore, I panicked. I didn't even know if I had been hit or not.

"I was breaking it up! I don't have a weapon!" I heard Kael's voice again and my eyes found him.

I was no longer thinking about shielding myself. The only thing on my mind when I saw an MP reach for his black baton was Kael. The officer's focus was on him as the other two officers approached. Kael was on the ground and about to be blindsided, as the officers got closer. *His leg!*

He would have direct contact with Kael and Kael wasn't the violent one here.

Another scream rang through the air; it was a woman's voice.

The officers turned to me. I looked at Kael again, then for Austin, who had found his way to the Bronco. He managed somehow to lift his drunk ass up inside and lie down. Hiding from it all.

While one of the officers stepped toward me and the others to Kael, I moved quickly, shoving myself in front of him. He grabbed me by the shoulders and tried to push me out of the way, but I put up a fight.

"STOP!" I screamed, recognizing that I had been the one screaming the whole time. "FUCKING STOP! HE DIDN'T DO ANYTHING!"

My pleas finally got through to two of the MPs, who then stopped the one with his weapon out. The tallest of the officers cursed and shoved at his partner, and I wondered how the hell these power-tripping assholes could possibly be protecting anyone. I couldn't fathom why they were even going after Kael in the first place.

"What the fuck is your problem? He wasn't even involved! He was trying to break it up! Give me your badge number or whatever I can fucking report you with!" I shoved the shorter officer who was holding the baton with everything in me. He lost his footing and stumbled back. The other two were staring at me but weren't moving. I couldn't control my anger. I tasted salty tears on my tongue and all I could think about was grabbing the baton from this fucker's hand and bashing his head in with it.

"Karina, no!" Kael's voice brought me out of my blind rage. "Come here," he said, softer this time.

Everything was still blurry as it slowed down, but Kael was safe now, though limping to the curb, calling for me again. I went to him and sat a few feet away, catching my breath and trying really fucking hard to calm down. Kael's hands were holding the bottom of his pants tightly around his ankle.

"Are you okay?" I asked him. I blinked away the tears that were stinging the corners of my eyes. I had dirt or something in them.

Kael nodded. "Are you?"

He had a cut above his eye, and it made murderous waves of anger flow over me to see him hurt. "Yes, but you're not. I want to fucking kill them. How dare they come at you!"

He groaned, still rubbing his ankle. Kael's hands were visibly shaking as he lifted them up and balled them into fists. After a few seconds, he opened his eyes and went back to rubbing near his ankle.

"Do you want me to look at it?" I began to offer.

"No. I'm fine." Kael stopped me in mid-sentence, yanking the pants all the way down to the top of his sneaker.

He looked past me, then to my eyes. "They're coming. Answer their questions and try to stay calm. If you don't, it will only incite them further."

The three MPs were walking over to us, so I didn't say anything until they began their questioning. I thought about calling my dad, weighed the possible pros and cons, but couldn't bring myself to do it. I heeded Kael's warning and tried my best to stay calm. It was so infuriating and difficult, but I managed for a while.

"Let me see some ID, soldier."

"So you're telling me you two just happened to show up here and you know the Fischer boy?"

"He's my brother. And like I told you, we came here to stop the fight," I snapped at them. Kael's hand touched my leg, gently squeezing. I again tried to be calm.

While they wrote whatever bullshit down on their little note-pads, I glared a hole through their skulls. Kael was silent, but I could feel that he wasn't okay. I had finally caught my breath, and the shock of it all was beginning to set in the longer we waited for them to continue their interrogation. Kael answered everything with an even tone, despite the situation and the fact that he'd done nothing wrong and was nearly fucking beaten by them. If anything, I should have been the focus of their animosity, having screamed and put my hands on an officer. That should have landed me in the back of a car pending an arrest. But no—no consequence for me, it was only about Kael.

Apart from Kael, they seemed to be more interested in how we knew Austin than in the fact that Austin was the one who'd caused all of this. In that moment, I couldn't have cared less about my escape-master brother, who needed to pay for his crimes. I almost told them where he was hiding. I was that mad. Kael sat there with such stillness. He barely blinked as he answered their questions in a controlled, flat, but polite voice. He refused to let them get the best of him, I assumed. I wished that one day I would be as emotionally disciplined as Kael. His eyes were steady but somehow I felt that he wasn't as calm inside as he appeared to be. The cold night air made little puffs of smoke come out of all of their mouths. I decided that the three of them were now my mortal enemies and I would NEVER forget their names: Solomon, Kruger, and Deek. Especially Solomon, the troll-like man wielding a baton with an evil behind his eyes that enraged and terrified me. Give a man power and he'll rule, then ruin the world, my mother always told me.

She was proving to be more right every day.

The temperature had dropped significantly since we'd arrived. I had lost track of what time it was and how long we had been there. I was still in my work clothes, but my adrenaline kept me from being cold. I paced next to Kael as he still sat there, his legs extended in front of him.

The other guy involved in the fight had already left without being questioned; it was only Kael's identification they had collected and scanned. Their awareness of Austin's name triggered a connection to our dad, so they didn't even bother to look for my brother. Nor did they seem to care who Austin's assailant was, and they didn't go after him either.

When I quietly told Kael it wasn't fair, that this was all completely wrong and had to be against regulations, he explained that if I wanted to survive here next to an Army post my whole life, I shouldn't question authority, that it wasn't safe. Things were the way they were, and I wasn't going to change it.

"If you want to fix things, go for something that's possible. Smaller. You're not going to change what's ingrained into American culture."

"And that's it. You're just going to take it?"

"You know you're lucky that after putting your hands on an officer you don't have a bullet in your head. If I had done that it wouldn't be the case." Kael's eyes darted from my face to the night sky, but when the men looked back at us, he was composed again.

The questions continued and Kruger rolled his eyes at me when I got choked up talking about the situation with my brother—his getting mixed up with the wrong girl again, drinking too much, getting jumped by the not-ex ex-boyfriend. He was scribbling down everything I was saying while holding a recording device between his middle and index fingers. It felt like hours had passed. My brother was lucky to have slid off.

We were close to being able to leave the scene when the MPs put away their notepads and got back into their patrol cars. Kael stood up when they reversed and pulled away. I felt like crying as they left, and my chest heaved as their cars got smaller and smaller in the distance. I couldn't believe the way they behaved and the way they'd treated Kael. It made me shiver thinking about the way their American flag patches glowed under the bright streetlights. My throat was dry and on fire when we climbed back into Kael's truck. The empty street seemed spooky now, eerily still, as if nothing had happened at all. Everyone was gone, except us.

# CHAPTER **FORTY-NINE**

"Are you sure you're not hurt anywhere?" I asked Kael again.

"I'm sure."

Austin was asleep in the back of Kael's truck with his mouth wide open. Or maybe he was blacked out, I didn't know for certain and the only reason I even gave a shit was because I wanted to cuss him out. His face was gray, his lips dry, and his palms were a little bit clammy when I reached back to check them.

"He's an idiot. Why does he do this?" I felt so exasperated.

"I think he's more than drunk," Kael observed.

"What do you mean?" I lowered my voice so Austin wouldn't hear us if he woke up.

"He seems like he had something more than alcohol. I've seen a lot of guys fucked up on all kinds of stuff. Mendoza's one of them. I know what I'm talking about, and this is more than liquor and weed. Mendoza doesn't do the shit anymore, but he was on pills for a while, too."

I looked back at Austin again. "I appreciate your concern, but he's not on drugs. Weed maybe, but that's it. I've seen him way worse than this. He's a professional partier. If he doesn't wake up by the time we get to my dad's, I'll wake him up."

"Fine. You know him better than I do and we've both had a long night." He gave in as we pulled onto my dad's street. I wondered how long it would take for word to reach my dad. Days? Hours?

I ended up waking Austin to have him sit upright while we drove through the gate. He managed to keep his eyes open long enough to have our IDs checked and then he fell back asleep for the few minutes' drive to our dad's. I thought about taking him to my house, but I didn't want to look at his face right now and, really, I wanted Kael to stay over tonight.

Kael swore he was physically okay and half carried Austin into my dad's house and up the stairs. Kael had just tucked Austin into his bed when I shook my brother's shoulder. He opened his eyes and groaned, and Kael took over, asking him questions to check his cognitive awareness: When was his birthday? What was his address? Austin answered each one in a slurred version of his voice, using our dad's house as his address. Kael shined the flashlight from his phone over Austin's pupils and felt his forehead before standing up from the edge of the bed. Kael really did everything in life so thoroughly, even taking care of my drunken idiot brother.

"You'll be okay, but you need to drink water tomorrow. A shitload. And lay off excess of anything. Trust me, man." He leaned down over my brother. Austin smiled goofily at him.

"Indulgence in anything never ends well. Get your shit together or you're going to fuck up your life." Kael was serious, and his focus was on Austin's drunk smile turning into a sad one.

"I know. I'm done drinking," Austin said, followed by, "Gonna sleep it off . . . drink water in morning . . ." His eyes fluttered closed.

"What was that about?" I looked at Kael with harsh eyes as we walked down my dad's lawn. Austin was barely coherent and didn't defend himself or make excuses like he usually would have. *My brother on drugs?* He could barely afford to get his hair cut, let alone buy drugs and keep up with his love of alcohol and Chipotle.

"I'm only trying to help," Kael said.

"Well, don't. Or at least talk to me about it first before you say something like that to him again."

"Really, that's what you're saying to me right now?"

I was defensive and Austin was my twin. He wasn't on heavy drugs. He knew better than that. He just drank way more than he ever should have and didn't know when to stop.

"I think it's best if neither of us talk," I said, trying to regulate my emotions, but not doing a great job of it.

We got into his truck and kept conversation to a minimum. His brows were pulled, his eyes deep in thought. I knew my behavior was unfair and I didn't know if I could stop it. I was hurt and embarrassed and not exactly great at controlling my acting out. Another thing to send my mom a thank-you postcard for if I ever got an address for her someday. This wasn't Kael's fault, I knew that. I needed to grow the hell up and stop lashing out. I would break the cycle, even though it was really fucking hard. Regardless of our sticky relationship, Kael and I were friends and I cared about and respected him enough to stop myself from doing what I would normally do, taking my hurricane of emotions out on everyone around me.

He had been through enough: the MP nearly took a nightstick to his already injured leg! The scene had been horrifying and the memory of it was a hundred times worse. It had to be a thousand times worse for Kael. But how dare I make this about me or Austin!

"It's so messed up of me to be rude to you right now. Let's not talk about my brother tonight? I'm sorry. We've . . . well, you've been through a lot. I'm really sorry for the way I responded. I know you're coming from a good place," I reassured Kael, reaching for his hand to calm me. I hesitated with my hand hovering above his, tempted but timid. His fingers reached up, wrapping around mine. They were warm and familiar, threaded through mine, and I felt grounded again. I didn't know if he would let go or not, but if he did, I would respect that and not touch him again. He didn't, though; he rearranged our fingers so he would drive safely, but he didn't let go.

"I'm sorry for all of this. Really sorry. I can't believe what just happened. You must be traumatized."

"Enough saying sorry. I'm used to trauma." He relied on humor to soften hard things, and it worked.

"I'm serious. You did nothing wrong. By standing up for my brother, you got forced into a shitty and dangerous situation. It's so fucked up how they have a little bit of power and they abuse it. We should have stayed at dinner and let Austin figure it out. You didn't have to rescue him."

"That's my job. Literally. To protect the freedom of civilians." He smiled. He was being sarcastic, but his words were still somewhat true. The irony wasn't lost on me.

"Do you really think that's what you're doing? In the Army?" I hesitated to ask, afraid that my words would come off as insulting. I didn't mean them that way, and I knew how sensitive a topic this could be for him. If he didn't respond, I would change the subject and not pressure him. But if he did, I'd be grateful for the insight into his beliefs.

He didn't answer right away, so I counted my breaths while he turned the truck on and blasted the heat. It was so loud and blew cold air that hadn't warmed up yet.

"I can't speak for every single service member, but I know that I try to do what's right, with good intentions. When you put enough humans in the same place, there are going to be some bad ones. But in my case, I never went out of my way to hurt anyone, I never abused my power like some do." The look on his face was one of a lost boy. A soldier away from war, but still not at home.

Nothing I could say would match the gravity of what he was saying. A simple *Thank you for your service* wouldn't do.

"And you're still willing to die for the cause?" I asked.

He lifted our connected hands to his lips. He kissed the back of mine and I closed my eyes. A small comfort.

"Yes," he said. The word felt like a flame against the back of my hand.

"Please don't." I opened my eyes to see him staring through me.

"It's not like I plan to. But there's—"

I interrupted him by moving our hands to cover his mouth.

"Let's keep it at that," I begged. I couldn't think about him going anywhere except across the state of Georgia.

"Deal." He leaned back against the seat. "For now, at least."

I didn't want to read too much into his comment. It felt like a warning so it made me pause, but I blocked myself from digging into it. I focused on him. On his warm eyes, his careful and callused hand holding mine. Even inside of the eye of a storm, he could make me feel like I was safely planted. It was all about perception, and mine could have used a dose or two of reality. But instead of searching for the ground, I was floating in the sky with the brightest star of all. My mom's voice echoed in my head as I leaned over and kissed Kael: *The brightest stars burn the fastest, so we must love them while we can.* She told me that only once, but all these years later I still remembered it.

I touched his cheek with my free hand, running my fingers over his skin. The soft scar tissue above his eye, but below the fresh cut there, the harshness of his jawline.

"Are you okay, *really*?" I asked, loading the question this time with extra meaning.

He laughed a breath through his nose and looked straight out of the windshield. "Maybe someday I will be."

"Let's go home?" I asked Kael, no longer wanting to pressure him with conversation.

He nodded in agreement, and I hoped he would come in and stay the night of his own accord, without me having to ask. We drove home in the most peaceful silence. My eyes closed again, and by the time we made it to my house I was dreaming of a place where I could keep Kael safe.

# CHAPTER **FIFTY**

I don't know what I'd do without my job. It wasn't only about paying bills—although God knows there was that. It was about turning
the key in the front door, switching on the lights, making sure we
had fresh towels and were stocked with oils. Each little task took
me out of myself and helped me connect to the world around me.
I was sure of my skills as a massage therapist and proud of what I
could do to help people disentangle the knots of their own lives. I
needed that more than ever today, as I tried to disengage from the
anxiety that hadn't gone away from last night. One minute I was
listening to music with Kael and the next I was being interviewed
by aggressive military police.

Mali understood why I was late. She had urged me to take the
day off when I called to tell her what had happened, but I couldn't
bring myself to do that. Kael didn't stay over at my house after
all. He didn't even come inside. He woke me up, walked me to
the porch, and touched his hand to the top of my arm as his
good night. We were back to just friends now that the moon was
replaced by the sun.

He texted me that he had discharge appointments on post all
day, and I guessed that meant he was getting closer and closer to his
release from the Army. He asked if I had to work today and I told

him yes, until late afternoon. He didn't ask what I was doing after work, so I didn't volunteer any more information. I was trying to keep things cool even though I truly hated being away from him. I was already embarrassed from having called him while I walked to work. He didn't pick up, of course, and I left a nervous voicemail that I tried to delete but pressed the wrong button and sent it. I also couldn't stop constantly checking my phone between clients and even once during a treatment for his answer. I took a few extra seconds after covering the client's eyes with a warm towel. And finally, halfway through my shift, I got a text from Kael—very brief and wanting to know if I had plans for dinner.

I had texted my brother, too, trying to figure out what the hell happened last night. It was unbelievably stupid—he could have been badly hurt or arrested. And Kael was nearly assaulted by the MPs, and risked ruining his good standing and discharge plans. I needed to make sense of why Austin had gotten himself in that situation over this girl. It was so stupid. I could barely stand it. I thought about going by my dad's and dragging my brother out of the house to interrogate him—but now that Kael was asking about dinner, I decided I'd much rather spend the evening with him than with my brother or alone with a frozen pizza and a half-bottle of wine.

Austin
**I'll come by tonight. If you want, come get me.**

Kael
**How late will you be there?**

I was excited to read another text from Kael during my shift, but now disappointed to see that Austin wanted to come over for the evening. I was scheduled to work until four, but I would slip out an hour early if I didn't have a walk-in by three. Maybe I would have time to see Austin before having dinner with Kael.

Kael texted that he wouldn't be finished with all of his meetings until after five anyway. I invited him to come over around six thirty p.m., and offered to buy him dinner to even out his paying for my food the last time. I didn't have money for much, but we could order in something tonight, and the next time I got paid, I could take him to a nicer place. Next time. The words sent a shiver of a warning through me. I really, really needed to stay in the present with Kael, or we wouldn't fit anywhere at all. There was no future and I doubted I would ever see him again after his discharge and the arrival of Elodie's baby. Phillip would be home and everything would go back to the way it was. I would be alone in my house again.

While waiting for my next client to undress and get comfortable before their treatment, I texted my brother to confirm that we needed to talk and that he'd better not fucking flake on me. I was more tired today than usual. I hadn't slept very well after Kael dropped me off. For some reason, I lay in bed thinking only of the shitty things in my life. I didn't have a typical family, or a loving boyfriend. I didn't have Instagram-worthy brunches with a big group of girlfriends. Not that I even really wanted that, but the option had never presented itself. But what I did have, for now, was Kael, and I started to reread his texts when I saw one from Austin letting me know that he got a ride and was on his way over to my house.

I would still be at work for at least an hour, but I told him my door was unlocked. Kael's by-the-books voice was in my head telling me to keep my door locked at all times, whether I was gone or at home. He seemed way too concerned, but I had downloaded the neighborhood security app when I moved in and it was pretty damn terrifying to get an alert every hour for a break-in or assault. Stolen dog, drunk driver, drunk soldiers fighting at a bar—it was so overwhelming that I turned my notifications off after three days. I knew the world was a lot darker than I wanted to believe it was, but I still wanted to have hope that we didn't need to shut our doors and lock ourselves away from our neighbors and community. I hated the idea that I couldn't leave my front door open with just the screen between me and everything outside. I wanted to hear the sound of cars, people talking and connecting as they walked down the little strip of shops across the street, the roll of thunderstorms, and the calm patter of the rain. Even honks and sirens were a part of the soundtrack of my life.

Austin was sitting on my couch, shoes off, hat on. I had thought about what I would say to him as I walked home from work. He looked bright and awake, much different from the way he looked last night, when Kael laid him in his bed. Austin pepped up when I walked in, grinning at me, already playing for my forgiveness. He was conniving back when we were seven, and even now not much had changed. Well, our family had changed a lot, our lives were turned upside down when our mother left us and a woman we didn't know moved into our house before our mom even had a chance to come back. But Austin was still a brat.

"How was work?" he asked.

I stepped over his legs. He was sprawled across nearly the whole couch, and I maneuvered to the small available space at the other end and sat down.

"It sucked. It was fine, but it sucked. What the hell happened last night?"

"It was a misunderstanding. I'll be fine as soon as I eat. What can you cook for me?"

I reached out to feel his forehead and rolled my eyes. "What can I cook for you? You should be asking what can you, Austin, make for me. And that's not an answer to my question. I need details and I need you to stop getting yourself and other people in trouble. Kael could have really gotten hurt, Austin. This isn't a game."

He pouted for a second before nodding. "I know, I know. Let me order food. I have fifty bucks. We can get pizza."

I shook my head. I definitely didn't feel like cooking, but my brother needed to eat. I wasn't going to let Austin leave here without him telling me what the hell happened last night.

"I have dinner plans and you need to save your money. Let's make you something," I suggested.

I stood up and waited for him to follow me into the kitchen. The sunlight pouring through the windows made that room at least ten degrees warmer.

"I have pasta and a few things in the fridge that are going to go bad soon. Let's use up what I have." I winked at him. "You should save your money for a haircut." I pointed to his uncharacteristically long hair. I sort of loved when his hair was long, the opposite of a soldier, away from danger. Or was he?

"How did you get here, anyway?" I opened the cabinet and pulled out a pot. I knew I had pasta in my pantry and tomatoes on the counter that were nearly too ripe.

"Martin dropped me off."

The pot slipped from my hands and fell into the sink. Water splashed up at me. "Martin?"

I turned the water off and looked at my brother. "How?"

My brother rolled his eyes and looked at me like I was making a mountain out of a molehill by asking him that. I had every reason to, especially after last night.

"I called him to say sorry for being a shitbag last night." Austin was that way. He would put you in a crappy situation but not entirely on purpose, and he would always actually feel bad about it.

"How did you get his number?"

"Mendoza gave it to me."

I sighed. My small circle was becoming more and more tangled.

"Are you and Mendoza close? I knew you were friends before, but have you stayed in touch?"

Austin nodded and the screen door creaked. Elodie's voice chirped through the house, cutting the conversation off before my brother could respond.

"Karina?"

"In here!" I answered, as she came in, her face looking more tired than usual.

"I got home just in time, it's about to pour!" She sat down at the table next to Austin and he gave her a big smile.

"We're making dinner. You hungry?" he asked her.

I laughed, turning around to them. "Correction, I am making dinner. For Austin. Pasta with . . . well, random stuff, but it'll be good."

I turned the stove on to boil the water and started to dig through the fridge to see what random vegetables I had to throw into the pasta sauce. Carrots. Even though Austin was like a child when it came to food, if I chopped them up small enough he wouldn't notice them. Hell, even if he saw me chopping them, he probably wouldn't notice.

Austin and Elodie started basic small talk, how unpredictable the rain was and how the weather people never got the forecast right, that Austin had a headache and that Elodie's hands were starting to ache each day after work. The pain was increasing quickly, and she was a little worried. Austin touched the tips of her fingers and she winced.

"Sorry." He let go, looking like a puppy who'd chewed apart a favorite shoe.

"It's okay," she assured him, verbally petting his head. "I have about ten minutes until I have to meet Martin; he's with Julien and Gloria."

I turned around faster than I meant to, coming comically close to chopping the tip of my finger off. I set the knife toward the back of the cutting board, facing away from me.

"Martin, Kael Martin?" I asked her, somewhat puzzled. He told me he had meetings on post until five, but he was with Austin maybe an hour ago; now he's somewhere with Mendoza's wife and baby, and Elodie is going to meet up with them?

Elodie nodded. "He picked them up from home and dropped them off at the doctor. Kael's been spending all his time on post for his discharge stuff. I offered to take them home since Mendoza's on twenty-four-hour duty. I haven't met Gloria, but I'm hoping to make mom friends." Elodie's voice became more and more exhausted as she finished her sentence.

"Oh. Yeah. Gloria seems cool." I turned back around and continued chopping the carrot, noticing that the water in the pot was beginning to boil. My mind drifted to Kael as Elodie and Austin started talking about some park she saw on Instagram. So Kael must have driven back and forth to help them out. Of course he did. I felt the little nudge between my lungs as I thought of how much I liked the softness of his actions and how they spoke infinitely louder than his words.

I realized that Kael and I don't talk much about his military life day to day. It's more about the big picture of his life, but even then, the conversation is mostly focused on me. Elodie seemed to talk to Kael every day, and I wondered what he might have told her about us. I thought about mentioning to Elodie how often I'm hanging out with him. *"Hey, Elodie, Kael and I are. . . friends . . . and we kissed more than once. I kinda want to kiss him again, but we're just friends . . . okay, thanks?* But since I can't even explain what the hell we're doing, there was really nothing to say to her.

Elodie's loud laugh suddenly interrupted my thoughts. Clearly, I had missed one of Austin's jokes, but I noticed how he had managed to charm her. The banter between the two of them was a pleasant distraction.

"Mom friends in the Army can be brutal. My mom got treated like shit by the wives around us. She hated it, that's for sure," Austin told Elodie. It felt a bit too personal, a bit too vulnerable for him to say so casually in my kitchen.

"It's hard. I just want them to like me, is that too much to ask?" she whined, laying her forehead on the wooden kitchen table. She lifted it and gently put it back down, not actually touching, but pretending to bang the table a few times for dramatic effect. "I feel like I'm in primary school again but this time it's worse, because I don't know anyone, they are speaking another language, and I can't even run home to my parents," she sighed.

I couldn't imagine Elodie not being liked by the women she desperately wanted to befriend. They were the only people who would truly understand her situation and be able to relate in a much deeper way. I was proud of myself for wanting my friend to be happy and loved and have as many friends as her little pure heart could hold; the thought of her happiness didn't make me jealous at all. Unlike my father, who needed to possess the people closest to him under the pretense of love. I tried really fucking hard to not be like him in that way. I wanted the things I love to flourish, uncaged and free. He made the mistake of marrying someone whose mind, body, and spirit were wild. She couldn't be owned, and he needed to collect things. While my mother couldn't be tamed, Estelle was primed to be a precious and pampered doll—a beautiful brunette with eyes for him and his world only, a prize he could display, polished and perfect.

"What time is it?" Elodie asked, eyeing the downpour of rain through the window. "Gloria was supposed to be here with Julien by now."

"Have either of you seen their baby? He's so cute." Austin strummed his fingers on the table.

"Only in pictures!" Elodie responded immediately in a high-pitched voice. "He looks just like his—" She stopped in mid-sentence and her face lit up; so did my brother's.

Elodie's hand shot up into the air and waved. I turned to see who they were looking at as the back door opened. Kael stood, half in, half out, dressed in his uniform, his cap hanging out of his front pocket. I quickly ran through my appearance in my head. I was still in work clothes, with frizzy, air-dried hair. Even though I'd planned to be a bit more polished when I saw him, when we made eye contact, my self-consciousness instantly disappeared. It was wild, the effect he had on me. All of the spiraling thoughts slid from my mind as he took a step forward and a small child walked in behind him. The boy had dark hair, wet from the rain. He was as cute as Elodie and Austin had gushed, and Mendoza's wife, Gloria, followed behind him. She was beautiful—of course she was— and radiant, despite the dampening rain. She had big, dark eyes and thick, long hair. She was dressed in a white turtleneck tucked into dark jeans. Her jeans were baggy on her frame and her smile oozed confidence and sweetness, almost as if she was an old friend, though I had never spoken to her.

"Hi." Elodie addressed the child first. "I'm Elodie." She was using a baby-talk voice and the boy smiled brightly. Okay, he was actually the cutest child I had ever seen. He looked so much like Mendoza, but also like his mother. Big, bright brown eyes and thick lashes.

Austin stood up to hug Gloria and I waved awkwardly. It was clear that Austin knew her well by the way he smiled at her and the fact that he wasn't hitting on her. My kitchen felt smaller than ever as Gloria glared at Austin and playfully hit his arm.

"I heard you got Martin smoked today for what you did last night. Get your shit together." She spoke to my brother like a sibling.

What Gloria said took a few seconds to hit me. Kael had been reprimanded and humiliated, publicly, at work, but wasn't going for my brother's throat? I guess no one was immune to Austin's charm. I was used to seeing women, even myself, hover over him and contort themselves to accommodate his varied behaviors and volatile personalities—outwardly strong, yet sometimes extremely fragile.

"I knowwwww," Austin whined, and ran his hands through his messy hair. "I'm sorry, truly. I'm not going near that girl again," he promised all of us. When his eyes landed on me, I mentally cussed him out in hopes that the whole twin-telepathy thing would work.

"You better. Are you coming over to grill with us?" Gloria asked Austin.

"Hell, yeah," he responded without hesitation.

"You can come, too." Gloria was looking at me. "We're going to chill at our house, if you want to join us."

It felt nice to be included, but I really didn't want to be around anyone other than Kael today. I didn't know how to respond in a way that wasn't rude. I wanted to keep open the chance of being invited again. My brain was failing me, not coming up with the words fast enough, when Kael spoke. He was answering Gloria, but his eyes were on me.

"Actually, we have plans. And we can't move them." He shrugged and looked at her.

"Next time, then." Thankfully, Gloria's smile was just as warm as it was when she arrived.

I nodded to Gloria, tentatively accepting her future invite.

I would be sure to thank Kael for saving me from my own social awkwardness when they left. Honestly, I wanted them all to leave, even adorable little Julien. I wanted to be alone with Kael.

# CHAPTER FIFTY-ONE

"Sorry, Kare. Next time, dinner's on me." Austin gave me a hug and said another quick sorry against my ear.

He was out the door before I could respond. I waved goodbye to Gloria as she left carrying Julien. Elodie double-kissed me and gave me a puzzled look before opening her umbrella and following Gloria out of the house. As their voices trailed off, Kael shut the door, locking not only the main door, but the screen door, too. Just like that, the kitchen was empty.

"Are you keeping something out or locking me in?" I asked him, sarcasm coating my voice.

He laughed and brought his gaze to meet mine. I nearly squirmed when he focused in. "Both."

I couldn't move the smile from my face, and Kael's doubled in size, bigger than I'd ever seen. Finally, a level-ten smile from Kael Martin! I won. I didn't know what, but in my head there were buzzers going off and neon signs saying !!WINNER!! and I knew that something special was mine. We stood there for a few seconds, taking each other in, the rain outside filling our silence. Kael's eyes went from my scalp to my socks and back up to my face before he spoke again.

"Hi."

"Hi." I smiled a smile that was so big that I couldn't close my mouth, even when I tried.

"How are you?" he asked, nudging his shoulder to mine.

"I'm okay. How are you? You seem pretty happy for someone who got smoked today." My brows drew together. I nearly apologized for my brother again, but Kael's voice in my head stopped me.

His smile stayed as he replied. "It's done now. I needed the exercise anyway." He laughed, and I felt relief and guilt at the same time.

"Kael, I'm—"

"If you say sorry, I'm going to . . . well, I don't know what I'll do exactly, but don't apologize for your brother," he told me in a voice so patient that I couldn't help but nod in agreement.

His face was freshly shaven, and his thick eyebrows were perfectly wild above his bright eyes. He was still grinning. Something about him felt different, lighter. I was confused, but so happy to be this close to him.

"Did you have a lot of meetings today?" I asked, shuffling my soft socks against the tile floor.

"I did."

"And played taxi?"

He nodded. "A lot of driving. How was work?" he asked, turning the conversation back to me.

"It was okay. Same as always," I told him, feeling the floodgates open in my mind. I tried to hold them up, but knew it was a lost cause.

"I was bored, honestly. I'm starting to feel a little . . . distracted at work."

Kael's brow lifted. "Distracted? How so?"

I felt my cheeks flush and my heart began to pick up speed. *You! You distract me!*

"Just life." I told half the truth.

Kael was good at reading me, so I looked away from him and stared at the boiling water on the stove. I had wasted my time cooking for my brother. Typical.

"What were you cooking?" Kael changed the subject. He was looking at the skillet of food on the stovetop.

"Kitchen-sink pasta, my specialty when food in the fridge is about to go bad." I waved my arm in the air. "For Austin, but he left, so I might as well not even finish it."

Kael took a step toward the hot skillet. "I'm starving. I didn't eat anything today because I was too busy."

"Oh, you don't want to eat my cooking, trust me. Didn't you want to get dinner somewhere?"

He shrugged. "I'm easy. I'm good with staying in, if you are. And this smells really fucking good, honestly."

A tiny compliment and my confidence was soaring. I pointed to the simmering pasta sauce. "Why don't you try it first?"

"It can't be that bad," he teased, grabbing the ladle from the counter. He dipped it into the sauce and managed to make such a simple act insanely attractive.

"I wouldn't be so sure," I confessed.

"I've eaten MREs."

I remembered my dad bringing home a spaghetti-flavored MRE for my brother and me to try after his first deployment. It was such a novelty to see food made out of powder, and Austin and I got so excited. For years I tried to hold that fond memory with my father as close as I could. I almost told Kael about it instantly, but I didn't want to bring down the mood by talking about my dad.

I smirked as he brought the spoon to his lips for a second time.

"It's really good. Let's eat this?"

"If you're sure"—I shrugged and turned off the burner—"after the day you've had."

"Who said I had a bad day?" Kael asked, stepping closer. He put his arms on both sides of me and leaned in. His face was inches from mine.

*Would it be weird if I kissed him?*

*Will he remember kissing me when he's back in his hometown, beginning his new life? Would he miss me? Would he remember me at all?* The thoughts hurt me.

"I—" I couldn't recall what he had just said to me. I was too distracted by how close he was.

"I've been smoked before; everyone has. I'm taking this as a farewell from the Army. Plus, look how my day has turned around." He licked his lips, and I mirrored his action without a thought.

"You promise you're okay?" I asked one last time.

"Me?" He tapped his chest with his finger. It landed on his rank badge, front and center.

I nodded. My throat was dry as a bone. "Yes, you. After yesterday, after today, in general. I really hope you're okay," I said, meaning it.

He smiled again. "I'm fine. Are you worried about me?" he asked playfully.

I shook my head, avoiding eye contact. He dipped his head down to make my eyes meet his.

"Karina, I think you *are* worried about me."

The kitchen, my very small kitchen, felt as if it were shrinking by the second.

"I mean, I was worried, yeah. Last night was pretty damn intense. I feel like you should run away from me as soon as you can, before something worse happens to you."

He smiled and chewed his lip again. The scar above his brow

had darkened; I noticed the change of color. Some days it was more raised, others more purple. The cut he got last night was less pronounced today. I felt a little relief.

"I've been to war twice before the age of twenty-one. I can handle MPs, and Austin is . . . well, Austin." He sounded like he knew my brother well and, once again, I felt left out.

"Karina, Karina, Karina," he sang my name. There was a softness to the way it sounded that made me want to close my eyes. So I did.

Kael's voice carried on. "You keep apologizing for things you didn't do. I thought we were going to stop doing that," he teased.

I loved this mood he was in. I wanted to stay in a cloud of it forever. I was blissful long enough to get addicted, enough to crave it again until reality caught up with me. What was I doing? Literally, what the hell was I doing? I opened my eyes, closing the curtain on my daydreamy moment with Kael.

I somehow managed a voice. "You sound like my old therapist."

"Is that a good or bad thing?"

I thought about it for a second. "Both."

"Well, if I were your therapist, I would surely advise you to stay away from men like me."

I watched him as he nodded and inched closer to me. I wished I knew where we stood.

"Far, far away," he whispered.

My eyes grew wider as he neared. His mouth was saying the opposite of what he was doing. Something inside me burned to know more, to know everything about him.

"And what if I don't want to stay away?"

"It's wise advice. But you're the one paying the bill," he said.

It sounded like a warning, so I moved my head back, putting a little space between us to think straight.

"What exactly is it that I'm staying away from?" I asked, "An upstanding citizen who drives women and their children home from the doctor and goes to war to fight for our country?"

"A man who has no capacity to know what's right or wrong anymore. Someone who tears things apart"—he paused, and I could feel his warm breath flush against the apple of my cheek—"and doesn't stay to put them back together."

Kael's fingers were warm when they caressed my chin, tilting my head to see his full face. His breathing slowed and the air between us became more serious. The stakes were growing with each second that passed.

"A man who's a killer," he whispered.

Adrenaline shot through me and I held his eyes. "I . . . I don't know what to say to that."

"You don't have to say anything." Kael's eyes were on my lips as I nodded.

He kissed me the way I've only read about in poetry. I now understood what all the poets and writers complain about when they lose their love. This was that feeling they all chased, missed, remembered, would die for another chance to feel again. His lips opened and his tongue slid across mine. I would never forget this kiss, it was now a part of my DNA, the intensity of emotion, a rush unlike anything else I could explain. I wondered how anyone could possibly live after feeling this even once.

Kael's hands lifted me up onto the counter and my legs opened and he stood between them. His hands gripped the tops of my thighs as he devoured me, body first, then mind. His ACU jacket was crunchy between us, but I could still feel his heart pounding as I put my hand on it, next to the pocket. The way his heart danced under my palm felt like he was playing a song made just for me. This connection with him, this consuming connection, was otherworldly. I had never desired to be this close to someone before, not even when I was a teenager and confused infatuation with love. Pages of all the romance novels I had read, every scene from the dozens of rom-coms, all flicked and fluttered in my mind. They finally made sense.

His hands were pressing against my back, holding me to his chest. My mouth and entire being were docile in his hands as they cupped my ass, my hips, my neck. Whoever he was and whether or not I ever found out wasn't on my mind as I kissed him for the second, third, then the tenth time. He carried me to my room, never letting his mouth leave mine, and I used my foot to slam the door behind us. I ignored the little bell going off in my head, reminding me that I shouldn't fall for this soldier. My body ached, begging me to give in to its desire, and as he landed us on my bed, I let my mind go mute and allowed myself to lose control for once in my life.

# CHAPTER FIFTY-TWO

The heat and the sun woke me the next morning. Its brightness came with the dawn of a new way to begin my day, with someone else here. At first, I was confused when I woke up with Kael, his body running his usual insanely warm temperature. My little room was hot and steam filled the windows. My cheeks flushed with prickly heat, and I looked at him next to me. His eyes were closed, and his lips were ever-so-slightly parted. He was still in his pants and boxers; only his T-shirt and jacket were missing. He proved to be a gentleman who didn't even try to sleep with me. I couldn't decide if that was a chivalrous thing or an insult to my ego. Although we hadn't slept together, it had been the best night of my life.

I was grateful for his eyes being closed, as I couldn't stop smiling like a lovestruck idiot. I really was a goner. This was going to end horribly. He was so beautiful, thoughtful, gracious, kind, and brilliant, and all of that overpowered the horror of not having a future with him. People my age hooked up all the time; why was my brain acting like we had exchanged vows just because we'd shared the same bed?

Being greedy with our limited time, I used the tip of my finger to trace around his chin; the squareness of his jaw was an art form in itself. As I studied his face I noticed it was marked with little scars. Every one of them made me curious to know where it came from. The one above his eyebrow was deep, along with the one below his lip. I touched it gently; the skin was soft and puffy. Kael rumbled a little and turned his cheek, mumbling something about rocket ships.

Kael draped his arm around me, pinning me to the bed. There was something incredibly safe-feeling about being with him physically. I couldn't understand it, but the world seemed so far from us, my walls felt ten feet thick, my house made from iron and stone, not brick and drywall. I wondered if I should wake him up. I didn't know what time it was, but since I didn't have to work today, I craved a few more minutes with him in the silence.

There were so many things I wanted to do, and they all involved Kael. I hoped Kael didn't have another full day of appointments. I really, really didn't want my dreamlike time with him to prematurely come to a screeching, lonely halt. I continued to stare at every feature of his face, his bare chest, the tattoo on his forearm, and the nearby deep scar in the perfect shape of a bullet hole. I shivered and hoped I was wrong about that one. Thinking of him hurt was overwhelming and scary. I tried to analyze how it could be possible to feel this connected to another person after such a short stretch of time. How did I live before this? How would I after it? It was going to be so much worse when he left now that he'd stayed the night with me.

There wasn't a dull moment the entire night, and as our voices had quietly filled my room with our secrets, I finally realized how insanely rare it was to meet someone who understood me. When Kael opened his eyes, my endorphins rose and I smiled back at his sleepy, so, so swoony grin. He buried his face in my messy hair and groaned, pushing his body against mine. Did he want to kiss me again or was he hiding in embarrassment? My heart pounded as he lifted himself up and faced me.

"Hi." He spoke softly. His voice was tired and deep.

"Hi," I whispered back, wondering what the sun would bring.

Kael didn't say anything.

My paranoia began to grow. "I'm sorry if—"

He rolled on top of me, his arms on both sides of my head. He dipped his head down to look at me. With his mouth, Kael erased my doubts and thoughts as his lips moved down my jaw, across my collarbone. I closed my eyes.

After having an uninterrupted night with Kael, I wanted a thousand more. I wished we could stay in my bed for a week straight. I tried to savor every second we had, to make sure I would have something lasting to hang on to when he wasn't around. When my thoughts started to spiral again, I began to count the number of times Kael breathed in a minute. I pressed my hand against his chest the way I did once before, so I could feel his heart beating. His tongue made a line from the base of my throat and back up to my lips.

I groaned as he gently opened my mouth with his and kissed me again. I lost count of them; each one was somehow better than the last. It could have been minutes or hours before he gently pulled away from my mouth and kissed my forehead.

I ran through the endearing things I'd learned about him last night. He can't stand the sound of trains and loves hard candy but has never had a cavity in his life. That the only toothpaste he uses is cinnamon—not only does he hate the smell of peppermint, which I knew, but also the taste. He doesn't like sports, and has never watched an entire football game start to end. His favorite season is winter. Kael opened up like a thousand novels written just for me, and I longed for the chance to read them all.

"What's going on in that head of yours?" Kael kissed against my neck.

"That you're a library."

"A library? Is that a good thing?"

I nodded and he turned onto his side to face me, wrapping both of his arms around me and pulling me close to his chest. He gently stroked my hair, and my heart exploded from the sweetness of it. I couldn't keep my eyes open long when his fingers started to rub my scalp in back-and-forth motions, right above my hairline, the exact same way my mother used to do. Her fingers would circle my head until it prickled and went numb, helping me fall asleep.

"What are your plans for today?" Kael asked after a few seconds of silence.

"Nothing, actually." I couldn't see Kael's face because my head was on his chest. His fingers were rubbing my head, creating that calm numbing sensation that was my favorite part. It was such an intimate feeling that I hadn't felt since my mom left. I started to tell him that, but he spoke first.

"If you're up for it, I wanted to show you my place. I don't have PT or any appointments today. The duplex is a complete mess and in the middle of being renovated, but I wanted to take you there." He sounded shy by the time he finished.

I couldn't hide the excitement in my voice. "You do?"

"Yes, of course I do."

"I would love to see it."

"Cool." He smiled.

"Cool." I kissed his grinning mouth.

"You need more days off. Imagine if we had an entire week to ourselves, no family dinners, no work in our way," he said against my lips.

His fingers moved from my scalp to the ends of my hair. I loved the way his thick fingers wrapped around my dark strands, gently twisting between and around them. I felt so dazed by his attention, so content and warm. I realized that I could actually sleep if I wanted to. That was a first for me, to be so relaxed that I could fall asleep before the sun went down. It had everything to do with him.

Kael started humming a song and told me about this little-known band he found in a bar in Kentucky after he graduated basic training and how he recently heard their song on the radio. I smiled as he hummed a few more bars and started to kiss down his chin, around his collarbone and shoulders. His skin was so soft under my lips and his body shuddered when I kissed the scar tissue that framed his shoulder blade.

Kael's phone started to ring on the nightstand. He jumped up and I moved away as he grabbed it, my eyes reading the screen.

"It's Mendoza," he said, showing me the phone.

I nodded as he answered.

"Hey, you—" Kael started to speak, but he was cut off by shouting. "Hey, hey, man, slow down." Kael's voice suddenly was different; he was now Sergeant Martin.

"Where you are?" Kael was out of my bed, sliding his shirt down his chest. He grabbed his jacket from the floor and put it on.

I didn't know what to do as I sat there on the bed and Kael moved around me. He was totally focused on Mendoza, in full-on mission mode.

"I won't tell Gloria or anyone where you are." Kael looked at me. "Don't go inside. Just wait outside. I'll be there in fifteen max. Don't go back inside," he repeated.

I got out of the bed and moved toward Kael. He held his finger up to tell me to keep quiet.

"I'll be there soon, everything's fine. Don't talk to or call anyone else until I get there, you could get reported," Kael instructed.

He seemed to have such great empathy, his soul glowed from the inside. It astounded and impressed me. He was showing me what a thoughtful man looked like: beautiful brown skin, a-thousand-seas-wide sympathetic eyes, and a considerate heart. It struck me that I hadn't seen this in a man before—at least not in real life. But Kael showed me exactly what compassion looked like.

"Is everything okay?" I asked him. He nodded.

"Mendoza, he's drunk and started saying these guys were spying on him. He's slipping and I need to get there."

"Spying?"

Kael sighed, rubbing his forehead with the back of his hand. "Paranoia from constantly being in situations where people are trying to kill you," he said.

His words rattled me.

"I'm sorry I have to go." He kissed my forehead, then my cheeks, then my mouth. "I'll be back as soon as I'm done there."

"Do you want me to go with you?" I asked, knowing the answer, but wanting to offer anyway.

He shook his head. "I told him I wouldn't tell anyone. If he sees you, he won't trust me. I need to get there before he starts a fight." His fingers moved quickly to lace up his boots. He stopped tying them for a second and looked up at me. "I appreciate the offer, though."

I had a really bad feeling about whatever was going on. My stomach ached as he stood up and met my eyes.

"Don't worry about me, okay?" Kael tried to assure me.

"Right." I rolled my eyes at him. We both knew that worrying was my specialty.

I followed Kael through the hallway, to the kitchen door. The sun was so bright, it clashed with my thoughts. In my mind a storm was brewing.

"Mendoza will be okay, right?" I asked him. I was aware that I barely knew the guy, but I could tell how much he meant to Kael.

He nodded. "Yeah, Kare. He's going to be okay," he reassured me, and stepped outside.

"Lock the door!" I heard him say.

I smiled at that and the way he called me Kare. Only Austin and my mom ever called me that and I really, really liked the way Kael said it so effortlessly.

After I watched his Bronco pull out of my driveway, I returned to my room and fell into bed thinking about how many soldiers had demons chasing them long after they had left the battlefield. Home wasn't such a safe place for them once they returned. I drifted off to sleep wondering how many demons were chasing my soldier, and if they were too strong for him to defeat.

# CHAPTER **FIFTY-THREE**

When I opened my eyes, it was early evening and the sun was setting; it took me a few seconds to realize that Kael hadn't come back yet. I went to our text thread and there was nothing from him. A bubble of uncertainty filled my lungs. I'm sure he was okay and just busy handling Mendoza. He wasn't ghosting me, I told myself again. As I debated texting Kael, Elodie sent a picture of herself in a pink sweater with her short blond hair in two low pigtails. How adorable! When I asked her where she was, she said she was at another FRG gig, a cookout this time. And that she'd been invited on a girls' trip to Atlanta to do some shopping. She was excited to browse for baby clothes and the latest gear—but even more excited that she'd been included spur-of-the-moment to go along. I nearly asked her if she'd heard from Kael, but I didn't want to seem overly interested; she must already be wondering what the hell was going on between us.

I threw in a load of laundry before turning to the unwashed pile of dishes and glasses in the sink. I hated hand-washing and reminded myself that one day I would finally buy a dishwasher. I hadn't done much and had slept most of the day, but my head ached and I took a Tylenol and gulped down a glass of water before making my way back to my room. I lay on the bed, staring at the ceiling, thinking of Kael. I remembered the first day I saw him in the lobby at work—the mysterious client who later refused to take off his sweats or let me touch his right leg. Now he wasn't a stranger, but he still hadn't shown me his legs, not once. He was always dressed from the waist down, and I cared too much about his trauma to force him to explain. There were so many other beautiful parts of him that he didn't keep a secret. Maybe he would tell me, or even show me the rest, when he was ready.

I remembered how close we felt a few hours ago. The way I held his hand in mine. Holding his hand like that . . . touching each of his fingers, tracing the little creases around his knuckles . . . his hand in mine was the best remedy to ease the paranoia of the secrets he kept. I loved his hands—how big they were, how strong. I thought of how they held me, touched me, comforted me. I dozed off again and woke up to Kael standing over me, watching me sleep. He looked like a prince out of a movie, wearing a white T-shirt and gray sweats. Maybe I was groggy, maybe I was losing my mind, but he was so beautiful and I missed him so much. I yanked on his arm, bringing him to me.

"Hey." He curled his body into mine. I clung to him like he had been away at war.

"How is Mendoza?" I felt unsettled but didn't want to ruin the moment now that he was back. Silence fell between us. He took a deep breath and I held mine.

"Did you enjoy your nap?" he asked, completely ignoring my question.

I had to make a choice. Press him for an answer about Mendoza and risk him closing off and turning distant or let him decide what parts of him I could access.

I nodded, trying to keep my emotions at bay. I lifted my head up to kiss him and his arms wrapped around me, hugging my body as close to his as it could get.

"I missed you. Too much," he said against my forehead.

And even though I knew this was too good to be true and the red flags were piling up, I held on to him and decided to take whatever it was he would give me. I should have remembered that not all fairy tales end in happily ever after.

## CHAPTER **FIFTY-FOUR**

With Elodie off on her weekend girls' trip, Kael and I played house for a couple days, never leaving limbo. I begged off work, ensuring with Mali that my clients would reschedule. Kael and I stayed in the house and ordered food when we felt like it. He made me want to do nothing except lie next to him all day. Not even having sex, just listening to his theories about the world, how it began and how it would end. When he sensed the conversation was too heavy and too bleak, he switched topics to show me a YouTube video on the conspiracy that Shakespeare had a ghostwriter. I rolled my eyes, telling him that insulting Shakespeare was a crime in my house, and he lifted his body on top of mine, offering kisses to avoid any penalty.

What I felt for Kael was something between sweet infatuation and total annihilation. It was powerful and raw. He was as fierce as an animal, and yet so kind and gentle. He was a bundle of contradictions. Even so, it felt secure and calm to be with him, not the chaos that being in love advertised. I was happy in this moment, when I stopped thinking about the short time we would have together. It was terrifying to let my guard down, but it was thrilling to immerse myself in this intimacy with Kael.

As he slept on my chest, and again when he woke up in the middle of the night asking for someone named Nielson, then shouting

Phillip's name, he was drenched in sweat. He pulled me close to hug him, moved my hair from my ear, and whispered: "Run."

A chill went through my entire body, but I didn't move. I hugged him back and gently rubbed his shoulder, telling him that everything would be okay, even if I knew that was a promise I couldn't deliver. Kael's war trauma made my problems and worries feel small and insignificant. I made a commitment to myself that, because of Kael, I would confront my fears and stop letting the terrible unknown control everything. I deserved to let go and live—really live. And he deserved the version of me who didn't need an answer to every question.

We had spent all the prior afternoon, evening, and night in bed, then finally it was Sunday morning and I had to go to work in the late afternoon. I absolutely had to show up today, or Mali would probably come to my house and drag me to the spa herself. Kael and I had baked Elodie's can of cinnamon rolls for breakfast and I made a pot of coffee that tasted like shit, but I drank it anyway. The rolls were gooey and warm and yummy, even sweeter when Kael kissed me with the faint taste of icing on his lips.

"When this ends, what do we do?" I asked flatly.

"What ends?" He was quiet as the seconds ticked by, but I sensed he knew exactly what I was talking about. "We remember this," he finally said, sealing his words with a kiss.

I had lost count of them at this point. I wanted to start all over and have another first, second, third kiss with him.

We were behaving so domestically; I had lent Kael a set of Phillip's PT clothing from Elodie's bureau to wear while he washed his sweats and T-shirt in my kitchen laundry. I pushed a pile of my laundry out of his way to make room as he transferred his wet clothes from the washer to the dryer and then went back to my room to put on my jeans and a comfortable baggy sweat-shirt. A few minutes later, Kael appeared in my doorway with all my clean clothes, neatly folded, and asked where they should go. I shrugged and motioned to the dresser, and he set them down on top, then followed me into the bathroom. While I brushed my teeth he swished some mouthwash around his mouth, opt-ing for something antiseptic and medicinal in lieu of my minty toothpaste.

Making breakfast together, doing laundry, sharing den-tal hygiene: *This is what people who get married do*, I thought to myself. And Kael had even convinced me to go to the mall to fix my laptop. More old-married-couple behavior!

The local mall was crowded, and the parking lot was stressing me out as Kael circled in his giant truck, looking for a space. When he finally found one, he slowly and stealthily parked backward in a tight spot right next to a tall light post.

"I hate malls," I said, as we walked through the noisy entrance. The ceilings were low, every wall was brown or tan, and the lights were so freaking bright that I wished I had worn a hoodie so I could crawl inside it. There were people everywhere. Kael looked around and turned his face to me.

"Do you want to go back to the car, and I can take care of the laptop?"

I smiled. "How can you be so selfless?"

"It's no big deal. I know a tech guy who works here at a kiosk. He's really fast, cheap, and won't be shady." Kael dangled his keys as a last offer for me to escape the mall adventure.

I shook my head and kept walking.

He read the doubt on my face. "I'll do the talking."

"Yeah?" I asked, hiding my face from him. I'd never had a friend, let alone a boyfriend, who paid this much attention to the way I felt and went out of their way to make my life easier.

Kael didn't say anything, he just smiled and grabbed my hand. He looked so good, and I was with him. He liked me, he picked me, and that made me feel beyond special. I wished someone from my high school who had made fun of my weight or acne could see me now. Well, I looked like shit still, and Kael was way out of my league. I kept slowing down, looking for a mirror and regretting not having put makeup on before we left.

"You okay?" he asked, squeezing my hand a little.

I nodded. "I'm just thinking of all the reasons that you're too good for me and why you should be embarrassed to be holding my hand in public."

Kael's laugh was deep, coming from the core of his body. "What?" He held our hands up in the air, in an out-of-character move for him. My tummy twisted.

I let my thoughts turn into words. "You're totally out of my league." His expression was one of both confusion and calmness.

"Who's deciding this? Just you?"

I nodded.

"You couldn't be more wrong," he said, as we passed a pretzel stand. The smell wafted through the air and my stomach grumbled. How could I be hungry after eating half a container of cinnamon rolls? There was a long line for the pretzels and the food court of the mall was beyond packed. Voices filled the space, all the way to the ceiling, with babies crying against the background noise of deep fryers bubbling and burgers sizzling as we walked past Wendy's. A couple in front of us were arguing over losing a receipt for a jacket the woman had bought the man. They were in their forties, maybe, and I watched them as we walked behind them. They went from bickering to laughing and back to bickering. I imagined being a fortysomething with Kael, arguing in the mall over trivial things. I had to rein in my thoughts; they were way ahead of me, running wild.

"Almost there," Kael reassured me, stroking his thumb over the back of my hand in his.

As we got closer, I unlocked our fingers and wrapped both of my arms around one of his, gluing myself to his side. I couldn't remember the last time I had been around so many people at once, but I was relieved to have Kael with me, We approached a kiosk that looked like a jewelry counter, but instead of sparkling rings and necklaces, its glass cases held tablet and laptop brands I'd never heard of. There was a row of smart watches and cell phones in cases plastered with "deal" stickers, several of them announcing, "Fix your cracked screen here for cheap!"

The line was short, only one person ahead of us. And when the woman spoke, I immediately recognized her voice. Sure enough, Kael did, too, and as he said her name, I clung like a flea to his side.

"Turner?" He used his free hand to tap her shoulder.

"Martin!" Her face lit up at the sight of him. Not that I blamed her, but I felt possessive and unreasonably jealous. My lungs burned as she reached for him like she was going to hug him. I let go of his arm, moving a few feet away, defensively; if they started to hug in front of me, my eyes were going to melt off my face. Kael reached for the baggy sleeve of my sweatshirt to pull me close, dodging the hug she tried to give him. Her arms fell flat at her sides as he laced his fingers through mine. Her eyes instantly went blank, hiding any thoughts she might have been having; she was a soldier, after all. In most romances, this would be the chapter where I find out that Kael has a secret past with her or, worse, he pretends not to know me. He was confusing me by doing the opposite of what I'd expected. Why do I always assume the worst?

"What are you doing here, of all places?" Turner asked Kael, not looking at me. She was smiling again, focused on him.

Kael held up my laptop with the arm that wasn't holding my hand. "Her laptop is fucked up, so we came to fix it."

*We.* I breathed a sigh of relief.

Turner straightened her stance, and I was a bit terrified of how small I felt next to her. She was wearing makeup today and had her civilian clothes on, unlike when we ran into her at the commissary. Not that she didn't look great in her uniform, but wow, her personal style was cool. She was wearing a black halter that tied across the back, with cutouts on the sides that exposed a lot of skin. Her jeans were loose everywhere except her hips and butt. She looked like she belonged on an Instagram account full of "look at me" vacation pictures or in an engagement photo shoot with a man like Kael. She was definitely on his level, unlike me with my sloppy clothes and blotchy skin. I inched a little closer to Kael.

"This is Karina, you've met her," he introduced me.

I waved, offering a quiet hello.

She seemed to analyze every feature of my face and clothes. "Oh, Fischer's sister! Now I see it," she said, laughing. I hated that I didn't get her joke.

"You know my brother?"

She nodded, flipping her dark hair over her shoulder. Her fingernails were perfectly manicured and painted a light pink, skating the line of dress regulations. She bit the edge of her lip and wrapped the ends of her glossy hair around her finger, the perfect metaphor for my inward spiral.

"Of course I know Austin! Who doesn't?" She said it in a way that felt like it meant something more. "And your dad. He—"

Kael interrupted whatever she was going to say. "Ray! My man!"

he called out to an older Black man with a thick gray moustache standing behind the counter.

"Martin. Haven't seen you in a while," Ray said in a raspy voice, obviously happy to see Kael. "I barely recognize you out of uniform. What brings you in?"

Kael gave Turner a quick nod goodbye and turned his attention back to me and Ray to explain what was wrong with the laptop. Ray said it would be an easy fix but that he was so backed up with work, it would need to be left there for a day or two.

"Friends and family discount." He winked, and Kael handed him his credit card without giving me a chance to protest. Not that I would have: I was still inside my head, wondering if Kael had dated Turner or, worse, had slept with her. Actually, I didn't know which was worse, but I'd surely prefer neither. This growing web of acquaintances connected to the people in my life was rattling me.

# CHAPTER **FIFTY-FIVE**

My shift that afternoon was long and I could barely keep my eyes open. It was now evening and I had already had three scheduled appointments; Stewart, who was one of my favorite clients, would be the last. Going to the mall this morning with Kael had depleted most of my allotted daily energy, but the way he'd held my hand the whole drive home had replenished it. I wondered what he was doing now. I hadn't heard from Kael since he dropped me off at home. He mentioned he would be going back to his place, and I wished we had had time to go there together. I wanted to see where he lived, where he slept—I just didn't want to miss a chance to know more about him. But now I was feeling self-conscious about texting him. I didn't want to seem clingy. It wasn't such a big deal to text him a quick "hi." I knew that, but I didn't, of course, and I watched the screen of my phone and the clock on and off until Stewart finally came in.

During her treatment, Stewart told me all about her upcoming move to Hawaii. On top of the perk of getting to live there, her long-awaited promotion to staff sergeant had also come through. And she spoke enthusiastically about her partner, Stacey, who ran a small business, designing and selling these cute floral dresses.

"She's going to set up one of those little shops right on the beach. She's convinced she's made for beach life," Stewart said and beamed. She was optimistic that Stacey's business would surely do better in a year-round beach town than it did here near the border of Georgia and Alabama, almost five hours away from the coast.

Stewart kept talking a mile a minute, her head in the cradle and her voice muffled. She winced as I applied extra-firm pressure. She was always full of knots, but she could handle the pain better than most of the people I'd had on this table.

"I've heard the housing on post is really nice, and very afford-able." I shared what I knew from my father and a couple other clients.

"I reminded Stacey that we're going to be living *by* the post, since it wouldn't be easy to live *on* post," Stewart said between her deep breaths absorbing the body work. "I did find a cute house only a few miles away. It has a small garden for the dogs."

I felt bad for not thinking about what I had just said before I said it. I knew that, in reality, gay couples weren't particularly welcome living on post together. It blew my mind that Stewart could serve her country the same way a straight woman or man could, but she might be denied the community support that a straight soldier would have. Seemed to me the "don't ask, don't tell" protocol really meant "don't care, won't respect." The military needed to catch up with the times. Things were changing slowly, but overall, the Army hadn't been very supportive of the LGBTQIA+ community. Too many men in charge still believed that being homosexual had no place in the military. These were sometimes the same men who swept sexual assault under the rug, not to mention an overwhelming number of disappearances and suicides of service members in every branch. I worried about all of the challenges that Stewart and Stacey would face, even if Hawaii seemed like a more accepting place to live than some other military bases. I listened to Stewart talk for the rest of our session, but underneath her every word, I felt a sense of sadness. I wished this world were more fair for Stewart and her partner and for all the other people I didn't know, but who were suffering for their own reasons.

I felt a little guilty that I was eager for the massage to finish so I could check my phone and see if Kael had texted me. I needed to connect with him any way I could. I needed to feel closer to him. Even just to see his name on my phone screen. To reread old texts he had sent me.

Three more minutes.

That seemed excruciatingly long. I didn't think Stewart would notice that I was already doing a sort of cooldown on her, gently moving my hands over her skin to relax her after the deep-tissue massage.

I waited it out for one more minute and ended her session with two to go. I made a mental note that I would add five extra minutes to her next session. I grabbed my phone from the shelf the moment my hands left her body.

No new messages, but I did have a missed call from my dad. Well, that could wait. I didn't feel like talking to him. The only thing on my mind was how Kael's mouth tasted like his coconut ChapStick and how hard he laughed when I tripped over a piece of tile in my bathroom that he promised to help me fix. Our scrambling bodies had moved from my bedroom to my bathroom, to the kitchen and back to bed, still not able to let go, to stop touching, to stop exploring each other. We had become masters at intimacy, without crossing the line into fully hooking up.

"Karina?" Stewart's voice made me jump. Talk about the real world. My phone dropped to the floor, the picture of Kael and me open on the screen. Bright as hell in my dark room.

"Oh my god, sorry!" I hid my face under my hair as I bent down to grab it. "I'll let you get dressed. See you in the lobby," I told her, leaving her in privacy.

When I stepped into the hallway, I had to bite my lips to stop myself from laughing. Typically, I would freak out over something like that and die from embarrassment. Was Stewart uncomfortable or thinking that I had lost my mind? This time, my brain didn't go there the way it normally did. It naturally thought about how obsessed I was becoming with Kael and how big his smile would be when I told him about my phone mishap with Stewart.

# CHAPTER FIFTY-SIX

"It's so good to see you like this," Stewart told me, squeezing my hand as I passed her a pen and her receipt.

I smiled and we both laughed. I felt that I had shared something very personal with her.

"See you next week," she said.

I was pleased for Stewart and the change ahead, but I was going to miss her a lot. And business-wise (usually an afterthought for me), I could hear Mali lecturing that losing a client as reliable as Stewart was going to affect how much money I would be bringing in each month, and what was I going to do about that?

I cleaned up my treatment room as fast as I could while still being thorough. I threw towels in the laundry and checked the bathroom to make sure it was clean enough and that the caramel apple–scented wax burner didn't need another cube. Oh, how I loved the fall.

I didn't wait for Elodie to finish with her client. I had managed to miss her return home this afternoon, and was relieved not to have to answer her questions about Kael. I just shouted a general "bye" in Mali's direction and left. I checked my phone as I walked outside, turning into the alley. On days like today I was thankful that my house was only a five-minute walk from work. As I skirted around a pile of new mattresses outside of Bradley's shop, I started to text Kael to see what he was up to. I stared at the phone, feeling the chill of cool air; it felt like rain was coming. I really hoped that I would see Kael tonight. Seeing him would instantly lift my spirits. He was the brightest star in my muted gray life.

The texting bubble popped up, three little gray dots were there, then they weren't.

I looked up from my phone and down the alley. I could see Kael's Bronco parked on the street right in front of my house. I used my hands to brush my hair back into a ponytail and straightened my shoulders, excitement bubbling through me. But when I reached the end of the alley and went to cross the street to my house, my eyes landed on a black Buick parked in my front driveway. I didn't need to see the *US ARMY* sticker on the bumper to know it was my dad's.

I felt as if someone had poured a bucket of cold water over me. I was nervous now. Unsettled. I almost wanted to turn back around and hide behind the line of dumpsters in the alley and wished I could text Kael to tell him to get rid of my dad. But I knew that was something I had to do.

I walked faster and saw the screen door open when all of a sudden my dad's voice boomed through the yard. I could see the shape of my dad in my doorway, his back turned to me. His hands were raised like he was yelling. Kael's voice was next.

"You don't have a fucking clue!" Kael shouted.

Chills ran from the tips of my fingers to the tips of my toes and something in my brain, some minuscule detail of a buried memory, told me to stop there, right before I reached the lawn. I stepped next to Kael's truck for cover, wanting to assess what was happening.

They were going at it. And they were going at it hard, each word a blow.

"How dare you try to keep my daughter from me!" my dad accused. "You need to stay away from my family."

Kael held his ground, and his voice was firm enough to make me want to hide from what I was hearing.

"Maybe she doesn't want to be around you. Have you ever thought about that?"

"You've got some nerve showing up at my house, Martin. Especially after what happened in Afghanistan. Why do this when you're about to get out?"

"You don't give a fuck about me getting out, this is about you keeping your hands clean and your retirement."

The rest of the words flew around me too fast to catch until I heard Kael say, "You're a fucking criminal!"

*Afghanistan. Criminal. My daughter. How dare you. Stay away.*

I leaned in to the side of the truck and crouched down small, a feeble attempt to protect myself from what I was hearing. I couldn't make sense of all of it, other than to realize that my dream of happily-ever-after had just ended. And a nightmare had begun.

# CHAPTER FIFTY-SEVEN

I walked toward my porch. What was this? What was happening?

I could barely feel the ground beneath me as I moved across my lawn. My heart ached and with every breath I became more certain that something was very wrong. I hated that my mind was already doubting Kael. The fact that he knew my dad—before I introduced them at dinner—and that something had gone on between them. He never mentioned it, and that confused and hurt me. *And my dad, of all people?* Could I trust either of them to tell me the truth? The steel wall around me that I'd lowered over the last couple of weeks was rising again. My defenses were on high alert.

As I climbed the porch stairs my father stepped into the house, still with his back to me. When Kael caught my eye, my dad tracked his gaze and turned abruptly.

"Karina," my dad boomed, pointing at Kael. "Why is he here, in your house? Why the hell is this guy sitting inside your home when you're not here?"

My heart was pounding. *What the hell is going on?* Kael was starting to look different, like a stranger again. Something about the way he stared forward, not appearing to even blink, made my blood run cold. My father's stern voice made me want to vomit.

"I overheard everything you just said. Tell me what this is

about," I demanded, and when neither of them spoke, I startled myself by yelling, "Tell me what the fuck you're talking about, right now!" I had never screamed in my house before.

Kael reached for me, but I jerked away. "Karina, I can tell you what's going on, your dad's—"

With an icy tone, my father cut Kael off before he could finish. "You've already overstayed your welcome, Martin. She's my daughter, and I don't need *you* to speak to her. Karina, we can discuss this when he leaves—which will be now."

"No one is leaving until I get an answer," I snapped at my dad. My hands were shaking. My whole body was shaking. "This is *my* house." I wasn't sure if I was telling them or reminding myself.

My father's eyes bore into Kael's. "You're so close to that medical discharge you want. And if you don't watch it, we'll all be fucked! Your career will end before you even leave Fort Benning. What are you going to do with a dishonorable discharge, boy?"

"I'm not your fucking boy. And I'm not fucking afraid of you." Kael stood, his back straight while talking to my father. It shocked and impressed me. "There's nothing else you can do to me, or to Mendoza, to any of us."

"And how much blood is on your hands, Sergeant Martin?" My dad growled at him before turning to me. "Did he tell you he's on the verge of getting himself a dishonorable discharge? What kind of future would you have with him, Karina?"

Kael's attention was on me, and his eyes were glassy like he was holding back tears of anger. "It's him, Karina. He's a senile narcissist who has convinced himself he's some sort of god and he's nothing." Kael's veil of composure was gone.

I stood there between them as their truths swirled around me, trying to stick.

"Are you denying that you came into my office, shivering,

your leg all bandaged, and signed your name on the bottom of that page, Martin? You signed official documents, you even got a promotion after that. You signed it. Mendoza signed it. Lawson signed it. All of you! And now you decide, almost two years later, to come back and try to backtrack?"

My dad was in full-on officer mode. It was sickening to watch the way he knew just how to warp the tone of his voice to whip soldiers into submission, like he sometimes did with Austin and me.

Kael spoke in a detached, steely voice. "He was sent into the wrong house. Shots were fired at him because no one did a proper surveillance. You know that you neglected your command, keeping yourself entertained back at camp while Mendoza, Lawson, and I went in. He didn't know who was inside when he fired!"

"Soldiers and civilians die, on and off the battlefield. It's a part of the job. It's what you signed up for. I'm sorry this happened to your friend. At least he's still alive, unlike most of mine."

In this moment I saw clear as day why my mom grew to hate the man standing in front of me. His skin was ashy and fell in loose folds around his jaw. That, combined with his shock of white hair, made him look like the ultimate villain. Like the kind of man who conjured up demons or ate children alive. Compared to him, Kael looked wounded and hurt, more hero than antihero. He looked no older than eighteen.

"I did what I had to do to help you, all of you." My dad pointed an accusing finger at Kael. "I watched you pull a body into camp, barely able to walk yourself. I did what I believed to be right, and I have a hell of a lot more experience with this than you do."

"You were protecting your own position! You didn't give a fuck about us or our lives! You only cared about your retirement and not jeopardizing your legacy," Kael snarled at my dad. "Tell your daughter how you used the lives of young men and women to get promotions and medals. Tell her how you constantly threatened us, making sure we never so much as whispered your name. My fucking friend is losing his mind over the guilt and he can't even talk to anyone about it." Kael stepped toward my dad. They were now to face-to-face.

"Are you hearing yourself, Martin? You're a soldier. I'm a soldier. We've seen and done things most people can't dream of. If you're haunted by what you've done, you're a piss-poor excuse for a man."

Kael stood silent as my father continued his demeaning rant.

"You know what will really haunt both of you? If he can't feed his family and has no paycheck, no healthcare, nothing. That's haunting." My dad's thick finger pressed against Kael's chest. I took a sharp breath, Kael didn't react. "You really want to get back at me, Martin? Sleeping with my daughter isn't the way to provoke me."

Kael didn't flinch, but my nerves and anger erupted.

"What the hell are you talking about?" I exploded. "You don't know anything about us or what we're doing!" My dad had the nerve to slap us both with an accusation that wasn't even true.

"This is bigger than whatever childish game you two are playing, Karina. This man can't be trusted. He's an unreliable liar. He's put people in danger, real danger—you and your brother should keep your distance."

My dad's golf shirt was pulling, untucking from his jeans, and his skin was red, all blotchy. Like a liar, or an innocent man on trial. I couldn't tell. Like my mom said, there's always more than one lie for every truth. I looked at Kael again.

"At this point you don't even care, do you, Martin? You have your bags all packed to move up to Atlanta and, what, are you going to take my daughter with you?" He laughed, then continued, "I know you bought a house there. Word travels fast around here. You know that better than most."

Words burned in my throat, failing to escape. There was no way that what my dad was saying was true.

"You bought a place in Atlanta?" I turned to Kael, but he was speechless, and my confusion turned into devastation. "Did you?"

I couldn't hide my shock as he nodded.

"When were you going to tell me?"

I wanted to touch his face and turn his cheek toward me so he would have to face me, but I was too stunned to move.

"You knew I was leaving," he said simply, as if we were discussing what to eat for dinner. His jaw was clenched, but his mouth was flat, nothing to read. I couldn't tell if he was putting on a show for my father, acting like he didn't give a shit about me, or if he just really didn't. He was just the other day offering to take me to his place, here in town. Not in fucking Atlanta. I hated being gaslit. But I wasn't even sure that's what Kael was doing, since there was zero emotion is his eyes; he didn't even care enough to manipulate me.

"That doesn't answer my question, Kael. When are you going?"

"Soon." He barely spoke.

I couldn't breathe, but managed to ask, "When?"

"Not soon enough," my dad replied for him.

I couldn't look away from Kael, not even to tell my dad to shut the fuck up. When I searched Kael's eyes, I couldn't find what I was looking for. I couldn't find anything.

I felt my anger too intensely to control it. I needed a reaction from him, so I pushed against his chest, but his body didn't move at all. Even the way the fabric of his uniform felt against my palms triggered me. The green and tan had always been an omen to the bad shit in my life.

I pushed Kael's chest again. I needed reassurance that the person I'd come to know was in there somewhere, that I hadn't invented this. As my hands touched his chest, his grasped for mine, latching on to my wrists.

"Do not touch me like that," he said calmly, looking into my eyes as he lowered our hands, then let go of mine. The words went straight to the deepest part of me and filled me with shame. He took a step away and stopped near the entryway of the kitchen.

I immediately shrank. What was I even doing? I couldn't believe that I had just pushed him like that, and in front of my father. No matter my anger. I couldn't look at my dad because I was afraid that I'd see more of myself in him than I could accept. I apologized to Kael immediately and loudly, but he didn't seem fazed. He was blank, shut down, a vacant soldier replacing the man I had come to know.

Kael was slipping away from my little living room.

"None of us are right in the head anymore." Kael's words tore me open and I struggled to stay in self-preservation mode.

I didn't believe Kael was being honest with me, and my dad was a notorious liar. I felt like I was in a fun house, mirrors cut in weird shapes, bent to confuse you with a distorted version of reality. *What you thought was reality.* Everything around me was warped.

"Both of you, just get out." My voice was shaky in its delivery, but the words came out confidently.

Kael remained unfazed. *Wow.* The pain lashed at me again.

My dad persisted in pushing my boundaries.

"Karina, we need to resolve this before it becomes more of a problem."

"This isn't my problem. It's yours." I pointed at both of them and said the words through gritted teeth.

Kael barely made eye contact. I couldn't believe his audacity to not even look me in the fucking eyes.

"Get out. Now," I said to them both again, but I was looking directly at Kael. He was still staring straight ahead as Elodie's voice rang through the chaos.

"Martin! You're here again!" she chirped, having no clue what she had just walked into as she bounced across the living room to give Kael a hug. Her face shifted from excitement to confusion as he stood unmoved by her enthusiasm. He suddenly took a step, then another, and his body moved like a robot, not stopping or even glancing toward Elodie as he walked out the front door.

I couldn't bring myself to watch him leave, so I focused on my father.

"You, too. Get out." I looked directly into my dad's beady eyes and gestured toward to the door.

Kael's truck roared in the background. I felt sick to my stomach. My father looked at Elodie, opened his mouth, then snapped it shut. He was summoning his outward charm—something he had mastered for the sake of appearances.

"I heard your soldier will be home soon." My dad's tone was soft as he touched Elodie's shoulder. They weren't close, but he had always been nice to her when she tagged along for dinner.

"I hadn't heard this, is that true?" She sounded genuinely shocked at the news. Her eyes blinked a few times as my dad nodded.

"I'll be going, good to see you, Elodie." He managed a smile for her as she awkwardly waved goodbye and disappeared into the kitchen, leaving me alone with my dad.

A scowl returned to his face as he addressed me. "I'll see you on Tuesday." His tone told me that it wasn't a request, it was an order.

This, whatever the fuck this whole thing was, wasn't close to being over. Instead of feeding his ego and airing my grievances as I felt them, I waved at the door again, not giving him the satisfaction of taking any more of me. I held my breath until he was gone and made my way into the kitchen, where Elodie was pacing was back and forth, waiting for me. Her arms immediately went around my body, and for the first time since I met her, I didn't have the energy to pretend that everything was okay.

# CHAPTER FIFTY-EIGHT

When I woke up the next morning, my head was throbbing. I couldn't exactly recall how I got to my bed last night but had a faint memory of Elodie's voice shushing my sobs as they wore me down to sleep. I remember her standing in the doorway with a look of pure worry on her face, the thin line of hallway light disappearing with her as she left the room.

I had tossed and turned the entire night. My room was too hot, then too cold. I curled into a ball to comfort myself, covering my mouth to calm the heaving; I had no tears left, but my body seemed to think that I did. I couldn't stop. As soon as I would slip into near-sleep, Kael's face would flash in my mind. When I couldn't sleep, I checked my phone, too many times to count. My finger hovered over his name repeatedly, deliberating whether to block him or delete his number, but at the same time desperately hoping for a single text from him. Nothing. And I had the strength to do nothing except toss my phone to the other side of my bed.

Even in my dreams, I couldn't escape him. Was my heart actually broken? Was Kael a liar? He wasn't even part of my life a few weeks ago. My reaction to all of this was an overreaction. I was preparing to lose him eventually, but this felt different from the loss I knew was coming. I imagined that pain would be a longing ache for him, inflicted by distance, something remedied by texts and calls here and there. But this was altogether different.

I stretched my arms out in front of me as I lay in bed. My body felt sore everywhere. The morning was misty and overcast, and I couldn't guess the time. How long had I slept? I found my phone under one of my pillows and squinted through puffy eyes to read: 8:24. I needed to get up and ready for work at eleven, but didn't know how I was going to deal with today's shift. I untangled myself from the disheveled mess of sheets and comforter and got out of bed. As I walked out of my room to the bathroom I heard the TV in the living room and knew Elodie was already awake. After a quick check of my face in the bathroom mirror, I splashed my cheeks with water in a futile attempt to revive myself. Kael's tube of cinnamon-flavored toothpaste sat unopened on the counter. I cringed, feeling a pang of regret. He never even had the chance to use it, but maybe that was for the best.

As I stepped into the hallway, I heard Elodie giggle, clearly amused by whatever she was watching. That laugh always lifted my spirits when we hung out and binged on TV. She had kept me from plummeting last night. She hadn't asked any questions, she just hugged me as we sat on the couch as I cried. She was here for me last night in a way that I had never felt in a friendship before. I wanted to thank Elodie and say that I was sorry that I hadn't told her about what was going on with me and Kael.

"You're awake." She smiled, turning toward me as she lowered the volume on the remote. Head hurt. It felt like it had been days, not hours, since Kael and my dad were here. Elodie looked surprised as I practically crawled to her on the couch, snuggled up next to her, and wrapped my arm around her. She covered me with the blanket she was using, and I cuddled in closer. We didn't say anything at first and I couldn't think of where to begin or just how much I wanted to say. I owed it to her and myself to at least try to explain what was going on.

"Do you believe in coincidences?" I asked.

"Coincidence is simply what happens." She paused. "Are you asking me about serendipity?"

*Serendipity?* Kael coming into my life seemed like a series of unfortunate events. I didn't want to admit it was anything more than that.

"A coincidence is like bumping into an old friend at the movies or thinking about someone you haven't heard from in a while and then seeing their name pop up next to a text." Could it really be a coincidence that Kael and my dad and Austin and Mendoza and Phillip and everyone, literally everyone, were connected? I took a breath and continued, "The fact that my dad and Phillip and Kael are all in the same company feels like a bizarre circumstance."

"It does, but you get to decide what that means for you, Karina."

I stared at Elodie as she spoke, trying to take in how wise and comforting she was. People often underestimated her ability to read situations. Yes, she seemed young and bubbly, and adorably French, but her instinct and perspective blew me away.

Though I was ashamed to admit it, my first impulse was to lie again, to protect myself, but Elodie was trying to be a friend to me, and I desperately wanted to let her.

"Kael was here the whole time you were gone, and we've been seeing each other, well, not dating, but we were hanging out since the day we met." My cheeks flushed, I barely had any energy, but the bit I did have was pure guilt.

"Did you sleep together? I'm not judging, only curious," she asked me.

I shook my head. I couldn't meet her eyes anymore, so I leaned my head onto her shoulder again.

"We didn't. He didn't even try." I stopped mid-thought and had a realization. "Wow, that should have been my sign. He didn't even want to sleep with me."

"Be glad you didn't, then," Elodie said softly. I nodded in agreement.

A little corner, all the way in the back of my heart, the only part that hadn't gone numb, began to ache again. Kael's face flashed through my mind, him smiling at me, us in my kitchen, us falling onto my bed. The way he paid attention to the smallest things I said, the way his eyes lit up when we shared a favorite song.

"I think the other things we did were more intimate than sex. If we had only hooked up, this would be so much easier to get over." I shuddered. How did I get myself into such a mess?

She took that in. "Yeah, the sex is the easy part, isn't it?"

We nodded at each other.

"Do you want me to tell you that I think you shouldn't see Martin anymore and that things sometimes don't happen for a reason?"

I sat quiet for a moment.

"I don't know why it feels like my world is ending," I said softly, as Elodie's hand stroked my shoulder and down my back. I felt like a child curled up next to her. "I've only been this hurt once in my life, when my mom left. Maybe I should just get used to the fact that everyone who comes into my life will leave at some point." I saw my life as a revolving door. I got over my mother. I would surely get over this.

"What am I even saying?" I continued, closing my eyes. My mother's face flashed behind my lids. "My mom leaving was so much worse. Kael's a stranger. I can't believe I'm even comparing them."

Elodie breathed in a deep breath. I couldn't look at her when she spoke. "Loss can't be measured in that way. If it was that simple, life would be much easier."

Her words sat with me, and as they settled, I felt a bit of relief in my lungs.

"People are selfish." I sighed. "I've always known that. I think I lost my mind a bit."

"People do things they don't plan to do when they're in love."

I let out a cackle, overcompensating for the possibility of truth there. "I'm *so* not in love."

"Well, it might feel just as painful as if you were," she said, pursing her lips. "I thought Martin was a nice guy. I really did, I'm sorry that I introduced you to him."

The size of Elodie's heart was so admirable. I wondered if things would have been different had I confided in her about Kael from the start. None of this was her fault, and I wanted to tell her that.

I sighed. "I lied to you about Kael, I'm the one who's sorry."

She shook her head and a piece of her hair fell from the low ponytail resting just above her neck. She tucked it behind her ear.

"Karina?" Elodie's bright blue eyes met mine. She lifted one hand and rested it on her stomach. "Do you think your dad was telling the truth that Phillip will be home soon?"

My heart ached. "I wish I knew. Has Phillip not mentioned this to you?"

"No, he didn't." Elodie's tone was solemn. "Did Kael say anything?"

I shook my head, but wished I had something to tell her. It made me worry how easily she could be hurt, and with people like Kael and my dad around her, I wanted her to be more guarded when it came to trusting others. If I ever found a way to look at my father again, I would try to find out what was going on. It was the least I could do for my only friend.

Elodie tapped her finger against the tip of my nose, making my eyes close and my face crinkle. "Let's not change this to me." Her smile was a sweet and knowing one, and I realized I hadn't even asked her about her trip!

"Okay, but first you have to tell me about Atlanta. Did you have fun? Were The Wives nice to you?"

She smiled, giving my arm a playful squeeze. "Absolutely fun! But it was very crowded everywhere and the shopping was too expensive. I had a good time, but it will be curious if they ask me to hang out again."

"They will." I looked up at her. "If they don't, it's their loss anyway."

"You need to eat," Elodie exclaimed, jumping up from the couch. She disappeared into the kitchen and returned a moment later with a bowl of Cheerios with sugar sprinkled on top. Elodie knew it was my favorite breakfast, something my mom had made any time of day or night when she knew I needed a pick-me-up. It was still my comfort-food ritual.

I looked at the time on my phone: it was already 9:45, and I was due at work at eleven. How was I going to work a shift today? I was in no mood to be with anyone.

"I am going to call Mali," I said between bites of cereal. "I know I've taken time off this week, but I just can't go there today. I know Mali's going to freak, but I just can't do it."

"Don't call her! She'll kill you. And she's already mad at me for not working my full week," Elodie exclaimed, eyes wide. "I'm off today, I can cover for you."

"Are you sure?"

"Yes, I decided already. You helped me so much when I was sick from the baby." She smiled. "I'm going to shower now and get ready."

After Elodie left, I had the house to myself and could either crawl back into bed and be miserable or try to keep myself distracted while still being miserable. Giving other people the power to make me feel this way was exactly what I had been avoiding my entire life. Kael made me break my own rules.

I should have known that, sooner or later, he would reveal himself to be exactly what he was, what we all are, the most selfish of creatures. I'd never met a person who wasn't selfish. I shouldn't have ignored that little voice inside that told me we were headed for nowhere fast and we were going to run out of gas anyway. The problem was he made me feel comforted and understood, less alone in the world—the highs of being with him were so consuming that the voice of reason in my head was drowned out. It was fucked up the way he cracked me open, turned me into a freaking maple tree, my deepest private thoughts pouring out of me and into him. He soaked them up, but kept the tap closed when it came to himself. And he turned out to be just another liar in my life.

Even so, it was a hard pill to swallow. My body clung to the memory of his touch, the hot flash of his warm lips brushing my skin, his mouth trailing down the nape of my neck. I lifted my hand to touch there. Even my own touch reminded me of him. When he touched me, I didn't know where I ended and he began.

Time was going impossibly slowly; it was barely eleven in the morning on Day 1 post-Kael. I couldn't get him out of my mind:

he made his home there with a constant presence—and worse than that, there were traces of him were everywhere in my house. As I dug through my drawers for something light and easy to wear, I saw the satin pajamas. And his gray PT shirt was folded neatly next to them. Even my fingers ached for him. *Fuck him, honestly.*

Maybe if I cleaned myself up, had a shower, and brushed my teeth, I might feel a little less zombie-like. At minimum, the tasks would distract me. I walked to the kitchen to throw my dirty laundry into the washer, then went into the bathroom, where I grabbed Kael's stupid gross toothpaste and tossed it into the trash can. When I missed, it hit an already loose wall tile that cracked into pieces, hitting the floor. Fuck this house, and how it knows just how badly I need him to fix my life.

And then I thought about my own advice to my childhood friend, Sammy, after she and Austin broke up for the fourth time. I reminded her that he was only a teeny tiny little part of her life, that in five years he wouldn't matter. No one in our school in Texas would matter to us. Not even the cool kids would matter when we were grown-ups. She said she'd never fully be able to forget him because he was my twin and our laugh was the same. We got distant after she and Austin split, and her marriage soon thereafter made it harder to keep in touch. Eventually she faded from my life like everyone else had.

I turned on the music and looked into the mirror. My dark hair washed out my tired face more than usual, and I thought about coloring it. I crouched down and opened the cabinet. Sure enough, I had a box of dye. A lighter brown than my hair was now, but not too drastic of a change.

Screw it, I decided.

I had the house to myself for the rest of the afternoon and I'd been thinking of changing my hair for a while anyway; it would be a few months until I could afford to go to the salon to get it done. I ripped the box open and followed the instructions, even though I knew how to do it by now. I mixed the dye, shook the bottle, and applied it carefully to my hair over the sink. I had lost count of how many times I'd changed my hair color in my life. My mom let me use temporary dye, a dark blue, when I was twelve. I would never forget the look on my father's face when he came downstairs to see my mom and I both with deep blue streaks in our hair.

I set a timer for twenty minutes on my phone and rummaged through my cabinet to see what other luxuries I had. I found a face mask to use after the shower and grabbed my nail file and tweezers. I leaned my face to the mirror and brushed my eyebrows with a little brush meant for tooth flossing. My thick brows could definitely use a little shaping; I held the tweezers up and brought my face closer to the mirror. In my reflection, my hand was shaking, so I traded hands. The right hand was even worse, and because I had already committed to hair dye with no guarantee of the outcome, I didn't want to risk messing my eyebrows up, too. I wasn't *that* far gone.

I stood outside the shower, impatient for the water to heat up. Steam began to fill the bathroom after only a few seconds, and that annoyed me. Another reminder of Kael—Mr. Fucking Handyman. Fuck the shower. The water was warm and the pressure luxurious, and I decided to take the longest shower I could. I applied a conditioning mask to my hair and shaved my legs. Holding the razor made me think of Kael in front of my mirror and how often he had to shave due to regulations. *How hard was it going to be to untangle him completely from my memories?* I closed my eyes and let the water spray directly onto my face. I asked the universe, but since it felt like no one was listening anyway, I answered my own question. It would be as easy as throwing away his toothpaste and never going near post until he was gone. I was done breaking my own rules and would just focus on my job and getting my shit together. I didn't have the time or energy for chasing liars in ACUs around, and this was the end of it.

# CHAPTER FIFTY-NINE

The shower had helped me feel relaxed enough to take a nap. Sleeping the day away made me feel better, but I still looked like hell. I had fallen asleep with wet hair and, even though the color was more flattering than I had expected, I woke to a frizzy mess; the way I looked now went right along with the mania I felt. I threw on black sweats and a baggy black T-shirt and pinched my cheeks to bring a little color to the surface.

I heard Elodie's voice as soon as I stepped into the hallway. If her shift was already over, I must have been asleep for a long time. It sounded like she was hushing someone in conversation, but when I peered around the corner, she was alone in the dark living room with her laptop on her lap. A man's voice was coming through the speaker.

"Don't lie to me," he said in an accusatory tone.

I thought I heard him wrong, but he said it again. This time his words seemed even more demeaning. I didn't want to intrude, but I was concerned for Elodie.

"Cooper's wife told me that you were over there. His wife tells him everything, unlike mine."

*Phillip? Shit.*

Elodie was crying. I had to hold on to the door handle of the hallway closet to stop myself from butting into the conversation and her business. I didn't know what Phillip was talking about, but I knew I didn't like the sound of his voice. I had never seen that side of him or heard it. I couldn't tell if his wife was used to it or not. I immediately wondered if Phillip was, like Kael, not what he seemed.

"I'm not lying," she pleaded. "We stopped there for an hour at most. We went to the meetings, then to that house. There weren't any guys around."

My phone in my hand dinged as my brother's name popped up on my screen. I knew Elodie must have heard it, but I tapped my fingers against the wall, just in case, to let her know I was coming into the room. She perked up and wiped at her tears.

"Phillip, Karina's just walked in," she cautioned him.

"Hey, Karina," Phillip said, his voice nice and friendly, a complete transformation from what it had been.

I threw him a bland "hey" and walked into the kitchen. My intrusion seemed to stop their conversation. I decided to stay out of the living room and wait for Elodie to finish. Dishes were piling up in the sink. Wet laundry had accumulated in the washing machine and I opened the dryer to clear it, feeling taunted yet again by Kael as I placed folded clothes in the basket. I couldn't even blame the mess on my emotional despair because the breakup had happened barely twelve hours ago.

Elodie signed off Skype and met me in the kitchen as I stood washing the dishes. She didn't seem ready to say anything for a few minutes, and I kept myself busy cleaning up. I gave her a moment to herself as she sat silently at the table.

"Everything okay?" I asked eventually. "Is Phillip coming home?"

She shook her head and I went to sit down across the table from her. Elodie's eyes were bloodshot; the tip of her nose was red as fire. I didn't want to press her, but she was obviously not okay.

She handed my question back to me. "How are you feeling, Karina?"

"I'm fine. Don't let the hair fool you. Elodie, you know you can talk to me."

"You have your own problems." She tried to smile.

"We've done enough talking about that. I'm here for you, too."

She nodded. "I'm okay. It's only Phillip imagining things when he hears the other soldiers talk. Why is there so much drama? Don't they have anything better to do?" She sniffled and rubbed her nose. "How are *you*?"she asked, reaching a hand across the table. I pretended not to notice as I lowered my hands onto my lap.

"I'm all right. Just tired," I lied.

If she could lie to my face, I could do the same.

# CHAPTER SIXTY

I spent the next day working in the morning. I was getting used to the bags under my eyes, but I finally felt a little more alive. I whizzed through my shift—three clients back-to-back—and got higher tips than expected on all three. I was feeling pretty good as I walked down the street to my house. The sun was bright, and I felt more energetic than I had for the last couple days. I thought of the many ways I could spend my afternoon off. I tried to remember the things I liked to do before I met Kael.

I walked into my bedroom and looked at the stack of books on my dresser. I had read most of them and didn't feel like starting a whole new story, so I decided to grab one of the poetry books I had bought while browsing in a favorite bookstore in Atlanta. Right now, poems suited my mood—the perfect length, room for my own emotions, and I could skip anything that made me think too much. I desperately wanted to distract my brain from reality.

It was the perfect temperature outside today, warm enough not to have to wear a jacket, but cool enough that I could wear a long-sleeved shirt and shorts and be comfortable. I pulled my hair up, grabbed a few things—my phone for music, a pillow from the couch, and the poetry book *Lost and Found*, and headed out to the porch. I sat down on the cool concrete and wished I had a swing. Another item for the "one day" list. One day when I redo the porch, I will make it big enough for a swing. One day.

As I skipped from page to page in the book, I felt like every single poem was being read to me in Kael's voice. He was everywhere. He had become everything.

*In the hollows under his eyes, I found a map*
*in the stars that dipped into his cheeks, I found solace*
*in the bow of his lips, there was truth*
*in the rise and fall of his chest, I found myself,*
*and if you ever need me, that's where I'll be.*

I closed the book and tossed it, watching as it went skidding across the porch. The stars reminded me of Kael, the mention of his dimples, the truth I'd believed from him that wasn't there after all. The feelings were too close and I wanted these words as far away from me as they could get. I stood up, took a few steps, and kicked the little white paperback, watching it disappear into the patch of weeds next to my porch.

Then I felt guilty. It wasn't the poet's fault that my first real connection with someone was so short-lived I stepped down off the porch to retrieve the book, digging my hand into the stringy weeds that surrounded the concrete slab. They were too long, too unmanageable; unpredictable vegetation was overgrowing my yard. This little house was what it was. I knew what I was getting when I signed on the dotted line for the basically abandoned house at the end of a commercial strip. It was the only thing in my life that wasn't going to turn out to be something that it wasn't.

I began to pull at the weeds in the yard. They were everywhere, the more I looked. I needed a distraction and had the rest of the day to do as I pleased. Minutes went by and I moved on from the weeds to sweep the gravel back into my driveway. I had decided to ignore this week's Tuesday family dinner obligation. No way was I going to deal with that.

At first, I thought the dark blue Bronco pulling up to my house was a mirage. The sun was already setting and I seemed to have lost track of time. My mind was obviously playing tricks on me. I stood up and stared, watching unwaveringly as Kael parked in front of my house in his usual spot.

When he got out of his truck, it dawned on me that he was at my house for the first time since the blowout with my dad. I had so much to say, but couldn't think of anything that would help the pain I felt in my bones.

"Karina." His voice danced around me, almost hypnotizing me.

I opened my mouth to speak and heard my dad's voice in my head, followed by Kael's, then my dad's again. I couldn't sort out my own thoughts, and I still couldn't make sense of everything that they had said, even though I had replayed it over and over in my mind. I realized that I wasn't prepared to face Kael. Not tonight. I needed at least one hundred hours to mentally prepare to see him.

"For so many reasons, you can't be here," I told him just as he reached the grass. My back hurt as I stood there with one hand on my hip and one blocking my eyes from the blazing sun that had nearly set. Why was the sun so bright? Even nature was taunting me at this point.

He stopped and looked at me, seeming uncertain what to do next. Still too close. He held out my laptop with an extended arm and I quickly grabbed it from him. The last bit of me that he could have was now back in my hands.

"Karina, can't we talk? I just want to explain myself," he pleaded.

I had barely caught a glimpse of his face, and the emotion in it made me move my hand down to shade my eyes like a coward, so I couldn't see his face.

He was staring at me, I could feel it though I avoided his eyes. He was attempting to register everything I was feeling, absorb it, and read me like a fucking book, and I regretted that I had ever given him this type of access in the first place.

"You had the chance to explain yourself and didn't," I said flatly.

"I didn't mean to hurt you, Karina. You must know that." The cool condescension in his voice sent me over the edge.

I threw my hands in the air. "Atlanta! You're kidding, right?"

He shook his head.

"Actually, *Martin*, I don't know anything about you at all." I wanted to hurt him with my words, so I didn't allow myself to filter my thoughts. "Everything you've told me seems to be part of a story that I don't know. You've humiliated me, like it's some kind of joke that everyone else knows who you are and what you do but I don't. You may think I'm naïve, but you are exactly the kind of person I've tried to stay away from my entire life. You need to leave . . . you need to go."

His eyes went wide as if he were stunned, and the selfish satisfaction I felt from his reaction outweighed the pang of guilt I felt for purposely hurting him. He must have found something in my expression when my eyes finally met his that told him to back off, because he put his hands in the air and turned around and walked away.

# CHAPTER **SIXTY-ONE**

When I woke up the next morning, I was even more miserable than I'd been the day before. Would it really get worse every day? For how long? I washed my hair for a while, rubbing my scalp to ease the ache. My neck felt so stiff, my skull so heavy. It wasn't fair that I was made to feel both physical and emotional pain. What sort of God, or universe—or whatever is up there—allows that? It was just cruel. An unfair punishment. I'm not a crier usually, but I couldn't hold it in last night, and honestly, I'm not sure if it helped or was a waste of time because I still felt like shit inside and now my head was pounding, my eyes swollen, my skin blotchy and uneven.

The longer I stared at myself in the mirror, the more hesitant I felt about going to work, but Mali's staffing and my bank account were both running short, so staying home wasn't an option. I did what pre-Kael Karina would do and dabbed concealer under my eyes, put my hair up, and got dressed. I wore all black to accentuate my mourning and appreciated the morning's clouds and rain as accompaniment to my mood.

Elodie was still asleep on the couch when I went into the kitchen. I was going to eat a bowl of cereal and make a pot of coffee with the little bit of time I had before work, but I didn't want to wake her up. Instead, I opened my back door and took a breath, letting the humid air fill my lungs. I closed my eyes and listened only to the rain, letting my thoughts float away with the clouds, until my phone alarm started to vibrate in my uniform pocket. Everything would be fine. Time for work had come, yay. I had left my umbrella leaning against the dryer. I grabbed it and, holding the back door ajar, I tempted fate by opening the umbrella inside the kitchen. Bad luck, but who gives a fuck! At this point, why did that matter? Things couldn't possibly get worse for me. I rolled my eyes at how dramatic I was being and walked out the door. I thought of Kael when I looked at the lock, and damn it all to hell, I locked the door.

I walked around the side of my house and halfway across the yard before something caught my eye. Kael's truck was parked in the street in front of my house. *Is he really here again?* Maybe he had parked and gone somewhere . . . or was he waiting there for someone? I couldn't tell and thought for a moment to just keep walking past, as if I didn't notice. The rain felt like it picked up as I passed his truck at a safe distance. I could barely see him through the rain falling on the glass, but could make out the same gray sweatshirt he was wearing when he came here last night.

Did he stay the whole night? My view of his face was distorted by water running down the window, but I could see that his eyes were closed. I had no clue how long he had been there, sleeping in front of my house; my resolve to tell him to fuck off and never speak to me again was wavering, as I stared at his beautiful and calm face, nearly forgetting all of my feelings. I remembered this look from the nights we spent together. It made my chest ache. I wondered if he had slept okay. *Ugh, for god's sake, Karina!* The logical part of my brain crushed the romantic part as I turned away and rushed across the street.

So what if he'd slept in his truck for one night? He was responsible for this massive hole in me and I was supposed to forgive him just because he made himself uncomfortable for one night? I'd been miserable without him—frankly, uncomfortable my entire life before him, so I hoped he slept like shit in his truck after all. Why should I feel bad for him? This was infuriating! The amount of empathy I had for him pissed me off. If only I could give myself the same grace that I tended to give other people.

The street was empty except for my neighbor Bradley's truck. I took a few backward steps, scanning for Bradley as I crossed the street and moved into the alley. Water was suddenly squishing into my work shoes and was soaking me, but I really just didn't care. I looked back at Kael's truck through the rain. I couldn't see him, but I knew he was in there, and that was enough. I hated that for a moment I'd worried if he was cold inside his truck. *Serves him right,* I thought to myself, trying to let anger overpower the rest of my emotions. Immaturely, I lifted my middle finger into the air at him, and even though I knew he wouldn't see it, it still felt like a tiny, victorious act of aggression.

"You need an umbrella? You're goin' to get sick out here like that!" Bradley's voice startled me, and I snapped my hand back down to my side.

"I have one! Thanks!" I yelled back to him.

How mortifying if he saw me flip Kael off. I lifted my hands, realizing they both were bare. Sure enough, when I looked across the street, my umbrella was sitting opened on the pavement next to Kael's truck. *Shit.*

"I'm okay!" I shouted through the pouring rain. No way in hell was I going to go back and get it now.

Bradley's face showed concern, but he left it at that, yelling back a simple "If you say so!" before he climbed into his truck.

I practically ran to the back door of the spa; thankfully, it wasn't locked. I was soaking wet but hardly cared; I felt numb, nothing really mattered. My mundane boy and daddy problems were nothing compared to the problems other people had. I knew that. We were all just living on a giant rock, floating in the sky, anyway. By the time I entered the building, I had pretty much shut down, and Mali greeted me with dry towels and a warm hug. She also gave me cotton slippers and put my socks and shoes near the dryer vents. Her small efforts were entrancing and comforting and made me feel like I was in a bit of a daze. It was out of character for her to behave this way, and even more out of character for me to accept her gestures without complaining.

It took me until late afternoon to find my usual professional rhythm at the salon. I was relieved that I didn't have any of my regular clients today. They would have noticed immediately that I was not myself. It was easier to get through the day with a wall around me. My guard was tested when I stepped into the reception area to find Mali with a scowl on her face, cussing under her breath. I searched around the lobby for the source of her anger and found my umbrella, dry, closed, and propped neatly against the glass window near the door.

I turned around and made it back to my treatment room before I broke into tears.

Life went on like that, both numb and excruciating, for a stretch of days. I worked. I slept. I cried. I may have watched a couple of movies with Elodie. I can't remember any of their plots. I knew a Tuesday had passed because both my father and Estelle called me. I didn't bother to call them back and ended up powering my phone off for a full twenty-four hours to see if I could get my life back on track without the distraction of the outside world. This is what my soul needed, to stop comparing my life to everyone else's online perfection. I needed to find my roots again and remember the life I was building for myself before I met Kael. My self-sufficient bubble. I wasn't made to fall for someone and then crash on the other side of it.

I'm not sure when it was, how many days post-breakup, that I had come home from work to find Austin waiting for me on my porch. My brother was easy to spot from a distance; he was fidgeting, tapping his fingers against his knees. His face was blotchy red and his blond hair was a mess, making his features melt into something close to our father's. There were no cars in the driveway or parked on the street, so I couldn't figure out how he got there.

"What's wrong? Are you okay?" I asked, mildly panicked, and sat down next to him.

He shook his head.

My brother's eyes were bloodshot and swollen like he hadn't slept in days. His lips were dry and cracking, with little slices of red along the bottom one. He was even more disheveled than usual. Yet what would make most people unattractive only added to the many things that women found endearing about him. He was dressed in a white sweatshirt with *Riverdale High School* printed above a pocket on the left side. *Riverdale High School?*

"Is that Kael's shirt?" I tugged on his sleeve.

"Huh?" Austin looked down at his sweatshirt and nodded.

My entire body shifted. Kael somehow snuck himself into my house via my brother. There was hardly a place where I was safe from reminders of him.

"Where did you get his shirt?"

"I was at his place and wore it."

Before I could respond, he began to speak. "Let's not fight about him, K. I already got into it with Dad." Austin dipped his head down between his knees.

I didn't know what to say. I wanted more answers, but I could feel my brother's energy was depleted, and he, unlike me, had never been able to suffer in silence.

"To be honest, I'm tired of being back in Benning. I just want to go somewhere else. Not to Uncle Rudy's again, just . . . somewhere else. Don't you ever feel like that?"

"Yeah," I said and sighed. "But I bought a house here, so I couldn't go anywhere if I wanted to."

Austin rolled his eyes. "That's not an excuse. You know in this market you could sell and make more than you put into it."

"Since when are you savvy about the housing market?" I asked, playfully challenging his authority. "Where would you even go if you left?"

Austin was a nomad, where I was a settler.

"Arizona. Barcelona," he daydreamed.

"You can't even point to Barcelona on a map."

"Yeah, I can." His light eyes were facing the sky, half opened. "And Berlin. Rome. Anywhere. Hell, I'd go live in a van on the coast. I really can't stand being this close to Dad."

I agreed with him. But we were two totally different humans, even if we'd shared a womb. It was easy for him to abandon all logic, I just couldn't.

"Do you even know where your passport is?" I asked.

"Yes. And yours. They're both at Dad's, in the drawer." He gave me a sneaky look, like he had found the entrance to Narnia.

"If only." I laughed.

He leaned against me to reach his phone when it started to vibrate in the pocket of his joggers. A number that wasn't saved was on the screen. He seemed surprised and agitated, and he immediately ignored the call. When he looked up at me he shifted uncomfortably. Something was up; I could read Austin like a book.

"Who was that?" I asked, when he stopped my hand in midair as I tried to reach for his phone. "Was it Katie?" I rolled my eyes.

Austin's face broke into a smile, and he shook his head. He almost looked relieved. "No. God, no."

My mind wandered to being in my old bedroom at my dad's, with Kael, the first night I met Katie and embarrassed myself insulting her, which seemed so trivial now. After the fight, Kael's run-in with the MPs, and everything that's happened, I was relieved to hear that Austin had moved on from that chaotic woman.

I was brought back to reality with Austin's leg shaking the way it did whenever he was nervous. It was getting cooler outside, and I wanted to go in.

"Do you want to stay here for a little bit?" I looked at Austin and, for a second, I could see our mom in him, something around the eyes, about the shape of his mouth. We'd always be a mash-up of our parents, and that horrified me.

"No." He sighed. "I don't know. I need to figure my shit out. I can't do that from your couch."

"It's cheaper than Barcelona, and besides, how the hell would you even pay for a trip like that?" I joked.

"Actually, I was thinking about staying with Martin."

His words punched me. A sucker punch.

"Martin?" I was going to make him say his name.

"Kael."

"Since when are you two friends like that? You're wearing his clothes and now moving in with him?" I couldn't even hide the hurt in my voice.

"I don't know, a week or so." He laughed. I couldn't breathe.

"He's been at Mendoza's a lot. Plus, Elodie is already sleeping on your couch, there's no room for me here."

"Elodie can sleep in my bed."

"Martin has an extra bedroom and I sort of already took my stuff there."

"Seriously?"

I couldn't believe him.

"Look, I know something happened between you two and I know how it blew up with Dad. And that's all I know. You know Dad is a fucking bald-faced liar, so don't let him get in your head. Once he's in, he won't get out." He looked me straight in the eyes. Daring me to be honest.

That was a dare I wouldn't take.

"So unless there's more to it, or Martin did something to you that I don't know about, I don't see the problem with me crashing with him. He's the only one outside of Mendoza who just chills at home and doesn't bring girls around every night. He doesn't get in trouble. He's being really good to me, Kare."

I wanted to throw up. I was relieved and devastated. It was a wretched combination.

"I'm not saying not to be friends with him." I let out a breath of frustration. "I just . . ." I couldn't think of a valid reason to tell Austin not to stay with Kael unless I wanted to tell him how Kael made me feel.

"If you don't want me to, say it. Just know that I can't stay at Dad's anymore, Kare. I can't do it."

I nodded. I understood needing to get away from our dad. Austin should stay at Kael's house, *Martin's* house.

"Dad's calling me again." Austin sighed, changing the subject, looking at his phone. "He's so suffocating."

"Are you going to answer?"

"No."

A car drove by and a little boy in the backseat waved at us. Austin waved back, even smiling for the child.

"I got a job, too," Austin told me a minute or so later. The sun was going down and the sky was changing colors around us.

"Really?" I pepped up for him. "That's great news," I meant it. He hadn't had a job since he got fired from Kmart for calling out too much. I wasn't sure what job could possibly hold my brother, but I was happy he had one.

"Where is it?"

He hesitated. "It's with Martin. He's flipping that duplex he lives in, you know? He's really fucking smart, man. He's paying me and Lawson to help him. I'm going to get more hours in than everyone else, since they all have to work during the week. It's just like tearing up carpet, shit like that. And, Kare—I got myself honest work without having to join the Army, no breaking our treaty," he said with a teasing smile.

"Not funny." I playfully pinched his arm. I really didn't know what to say, but I felt the ice inside my chest melt a little as I thought of Kael and how much he had helped my brother. I had to remind myself why I needed to keep Kael distant: he was moving to Atlanta, bought a house and hadn't mentioned it, not even once. I wondered if Austin knew about that.

"Has he told you about Atlanta?"

"Yeah, and I was the one who told Dad about it. Which is what caused this whole thing with you and Dad, I guess. Even though Martin took the blame for me with that shit with Katie, Dad still has some grudge against him. It's fucked up."

"What do you mean he took the blame?"

Austin sighed and ran his fingers over his hair. His blue eyes were bright, even though they were bloodshot. "He took all the blame, didn't even mention my name to anyone, and probably jeopardized his discharge."

As the words sank in, I couldn't help but shift my perspective on Kael. Why was he being kind to Austin? Was it for me? I shook my head, answering my own question. This was Kael. The kind of person he was . . . or is. He's a good person, despite his lies. And I had to recognize that everything wasn't about me. I knew deep down that he was truly a good person. He just wasn't *my* person, and I'd have to come to terms with that.

"Kael and Dad have more of a history than we know," I told Austin, reminding myself why I couldn't see Kael anymore.

My brother looked at me with a confused but sarcastic expression. "Well, they all deployed together, you know that. They're in the same company." Austin shrugged as though he were telling me the score of a football game, like I gave a shit.

"You knew that?" I asked.

He nodded, sticking his neck out and hunching his shoulders as if to say *Duh!* "How else would I know these guys?" Austin studied my face, and after a second his eyes widened. "You didn't know that?"

I shook my head. "No, but I guess it makes sense."

It *was* all starting to make sense, but once again I was the last to know. Why hadn't anyone told me?

"My fight with Dad was about me working with Martin. You know Dad hates anyone who challenges him, and that's what Martin does. It's almost like Dad's intimidated by him."

I looked up at the setting sun, staring at it long enough to see stars behind my lids when I closed them. I needed to be happy for my brother, even if he was intertwining his life with the one person I was trying to detangle mine from.

"You two are a lot alike, you know that?" he said, a smile on his face.

"You better not be talking about Dad."

He laughed. "Martin."

I shook my head. "That's so not true."

"Whatever you say, Kare." He lay back on the porch and closed his eyes.

"Anyway, enough about Kael. I'm happy you have a job, regardless of how I feel about your boss." I leaned back on my elbows and scooched next to Austin, resting my head close to his. We were almost kids again.

"Thanks," he said. "I won't bring him around if you don't want me to, but he's really helping me out."

I didn't know what I wanted when it came to Kael. I stared at the sky, begging for the stars to come out and play. I wanted to know that I could count on them to help me find my way. I wanted to be certain of something.

"Or we could all hang out, unless that's too awkward for you." Austin's suggestion was jarring, and my defenses kicked in.

"It's fine. I'm seeing someone anyway." The words slid from my tongue, as devious as the lie itself.

"You are?" he asked.

"Yeah. I don't want to talk about it." I wasn't a good liar, so I didn't want any questions.

"Okay, seems a bit random, but sure." He nodded, seeing right through me even with his eyes shut.

It would have been totally out of character to have another guy lined up already, but it was even stranger for me to lie about the whole thing when I knew damn well Austin could sense when I wasn't telling the truth.

"So you won't be mad that he's picking me up here like any minute?" He said the words fast, as if it would change their meaning.

"Austin." I whined his name, twisted it around my tongue. "Fine. I'm going inside. You really need to get a car."

"I will, now that I have a job." He beamed, easing my pain a little.

I heard the roar of Kael's truck without seeing it. My body didn't react at the same lightning speed as my mind; I needed to force myself to go inside the house before he turned onto my street. I wanted to avoid another run-in. I wasn't ready to face him, especially after hearing the kind things he was doing for my brother. I needed time—a long time—before I had to see Kael again.

He was out of the truck and walking up the grass before I had moved even an inch. A faded baseball cap covered his eyes, matching his all-gray outfit—a hoodie and matching joggers. His white sneakers were too clean for this shitty weather, even though the sun decided to come out for the first time in days; maybe I should have taken that as a warning.

"Karina." Kael's voice was punishment wrapped in silk.

I couldn't speak through the lump in my throat. My tongue felt so heavy. I looked at him, but didn't verbally acknowledge his greeting.

He seemed the same, unaffected, and it surprised me. He didn't look miserable, and that pissed me off. It was a short time but it felt like forever since I had touched him. It didn't seem possible. My body was a traitor, recalling his warmth as he stood in the yard. I hated that I immediately noticed how good he looked. I wondered if he noticed my hair color or cared.

My brother stood up, blocking my view of Kael for a second. Just what I needed to help me snap out of it.

"See you later," I said to Austin, as casually as I could manage without acknowledging Kael. I stood up, stepped to the screen door, and grabbed its handle without looking back to see Kael's expression. I deserved an Academy Award.

Once inside, I turned the lock on the door. I pressed my body against the cool wood. It was an attempt to stabilize myself, to keep myself upright. It didn't work well, but I got to my room and slammed the door. I crawled into my bed and wrapped my comforter around my body to hide like I had done my whole life when things were bad.

That's where I stayed until Elodie came home from her doctor's appointment after work. The sun was down, my room black as night, and when she found me hiding from the world, she climbed into my bed. She lay next to me, both of us on our backs, looking up at the ceiling. She turned the flashlight on on her phone and shined it upward. Elodie held a picture of her sonogram from her appointment in the beam of light. It was in black-and-white and seemed to make her so happy that her hands were shaking as we both admired it. Her little avocado was now the length of a banana. She was so thrilled that she began to cry, and I joined my tears with hers. Even though we were crying for extremely different reasons, it felt so nice to have her inside my lonely bubble of life.

# CHAPTER SIXTY-TWO

Over the next week it was hard to dodge my many thoughts about Kael. Austin sent me update pictures of the interior of the empty side of Kael's duplex at least once a day, and the look of pride on his face made my soul happy. I'd never admit it, but I was starting to look forward to the pictures, sometimes even allowing myself to hope Kael would be in the background of one.

I had gone through the motions of another week, and skipped Tuesday dinner again, which raised questions about birthday festivities for Austin and me. A celebration, orchestrated by Estelle, was the last thing I wanted. I wasn't going to mention my upcoming birthday to anyone and hoped Austin would take a similar approach or at least not try to involve me in whatever plans he was making.

Each time I sat on my porch after a shift, I wished for the sound of Kael's truck to rumble onto my street. The sun and the moon changed places, again and again, day after day, and I checked my phone too often, hoping for a word from him, but nothing came. I had told him to leave me alone, so what did I expect? I wondered if I should text or call him, but I couldn't lose the last little bit of pride I had by reaching out first. It wasn't that I was playing hard to get, I just didn't know what the hell to say even if I did. Was he already tired of chasing me? Did I want him to chase me? *No*, I answered my own question. I wanted him to find me and keep me; that was the problem. Life was just complicated now.

I was booked to work most of the day and evening. I welcomed the distraction and the Sriracha noodles that Mali brought for me and Elodie. Elodie kept hiccupping, claiming the noodles weren't too spicy as her nose ran and her eyes watered. After her shift she was going to an FRG meeting and a weekend cookout; I was glad that she was keeping busy lately, especially since she wasn't hearing from Phillip enough.

The first appointment of my shift was Stewart, and I was so relieved to find her already checked in by Mali and lying face-down, asleep, on the treatment bed when I entered the room. Without having to make conversation, my thoughts roamed back to Kael. What was he doing right now? How was his discharge going, or did he lose it because of the incident with my brother? The thought made me feel sick.

My workday progressed uneventfully, but my mind was doing laps, trying to solve the puzzle of my confusion over Kael. I went through the list of pros and cons—what was right and what was wrong about him—and only felt more indecisive. Maybe there was more to the story than I allowed Kael to explain? I considered texting him to see if he was busy, to see if he still wanted a chance to explain himself, but I couldn't bring myself to do it. I had three appointments left, and after giving the first two clients their treatments, I typed a text to Kael and deleted it, typed and deleted again, then tossed my phone into the drawer where I kept the dry towels.

After the last client, I retrieved the phone from the drawer and typed the text to Kael again. Something simple and not desperate, I reminded myself. I just wanted to know if he was really going to lose his discharge, that was it. Mostly.

**Hey, do you want to come over after work today? I get off in an hour. No pressure.**

Before I could stop myself again, I sent it, and before I could hide my phone the little typing bubbles on Kael's side appeared. I held my breath and they disappeared. I waited a few more seconds and nothing came. Great, now I look even more like an idiot. I shouldn't have texted him. I definitely, certainly, surely, truly shouldn't have fucking texted him. Even if he was nice to my brother.

I was so glad this long day of work was finally ending. Other than my scheduled appointments, the salon had been slow all day. I was the only one with evening clients, and I agreed to close up. There were no more clients on the schedule sheet, and I doubted anyone would be walking past the mostly-closed stores within the next twenty minutes, so I straightened up my room for the night and got stuff ready for the morning. The cleaning company had been in the prior evening and everything was in pretty good shape. I just had to organize a few things and make sure all the candles were out and clean towels were stocked. I turned the lights off, one by one, before locking the back door—padlock, too—and shutting off the front desk light.

When I saw a shadow approach the entrance, I practically jumped out of my skin. I think I may have screamed a little, too. I stood still, trying to catch my breath and slow my heart rate. The shadow moved closer into view, and that's when I saw that it was a man—a young one, but not a boy. Maybe a soldier, given the haircut. It was a little late for someone to just pass by. And I didn't recognize him, which made me uneasy.

I had been alone in the spa at night only a few times and it was always fine, but for some reason, this man gave me the chills. He tugged at the door and I stepped into view, flicking the reception area lamp back on. I turned the flashlight off on my phone and kept a little distance from the door.

"Hey, sorry, are you closed?" he mouthed through the glass door. His voice was friendly enough.

"Yeah, we are."

"Oh, sorry. I think I did something to my back during PT and was hoping you guys would still be open. Do you know anywhere else around here that's open late?"

He seemed legit, friendly enough, and I immediately felt guilty for the way my imagination had instantly conjured up the worst-case scenario. I'd had a rough week and was obviously still a little wonky. I smiled at him to make myself feel better about branding him as a serial killer. I wasn't going to stay for another hour—even though we really did need the business, and lord knows I really needed the money. Instead, I opened the door slightly and proposed a compromise.

"I don't think anyone is going to be open past nine, but if you want to come in first thing in the morning I could be here extra-early," I offered. I wasn't just saying it to get the business; nothing except Walmart and fast food joints were open late in this town.

"I think I can get out of PT in the morning. Can I come in and put my name down?"

"Sure."

The man stepped inside and looked into my eyes. It was a little off-putting, but honest, too, in a strange sort of way. He followed me to the desk, and I grabbed the paper version of the schedule, since I had already shut the computer down. I looked at my day tomorrow.

"I have a ten-o'clock opening and a twelve, but I could come in at nine or eight thirty for you, since you came all this way tonight," I told him.

"Let's do eight thirty so it will be extra-quiet in here." He turned to look at the hours of operation painted on the front door in clear white letters.

"Okay." I swallowed. "Eight thirty it is. Can I have your name, please?"

"Nielson," he told me. I wrote it down. It sounded familiar, but I knew I had never seen his face before. I knew faces.

"Are you . . . you know, going to give me that kind of massage?" His voice crawled over me like tiny little spiders.

My stomach dropped. "What did you just say?" I snapped. I looked at the camera again, this time in a really obvious way. This time he noticed.

I wanted to throw up. I wanted to run. But I reached deep for my courage and held my ground.

"I'm going to have to ask you to leave," I said, as firmly as possible. Then I reached for the landline and lifted it halfway to my ear.

He gestured in mock surrender, smirking. I thought I saw a flash of metal in the back of his jaw when he laughed. "I'm joking! Sorry, bad joke. Sorry, sorry." He held his hands up. "No harm done."

I stared at him silently, not lowering the phone, and hoping he couldn't see my hand shaking or the way my knuckles were stretched and white, holding on to the phone as tightly as I could. It had been a while since someone made an offensive comment like that, and I didn't find it funny, at all. After the longest few seconds of my life, he retreated, walking backward, keeping his eyes on me as he moved toward the front door.

Those icy blue eyes and taut pale skin were much more threatening now that he had been so inappropriate.

Just before he backed out of the door, the man smiled again, like he had a thought pop into his head.

"You're Fischer's daughter, right?" An alarm sounded in my head. Who was this guy?

"What?" I managed.

The bell on the door chimed when he leaned his back against the door frame.

"You look just like him."

I was stunned into silence. My heart was pounding out of my chest. *Please, please leave,* I silently begged him. He turned around and hovered in the doorway. And in that moment, just as the door was slowly pulling closed, Kael appeared on the sidewalk. I thought I was going to pass out at the sight of him there.

Kael was illuminated under the streetlights. I wasn't alone anymore.

"Martin?" The man knew Kael's name. I don't know why this web just kept surprising me.

Kael's eyes searched my face.

"Are you okay?" he asked me, as he walked directly toward me, ignoring the man.

I nodded, confused, but felt my heart slow; the effect Kael had on me hadn't diminished one bit. It was such a relief to have him here. Not only because of what had just happened, but because I wanted to see him. I knew I wanted to see him. I felt the air disappear from my lungs. They burned and my heart sped as I looked at him. His eyes took me in slowly before they darted around the lobby and he stepped inside. The man, Nielson, had taken off by the time I looked past Kael a moment later.

"What are you doing here?" I asked him.

He was dressed in all black, except for his typical stark-white sneakers. His hair was freshly buzzed and he was undeniably handsome, as always.

"You texted me. Did you not want me to come?" He took a step toward me.

I scoffed. "You didn't reply." I pulled my phone out of my pocket and checked again. Nothing.

I held the phone up to show him the blank screen. Just my wallpaper of a sunset was there.

He shrugged his broad shoulders and looked into my eyes. "I came."

"Why?" I was getting emotional already. I tried to reel it in and give him a moment to speak.

Kael's expression softened and he shook his head slowly. I wished I could read his mind. "I'm sorry, I should have responded to your text. If you want me to go—"

I held my hand up. "No, I don't want you to go," I admitted.

The corner of his full lips twitched and pulled into a half-smile. "Good."

I laughed, surprising myself. God, it felt so good to be near him. I grabbed my purse and walked toward him. I wanted to hug him, I wanted to hold on to him, I wanted to yell at him and laugh with him, I wanted to cry and scream and giggle and sit in silence. I didn't have a fucking clue what I wanted. I didn't know what to say to Kael or what the first step should be.

He seemed to sense my hesitation as he pushed the door open. "Shall we?" He waved his hand for me to go first.

I followed him outside and locked the shop door, forgetting about everything and everyone except Kael Martin.

# CHAPTER **SIXTY-THREE**

Kael opened the door and I climbed into his truck. The familiar smell of him saturated my senses; my nerves were unwinding second by second. I tried not to think about how much was left unresolved between us or how much I wanted to know what was going to happen next. I didn't know what the hell to say or do, so I just sat there, leaning my back against the seat, trying to gather my thoughts.

Kings of Leon's first album was playing low through the speakers. I rolled down the passenger window to get some air. It smelled a little like fresh rain and earthworms. It helped calm me. The wind blowing, Kael driving, the loud thrum of the engine in this beast of a truck. It all helped calm me.

"Are you hot?" Kael's voice was smooth as he put his seatbelt on.

"No. I'm okay."

He smiled at me and I had to look away. I hated that my guard was slipping and slipping fast, but I felt a burst of relief when he looked at me, head tilted and lips parted. His eyes stayed on me. I could feel them but didn't meet them.

"What?" I asked him, tucking my chin to my shoulder to hide my mouth.

"It feels good to breathe again," he responded, and as I turned to look at him, his eyes were locked onto mine. I didn't know how I could look away.

"You can't just say something like that," I teased him softly.

"I thought you wanted answers from me."

I stared out the window as he continued to drive. "I do."

Silence passed between us as he turned onto the main street, heading the opposite way from my house. I didn't ask where we were going.

"Where do you want me to start?" His voice was so calming, so deep and comforting, even in this raw and uncertain moment.

"Well, how many lies were there?"

Kael sighed and the turn signal dinged as he waited at a red light. His eyes were on the road in front of us.

"I didn't tell you about knowing your dad because when I went there that first week, I had no fucking idea that he was your dad, honest to God, Karina. I didn't know before we walked in. I didn't know anything about you. Yeah, I knew he had twins, but I didn't know you or your brother. I thought you were just Elodie's friend."

Kael's words gave me a hint of reassurance, but didn't address why he had stayed silent about it for days and weeks after. "You've had plenty of time to talk to me and tell me what happened with my dad. But you never did."

His jaw clenched, but his voice came out even. "At first, I didn't tell you because you seemed so kind and my history with your dad was really complicated. It seemed easier not to get into all of that. Then we kept hanging out and then I started to—" He stopped as a flash of light illuminated the windshield.

He had swerved into another lane. A horn blared as Kael jerked the wheel to straighten the car and I caught my breath.

"Fuck, sorry." Kael was looking straight ahead, his hands strangling the steering wheel.

"Are you okay?" he asked.

His chest was moving up and down like he was bursting with adrenaline and fear.

"Let's just pull over here." I pointed to a Dollar Tree across the intersection. He parked the car, but kept the ignition on. He switched the music off and turned his body to me.

"Are you okay?" he repeated. I nodded and he sighed, blowing air out of puckered lips.

We sat under the dim parking lot light and looked at each other, barely blinking, before I spoke, breaking the silence.

"Atlanta? Were you really not going to tell me that you bought a house there? You made me look like such an idiot in front of my dad, and you know how shitty that was for me."

"I just closed on the property, literally the day your dad came to your house. I don't know how he even knew that, but I had every intention of telling you that day. I came hoping to celebrate with you, actually. Hell, I even thought about trying to convince you to go with me . . . . The house is in bad shape, it'll take me at least a year to get it ready to live in or sell."

"Okay . . ." was all I could come up with. Deep down I really believed that he was telling the truth. I didn't know why, but I just had a gut feeling that he wasn't lying to me. Not about Atlanta, at least.

I took a deep breath, but kept eye contact. "Okay, so even if that's all true, what about my dad? And Mendoza?"

"Mendoza is another story for a different day, but just try to put yourself in my shoes, knowing that my friend is deteriorating in front of my eyes and so fucking quickly. I wasn't trying to keep it from you, but I've been really focused on helping him get by. Bringing other people into his shit would only make things harder for him. We're all fighting the same battle with PTSD, but he's losing, so I tried to keep everything and everyone around him as normal as possible, to help him feel less crazy."

His eyes left mine and stared at the seat between us. My heart ached and swelled. It wasn't my place to force Kael to tell me about Mendoza's mental health. I felt like shit for even attempting to use that against him when this was really about my dad and the house in Atlanta.

"Okay," I repeated. "And what about my dad? You're telling me there wasn't ever a time to tell me from that first day until now?"

"No, there was. And honestly, I'm sorry that I'm such a selfish person." He rubbed his hand across his chin and pulled at his lips. "I was selfish, that's it. I knew you wouldn't want anything to do with me if your dad told you, which I figured he would. So I just kept taking more and more of your time. Karina, I have felt nothing for so long, I started to think I wasn't capable of caring about anyone this way, so I got addicted to this feeling."

"What feeling?"

His hand was warm when he lifted it to gently grab mine. He pressed them both to his chest and I felt his heart pounding.

"I'm not even sure what it is, it just feels so good. And I'm a selfish fuck who wanted to keep getting this feeling from you before I left. I didn't mean to hurt you, I really, really didn't. I waited each day like a madman for the other shoe to drop, for you to find out that I lied about knowing your dad, but each time I saw you, everything disappeared except you and me. I know this isn't enough and I won't ever be enough for you, but I just wanted to explain myself and apologize for not doing it earlier."

He dropped our hands but I grabbed his again. My eyes were stinging, and my head was foggy and I didn't know up from down, but I knew I wanted to hold his hand.

I moved toward him, closing the space between us. A pile of

papers and a bookbag were in the way, but I pushed them toward the door as Kael held my hand, firmly.

"I'm really sorry, honestly. And I get it if you just want me to go away." He rounded his shoulders, deflated, and I had the strongest urge to comfort him.

He was so close now that I could smell the faint earthy cologne he used and I could feel the warmth radiating from him. I ignored the storm of doubts left in my head, stepped over any remnants of red flags, and pulled my hand from his to bring it to his cheek.

His skin was so soft, so beautiful and familiar. I felt warm and glowing from the inside out and couldn't think of how to say that to him. I used my body instead of words to show him we would be okay. I climbed onto Kael's lap and he groaned as I wrapped my arms around his back. The sharp fear of rejection disappeared as he dug his hands into my hair. I could feel the relief flowing from both of us so intensely that I thought we would shake the truck.

His hands held on to my hips, roaming around the tops of my thighs without a word between us. Somehow this would work out, we were supposed to be together. If we weren't, it wouldn't feel this good, we wouldn't be able to communicate like this, without saying a word. The connection wouldn't feel this intense and electrifying if we couldn't figure it all out. I refused to believe the universe was that cruel. I brushed my thumb across his cheek just below his eye.

"I don't. I don't want you to go away ever again," I whispered, as his eyes fluttered open to look into mine.

"Are you sure? I'm trying to warn you," he said. He brushed a piece of my hair out of my face and tucked it behind my ear. "I like your hair, by the way." His voice was a whisper by the end of the sentence, and my hands were shaking as they trailed over his bottom lip and he made a noise again, encouraging me. I pressed my lips to his, letting all my guard down now, letting all the pain rush out of me, all the anxiety, the loneliness; it all melted out of me as he kissed me. His hand went around the back of my neck and his lips opened mine wider to taste more of me. I never, ever wanted to be away from this man again, no matter how many coincidences and unanswered questions surrounded him. No matter what demons he was running from or chasing. I couldn't lose this, not again. I hugged him tighter and he said sorry between kissing me and pressing his hands to my cheeks, and I shushed him, begging him to take me home.

He didn't stop kissing me, exploring me. I was completely melted by his warm hands and mouth.

"Okay, okay," he eventually said, kissing my forehead. "Let's go home."

The way he said "home" made me feel so comforted. I had always thought of home as a place, but it's a feeling, I decided in that moment.

I stayed as close to Kael as I could during the short drive to my house. We turned onto my street, and he drove more slowly before pulling up to his usual spot. I felt a mix of nerves and elation, and a rush to get inside with him. I missed having him in my house, and I think he knew that. He gave me a shy smile and courteously picked up my handbag, to move it out of my way. In my rush to climb out of the passenger door, I knocked the thick packet of papers to the floorboard.

"Sorry, I dropped these. I hope I didn't mess them up," I said, as I stacked them neatly. "Is this for your discharge?" There was an Army folder on top with the typical Army star. Kael stilled next to me. I felt the shift in the air around us as I realized what the packet said.

"Who's enlistment packet is this?"

Being nosy and not thinking anything of it, I started to open the folder. That's when Kael reached over, trying to grab it from me. "Who's signing their life away?" I teased, as his eyes fell to the paperwork in my hands.

And then I read the name on the first page.

AUSTIN TYLER FISCHER

# CHAPTER SIXTY-FOUR

Now it was Kael's turn to call my name. Kael's turn to bring me back to earth.

"Karina. Karina," he said. "Listen to me, Karina. There's an explanation—"

His words were gibberish. I could make out my name, but that was it. I could barely feel my body. The truck was parked on solid ground but felt like it was dangling over the edge of a cliff. "What is this, Kael?" I managed at last.

When he didn't answer me, I screamed.

"What is this! What the hell is this?" I slammed the folder down onto the seat's empty space between us. "Do not move any closer to me until you tell me what this is and why it has my brother's name on it!" I was every emotion: fear, anger, disgust, contempt.

Had Austin really joined the Army? No fucking way that was what this was. I must be missing something. Kael stared at me blankly, I could see him doing it again, closing himself off like he did during the fight with my dad.

"Don't you dare shut down! I want answers," I insisted. *Austin!* I dug in my purse for my phone and, finding it, searched the screen to pull up his name. My head was spinning so fast that everything was blurry when I tried to call him. Of course he didn't pick up.

"This can't be true, Kael, didn't you just give him a job? You . . ." I could barely get the words out. "You convinced him to enlist, didn't you?" I spat at Kael as I yanked and pushed the door of the truck open and stepped outside.

I coughed, my lungs failing me as the world around us spun. "Oh my god." It sank in. "You did this because of my dad . . . oh my god." I held on to the door of the truck and Kael ran around to my side but kept himself at a safe distance.

"This doesn't have anything to do with your dad. This was me helping your brother with his future! I did this because he needs to stop fucking up his life. His words, not mine."

I wanted to scream at Kael. He was a marble statue—beautiful, but cold.

"You knew how I felt about Austin, and the Army, and the agreement we had that he would never enlist. You knew how much it would hurt me and you still did it. Oh my god, I'm such a fuck-ing idiot." I glared at him. "You're so fucked up." I put my head in my hands to not have to look him in the face.

It wasn't worth trying to rationalize. People, some of them, hurt others as a way of masking their own pain, but some people just hurt other people simply to do it. I didn't need to know anything else about Kael to know that he must be one of these people. All of the helping-Austin bullshit, all of the hours we spent and secrets we shared, it was all fake. I wrapped my arms around myself. I was going to be sick. Kael had the nerve to reach for me and I jerked away, moving from the street to the patch of grass next to the sidewalk in front of my house. I felt unstable in all forms of the word. My body and mind were no longer connecting.

Even though I couldn't speak, I kept backing away, nearly tripping on the edge of the sidewalk.

"Karina! Please—" Kael pleaded. I held my hand up, silently begging him to stop.

"Get away from me!" Tears soaked my face and I brushed aside strands of hair stuck to my wet cheeks.

"Go!" I screamed, not caring that it was dark out or that I would be alone on the side of the road. I just wanted to be as far away from him as humanly possible.

And of course, because the universe hated me, the moment my shoes touched the ground and I yelled at him again to drive away, the sky started to cry with me, covering me with thick tears of rain from head to toe.

I collapsed in the grass after he pulled away and stayed there until the moon glared at me to go to my own bed and leave hers. There were no stars to dry my tears.

# A Note from the Author

An early version of this story was originally self-published as the novel *The Brightest Stars* (2018). Now, several years later, and after many months of writing and rewriting (more than thirty thousand words are new!) and a deeper exploration of character and story, I have reconceived a book that I am proud to relaunch. There was so much more that I wanted to share with readers.

During the pandemic, I had a lot of time for inward reflection and thinking about the issues that are most important to me. I know we all have gone through our own version of this in some way, and for me, it became really clear that a part of my voice, a part of myself, wasn't fully expressed in my earlier drafting of this novel. I didn't know where that piece of me had gone, but I couldn't find it inside the pages as I turned and turned, and the novel ended. So I decided to revisit this story and these characters thoughtfully, and with great energy and affection. I truly believe you will find more of me, Anna, inside this "revisited" story. I've titled the new novel *The Falling*— and the books to follow in the Brightest Stars Trilogy will be *The Burning* and *The Infinite Light of Dust*.

I can't wait to continue with you on Karina and Kael's journey to discover themselves as they discover one another. Thank you for continuing to believe in me and coming on this journey as we learn together.

<3 Anna

# Acknowledgments

This is that awkward part of a book where I pretend I just won an Oscar and name the first people who come to mind, so bear with me as I try to give these wonderful people in my life a tiny bit of the recognition they deserve.

Anne Messitte: It was more than fate when our paths crossed but didn't connect in the early days of my publishing, because now they have at the perfect time. I'll never forget the day I met you at a Greek restaurant in NYC and was just absolutely blown away by your deep understanding of romance and the audience of readers who embrace these books. I felt an immediate connection with you. I not only wanted to work with you on my stories, I wanted to listen to you talk for hours about the community of readers and how to serve them best. It was refreshing and has been the best ride starting this big dream with you! Thank you for your endless hours and unlimited capacity to help me run my first company. I can't thank you enough for making me dream even bigger and become a better writer with each book we do together. You understand me, and that's priceless.

Flavia Viotti, agent/manager/business partner extraordinaire: You are such a badass and one of the hardest-working people I know. I'm so honored to be working with you and can't wait until our dreams come true. You're a force and I'm sooo here for it. I can't imagine my life or career without you. Since the day we met, I knew I wanted you in my corner and have never looked back. I hope I can one day live up to the way you see my potential, even if it takes one hundred years.

Erin Gross: You complete me. Literally. Thank you for being my right and left hands, brain, arms, etc., etc. You're the best and we are taking over the world together. You're so innovative and literally work through your sleep. I heart you so hard. I've known you since the very beginning of my career and you've always rooted for me and seen what even I couldn't see. Here's to the next decade.

Kristin Dwyer: This is our tenth book together! Whatttt. You're the bomb and I can't wait for eleven, twelve, ninety-nine. You've helped guide me as an author and held my hand as I have navigated my career since day one (literally). You're the OG and I heart you so much.

Douglas Vasquez: It's so hard to believe that we met at a signing in Brazil all those years ago. You started as a fan and now are one of the closest people in my life. You understand me and root for me and it means the world to me. Here's to taking over the world in a fresh, exciting way. I couldn't do this without you.

S.M.: I didn't get enough time with you and some days I hate you for that. Others, I remember the way you taught me about myself, and that you were the first person who ever told me to write my thoughts down. You told me I should be a writer long, long before I ever could have dreamed of it. You taught me so much about myself in such a short time and I wish I would have had more time with you, or would have known just how deeply you were hurting. Until I see you again, I will write you into my novels and dream about what your life could have and should have been like.

Vilma Gonzalez: We will be the Tae to each other's Yoongi and carry each other around to beautiful places in our next lives.

Eric Brown: Your wise counsel and the many hours spent to ensure the solid foundation of my company are truly appreciated.

To the dedicated team at Wattpad who have helped me produce and present Frayed Pages x Wattpad Books, especially Tina McIntyre, Deanna McFadden, Patrick McCormick, Delaney Anderson, Lesley Worrell, Amy Brosey, Rebecca Mills, and Neil Erickson. And to Aron Levitz and Ashleigh Gardner for all the years of collaboration and for supporting the partnership that's created this unique co-publishing imprint.

To all my publishers around the world, the editors, the sales teams, the cover designers, everyone who spends any of their precious time trying to help my dreams come true, thank you!! Your time and dedication doesn't go unnoticed.

And to my small circle of friends who have been here for me through the world changing, you are the glue of my life.

# About the Author

Anna Todd (writer/producer/influencer) is the *New York Times* best-selling author of the After series, which has been released in thirty-five languages and has sold more than twelve million copies worldwide—becoming a #1 best seller in several countries. Always an avid reader, Todd began writing stories on her phone through Wattpad, with After becoming the platform's most-read series with over two billion reads. She has served as a producer and screenwriter on the film adaptations of *After* and *After We Collided*, and in 2017, she founded the entertainment company Frayed Pages Media to produce innovative and creative work across film, television, and publishing. A native of Ohio, she lives with her family in Los Angeles.

@annatodd

@imaginator1D

Anna Todd's **Brightest Stars** trilogy continues . . .

BEST-SELLING AUTHOR OF *AFTER*

ANNA**TODD**

# THE BURNING

## A BRIGHTEST STARS NOVEL

"Anna Todd has done it again!"
—Colleen Hoover, best-selling author of *It Ends With Us*

An excerpt from Book Two, *The Burning*—

# CHAPTER ONE

**Kael**

My truck roared down the small street. I continued to hit my hands against the steering wheel as I drove far enough down the dark road to be out of her eyesight. I slowed to a stop on the gravel pull-out at the end of her street and stumbled out of my truck. The ground was soaked with unforgiving rain and as I looked into the darkness, I couldn't see more than ten feet in front of me. It had been less than five minutes since I left Karina at her house, but the guilt weighed enough to feel like thirty years.

Reaching for my phone, I called Austin first. My hands were shaking intolerably, and the rain was soaking my phone as I waited for him to pick up.

"Hey man— what's up?" he asked in a casual tone. The sound of his nonchalant voice immediately triggered my anger. Even if I knew both of us did the right thing, I needed someone to be pissed at and I could hear women's voices and music in the background of wherever the fuck he was.

"Your sister found out," I flatly told him.

Silence.

"Found out what?" he asked. I knew he wasn't that damn clueless. He was in shock, not that ignorant.

"Where are you?" I was beyond impatient.

He paused, took a deep breath in before responding. "I'm at Mendoza's. What did you mean by my sister found out? Tell me it's not what I think it is."

"It's exactly what you think it is. I'm on the side of the road and I didn't call you for a heads-up Fischer, I called you to tell you that your sister is devastated and could really use you right now."

"Did you tell her? I thought we were—"

Before I could help it my fist slammed against the hood of my truck. "It doesn't fucking matter who told her, what are you going to do about her right now?"

"I don't even have a car, what can I do?"

"Are you drunk?"

"No…" He was lying. "Yeah, I mean, I'm not sober. But it's not like I knew this was going to happen and got plastered so you had to deal with her. Maybe call Elodie? But she's been working all day, so—"

I ended the call before he offered another not-thought-out solution.

The rain took a short break, long enough for me to consider driving back down the road to beg for her forgiveness, to explain why I did what I did. The weight of the world pushed against my shoulders as I imagined her at home alone, sitting in the dark kitchen feeling completely betrayed. I made the choice when I met her to try my best to take care of her, to make her life better, easier, but all I've done is fuck it up.

Even if I still stood by helping her brother get into the Army before he could tank his life in a serious way. That's what this was, the sacrifice was temporarily hurting Karina, but in the big picture of her entire life, her brother being alive and breathing would matter more to her than the feelings she thought she had for me. In a year from now, she would be proud of him instead of mourning him. After a month or two she would barely think of me. She deserved to have that and I didn't deserve to have her, so this was the way things would be. She will never leave my mind, but isn't love supposed to be about sacrificing? I didn't know, I had never loved anyone before, but it felt right. It felt wrong, but so right.

I hoped to God Elodie was home and could comfort her. I thought about calling her but I didn't want to admit what I had done and I knew Elodie had become attached to Karina's brother lately and she would be pissed at me too, so I took the easy way out, climbed into my truck and drove to Mendoza's. The solution wouldn't be there, but I knew a bottle of tequila would.

Mendoza's house was lit up, every single light seemed to be on. All the other houses on the street were dark and quiet. I parked in the driveway right behind his van and took a breath before getting out. Soon, I wouldn't be able to come here when shit went wrong. Soon, I would probably only see him at funerals or weddings, or maybe never again. That's how it was in a soldier's life, you had unbreakable bonds, but when people got out, they usually moved back to where they came from and hardly ever looked back. Well, they looked back all the time, but physically never came back.

I heard his voice before I saw him.

"Your truck keeps gettin' louder. I can hear it a damn mile away." He greeted me with a soft smack to my shoulder.

"Yay, you're here!" Gloria hugged me and I tried to force a smile. Suddenly I wondered why the hell I was there. I didn't deserve the comfort of friends right now when I knew Karina had no one. Carefully moving out of Gloria's arms, I tried to think of an excuse to leave even though I had just arrived.

Fischer's voice rang through the living room. "Yoooo," he slurred.

He was lazily sitting there, his arm stretch across the back of the white sofa. His eyes were barely open.

"How drunk are you?" I questioned, moving closer.

He laughed a little, tilting his head. He looked so much like Karina that it made me want to throw up.

"Nah, I didn't drink." He nodded toward Mendoza and Gloria who were being grossly affectionate in front of us.

Mendoza kissed Gloria's forehead. "He hasn't drank since he got here. But he's on some shit, that's for sure."

Gloria rolled her eyes and shot Fischer a look of disapproval. Fischer smiled and stretched his neck. He was definitely high out of his mind. "What are you on?" I pushed his shoulder and he moved like jello.

"Some soldiers dropped him off here like that but I don't know them. I think he bought pills from them."

"Again?" I groaned. This motherfucker was really driving me crazy.

I kneeled in front of him and I saw Gloria and Mendoza leaving the room in the reflection of the window behind Fischer. There was a plastic baggy sticking out of the pocket of his sweats. I grabbed it and he tried to stop me, but his reflexes were too slow from the drugs. Long white rectangle pills and traces of white powder from them danced as I shook the bag in front of his face.

"You won't be able to do this shit soon. They're going to piss test you regularly and they will kick you out or lock you up if you don't pass."

"I know, I know. I just wanted one last night to celebrate," he groaned. There was a sadness in his voice that almost made me feel for him. Almost.

"Your sister is completely destroyed right now and you're here high as a kite, not having to feel shit."

He closed his eyes. "You're here, too. Not with her."

"She wouldn't let me stay," I defended myself.

This irresponsible asshole gets to numb himself with drugs and I have to just deal with it, so does she. It was unfair and infuriating. Times like this I wish I could show Karina why I helped her brother enlist, why his life was in danger, and why all of this was for her, whether she could see it yet or not.

"You and I both are the last people she would want around her right now." His voice was fading, his eyes bloodshot slits. "Maybe ever. And look, I know I'm a fuck-up, but tonight just leave me alone with my mistakes? Please, bro." His desperation bled through his intoxication.

I didn't say another word as his head slopped to the side. I just sat and stared at him, hoping I was doing the right thing. I watched the rain through the window as he slept—or passed out—and Gloria and Mendoza never came back in.

# CHAPTER TWO

"Whose food is this?" I tossed the dirty bowl into the overflowing sink.

No one answered and I didn't even know if anyone was home except me. Gunk-encrusted dishes stacked in a chaotic pile filled my usually clean sink. There were beer bottles, half empty and fully empty on the counter, wadded-up potato chip bags, and crunchy pieces of instant ramen noodles in their foil wrappings, with flavor packets torn on the corner dotted with "chicken"-flavored crumbles of seasoning. For a couple of weeks now, things had been going downhill. I had never allowed my place to look this disastrous, but I couldn't find it in me to give a shit lately. I used my teeth to tear open another packet and pushed a pile of empty take-out containers out of my way. I was fully aware that the trash can was merely three feet away, but it didn't matter. Not much mattered these days.

I filled a bowl with water and pushed the noodles down enough to be covered before lazily putting my dinner into the microwave. I grew up eating these cheap ramen packets, ten cents apiece. Most of the time, I didn't bother to cook them and just dumped the uncooked noodles into a Ziploc, poured the seasoning in, and took it to school. I spent more time making my sister's lunch when she got tired of being in the "free lunch" line. Whatever I could do for her, because she was the brains of the family and needed the fuel more than me. Our mom's work schedule of two jobs didn't allow the luxury of some families. Time-consuming lunch preparation, perfect packages strategically including every section of the food pyramid, handwritten notes wishing us a good day, expensive sodas and name-brand chips... We didn't have any of that, but we had a mother who woke up before the sun and barely got a meal herself before her night job.

I used to be bitter about it and wish I had what the privileged kids I saw on TV or met during football game parties at the rich white schools had. Being what was considered talented at football gave me opportunities to mingle with kids who lived in wealthy Atlanta suburbs. I got invited to big houses with pools in the yard and once, a kid gave me a brand-new pair of Jordans just because he already had a similar pair. It would have been easy to feel like he was looking down on me, but I didn't really care since I knew I could sell the shoes and buy my sister a new school uniform and take her to the movies with the money. New cars and fancy new Nikes, but none of them seemed to know what sacrifice was. Not one of them knew what it meant to work for what they had and it made me appreciate my mom more. Even though she couldn't go to my games often because of her work, I knew that the reason I could play was her. Karina melted into my thoughts. One of the things I respected about her the most was how hard she worked to have what she wanted. She could easily ask her dad for help, but she never did. If something was broken, she would fix it. She was proud that everything she had was from her own two hands, literally, and it made me feel connected to her because I value working for what you have more than most people my age.

The familiar smell of the ramen made me want to call my mom or my sister, but I knew I wasn't in the right head space right now, and they had more important shit going on in their lives than me sulking on the phone and lying that my life was going great.

I heard the sound of the front door shut as I inhaled a mouthful of noodles. I knew every sound of this place, and most places.

"Yo! You home?" Fischer's voice rang through the duplex, bouncing from one wall to the other.

He walked into the kitchen before I bothered to answer him. His face was blotchy and his light hair a mess. Blue circles swelled under his normally bright eyes.

"You look like you feel like shit," I told him.

He nodded. "Because I do."

"Good."

Fischer lifted his T-shirt up and wiped his face with the bottom of it. "I am so out of shape. Basic is going to kill me." He plopped his head down on the counter.

He was leaving in about two months and started trying to get into shape about a week ago.

"Yeah, and I'm sure the drugs help," I reminded him.

He shook his head. "You'd be surprised." His grin was sarcastic and charming, even if we were joking about something heavy.

"Have you talked to your sister yet?"

He groaned. "You ask me that every day."

"Have you?" I poked at his sweat-covered arm with my spoon. "Huh?"

He rolled his head, whining. "This is like having two annoying siblings annoy you at the same time."

"Good. You've completely ghosted her since she found out about you enlisting."

I was envious of him that she bothered him. She hadn't texted or called me once since that night. I kept checking her social media and for the first week it was great, but she eventually blocked me. I wondered if I accidently clicked something and gave away my stalking, or if she just didn't want to risk coming across me.

"So have you or not?"

He shook his head. "Every day that goes by makes it harder. I don't want to face her right now."

"Have you ever thought about how she must feel?" I sat my bowl down on the pile of dirty dishes as Fischer leaned up to face me. "It's for the best. You know that. If you explained to her why you did it, I think she would be more understanding. She wants the best for you, truly. She's probably so hurt now that it's been so long and you've avoided her."

"What does it matter to you how she feels? You hurt her too, so don't give me that shit about thinking about how she feels when she's really probably more heartbroken by you than me."

A small hole opened up in my chest as he spoke. I knew he was wrong, but the idea of hurting her and betraying her trust had been feasting on my corpse for the last two weeks.

"This isn't a competition of who is worse. We both fucked up but you're her brother, her twin brother, and I'm just a guy she halfway dated and hates now."

He stood all the way up. "Bullshit. You know you're not just a guy to her. We should have told her, and you're right, I'll be the one who has to face her and deal with her pain and you'll be able to run off to Atlanta soon. I'll have to see the disappointment on her face and you'll never see her face again."

I reached for his shirt and balled my fist around the fabric. His green eyes went wide and he raised his hands up in the air.

"Sorry. Fuck. Sorry, Martin. I just feel like shit about it and am pushing it onto you. I'll go to her house tomorrow. I don't know how much longer I can avoid her anyway. It's killing me day by day." He sighed and I let go of him.

"I don't think just showing up at her place without a warning is a good idea."

"If I call her, she might be working or not answer. She's texted me too many times for me to say sorry over the phone. I need to just face the music." His voice was shaking and I knew even though his words sounded like he barely cared, he absolutely did and hated disappointing her. We had that in common.

As selfish as it was, I felt like I knew Karina more than he did, which I knew wasn't true, but it made something inside me feel satisfied or fulfilled. Like the time I spent with her wasn't a dream or a waste of time. I would rather have felt that feeling at least once in my pathetic life than never at all, and since people like me didn't get a fairy-tale ending, I would take what I could get and leave it at that. I'd already been pushing my luck by having someone like Karina give me the time of day, and now the time had run out and I needed to get over her. Having her brother around me constantly didn't help me forget her, but maybe that's why I decided to spend my time helping him make his life better. I couldn't do that for her, so maybe doing it for him would repent some of my sins?

I needed to work on controlling my temper and I knew my anger wasn't directed toward Fischer, just like his anger wasn't directed toward me. We both hated ourselves. That was the thing we had the most in common.

# ANNA TODD'S
# BRIGHTEST STARS TRILOGY

### BOOK ONE
## The Falling
Available Now

### BOOK TWO
## The Burning
Coming Summer 2023

### BOOK THREE
## The Infinite Light of Dust
Coming Soon